Learn how
Read book one in the Endosym series.
Available from Amazon.com

ENDOSYM

BOOK ONE

THE DARK FACE OF EVIL

By J. Henry Thomson

PEOPLES OF WEST AFRICA BELIEVE THAT DEMONS HIDE IN THE DARK FORESTS. Sometimes a demon and a man becomes one creature, an *endosym*. The *endosym* is a malevolent thing that dares to rage havoc on the village.

Hank Martin, his wife, Lindsey, and their teenage son Tim arrive in Liberia, West Africa where Hank will be the defense attaché' at the American embassy. What began as the ideal tour for the Martins escalates into sheer terror when an incident from Hank's past haunts his dreams and becomes reality.

Hank is forced to choose between the interests of the United States as it negotiates for the vast oil reserves hidden beneath the Saint Paul River Delta and the destruction of an evil that permeates the government of Liberia to the very doors of the President's office.

This is a battle that if Hank does not win will cost him far more than his career; it will cost him the sacrifice of his son to the *endosym*.

THE DOORWAY TO THE OTHER WORLD WILL OPEN

ENDOSYM

THE PLANTATION
Book Two

By J. Henry Thomson

8-6-15

J. Henry Thomson retired as a colonel in the United States Army. He is a decorated combat veteran with service during both Vietnam and the Gulf wars. He has served in airborne and special operations units and has commanded soldiers from platoon to brigade.

Thomson spent more than three years in West Africa and lived twelve months in the jungles. He has worked with the governments of Spain and Brazil on counter terrorism, mines and explosives; and with Delta Force and the Central Intelligence Agency. He lives with his wife in the state of Washington. He is the author of book one of the Endosym series *The Dark Face of Evil*.

ACKNOWLEDGMENTS

WHEN WRITING A NOVEL, THERE ARE ALWAYS THOSE INDIVIDUALS WHOSE contributions make the novel come to life.

A special thanks goes to Yelm, Washington Police Chief Todd Stancil who provided an insight into law enforcement work.

Then Dianna Main, John Main and Larry Hicks who read the draft and told it like it is.

Dave Raymond, thank you for explaining the concept of flying helicopters.

My brother-in-law Dick Raymond, you are an awesome Webmaster.

As always, my editor, Irene Hicks, who provided the energy, unflagging support and encouragement got me through the difficult periods. Without her constant efforts none of this would be possible.

HE MUST BE HALLUCINATING. HE LOOKED AGAIN. THREE THINGS — NO, NOT things—but demons, stepped out of what appeared to be a black pipe. They seemed human, yet something beyond human. Two horns sprouted from their large, hairless heads. Their long, pointed ears dangled almost to their shoulders. Their bodies seemed human in shape except for one feature — tails that began at the base of their spines. The sharp tips dragged behind, leaving their mark on the surface of the Earth.

Johnsonville, Virginia August 18, 1861

IT TOOK THREE DAYS FOR COPIES OF THE *RICHMOND HERALD* TO REACH Staunton, the county seat, and another full day for Amos to locate one paper and carry it back to the plantation. He rushed to the door and handed the newspaper to the houseboy, hoping to avoid the master's wrath. More than likely, his punishment for taking too long would include a whipping.

News travels fast, thought Nathanial Johnson, but not fast enough. Now with the front page spread out in front of him, Johnson ran his finger across the bold print as he leaned forward at the broad oak desk. Here in the mansion's second-floor office, he maintained paperwork, inked records, and kept books on animal husbandry and agriculture. In his right desk drawer he stored the ownership titles for his sixty slaves – those purchased and those born on his land.

Johnson's lips moved silently as he again read the bold headline: "Militia Mobilized, Ordered to Report to Charlottesville." He had known war was coming, but he didn't think it would happen so soon. It had been only five months since the first shot was fired at Fort Sumter, South Carolina on April 12, 1861.

"Yes," he said out loud. "Now it's time for war."

One hundred miles from Richmond, war had finally come to this peaceful valley in the Alleghany foothills. The United States fought within itself, yet the brave men from the righteous Confederacy would quickly defeat the Union army. Johnson knew it was meant to be. The North was hell-bent on destroying their way of life, his livelihood, and everything that fine Southern gentlemen held dear.

How dare those Yankee bastards tell him and his neighbors that they could not own slaves? They didn't understand – or refused to understand – the issue. The slaves were his property. Furthermore, the black slaves were incapable of surviving on their own. Letting them go their own way would be as dumb as taking a domestic dog that had been raised all its life on a farm and releasing it in the woods to compete with the wolves for survival. The Negroes lacked the intelligence to live on their own.

If the fight was to come, so be it. Johnson looked to his left where his Confederate jacket hung from a peg on the coat tree. The bright stars of Brigadier General were affixed to the lapels. The South needed leaders, and, as one of the most powerful landowners in Augusta County, Johnson was prepared to quickly bring this conflict to an end and send those Yankees running north with their tails between their legs.

The windows in his office stood wide open on this late summer day, yet no cool breeze brought any relief from the insufferable humidity. Johnson stood as he heard the yapping of the dogs and the clip-clop of an approaching horse and rider. He looked out the window. His son, Beauford, wearing his gray military uniform, jerked the reins and pulled to a halt.

The boy was just twenty years old. In less than a week, Beauford and every able-bodied white man in the county would ride off to Charlottesville to take their places in the proud Confederate army.

The boy was tall and broad shouldered, Johnson thought, just like his father at the same age. So much had happened in the last two decades.

Just twenty years ago, in what had seemed like months, not years, Johnson had brought his young family to the valley. In the spring of 1841 when Johnson was thirty-five years old, he arrived in the valley with a young wife and six children. He took every penny of his inheritance after his father's death to purchase the four hundred acres fifteen miles west of Staunton.

The Johnson family had left Richmond along with six other white families, one hundred fifty slaves, a hundred head of cattle, forty horses, sheep, goats and swine. In addition to the wagons that carried the families, they had ten wagonloads of building materials and supplies. They had traveled west through Charlottesville, crossed the Blue Ridge Mountains and spent several weeks in Waynesboro, replenishing their stores before heading farther west. Elizabeth was carrying their seventh child, Beauford, who was destined to be the first white child born west of the mountains.

When they reached the valley, Johnson knew that he had arrived at the place where he and his family could live and prosper for the rest of their lives. He built the main house next to a stream that wound its way through the property. The front of the house would face the east to catch the rising sun; the back would border the stream. Out of sight of the main house, the slave quarters were built behind the main house.

The four-level main house contained more than nine thousand square feet of living space. The lower level was dug into the hillside. A large storeroom under the house took up twelve hundred square feet. An open-air kitchen was built next to the stream. It was joined to the lower level by a covered walkway. Slaves brought food via stairs to the dining room.

Double doors of solid oak provided the entrance to the second level from the wide, front porch. A large, formal ballroom was located to the right of the entry. A library, a living room, and dining room completed the second level.

A wide staircase off the foyer rose to the third level. Hidden from sight, a second small staircase led from the kitchen and dining room. Most of the family's activities took place here. Besides the office, the floor consisted of a sewing room, the children's playroom, the master bedroom, a sitting room, and two additional bedrooms. The fourth level provided space for three more bedrooms and a large storage area.

The house was built to last three hundred years. From virgin forests, eighteen-inch thick beams supported the upper levels. Above the hard dirt floors of the lower level, the upper floors had four-by-twelve-inch hardwood planks. Granite blocks cut from a quarry on the property formed the building's foundation. Bricks for the six fireplaces were shipped from factories in Richmond.

For the next twenty years, the plantation had grown and prospered. As more families moved into the valley, the town of Johnsonville, Virginia was established. It served a population of two hundred fifty whites and two hundred black slaves.

Johnson watched his son take long strides as he neared the front porch. The young man paused momentarily to acknowledge thirteen-year-old Tillie, Carla's daughter, who ran up to greet him. From his office window, Johnson admired the girl's budding breasts beneath her white cotton dress. He smiled with approval when Beauford patted the girl's rounded buttocks before she scampered away.

Johnson laughed to himself, "Good for you, boy. Already sampling some of the stock." It was healthy for his son to fornicate with slaves. It would help him to learn ways to satisfy himself with a woman. Hell, Johnson himself still enjoyed Carla, Tillie's mother. Yet Johnson was discreet. If Elizabeth found out, she would threaten to cut off his manhood.

Beauford knocked on the office door.

"Come in, son, have a seat," said Johnson.

"Good morning, sir. I have the information you wanted about the ceremony tonight."

"Good, did you have any problem finding out who is responsible?"

"No, sir, the whip worked great," grinned Beauford.

"What did you do with him afterwards?" asked Johnson.

"He's over at the Hendrickson barn tied up in the loft," answered Beauford.

"We'll release him after we teach these heathens a lesson. I just can't believe that our slaves are participating in idolatry. We taught them the Ten Commandments, and I've told them that I will not have them blaspheming the Lord," grumbled Johnson.

"It's because of that slave that we bought last year. He was an African boy, and he learned witchcraft over there. Now he's teaching it to our slaves," said Beauford.

"Well, after tonight, they will never practice it again. We'll teach them a lesson they won't ever forget."

"Beauford, notify all the folks in the valley that tonight they need to be here at midnight. We're going to show our slaves what the wrath of God really means."

1

*The derelict mansion on the Johnson
plantation faced east, toward the rising sun.*

BUT THE SUN WAS NO FRIEND TO THE DILAPIDATED STRUCTURE.
Clearly the ravages of time and weather had stolen its grandeur. Even at
ten o'clock in the morning, the outdoor thermometer registered eighty
degrees. It would be another day with the muggy heat rising into the high
nineties, making this the hottest summer in decades. Later, dark clouds
would move in, bringing thunder and lightning, but little moisture. The
summer drought had already shriveled the hardiest of weeds. Muddy
pools of stagnant water marked the path where a stream had once flowed
steadily for as long as anyone could remember.

The building's thick walls creaked as the temperature differential
between sweltering sun and cool interior pulled at its joints. Creeping
vines clung to the brick exterior, on a mission to overcome the thick
blanket of moss that covered the slanted roof. Wide planks had been haphazardly nailed to the window frames, concealing the interior. A twelve-
inch metal hasp and heavy padlock secured the double doors. One side
of the front steps had collapsed. Several inches of dried leaves and broken
branches piled up along the crevices between the building's tattered wall-
board and sagging porch.

In its glory days, the huge dwelling would have been one of the most magnificent structures in the valley. Now, like the young beauty who one day looks
into the mirror and discovers she has been transformed into an old crone, the
once-prosperous Johnson plantation had become an ugly blight on the landscape.

A rough roadway wound its way to the neglected building. No longer lined with carefully tended gardens, clumps of wild grasses and unruly weeds were gradually eroding the once-grand entryway. A foot or two of faded yellow tape – a remnant of a crime scene investigation – hung limply from the porch railing.

A large gray squirrel raced along the rotting lumber, jumped to the uneven wood slats, and then scampered down the broken steps before coming to an abrupt halt on a broken tile in the slate walkway. The young male, nearing its prime, raised his bushy tail and surveyed his location. One large acorn, a product of the single large oak, promised a rare treat in this parched land. He sniffed, jerked his head to the right, and stood stock-still.

Several other squirrels scampered in the branches of the nearby oak, yet none ventured near the steps. A magpie whistled at the bold rodent. Never before had this young creature gotten so close to the decrepit building. In fact, the older squirrels avoided it completely. But this youngster dared to test his luck. The acorn was large and tempting. He jerked his head to the left and sniffed again. The scent of man was barely detectable. He cautiously moved forward, ignoring an urge to abort the quest.

The thing under the porch watched and waited. It patiently rested in its dusty hideaway. It had not moved for hours. The squirrel moved forward. The thing tensed. The squirrel hesitated, and then bolted back to the safety of the porch.

Unconcerned, the thing had no regret. If not this squirrel, it would be another.

But greed would win out. The squirrel dashed forward, grasped the acorn in its paws and pushed the precious morsel into its jaws. The chiseled teeth cracked the nut. The squirrel had only seconds to savor the fresh pulp. It never saw the white mouth and flashing fangs as the copperhead struck, injecting a fatal dose of poison into the rodent's body. After an agonizing scream, the squirrel went limp, its life force gone. Four feet in length, weighing more than fourteen pounds, and with a head larger than a man's open hand, the serpent was the inevitable winner in the contest for survival.

The snake quickly swallowed the squirrel, then slithered back under the porch and disappeared into the cool darkness.

2

On patrol in downtown Johnsonville,
things were slow, even for a Tuesday.

PATROLMAN JIMMY JOHNSON LOOKED ONCE AGAIN AT HIS WATCH, the third time in as many minutes. He'd started at midnight. Now it was half past one o'clock in the morning. He had another six and a half hours until his shift ended at eight o'clock. He'd been sitting in the lot of the Baptist church with his lights out and engine idling for the last twenty minutes. Only two cars had passed.

It was a good place to hang out. The black and white police cruiser faced east, looking toward the hill where Johnsonville Avenue led into town. Halfway down the hill was the thirty miles per hour sign, right at the city limits. It was another warm night, the temperature still in the mid-seventies. The green light on the radar detector began to flash.

"Looks like I got me my first customer," the officer said out loud.

He'd first seen the car's lights as the vehicle crested the hill. He figured it was a compact car, judging from the spacing of the headlights. They were the round, old sealed beams. The speed limit was fifty up to the sign, but this car went faster, rather than slowing down. The detector read fifty-five, then sixty, and then seventy. At the thirty miles per hour sign, it was going a good eighty miles per hour.

"Shit," cursed Johnson as he dropped the gearshift into drive and switched on the emergency lights. He hit the gas. With gravel flying, he pulled out on to the road, catching a glimpse of a small, red convertible as it flashed past. He gritted his teeth and gripped the steering wheel with both hands. The car slowed as it passed closed shops, turned left on Second Street, went another two blocks and stopped along the curb next to the police station.

The patrolman pulled up behind the vintage Sunbeam Tiger. Built in the sixties, it sported a small block Ford V-8. Even after all these years, this was one fast car. He got out of the cruiser, adjusted his flack vest and walked up to the driver's side.

A thin, white man in his mid-forties sat behind the wheel. He had short blond hair, graying at the temples. Without hesitation, the driver opened the car door and stepped out onto the sidewalk. Johnson did nothing to stop him. The man was five feet, eleven inches tall, three inches shorter than Johnson. He wore a blue uniform, white shirt and black tie. A police utility belt with a holstered .40-caliber Glock was visible at the waist. Three gold stars were affixed to each side of his shirt collar.

"Morning, Chief Bishop," said Johnson.

"Good morning, Jimmy. What did you clock me at?"

"Eighty."

"My speedometer must be off. I was doing eighty-five when I hit the thirty miles per hour sign," said the chief. "Mind if I ride with you when you check the bars at two o'clock?"

"Not at all, Chief."

Chief Brian Bishop slid into the passenger seat. Johnson dropped the cruiser in drive and slowly pulled out.

"Quiet night?" Bishop asked.

"You're my only speeder," said Johnson. He thought he detected a slight odor of alcohol on Chief Bishop's breath and wondered if his boss was not only speeding, but also over the legal limit for alcohol. Not that he would do anything about it. If it hadn't been for Brian Bishop, he would never have landed this job.

Johnson was born and raised in the colored section of Johnsonville. After graduating from high school, he had enlisted in the army and served six years as a military policeman. When his enlistment was over, he came home. He was looking for a job when Chief Bishop called him.

Bishop himself was hired just two years earlier following the firing of the former chief. Johnson remembered that when he was a kid, all the cops were white. Typical of many small southern towns, only "the good ol' boys" made the force. They bullied black people and looked the other way when the rich white folks did something wrong. Bishop had turned the force around. He required all his officers attend the Virginia State Patrol Academy, got rid of the fat, lazy officers, and hired two black officers, Johnson being the first.

Bishop had also been an MP and retired as a major. Although he liked his booze, he ran a pretty decent shop. The chief would go out on patrol with his men, and he actually listened to their concerns.

Recently, the city council voted to close all five of the town's bars at two o'clock in the morning. Bishop required his night shift officers to make the rounds to see if the bars were complying. Johnson and his chief had just finished their stop at the fourth bar. At Bobby's Bar, they had to ask one guy to leave.

Although Johnson had been enforcing the ordinance for the past six months, he still felt the white guys' resentment when he walked through the doors. Sure, it was the twenty-first century, but even now a few bar owners might as well still have the sign "No Coloreds" because no black man would dare go into the bar. Bobby's was definitely an all-white bar.

After Bobby's, only one bar remained.

"Well, I guess that leaves Ginger's Bar," said the chief.

"Ginger's Bar?" asked Johnson.

"You know, the bar in Shantytown."

"Aw, chief, I don't think you should go to Ginger's Bar."

"Why?"

"White people never go to Ginger's."

"Jimmy, I doubt if black people go to Bobby's, but you have been going there every night at two in the morning for the last month."

"That's different. They look at me as the police, not a black man."

"What's the difference?"

"Chief, there is some bad people at Ginger's. Let me go in and close it down while you wait in the car."

"Sorry, Jimmy, that's not the way it works. Head for Ginger's," ordered the chief.

They drove into Shantytown. Even after two years in Johnsonville, it amazed the chief that something like this could exist in rural America. It was like driving into the past. Most of the homes were run down. Junk cars lined the streets. Several houses had boarded-up windows.

Ginger's didn't look like much. An old two-story house had been made over into what passed as a business. A sign on the front flashed on and off with the word "-inger's." The G was dark. The cruiser bounced as it hit one of the potholes in the dirt parking lot. Johnson pulled into a wide spot between three cars and an old pickup truck. Even before they opened their doors, they could hear the blare of hip-hop music coming from the wide-open doors. It was now quarter to three. The bar should have been closed forty-five minutes ago.

The chief stopped momentarily, noting the strong odor of cigarette smoke, spilled beer and unwashed bodies. Two strikes against them, thought the chief. Not only are they in violation of the closing order, they aren't abiding by the no smoking ordinance. He looked around.

A white-haired black man behind the counter looked up and froze in place. Four men stood silently by the pool table, each with a partially consumed bottle of cheap beer in his hand. One glanced up and stared at the black officer and white man who had interrupted their game. He leaned to his right and whispered to another, larger man.

The big man had a ragged scar that ran down his right cheek, and his muscular arms were heavily tattooed. He dared to break the silence.

"What's happening?" he said, glaring at the deputy.

"It's past closin' time, TL. You guys need to go home."

"Yeah, sure," growled the big guy. "Hey, Willie, there's a white honkey in here. Throw him out."

"Sure, TL."

It was hard to tell who said that because Bishop didn't see anyone's lips move. He whirled around to the dark corner behind the cue rack.

"Holy shit," Bishop thought, trying to control his first reaction.

Out of the shadows came a huge black man, maybe six feet, ten inches tall or better. Bishop sized him up at more than four hundred pounds.

"TL says you gotta leave," said the man called Willie.

"Sorry, Willie. That's your name, right?" asked the chief as he moved forward and stood side by side with his officer.

"That's my name. What's you be sorry for?"

"I can't leave until the bar is closed down," said the chief, his eyes fixed on Willie's face.

"Willie, throw that asshole out!" shouted TL.

Willie stumbled forward, grasping the edge of the pool table to steady himself.

"Willie, if you don't stop, I am going to arrest you," said the chief in a steady, calm tone of voice.

Someone else yelled, "Go on, Willie, throw the whitey out."

All four of the men at the pool table begin chanting, "Throw whitey out. Throw whitey out."

Suddenly Willie sprang forward. He reminded the chief of an angry, charging bull.

The chief recalled his Fort Leavenworth judo instructor's words, "Use your opponent's weight and momentum as leverage." As Willie reached forward, the chief grabbed the man's right wrist, rotated his hips and sent him flying over his shoulder. The glasses behind the bar rattled as Willie crashed to the floor.

The chief was on him in an instant, fitting his knee in the small of Willie's back. He snapped a handcuff on the wrist and pulled the left wrist over the right, cuffing them together. The man's wrists were so large that the clasp barely fit into the last link.

"On your feet!" ordered the chief. Willie slowly got up. Even though the chief expected him to continue to resist, Willie bowed his head and stared blankly at the floor.

"Yes, sir," he whispered.

The chief saw that his patrolman had his hand on the butt of his service weapon.

"Harry, you close this bar right now!" said Johnson. "And, TL, I don't want any problem from you or the boys. You got it?"

"Sure, Jimmy, sure. No problem," answered TL. "Let's go over to my house, guys." Without another word, the four men walked through the front doors and disappeared into the night.

Both officers escorted Willie to the patrol car. He was so big that they had to tell him to sit sideways in the back seat. The two policemen rode in front. The chief's hands began to shake. He held them together tightly until the shaking stopped.

"Well, that was a little more exciting than I expected," he said. "Let's take this guy down and book him."

"Yes, sir," said Johnson.

The chief took a second look at his patrolman. Something wasn't right.

"You know the guy in the back?"

"Yeah, Chief. He's my cousin."

"Christ, I suppose his name is Johnson, right?"

"Yeah, Chief. He ain't really bad, just a little drunk. Willie wouldn't hurt a fly."

"Maybe not, but he sure could squash one," mumbled the chief. "Where does Willie live?"

"Two blocks over," said Johnson.

"Take me to his house."

"His house?"

"Yes, his house."

When they got to Willie's street, Johnson pulled up at a white house. "That's Willie's house?" asked the chief.

"Yeah, Chief. Willie and his wife, Jasmine, live there. They don't have no kids, but his grandmother lives with 'em," said Johnson.

"Let me guess, the Grandma Johnson everyone in town talks about?"

"Yes, Chief, that's his grandmother."

The manicured lawn and a sidewalk bordered by purple petunias made this house stand out in the otherwise shabby neighborhood.

"His grandmother must be quite the gardener," said the chief.

"No, Chief, Willie does the flowers. He used to work for the parks department before they had to lay him off following the budget crunch," said Johnson.

"Funny, he didn't strike me as a gardener," said the chief as they opened their doors.

"Get out!" he ordered, noting the fear in the big man's eyes. Turning to Johnson, he said. "Tell him I'm not going to hurt him."

"Get out, Willie," said Johnson, guiding the large man out of the back.

"Turn around," the chief said. He unlocked the handcuffs. Willie rubbed his wrists together and looked up in disbelief. He had been taken home, not to the police station.

"Go home and sleep it off, Willie," the chief said softly.

Willie lumbered up the walkway.

"Willie?"

"Yes, sir?" he asked, again lowering his eyes. "When someone tells you to do something stupid, don't listen to them. Do you understand?"

"Yes, sir," Willie said, a faint smile coming to his lips. "Yes, sir."

"Let's go back to the station, Jimmy. I think I need to go home and have a drink," the chief murmured as he leaned back and closed his eyes.

"Yes, sir, Chief," grinned Jimmy as he pulled away from the curb. "Yes, sir!"

3

Overlooking New York's Central Park, a black man of indeterminate age stood at the window in his newly acquired penthouse. With the downturn in the economy, the luxury apartment was a steal at forty-eight million dollars.

He admired his reflection in the glass. Hands positioned firmly at his belt line, he lifted his broad shoulders and breathed in deeply – clearly this was an uncommonly magnificent specimen of humanity. By most standards, he was not tall, perhaps five feet, nine inches, yet he appeared much larger. Weighing around two hundred fifty pounds, his bulk would strike fear into the hearts and minds of those who would test his power.

Bullet-like, his shaved head joined with his thick neck, forming a single unit atop the broad shoulders. His ears were small and close to his head, adding to streamlined effect of his firm cheeks and polished forehead. But, clearly, his eyes were the single most impressive characteristic. The eyes, even the irises, were totally black. Most people looked away when they first encountered him. Few had the confidence to look into the piercing orbs.

And the tailored suit – purchased for thousands of dollars – completed his image. How impressive, he thought, and how good he looked in the iron gray fabric, complemented by the ivory-colored shirt and crimson tie. The penthouse was the perfect setting for this extraordinary example of a human being.

He smiled again at his reflection. Six years had passed quickly. Anyone who knew him in Liberia would not recognize him today. He had shed nearly one hundred pounds through extensive workouts and diet. He was the powerful being that would now carry on the cause.

His mind drifted from self-admiration to assessing how far he had come in the time he had spent on Earth. He congratulated himself on his progression. Soon, he would win the greatest victory ever known. The *endosyms* would wage outright war against mankind and evil would triumph. It was just a matter of time.

This man-demon had transformed himself many times throughout the centuries. For thousands of years, he had hidden from humankind, cowering in ignorant fear. The demon that had entered his mind and body hadn't begun to realize its power.

Thousands of years ago, he was simply one among the many warriors who engaged in endless conflict on the African continent. His warrior band had fought an Egyptian priest who had been trapped inside an enormous underground cavern. The priest, the self-proclaimed leader of the demons, must be killed.

In the heat of battle, the warrior had brutally forced his sword into the priest's gut. It was surely a fatal blow, but the evil creature did not die. Instead, the priest turned to confront his attacker. About to strike the warrior, the priest's foot had slipped on the bloody floor. At first, the priest collapsed. Then he rose awkwardly to his hands and knees. He raised his head to focus on the warrior. It was a fatal move. His thin neck stretched out within an arm's length, directly in front of the warrior. It was so easy and so inevitable. With a single blow of his sword, the warrior sliced through the flesh and delicate bone. The head separated from the body and tumbled to a stop against a boulder.

Instantly, the warrior felt a strange demon-power enter his being. Frightened beyond reason, the warrior ran down the length of the dank tunnel until he emerged into the light. Now a crazed being without direction, he lost himself in the jungle. No longer a lowly warrior, he drifted aimlessly, unsure of his purpose or identity. When other creatures died, he continued to live. A naked and unkempt creature, he fed on the uncooked flesh of small animals. He had no concept of time. All he knew was that he must hide from humans.

He lived on for centuries, never experiencing the finality of death. Some six decades ago, three nomadic hunters attempted to capture him. He killed the humans with his bare hands. As they died, their essence entered his body, and he felt renewed. Strangely, the human part of his being took charge. He donned the humans' clothing. He wandered into a native village. The villagers assumed that he was a crazed man and offered him food. An old woman, Shana Sarday, took pity on him and gave him meals and a place to sleep.

Gradually, he learned the language of the village people and again learned to use the power of words. At the same time, he developed an urge to slaughter more humans, as he had the three hunters. But he was smart, and he kept his hunger hidden from the villagers.

West Africa was rife with people who practiced bloody sacrifices. He began to withdraw from the villagers and joined those who relished participating in the killings. Each sacrifice seemed to increase his sense of power.

He called himself George Nay Sarday. He assumed a leadership position at the University of Liberia. He believed that he was destined to rule the nation and eventually conquer all of humankind. He almost reached what he thought was his destiny. When the coup d'etat succeeded and the rebels upset his quest, Sarday was forced to flee the country.

"Damn," Sarday said, a self-satisfied smile spread across his face. What at first seemed to be failure, led to his current status. He had become a bold and inventive African man who could re-direct the foolish Americans into following his pathway to enlightenment. They would hand over their wealth, and Sarday would reward them with a new church, one that could provide these lost souls with a sense of belonging.

New York was only the starting point. Soon, he would have access to the human beings who would be primed for sacrifice. Their deaths would serve to increase his powers and take him even closer to his goal — destruction of the entire human race.

When Sarday escaped from Liberia, no one on Earth knew that he had become an endosym, a man-demon. Sarday and his henchman, Oscar Jalah, had slipped out of Liberia during collapse of Steven Dowling's administration. The unfortunate Jalah was on Liberia's most-wanted list. Charles Morray, in his second term as president of Liberia, had vowed to track down all those involved in atrocities during Dowling's reign of horror. But Liberia had no DNA or fingerprints for Jalah. It was an easy move to acquire a Jamaican passport and identity for him.

Yet he, Dr. George Nah Sarday, former chancellor of the University of Liberia, had remained in the shadows. Despite Morray's claim that he had witnesses to Sarday's involvement, he was unable to provide proof.

Sarday used his forged academic credentials and easily found employment in the United States as assistant professor of African Studies at New York University. With the funds he had in Swiss and Cayman bank accounts, he could move in the most elite circles, socializing with the rich and famous.

In his classes, he introduced Dacari Mucomba, identified as an ancient sacred being. Sarday claimed to be in communication with this being that could change men's fortunes. He wove fact and fiction into mesmerizing stories that gained him a large following, not only at the university, but also with thousands of believers who followed his Internet blog.

Even he was surprised to discover that America was fertile ground for those who searched for a leader who would bring them wisdom and wealth. Here in this advanced civilization, channelers earned millions by promoting New Age religions. Their gods were derived from the stories of the ancient horned beings. It was a perfect environment to come out from the shadows and to operate in the open.

When his book, Dacari Mucomba, the Path to Power, became a bestseller, he was catapulted to celebrity status and became a naturalized citizen of the United States of America. Each new venture compounded his success. Yet he lacked a physical center to further recruit even more believers. Once he had a location to open a school, preach to his followers and recruit new believers, he would be poised to spread his teachings throughout the world.

On the library table, Sarday caressed the message that would be the answer to his quest. Jalah had done his research well. He had found the perfect location for the religious center – an old Southern plantation in the town of Johnsonville, Virginia.

Yes, this would be the place that would bring thousands of believers the wisdom and fortune they were seeking. And Sarday would be one step closer to reaching his destiny. But, more important, he believed that he had found the secret that would open the demon's world creating more *endosyms*.

He couldn't resist reading Jalah's report once again.

PROPERTY FOR SALE: *The Johnson Plantation*

Sixty acres with house and outbuildings for $2.2 million

This property is located outside the Town of Johnsonville, Virginia, in the foothills of the Alleghany Mountains. The town was named after its founder Nathanial Johnson.

In 1842, Johnson and several other white families traveled west one hundred fifteen miles from Richmond Virginia. With them were one hundred slaves. The Johnson family settled in the valley prior to the outbreak of the Civil War.

Following the death of Brigadier General Nathanial Johnson during the battle of Shiloh, his oldest son attempted to run the Johnson plantation. With the slaves freed and no one to till the land, the farmland lay vacant. The Johnsons became as poor as the former slaves who, even today, work as sharecroppers.

In 1914, Walter Smith, an executive for Reynolds Tobacco, purchased the property. The Smiths restored the plantation to its original glory, but elected to sell off all but sixty acres of the adjoining farmland.

During the Great Depression, Smith, who had lost his fortune in the stock market crash, was believed to have murdered his wife then committed suicide. His body was found lying face down at his desk in the library. His wife, Mary, lay on the floor nearby.

Their daughter and only child, Martha, returned to the plantation after their deaths where she became a recluse. For seventy years, she seldom left the plantation. The townspeople called her Crazy Martha. Sometime in mid-April of 1999, Martha, well into her nineties, fell down the basement stairs and broke her back. She died alone of dehydration and starvation.

The Smiths had no other children, and the plantation had remained vacant for seventeen years. It became a Mecca for teenagers who dared to spend a night in the supposedly haunted plantation.

Then three years ago, six teenagers held what was rumored to be a drug party on the old plantation. Something went wrong. Bad crack cocaine; alcohol and a Samurai sword were found in the bloody kitchen.

When the bodies were found, they had been in the ninety-degree heat for at least five days. The corpses were infested with maggots, their eye sockets dark with rot, and their fingers and toes gnawed to the bone by rodents.

The plantation was boarded up. A distant relative placed it on the market at a reduced price of two million two hundred thousand dollars.

This was the place; Sarday was sure of it. He picked up his cell phone and punched in the contact.

"Yes, sir," answered Jalah.

"Oscar, make the arrangements for me to see the plantation property in Johnsonville as soon as possible."

"I'll get on it immediately," said Jalah.

Sarday smiled. Soon, very soon, he would have the power to control these foolish humans.

4

AT JOHNSONVILLE JUNIOR HIGH, CHIEF BISHOP PULLED THE UNMARKED cruiser into the principal's parking spot. He climbed out, punched the button on the key fob to lock the doors, and walked into the school.

The long, tiled hallways were empty. Most of the students had left more than an hour earlier. The school was quiet, but for the stop-start of discordant notes coming from the band room. He opened the door to the main office.

"Good afternoon, Chief," said the principal's secretary.

"Afternoon, Susan. How are things going today?"

"Not bad," she answered. "Mrs. Bishop will be done in a few minutes. She's going over an evaluation with an intern teacher."

Seated, he could see through the office window. Ann looked up and smiled at her husband. A short brunette, Ann, even at forty-five, was an attractive woman. Bishop believed that marrying her was the single best thing that had ever happened in his life.

Soon after they had met at UCLA, they both knew that they wanted to spend their lives together. Her career in education and his in the military would make a good match. Still a college junior, Ann needed to complete her degree. Brian took a one-year deferral of his ROTC commission to complete his master's degree in law enforcement.

Their first assignment was at Fort Leonard Wood, Missouri for the military police officer basic course. For the next twenty years, she had followed him from post to post. At the posts where they were assigned, she taught school. She earned a master's degree and doctorate in education along the way.

When Bishop had been passed over for lieutenant colonel, he decided to retire after twenty years of military service. During his hunt for a new job, he saw an ad for the chief of police position in Johnsonville, Virginia, a city with a population of four thousand located fifteen miles east of Staunton, Virginia. The city was growing, attracting commuters from the Staunton/Waynesboro metropolitan area and even as far as Charlottesville, forty-five miles away. With an eight-man force, Bishop felt it was an ideal career transition. He applied for and was hired to head up the department.

With one of their daughters teaching school in San Francisco and their other daughter and her husband working in Washington, D.C., Johnsonville wasn't a bad place to start their retirement career. Ann found a position at Johnsonville Junior High as the assistant principal. A year later, the principal retired, and Ann took his place.

Ann's car was being serviced today, and she had asked her husband to swing by to pick her up after school. It had already been a busy day for Bishop. He had driven to Fort Lee in the morning to pick up prescriptions at the base pharmacy. He had also wanted to stop by the Class Six store to stock up on booze. It was cheaper than the local liquor store. Might as well do two errands at once, he thought.

In many ways, it had been a great day. He wore his police chief's uniform and drove one of the unmarked patrol cars. Normally, a retired major in civilian clothes got a "ho hum" from the MPs guarding the gate, but when he pulled up at the gate with three stars on each shoulder, it was a different story. Even his old boss, Lieutenant Colonel Roger Evans, the base provost marshal, had seemed impressed by his chief of police uniform.

Alone in his car, he could laugh out loud. Hell, he had a smaller staff than a second lieutenant platoon leader. But, no matter the size of the force, a police chief was still a police chief.

The only sour spot in the day had been at the liquor store. He had loaded six half-gallon bottles of Jim Beam into a cart. While standing in line at the cashier, he looked up to see an older woman staring at him sternly. Apparently, she considered it inappropriate for a law enforcement officer to be buying hard alcohol.

What was the big deal? He watched her leave the store and climb into a silver Lexus. A blue officer's sticker was attached to the windshield. It had the eagle, designating full colonel. Well, screw her. He would love to pull her over for speeding.

Ann's office door swung open. Out stepped the intern. She looked to be about sixteen years old. Must be getting old, he thought.

Later, as they drove out of the parking lot, Ann asked, "Did you get the prescriptions?"

"Sure did. I even stopped by the Class Six."

At the last sentence, he thought he saw Ann frown, but she quickly changed the subject. "Did the comptroller let you hire Willie Johnson?"

He had to stifle a laugh.

"Yes, since I had a one-officer vacancy, there was enough money to add him to the park department payroll. He'll be a groundskeeper with the priority of maintaining the grounds around the station."

"It's such a strange story," she said. "Here you arrest the man for trying to hit you, then he shows up and starts cleaning up the grounds and planting flowers around the station without asking for money," said Ann.

"Well, it worked out great for Willie and for the department. I now have one real professional-looking police station. Hey, how about we pick up a pizza for dinner?" asked Bishop. "Then neither one of us has to cook."

"Sounds good to me," Ann replied, stretching out her arm and rubbing his right shoulder. "Sounds like a real romantic date."

5

At the old mansion on the Johnson Plantation, the "for sale" sign had been posted for what seemed like ages. No real estate agent had sold it yet. Until now, no one had even looked at the place.

She inserted the key in the rusty padlock that secured the chain holding the gate closed. She twisted the key, yet the lock failed to open. She turned the key again, pulling down on the lock. But it still didn't open.

"Shit!" she mumbled

Carefully negotiating the ruts – no easy task in four-inch heels – she walked back to the six-year-old, cream-colored Cadillac STS. She popped the trunk, pulled out a can of WD-40, and returned to the gate. She sprayed the oil liberally into the lock and tried the key again. This time the lock sprung open.

MJ removed the chain and leaned against the gate. The rusty hinges groaned as she pushed the heavy metal gate back into the brush to hold it open. Back at the car, she returned the spray can to the trunk, picked up an old towel, and wiped her hands. She took a whiff at her palms, wrinkling her nose from the pungent odor of the oil that still clung to her skin.

Back in the Cadillac, she drove up the winding road. Untrimmed branches of the large oak trees overhung the drive, giving one the impression of passing through a leafy, green tunnel. As she crested the hill, the plantation spread out before her.

God! It looked worse than the last time she had been here. The front porch sagged even more. Several boards had come loose from the windows. Shutters dangled from second floor windows. Several windowpanes were shattered, the likely targets of kids taking pot shots with small-bore rifles. Missing shingles had opened up a four-foot wide hole in the roof. Climbing vines blanketed the north wall.

The house was a mess, and so was the yard. No one had bothered to spruce it up to make a better first impression. Weeds choked the front yard. Several spindly oak trees, none more than three feet tall, struggled to survive in the middle of the curved driveway. She sighed in disgust. Would she ever be able to unload this derelict?

MJ rolled down the car windows, turned off the ignition and glanced at her watch. If the prospective buyer was on time, she had a thirty-minute wait. She pulled a cigarette from the crumpled pack in her purse and reached for a lighter. She paused, reminding herself to empty the overflowing ashtray when she got back to the office. She lit up and closed her eyes.

Sounds of late summer almost lulled her to sleep. She listened to the faint chirping of birds and the buzzing of insects outside the driver's window. A gentle breeze rustled the oak leaves. An occasional click echoed from the cooling catalytic converter. Her mind wandered.

Mary Jane McDonald had lived in Johnsonville all of her fifty-one years. Her father, a distant relative of Nathaniel Johnson, the founder of the town, had been a tobacco grower. She first married when she was only seventeen; it had been five years since her most recent divorce. Like always, she was on the hunt for Mr. Right or Mr. Whatever.

She'd been selling real estate for the last fifteen years. She had bought her own agency and had been generally successful. However, she had found that the responsibility had its perks, but also its frustrations.

Like this place, she sighed. She had been trying to unload this monstrosity for more than two years. She then noticed the yellow tape attached to the porch railing. Damn, she thought. It never helped sell a place if the prospective buyer asks about that. How could she mask the awful truth? It must have been left after the cops had investigated the deaths of those teenagers several years ago.

She glanced again at her watch and then looked in the rear view mirror, willing her customer to drive up. She didn't like sitting here alone even for twenty minutes. Although she wasn't superstitious, this place gave her the willies.

Finally, she heard a car approaching. MJ quickly pulled out her pocket mirror and applied a fresh coat of lip-gloss. She ran her fingers lightly through her hair, noticing the dark roots. Time for another bleach job, she thought. A second look also gave her reason to pause. Her cheeks and the skin under her eyes were beginning to sag. It was, once again, time for Botox. After all, successful saleswomen have to keep up a youthful appearance.

The black Mercedes limo pulled up alongside her car. The front door opened, and a black driver stepped out to open the back door. MJ smiled to herself. At least the owner had a use for New York coloreds. She got out of the Cadillac, ready to greet the potential buyer. To her surprise, the only passenger was a husky black man. MJ paused, momentarily speechless.

"Miss McDonald, I presume? I'm Dr. George Sarday. I'm here to look at the property."

"Of course, Mr. Sarday," she mumbled. "But I am sure this place is not suitable. It's very rundown for the price." MJ was careful to keep a professional tone of voice. Truth be told, MJ never would never sell the old Johnson Plantation to a black guy – no matter how high the commission.

"It's Dr. Sarday, Miss McDonald, and this place might just be what I am looking for. Please, let me see the inside."

"I'll get the keys." MJ turned and walked back to her car.

Sarday looked around, and then turned to Oscar Jalah, his driver.

"Oscar, this is the place. I can feel it." Sarday walked toward the front porch. He detected a slight movement under the steps.

The copperhead sensed this man. Its small brain registered danger, not food. Its body tensed. It hissed a warning. The human bent down and looked directly at the snake. The creature reared back and bared its fangs. The human did not back down. It reached forward with its hand. The snake prepared to strike as the hand came slowly toward its head.

Suddenly, the tension shifted. The snake no longer sensed the warmth of the human. Instead, it felt a winter cold. It closed its mouth as the hand gently stroked its head.

"Be careful, those steps are loose," said MJ.

"That's OK, my dear. I'll be careful," said Sarday, a serene smile crossing his lips.

"I have the keys," said MJ.

The three walked up the stairs onto the porch and stood at the front door. MJ inserted key in the realty's padlock, pulled the chain through the door handles, and pushed open the double front doors. The large room, untended and unoccupied for years, smelled musty. Sunlight streamed in through cracks in the boarded windows. The light revealed books and papers littering the floor. Broken pieces of furniture were scattered about. Thick, dusty cobwebs hung from the ceiling.

MJ hesitated. She felt a sense of unease, not only with the house, but also with the two black men beside her. There was something about Sarday and his driver that made her skin crawl. It was more than her discomfort at being inside the old mansion with two black men; it was much more than that. It felt almost evil.

"It's in pretty bad shape. Maybe this is as far as we need to go," she said too quickly.

"Nonsense," said Sarday. "I want to see the whole house."

"I'll have to get a flashlight," said MJ. She turned and walked back to her car.

Her instincts told her to get in the car and get the hell out of there. But her business sense told her she had to show them the property.

"God, let's get this over with," she said under her breath.

They had made it through all the rooms on the first and second floor and had just entered the kitchen. MJ felt too warm. Dust particles filled her nose and mouth. She stifled a sneeze, pulled a tissue from her pocket, and wiped her nose. When she ran her hand through her hair, thick, dusty strands of cobweb stuck to her fingers. She felt the urge to turn and run, anything to escape, return to town, and wash down with soap and water.

What a waste of time, she thought, seething with a mix of fear and anger. This fool could never afford to buy the place.

"That concludes the tour," MJ said to the men. Her words came out more forcefully than she had intended. "As you can see, the place is not worth the asking price."

"Where does that door lead?" asked Sarday, ignoring MJ's comment.

"Just to the old cellar. When the plantation was built, the area underneath the main floor was an open storage area. In the early 1900s it was bricked up. There are no windows down there," answered MJ.

"I want to see it," said Sarday.

"But I told you, there is nothing down there," said MJ, perhaps too abruptly.

"Madam, I said I want to see it, and I expect you to show it to me," he growled.

"Very well," she conceded. "But if you break your neck, don't blame me."

MJ opened the thick wooden door and carefully descended the wooden steps, shining her flashlight a few feet forward as she cautiously descended. The two dark men followed close behind.

Unlike the stale, humid air upstairs, the basement was as cool as a tomb. MJ found her right hand shaking, and she shifted the flashlight to her left hand. Suddenly unsteady, she began to feel nauseous and somewhat dizzy. She felt heaviness in her arms and legs. Her fingers became weak. The light slipped from her hand, falling to the hard, earthen floor. The light went out and darkness closed in around her. She found it difficult to breathe.

Then she heard the voice.

"This is perfect. They worshipped us here long ago. I can feel their souls around me. I must have this place!"

MJ screamed. It was too dark to see who or what was speaking. It sounded almost inhuman. Her legs buckled beneath her, and she dropped to the cool floor.

Time stood still, or perhaps it raced forward. She couldn't be sure.

Then she heard a man shout.

"Police!"

MJ was instantly alert. A bright light temporarily blinded her. She raised her hand to shield her eyes. Where was she? What happened?

Then she remembered. Then it came to her: She was in the basement of the plantation.

"Brian, it's OK. It's me, MJ."

"What the hell are you doing in the cellar in the dark?" asked Chief Bishop.

"I dropped my flashlight," she said, bending to retrieve the light.

Finally, with the flashlight back in her hand, she glanced behind her, pausing to ask herself if what she suspected had actually happened. She thought for a moment that the black driver had reached into his jacket and appeared to grip a large pistol. When Sarday shook his head, the man withdrew his hand. She let the moment pass without comment, and the three went up the stairs and entered the kitchen.

"Gentlemen, this is Brian Bishop, our chief of police. Brian, this is Dr. Sarday and his associate from New York. I'm showing them the plantation," said MJ, regaining her professional demeanor.

"A pleasure meeting you, Chief Bishop," said Sarday, reaching out to shake hands. It's always nice to know that law enforcement is on the job."

"I saw the open gate and wanted to make sure we didn't have another vandalism incident," Bishop answered.

"I would like to thank you for showing us the property. It's perfect for my work," said Sarday. "As agreed, I will pay the owners their asking price of two million two hundred thousand dollars. You will receive my bank draft Thursday."

"But we haven't signed any papers," stammered MJ.

"Of course we did, my dear lady. You have the signed documents in your purse."

Frowning, MJ opened her purse and withdrew a fist full of papers. She checked the signatures. Clearly, it was her name and in her own handwriting. Next to it in bold, black ink she saw Sarday's name. She had absolutely no recollection of signing anything, particularly anything agreeing to a sale to this imposing, dark man.

"Oh, my, look at the time," Sarday said, preventing MJ from saying anything more. "I must be heading back to New York."

All four left the house and returned to their cars.

Sarday seemed to have dismissed MJ's very existence. He opened his own car door and slid into the backseat while his driver turned on the ignition. They left without a single word. MJ stared at the billowing dust cloud as her client roared away, heedless of the bumpy road.

MJ momentarily speechless, turned to look for Bishop. He stood a few yards behind her. He held his smartphone in his hand as he finished entering the license plate number of Sarday's vehicle. He glanced up and saw MJ staring blankly in his direction.

"Are you OK?" Bishop asked, noting her unusual hesitation.

"Yeah, it's just the heat. I'm fine. Go on. I can lock up," she said, regaining her composure.

MJ watched the officer as he turned to open his door.

Nice butt, she thought. He was tall and thin without the potbelly of most middle-aged men. His neatly trimmed blond hair only showed a hint of gray.

"Not bad," she told herself, sighing as she admitted to herself that this Mr. was happily married.

Once at a chamber of commerce after-hours get-together at the realty office, Chief Bishop had gotten rather friendly after one too many drinks. He had shown obvious interest in the cleavage she revealed in her low-cut dress. He even laughed out loud at her every word. She had sighed, smiled and looked him steadily in the eyes, but he had turned away from her to speak with the mayor. Too bad, she had thought. Just too bad, but that was the way her luck with men had gone lately.

MJ secured the padlock to the front doors and walked back to the Cadillac. She pulled the door open and slid into the driver's seat. It was then she noticed the dampness in her underwear.

"Damn, I peed my pants!" she said.

What the hell was wrong with her? She couldn't remember signing the sales agreement. No way would she have sold the place to that man, yet it appeared he was the new owner of the old Johnson plantation. She wondered if old man Johnson was rolling over in his grave. Imagine a black man buying the plantation!

She laughed nervously. Now, with wet underwear, she had one more reason to go home and shower.

Before she started the car, she lit up a cigarette and inhaled deeply, allowing the warm smoke to flow into her lungs. She had enjoyed a cigarette thousands of times in her lifetime. Inside, her lungs were scarred from the abuse. She had the classic smoker's cough and deep, gritty voice. Yet she ignored the physical warnings. Surely, the cigarettes helped calm her nerves, and she didn't intend to quit.

But today, something had triggered a change inside her left lung. One cell divided and became a cruel harbinger of disease. The carcinoma began its irreversible mission to overtake her body.

Within a matter of months, Mary Jane McDonald would be diagnosed with inoperable lung cancer.

6

At one of Johnsonville's most popular restaurants, a group of regulars joined the newcomers and visitors for lunch.

JERRY'S BURGERS HAD SURVIVED WHEN OTHER BUSINESSES JUST couldn't make it. The restaurant's success was largely due to the hard work of Jerry and Billy Jean Phillips who had opened the place in the new Johnsonville Plaza twenty-five years earlier. The two of them took pride in offering home cooking and in catering to the locals who came in regularly.

Folks often complained about all the changes that had come along in recent years. In the old days, one four-way stop took care of all the traffic. Now they had five stoplights. The lights really slowed folks down along Johnsonville Ave. The old Kroger grocery had been torn down and replaced by that big Super Wal-Mart.

No one could even count the number of fast food places that had sprung up. Recently, someone had tallied up three supermarkets, a nine-screen cinema, two Mexican restaurants, one Italian place, and a bunch of Asian ones. Old timers didn't give that sushi joint much of a chance, but the young kids seemed to keep it going.

Despite the competition and the ups-and-downs in the economy, Jerry's was always packed. Most folks agreed that this was the place to go for breakfast. For lunch, few could resist the famous Jerry's burger. People drove all the way from Charlottesville to chow down on those burgers. Low-fat food wasn't Jerry's specialty. That burger had more than a half-pound of Angus beef. For dinner, the menu specialized in old-fashioned Virginia country cooking from ribs to fried chicken.

Lori Benson balanced a tray with three burgers and an order of fish and chips. The plump blonde walked up to the booth where four men were seated. She checked her scrawls on the four orders before passing out the plates. The cheeseburger with fries and tartar sauce went to Harley Grossman, a local building contractor and president of the Johnsonville Chamber of Commerce.

Grossman didn't even look up as Lori set the plate in front of him. He was engaged in a heated conservation with Dick Raymond, the city engineer.

"If you ask me, I don't care if Sarday is a professor from New York or not, I think this channeling stuff is bullshit," said Grossman. "I don't believe anyone can communicate with some ancient leader from Egypt or wherever it is. Even if they could, who gives a damn?"

"Well, you have to admit that since he arrived in town, the old plantation has changed," said Raymond. "I've approved permits for over ten million dollars in site improvements, and it is only fifty percent complete."

Raymond got a burger and potato salad.

Bill Anderson, who owned the True Value Hardware store, piped up, "Whatever the case, this Dakery Mumba thing sure draws big crowds."

"Dacari Mucomba," corrected Raymond.

"Yeah, yeah, 'daiquiries', as folks call them," Anderson said, laughing at his own joke. "Anyway, there are some powerful folks that think Sarday has a message worth telling. Besides the movie stars, I hear that there is at least one senator and some important folks in town."

"Like who?" asked Grossman.

"Well, folks don't really advertise, but I heard that Mayor Bradley has been by the plantation for several events."

"Oh, come on, Bill, Bradley has to be political that's all. Besides, Sarday donated big bucks to the high school's scholarship fund. Right, Chief?" asked Raymond.

Bishop reached over in front of Raymond to take the plate of fish and chips that Lori had been holding and flashed her a quick smile. "My wife said that he gave a quarter million to the scholarship fund."

"Man, where does he get that kind of money?" asked Grossman.

"I hear that they pay ten grand for one of his channeling sessions. If you want a private meeting, you need a cashier's check for one hundred thousand bucks," said Anderson, gulping down a bite of burger. "Lori, can I get a refill on my Diet Coke?"

"Sure, Bill," she said.

$\overline{7}$

On her way to Johnsonville's old Negro cemetery, Michelle felt the deep pressure in her chest, particularly on the left side near her breast.

DESPITE THE COOL AUTUMN MORNING, BEADS OF SWEAT FORMED ON her forehead and ran in rivulets down her face. First, the front of her shirt, and then the small of her back, felt damp. How much longer would it be? The toll on her ancient bones was too much. They say a person knows when his time has come. She knew her time was near. If not today, it would be soon.

Maybe she shouldn't have left home this morning. Was it still morning? She wasn't sure. She had made this three-mile walk every year on the anniversary of Henry's death, thirty years ago. Mr. P, her old gray cat, followed along behind her. Unusual for a cat to tag along like a dog, but Mr. P was an unusual creature.

She could hear the roar of heavy equipment working in the distance. When she topped a hill to the north of the main house, she let out a gasp. The skeleton of a large building rose above the trees. The steel girders looked like the rib bones of a long-dead animal.

Shouldn't aught to come to pass, she thought. Just ain't right.

Only a year ago that African man had bought the plantation. All the old black folks just shook their heads, marveling that the world had changed so much that a real Negro could buy that old Confederate place.

This man, this Mr. Saturday, he be different, she thought. Dem white folks holds him in high regard. They come to him and axes his advice and pay him big money for his answers.

Word was out that he was going to build a big fence all around, leaving only a pathway to the old cemetery. All of Henry's kin were buried there. All you'd have to do is ask permission of that African man to visit the burial plots. For her it would be an easier walk. Before, she had to take the old trail from Shantytown through deep woods. Soon she'd be able to walk the paved road.

At last she saw the old slave quarters. Behind them in the hollow, a rusty metal sign marked the entrance to the burials. It read "Nigra Semetary." Inside the fence, a person could make out some individual graves, but most were overgrown with weeds. Since the African had bought the place, her people had stopped coming, for fear of being chased off.

Now the pain returned, only sharper and deeper. She couldn't take breath without gasping. Just like a poor bluegill thrashing around in the bottom of a rowboat, she thought.

She had already seen the slave quarters, hadn't she? They had faded from her sight and then come back into view. She felt dizzy and grasped the branch of a low-lying oak to keep her balance. The ground began quake under her feet. She leaned forward, ready to empty the contents of her stomach.

Suddenly, her knees buckled. Complete blackness overcame her.

"Oh, God," she whimpered. "Henry, I be coming to join you."

Then there was darkness and absolute silence.

8

The cemetery was located near the old slave quarters on the
plantation. That's where she was, wasn't she?

ALL SHE COULD HEAR WAS THE INCESSANT CHIRPING OF THE CICADAS.
So strange, Michelle thought. The large broad-headed insects live in the
ground for seventeen straight years. Then they come out during hot August
nights. By this time of year, most insects should be hibernating or dead. It just
didn't make sense. When she left home this morning, it was cold – cold enough
to freeze. A white icing had frosted rooftops, cars, grass and bushes. Had something happened to her brain? Why did she get the seasons messed up?

She turned on her side and winced. A sharp pain shot down her arm
from her left shoulder. When she moved to the right, it went away. Best
thing to do was to just lie there on her back. She opened her eyes, but
couldn't see anything but the dark.

Must be blinded, she thought. Alive, but blinded. She felt the heat
and humidity and sensed a coming rain.

Now she heard voices, chanting-like sounds from somewhere nearby.
The last she recalled was that she and the cat, Mr. P, had gone on their
walk to the cemetery to visit Henry's grave. She recalled that while
looking over at the old slave quarters, a pain had squeezed her chest too
tightly. Maybe she had suffered a heart attack. Maybe she was in the hospital. All she knew was that she was alive.

A flash of lightning brought a moment of clarity. She saw the tall oak
trees, thick with dark green leaves. No, not in the hospital, she thought,
but where?

Confused, she was sure that the leaves had been gone from the trees for weeks. If it was dark, it shouldn't be so blasted hot. A roar of thunder rolled and echoed through the valley.

The chanting continued. It had an old, familiar rhythm, like back in Haiti when she was a child. It was dream-like: the melodic voices calling to the ancient gods of *vodoun*, just like when she turned eleven years old and had been initiated into the rites. But that's all she had of the ancient beliefs. Her family had moved to New York, and she had met Henry Johnson. Had she stayed in Haiti, she would have become choir mistress of the voodoo, a *hungenikon*. Instead, she had started a new life.

She pulled herself slowly up to one knee. Then gradually she got to her feet. She hurt all over. Strange, that in a dream you could hurt. A second bolt of lightning lit up the sky. Seven seconds later, the thunder roared again. A fat raindrop splattered on her forehead, then another. A warm breeze came through, rustling the leaves.

Michelle tried once again to identify the source of the chants. She gasped. It couldn't be possible. The sound seemed to come from the old slave quarters, no longer ruins, but a shabbily constructed wooden building. A yellow light flickered from a window. The lightning flashed twice within seconds. The brilliant light illuminated the whitewashed walls inside. One door stood wide open, allowing her to make out a crowd of people, their backs toward her.

A teenaged girl stood by an open window. Michelle slowly made her way to the windowsill and called out.

"Where am I?" asked Michelle, but the girl didn't answer. "Girl! Where am I? Are you deaf?" she demanded.

When the girl continued to ignore her, she reached out to touch the girl's thin shoulder, but her hand passed through the girl's body, only stopping when it connected with the hard wall.

"I am dead," she moaned, as her passing became certain.

The spirit world had always been real to her. Her mother had brought her up to know the ways of the *vaudou*. She knew about the *petro* gods, and she herself was gifted with the skills of a healer, an *ogu-balindjo*. Many of the poor, both black and white, had come to her for medicinal herbs and spells that would drive away illness.

But this was different. The young girl and the people in the room looked solid and real. It was she – Michelle – who must be the spirit, not these people. She withdrew her hand and studied the girl. Light-skinned, she wore a white cotton dress that hung loosely from her shoulders. Michelle could make out a dark birthmark about the size of a quarter on her right shoulder.

"That's the Johnson mark," she whispered. Many of Henry's family had that same mark. Henry didn't have it, but their grandson, Willie, did.

The chanting continued. She stepped to the left of the girl. Nearly thirty people filled the room, women as well as men. All wore white cotton shirts, pants or dresses, just like the slaves wore in the old South. Several had removed their clothing and danced naked to the beat of a single drum.

In the center of the room, white flour marked the border of the *veve,* a circle that indicated the place where a sacrifice would be made. An exquisitely carved bronze statue, only ten inches high, stood in the middle of the circle. In one hand, it held an axe and in the other, a spear. From its head sprouted two sharp horns.

Michelle had seen only one such statue in her long life. It was of a god so powerful that few knew its name. It was *Ezu, the evil spirit of the Macumba pantheon.* It had been worshipped for thousands of years. Witches called it the horned god; Christians called it the devil.

The tempo of the chants increased. A single individual, a man wearing only white cotton britches, stepped into the *veve.* His greased body glistened in the flickering flames of a hundred candles sitting on shelves, in window ledges and along the floor throughout the room. He must be the *hungan,* the voodoo high priest, concluded Michelle. He held a struggling hen by its stiff, yellow feet in his right hand. In his left, he raised a sharpened blade.

In a single stroke of the knife, he slashed the chicken's head from its body. Blood spurted from the headless corpse while the wings continued to flap. Chicken blood splattered the statue, the priest and those standing close by.

Attention shifted from the limp body and sightless head back to the statue. It had begun to take on a red glow. The crimson light increased to encompass the entire circle. The people hung back, murmuring unintelligibly in low tones. The statue seemed to increase in size until it reached the height of a grown man.

Michelle stood still, straining to be sure she saw what she thought she saw – the statue's chest seem to go in and out as if it were breathing. It had become a man, a living being. It was a man, yet it was more than that. When the Ezu and a man become one, it is an *endosym*. Some would call it a man-demon.

Two horns poked out on either side of the large, hairless head. Its ears were long and pointed. Its face seemed Egyptian, sporting the artificial beard worn by pharaohs. The thing had a sunken chest, like that of an old man. Its potbelly protruded. Its arms were thin and long. Its legs were the opposite, strong and muscular. A loincloth covered the genitals. A long, pointed tail that touched the ground protruded from behind. An amulet, suspended from a golden chain, hung from the neck.

Suddenly, the creature began to move. Michelle held her breath, struck dumb by fear.

"My children, you have asked me to come," it said in a deep, resonant voice.

A blast from a revolver shattered the spell. The people fell to the earth, muffling their ears with their hands at the deafening sound. The red glow vanished. People screamed and struggled to their feet. In their rush to the far corners of the room, the statue fell on its side and lay abandoned on the dirt floor.

Four white men entered the room brandishing handguns. Two men grabbed the priest and dragged him outside. Other men, armed with revolvers, wood bats and short leather whips, forced the people to move out to the clearing.

Suddenly, the wind came up with amazing force, cracking branches and scattering leaves and broken sticks. One by one, the candle flames flickered and died, darkening the room. Only one candle remained. The single taper on the fireplace mantle still burned, leaving but a dim light that cast shadows within the room.

Several bolts of lightning and claps of thunder followed, each stronger and more frightening than the one before. The girl, who stood quivering near Michelle, ducked inside a darkened doorway. One of the white men, tall and muscular, stood no fewer than five feet from Michelle. He stared directly at her. She cringed, holding her arms tightly around her upper body, attempting to fade into the shelter of darkness. Certain that she too would be dragged into the clearing, she pulled back even closer to the wall, trying to make herself as small as possible. As the man moved toward her, he suddenly turned and walked away.

"He can't see me!" Michelle screamed, "He really can't see me!"

She moved, slowly and cautiously, toward the open door. Outside she watched even more white men coming forward, several with lanterns. The lights barely illuminated the frightened slaves. They were forced to sit on the ground, facing the large oak. Michelle squinted and stared intently, making out the form of the now-naked priest. His hands were tied at the wrists, one end of the rope left long and thrown up high over a thick tree limb.

Without warning, four whites grabbed and pulled on the rope, lifting the man off his feet. His body began spinning, twirling and swinging as he shrieked helplessly. In the dim glow of the lanterns, Michelle focused on the priest's face. His eyes seemed to bulge from their sockets, the white part large and the black centers pointed upward toward his hands. The rope bit into his wrists and stretched his arms almost to the breaking point. The weight of his body pulled him downward. The twisting intensified as he kicked. A strong wind blew up from nowhere. Its force added more intensity to the turning and swinging of the body.

Out of the darkness came different sounds – the creak of wagon wheels, the stomping of heavy horses and the jabber and laughter of men, women and children.

The frightened slaves huddled together. Some were still pulled to the sway of the priest's agony; others were drawn to the uncertainty coming their way.

Now two men garbed in gray military uniforms rode up to the cowering slaves. The white people cheered from their viewing point aboard the wagons. The older man dismounted. Michelle recognized him immediately – this was Brigadier General Nathanial Johnson. She had seen his portrait hanging in city hall.

A light rain began to fall, distorting the sharpness of detail in the mist. Michelle squinted, at first unsure of what was going on. Another flash of lightning revealed the wild anger on the general's face as he walked briskly to the assembled slaves. Michelle cringed at the sight of the intense ferocity in the white man's eyes.

"I warned you!" he scolded, his voice coming in loud bursts. "I warned you to turn away from idolatry. You continue to disobey and blaspheme the name of the Lord. You will now feel the punishment of his wrath. My son Beauford will teach you a lesson you will never forget."

The second rider dismounted, tore off his jacket and shirt, and stood naked to the waist. His well-formed body, damp from the rain, glistened in the lantern light.

Beauford turned toward the heathen who hung by his wrists. Michelle gasped as she caught a glimpse of the quarter-sized birthmark on his right shoulder. What would happen, she wondered, if next year during the Johnson Days celebration, her great grandson Willie tapped the mayor on his shoulder and said, "Hello, Mr. Mayor, we be kinfolk."

Michelle jumped, stunned by the crack of a whip overhead. Beauford stood tall, facing the group, whip in hand. Another crack and another collective gasp. Behind him, the white people laughed loudly and screamed for more.

Beauford, buoyed by the shouts, whirled to face the voodoo priest. His whip lashed out striking the man on the back, the sides and front as the body continued to twist and swing. A long gash opened on the man's back. Blood mingled with rain flowed freely down the buttocks and legs. Each time the whip tore flesh, the man howled in agony. Beauford brought his arm back and lashed out again, then again and again. Ten, twenty, thirty times the whip tore at the open flesh.

The rain shower intensified. Forked bolts of lightning crashed relentlessly from the thick, dark clouds. Blasts of thunder muffled the poor man's screams and the sobs of the slaves. The man's cries ceased. Mercifully, the poor wretch had passed out. But Beauford never faltered. He continued to raise his right arm and slash at his prey.

The whites continued to encourage the beating. "More, more!" they screamed.

A bolt of lighting struck a nearby tree. The momentary brilliance was enough to light up the man's back. Michelle saw streaks of white. She held her hand to her mouth to stifle the rising bile and turned away. The white was bone. The poor soul's shoulder blades stuck out from his back. The whip had stripped the flesh all the way to the bone. Beauford was whipping the man to death.

Michelle turned and ran as fast as she could to escape the gruesome scene. She skirted the building, lightly touching its rough-hewn siding to guide her way. She hesitated as she passed the room where the voodoo ceremony had taken place.

Out of the corner of her eye, she thought she saw movement. She stopped and took a second look. That same young girl who she had seen earlier was creeping into the center of the room. The girl bent over and picked up the statue of the *Ezu*. Removing her white headscarf, she wrapped the statue in the soft fabric. She stepped silently to the stone fireplace, glanced quickly over her shoulder, then bent down and removed a large stone from inside the opening. She inserted the wrapped statue into the hole and replaced the stone. She turned and walked toward the door.

Michelle struggled to speak, but couldn't form any words. Only low, guttural sounds came out. Then her vision began to fade. Finally, she descended into darkness.

Now, nothing. Nothing at all.

9

*The slave quarters again assumed their state of disrepair. Just
moments ago, they had been occupied. Hadn't they?*

EVEN THOUGH HER EYES WERE CLOSED, MICHELLE COULD SENSE A
bright, red light. When she dared to open her eyelids, she instinctively
raised her hands to protect her eyes from the intense light. Stark sunlight
had replaced absolute darkness.

Her old bones ached, but she was able to get to her feet. Mr. P rubbed
against her ankles, moving in and out between them in a figure eight, all
the while purring loudly. To her left, she saw the ruins of the old slave
quarters. To her right, stood the massive oak where Beauford had used his
whip to shred the flesh of the voodoo priest. The tree was larger than she
had remembered. It was leafless, as it should be. After all, it was autumn.

Common sense told her that she had likely passed out and entered
a dream world. It all had seemed so real, yet it couldn't be. She ran her
gnarled fingers from her hips to her knees.

She wondered how her dress could be damp when it hadn't rained.

Now the slave quarters lay in ruins. The roof had partially collapsed,
and the doors hung loosely from their hinges. Rotting lumber offered no
support to the decaying walls. Sunlight streamed through a gaping hole
in the ceiling. Michelle cautiously stepped inside. But Mr. P showed no
caution. The cat leaped forward and pranced into the large room.

A burst of flapping wings erupted as a dozen or so gray-white pigeons
took flight, escaping through the opening overhead. While Michelle stifled a squeal, Mr. P didn't hesitate, totally ignoring the birds. The cat

boldly moved forward, walked to the hearth, sat down and began licking a paw.

Now it came flooding back to her – this was the room where she had seen the girl remove a stone from the fireplace. She walked up to the hearth, bent over and peered into the blackened hole. She couldn't remember which stone had been dislodged.

"Which one is it, cat?" she asked.

The cat meowed and looked in her eyes. Michele patted the wide head and scratched under the cat's jaw. It resumed purring, then stopped abruptly and returned to its grooming.

This is foolish. There is no statue. It was only a dream, she thought. Nevertheless, she knelt next to the opening, brushed away cobwebs and began pressing the blackened stones. Almost ready to give up, Michelle imagined that one stone moved slightly. But she was wrong, or was she? She cursed her weak old arms and told herself to quit the foolish mission.

She stood, brushed her hands on her dress, and turned to leave. On the dirt floor, just inches from her foot she saw a broken board. She picked it up and wedged it under the stone and tried to pry it loose. The board snapped. She needed something stronger. She smiled when she saw a rusty metal hinge. She picked it up and returned to the fireplace. She jammed the hinge into a crack between the rocks. She worked it back and forth and side to side. The rough edges of the hinge tore at the fragile skin of her old hands. The swollen finger joints ached, yet she pushed harder. The stone didn't budge.

Michelle was about to give up for good when the stone moved slightly, ever so slightly. The movement rejuvenated her efforts. The block moved, little by little. Time seemed to stop. She continued to pry the stone block from the wall. Finally, she reached in and grasped its edges by the fingertips of her bloodied hands. With one desperate effort, she pulled the stone free. She lost her balance, fell backward, and landed on her boney hindquarters. It took a moment for her to catch her breath. There in her hands, on the floor between her legs, sat the stone.

The faithful Mr. P rewarded her efforts with a lick to her face with his rough tongue.

She pushed the stone to one side and weakly rose to her knees and peered into the dark hole. She could see nothing. She poked her fingers into the hole, only stopping when her hand hit the hard wall. She wiggled her fingers and tested the sides, the top and even the bottom.

"Nothing," she said aloud. "Nothing. All this work and then nothing."

Even though it was all a dream, she still couldn't fathom what had happened. It all had been so real. She let her hand drop once more inside the opening. She gasped. She felt a hollow spot beneath the hole. She scratched the spot with her index finger, testing for more evidence that this was the hole in the dream.

She felt what seemed like fabric, but it was old and frayed and scraps fell apart in her hand. Finally, she felt something bundled inside the old cotton cloth. She clawed at it until it moved enough for her to pull it out. Gently, she laid the bundle on the dirt floor and pulled on the wrapping. She put her hand over her lips and laughed out loud. It was a small bronze statue.

"Oh, my god," she whispered. It wasn't a dream; it was real. Somehow, she had been given a glimpse of the past. More than a glimpse, it was a vision of the truth hidden in the hearts of the residents of Johnsonville.

But why Michelle? She had always been the outsider. She and Henry had married seventy-six years ago, but that hadn't been long enough to be considered a native of Johnsonville. Henry had been a construction worker in New York when they met and married. When he was hurt on the job, they moved back to his roots in Johnsonville.

It was a bitter town where blacks and whites never seemed to be able to bury the past. Most of the black families still lived in the poor part of town, Shantytown or West Johnsonville as it was now called. What neither side realized was that they all shared a common sin.

It was not just the sin of the brutal execution that night so long ago; it was a greater sin. Michelle knew in her heart that the young girl she had seen that night was Henry's great grandmother. She also knew the girl was Nathanial Johnson's daughter by one of the slave women.

Even more disturbing, she knew that Henry's grandmother was the daughter of Beauford, Nathanial's son. He had begot a child by his own half sister, and this was the dark evil of the Johnson plantation.

Michelle placed the statue of the Ezu into her handbag, wiped her hands on her dress and stepped out of the slave quarters into sun.

"What are you doing there?"

Startled by the man's angry tone, she looked up to see a white man standing in front of her. He was held a heavy, black rifle in his hands, aiming it directly at her chest. It wasn't an old cowboy rifle; it was like the guns she saw in the movies her grandson watched on television. Willie called the gun an assault rifle.

"I come to see my husband's grave," answered Michelle.

"Well, it ain't in there," snarled the man, pointing the barrel of the rifle at the door behind Michelle.

The statue weighed heavy in Michelle's carrying bag. She struggled for words.

"I, I had to pee," she said. "I didn't want to do it out here."

"What's going on, Roger?" demanded a short, heavyset black man in a tie-dyed shirt who came up through the overgrown bushes.

"This old biddy was wandering around the grounds," responded the man named Roger. The man studied Michelle for a moment before speaking.

"I'm George Sarday. Who are you, and why are you here?"

"Michelle Johnson," she said. "I come to visit my husband Henry. He be buried there." She pointed toward the cemetery.

Sarday's demeanor changed abruptly. His frown became a wide smile.

"I am sorry, my dear," he said smoothly, "but from now on you must make an appointment to visit the cemetery."

Sarday took two steps forward. As he moved, Mr. P growled and hunched down as if he were about to pounce, all the while his tail twitched from side to side.

Sarday looked down at the creature and stopped in place.

"What's that thing doing here?" he demanded.

Michelle scooped up the cat in her arms.

"He be mine," she said, holding him close.

But then it was her turn to be unnerved. As she stared at Sarday, her heart almost stopped. For a split second, instead of the African man standing there, she saw an *endosym*.

Oh, my god, she realized – Sarday was an *endosym*.

She forced herself to recapture her composure.

"Can I go now?" she asked.

"Yes," said Sarday. "Yes, but remember, you must have permission to visit the graveyard."

Michelle, still carrying the cat, walked slowly up the old trail, picking her steps carefully on her way back toward Shantytown. When they got out of sight of Sarday and the white man, she set the cat down and began walking faster than she had done in years. If she had been able to run, she would have.

She expected to hear the crack of the mean-looking black rifle, but nothing happened. Once she crossed where they were putting up that new fence, she sat down on a pile of posts to catch her breath. The cat kept looking back the direction they had come. The fur on his back was still puffed up, and he kept up with his low growl.

"What is going on, cat?" she asked.

Mr. P looked up, narrowed his eyes and whisked his tail back and forth.

"We best be goin' home, cat. We best be goin' home."

10

On the way to the University of Virginia, the driver of a dark blue, six-year-old Lincoln Navigator moved from one lane to the other and back again through the heavy traffic on Southbound Interstate 95.

WEAVING IN AND OUT, THE NAVIGATOR'S SPEEDOMETER CLIMBED past seventy-five and was closing in on eighty miles per hour.

Suddenly, the driver had no choice but to hit the brakes. Up ahead, two vehicles – a Cadillac in the left lane and a truck in the right – were going side-by-side at fifty-five miles per hour. The driver closed in on the Cadillac, inching closer and closer until it was less than a car length from its rear bumper. The driver mouthed several words about the parentage of man in the car. Despite the close proximity of the Navigator to the Cadillac's rear, its driver continued at the same speed, refusing to move over. The Navigator's driver flashed his high beams then hit the horn. He then moved to within a few feet from the rear bumper of the Cadillac.

Finally, the Cadillac crept past the truck and pulled over to the right. The Navigator immediately accelerated, and the Cadillac soon disappeared from view. The vehicle resumed weaving in and out of traffic at speeds close to ninety miles per hour.

The shrill scream of the radar detector mounted under the Navigator's dash, followed by the detector's female voice exclaiming "K band-Radar" caused the driver to quickly drop the vehicle's speed to the posted sixty miles per hour.

Up ahead, parked next to the underpass was a Virginia State Patrol car. As the Navigator sped past, the trooper pulled out into traffic and followed.

"Shit!" exclaimed the driver. The trooper did not turn on his flashers, but continued to follow. Trooper Terry Tompkins called in for any wants or warrants on the Navigator's D.C. plate. The answer came back, negative. The car was registered to a William Henry Martin.

The trooper's radar had showed the Navigator decelerating to sixty miles per hour. Unfortunately, Tompkins had been listening to the dispatcher and had not gotten an accurate fix on the SUV's speed. He decided to stay behind the Navigator and at least put a little fear in the driver. For the next five miles, Tompkins followed the Navigator until it turned off at the 295-West exit. As the Navigator pulled off, the trooper dropped the chase and continued southbound on I-95.

The Navigator stayed westbound on I-295 to I-64 west, traveling until it reached State Highway 29 where it exited north towards Charlottesville and the University of Virginia.

Once off the interstate, the Navigator pulled into Burger King. The driver stepped out into the hot August sun. It was only eleven o'clock and the temperature was already in the eighties. It was supposed to reach close to one hundred by evening. The driver walked into the fast food restaurant. It was still early for lunch and only a few customers were inside.

The girl at the counter watched the young man walk up to her station. He appeared to be in his early twenties, wearing a light green T-shirt, Levi jeans and Adidas shoes. He was tall, close to six feet, six inches, with broad shoulders and a narrow waist. He wore his black hair in a military buzz cut.

She smiled, looking up into his green eyes.

"May I take your order?"

"I'd like a Double Whopper with cheese and a large Diet Coke."

"Do you want fries?" she asked.

"No, just the burger and Coke."

He paid with a twenty and held out his hand for his change.

"Have a seat. I'll bring out the burger when it's ready," she said. Then she handed him a paper cup.

He walked over to the drink dispenser, filled his cup, picked up a discarded copy of the *Charlottesville Herald* and sat down. Several minutes later, the young woman came over with a hot burger on a plastic tray.

"Do you go to the U?" she asked.

"Yeah," he answered.

"Me, too," she said. "Well, at least I will be next month. I'll be a freshman. I'm Stacey Crosby."

"I'm Tim Martin. I'm starting my senior year."

"Enjoy your meal. Maybe I'll see you on campus."

"Yeah, you never can tell. Thanks for bringing the food."

She smiled, blushing as she turned and walked back to the counter. The other female worker leaned over to Stacey, "Well?" she asked.

"He's a senior at the U."

"Did you get a date?"

"Are you kidding? When I found out he was a senior, I was so embarrassed I didn't know what to say."

"Tough luck, Stacey."

"Yeah, isn't it?"

Martin finished eating, walked back to the SUV and drove out of the parking lot heading west on First Street. He went twelve blocks and made a left turn on Magnolia. Two blocks up, he pulled into a twelve-unit apartment house.

Something didn't seem right. The parking lot was empty. Cans, bottles and paper littered the lot, the sidewalk and the lawn. At several apartments, newspapers were piled up at the doorsteps. The place looked totally deserted. Martin checked the address on the deposit receipt. This had to be the right place.

A large green poster was taped on one of the doors. Martin got out so he could read it. It was a notice of foreclosure. "So that's what happened," he muttered. The entire place was closed down.

"Damn!" he swore. "Damn, damn, damn." He kicked the door with sufficient force to bend the aluminum frame. He turned around, climbed into the Navigator and squealed out of the parking lot. Just as he got out onto the highway, the light changed. He slammed on his brakes, sliding to a stop.

"Now what?" he fumed. School started in two weeks, and he had no place to live.

Behind him, a driver beeped his horn. The light had changed. The impatient driver behind him honked again.

"Fuck you!" Martin shouted as he accelerated.

He drove around for several minutes, unsure just where to go. Then he turned onto the road that led to the main campus. He headed to Dunnington House, one of the three-story dorms on Alderman Road next to Scott Stadium.

He parked in a visitor space and bounded up the stairs three at a time. He walked directly to the registration desk.

"What's up, Martin?" asked Butch Lang, the dorm manager. The two were old friends from the Army ROTC program where both were battalion commanders.

"Butch, I got a big problem. Have there been any no-shows for a room?"

"Jesus, Martin, even if there had been, there's a waiting list of over fifty applicants. I thought you were living off campus."

"I was, but the bank foreclosed on the apartment complex where I was renting."

"Man, that's tough. I wish I could help, but you know how strict they are on following the rules," answered Lang.

"I know, but I've got to do something. Soccer practice starts tomorrow, and I need a place to crash, at least until I can find somewhere to stay. Hell, I'll sleep on the floor."

Lang thought for a minute then snapped his fingers.

"Wait a minute, buddy. If you don't mind sharing a room with a lower classman, I might be able to work a deal. We have one double on the third floor with an empty bunk. There is one small problem though."

"What's that?" asked Martin.

"Uh, your roommate's kind of tan."

"So what?"

"You know what I mean, like real tan, like black."

"Look, Butch, right now he can be green for all I care. I can't be choosey."

Lang paused, then passed a packet of papers across the counter.

"OK, buddy, fill out the registration forms."

Martin picked up a pen and got right to work. When it came to address for next of kin, he reached for his wallet and pulled out a folded piece of paper.

Lang had been watching him fill out the forms.

"You don't remember your parents' address?" he laughed.

"Dad just got reassigned to Hawaii."

"No kidding?"

"Yeah, he's one of the assistant commanders in the 25th Infantry Division."

"So, your old man finally got out of the Pentagon. Sounds neat. Hey, are you planning to go home for Christmas?" Lang asked.

"No, but I do plan to visit during spring break."

Martin finished the paperwork in record time. Lang picked up the keys with the room number on the tag.

"By the way, what's my new roomie's name?" asked Martin.

Lang checked the computer record.

"The guy's name is Dixon, Edward Dixon."

"I'll be darned," said Martin. "I know Eddie. He's a JV transfer and on the soccer team with me. He seems like a decent guy."

"Maybe so," said Lang. "But if you want my opinion, I wouldn't want to room with one of them."

Martin smiled, "It's not the first time I've shared a room with a black. Relax, Butch, they put on their pants the same way we do."

11

The black, unmarked Impala – a special pursuit cruiser – slowed as it turned into Blue Mountain Heights.

THE TINTED WINDOWS HID THE RED, BLUE AND ORANGE LIGHT BAR MOUNTED in the back window. The rear view mirror incorporated a red-blue strobe light bar. It had no outside spotlight common in regular patrol cars. The sleek cruiser passed through the development of million-dollar homes.

The supercharged LS9's 600 horsepower V-8 rumbled, even at thirty miles per hour. The special purpose six-speed automatic shifted into third.

Bishop loved speed and power. Clearly, this car had been designed for the high-speed pursuit in states like Nevada and was not needed or necessary in Johnsonville.

Being chief of police had its perks. When the four new cruisers were ordered, he had added a black, unmarked special pursuit car for the extra fifteen grand. No one in the business office picked up the additional cost on the two hundred thousand dollar order.

Bishop glanced down at the engraved invitation on the passenger seat.

The School of West African Spiritual Studies
invites members of Johnsonville Area Chamber of Commerce
to an Open House and Dedication of the School
from 4 to 6 p.m., August 14
Hosted by Doctor George Nah Sarday
Refreshments will be served
RSVP by August 10

It was part of the job to grip and grin at these city functions, and normally it was the same old BS. But this time, Bishop was curious to see just what improvements had been made at the old plantation.

Obviously, one of the changes was the entrance itself. In the past, cars entered the plantation from Old Johnson Road. The directions for the open house took visitors into Blue Mountain Heights, down 145th Street to Oak Avenue.

The chief turned right onto Oak. The two-lane, freshly paved road led out into the rolling hills north of the town. The road curved through five miles of undeveloped property covered with wild oak trees. Rounding the corner, Bishop came up to an eight-foot high chain link fence that paralleled the road. It looked like the perimeter of a maximum-security prison. The fence was topped with razor wire. Inside, ran a second eight-foot fence. Between the two fences the new owner had put in a paved access road.

As Bishop drove along the fence, a shiver ran down his spine. Something about this extra security chilled him to the bone. This was a security fence system that not only kept intruders out, but kept students, or whatever they called themselves, in.

Up ahead, the road came to an abrupt end. A metal sign with a left-pointing arrow was fastened to a double aluminum barrier. Under it was another sign identifying the place as The School of West African Spiritual Studies. The gates were wide open. Bishop slowed and came to a stop at the guard shack just inside the first gate.

A young, light-skinned black man moved toward the car. He wore a white short-sleeved gown that reached his ankles. He was barefoot, stood almost six feet tall and probably weighed less than a hundred forty pounds. Bishop detected a definite effeminate tone in his voice and movement.

The Anti-Discrimination Act of 2012 prohibited discrimination regarding one's sexual orientation. But despite the laws, Bishop still felt somewhat uneasy dealing with gays. Bishop grew up in Sacramento, not that far from San Francisco, where gay men were first out in the open.

Back at Jefferson High, one of the running backs on the school's football team was gay and proud of it.

Although Bishop knew the law, his strict family upbringing made him uncomfortable around gays.

"Good afternoon, sir. My name is Dwain. May I see your invitation?"

Bishop handed over the invitation. The guard scanned the guest list, checking it against the name on the invitation.

"Mr. Bishop, welcome to the school. If you would please turn over any weapons, I will keep them secure until you leave."

"I beg your pardon," Bishop replied, somewhat taken aback by the request.

"Your weapons, sir. No weapons are allowed on the school grounds."

"Jesus H. Christ, don't you know who I am?"

"You-you, you're Mr. Bishop," said the guard.

"Stupid piss ant, I'm the goddamned chief of police. I'm on duty, and I do not turn my weapon over to anyone, let alone you!"

Bishop was about ready to launch into another burst of profanity when he saw movement on the left. A golf cart was heading full bore up to the guardhouse.

Oscar Jalah, wearing a dark gray suit with a white turtleneck shirt, pulled up, stopped and stepped up alongside the guard.

"Is there a problem, Dwain?"

"Oh, Mr. Jalah, this man will not turn over his weapons."

Jalah flashed a broad smile at the chief.

"Chief Bishop, I am Oscar Jalah. We met a number of years ago when Dr. Sarday purchased the property for the school," Jalah said.

Then he turned to the guard, "Dwain, Dwain, the rule does not apply the chief of police.

"Chief, please accept my apology," he continued, pointing up the road. "Please go ahead and follow the driveway to the parking area. Someone will direct you from there."

"Yeah, sure. Thanks," mumbled Bishop. He dropped the gearshift into drive and pulled away from the guard shack.

The guard was confused.

"Mr. Jalah, I thought you told me to collect his gun."

"Not a problem, Dwain. I only wanted to jerk the police chief's chain."

Jalah watched the brake lights come on as the police cruiser slowed to turn a corner. He pointed his right hand toward the car, pointing his index and middle fingers straight out and curling his thumb as if to pull a trigger.

"Pow!" whispered Jalah. "Make my day, Chief."

The black cruiser wound its way through old virgin oaks. Their long limbs entwined, forming a leafy tunnel above the pavement. In several sections of the drive, the trees were so dense that even at four o'clock in the afternoon, the car's headlights came on automatically. When he pulled out into the open, he joined a line of several cars waiting to pull into the grassy field that served as a parking area big enough to accommodate hundreds of cars. He found a space at the end of a row, just part of his habit to park where he could make a fast exit.

He locked the cruiser and followed other guests toward two young women, each wearing long white gowns. One was a short black girl, and the other one was a tall blonde.

The blonde was the first to speak.

"Good afternoon, ladies and gentlemen. Welcome to the school. My name is Trisha, and this is Amanda. We will be your guides for today's tour.

"The School of West African Spiritual Studies was founded by Dr. George Nah Sarday, our spiritual leader and the founder of the followers of *Dacari Mucomba*. Dr. Sarday communicates directly with Dacari Mucomba, the greatest of the ancient African gods. Membership in the school is open to men and women who are willing to open their minds to the ancient spirits of Africa, the cradle of civilization. Our first stop on the tour will be the old slave quarters. Please follow us."

Bishop lagged behind the group, chatting with a couple members of the city council. As they started up an incline along a brick walkway, Bishop gasped as he caught sight of Trisha's naked body visible through the thin, cotton gown, silhouetted in the setting sun. Bishop was certain that she wore no undergarments – none at all.

They stopped at the top of the hill. Below, the old slave quarters stretched out next to a clearing. Not like they were two years ago, the last time I was here, Bishop thought, shaking his head. The quarters had been rebuilt and a second building added.

Trisha kept up her commentary as they walked toward the building. She explained that students were required to give up all their worldly possessions. All students, both men and women, wore only the ritual gowns. They went shoeless unless they were going to town. They lived in the slave quarters, sleeping on grass-filled mattresses, living as the slaves did two hundred years ago. They cooked simple meals in the old fireplaces and ate the same rations as did the slaves.

The next stop seemed to be a huge indoor riding rink. At least, that's what it appeared to be from the outside. On the inside was a large open hall, constructed of dark stained wood. The entire structure was roughly the size of a football field. The floor was covered with a light brown Astro Turf. High-pressure sodium vapor lights bathed the interior with a harsh light. A large stage ran entirely across one end. Images of the horned gods of the ancient world were painted on the backdrop. On the opposite wall was a huge pentagram. Rows of folding chairs faced the stage.

The two guides led the group to the seats next to where other members of the chamber were already seated. Each had been given an event program printed on parchment. Bishop pulled up a chair next to Harley Grossman.

"So, Brian, what do you think Sarday is up to?" asked Grossman.

"Hell if I know," answered Bishop.

"The mayor said that Sarday was ticked off about the critical letters to the editor in the *Johnsonville News*," whispered Grossman.

"I guess we are about to find out," said Bishop as the overhead lights began to dim.

First, they heard the drumbeat. Then rows of colorfully garbed dancers ran across the stage. All wore the reds, purples, blacks, greens, and yellows typical of African fabrics. The women wore the native flowing

African lappas, the bright cloth pulled tightly around their breasts. The men wore the same loose materials, but left their chests bare and the fabric knotted at the waist.

They began a low chant that rose to a powerful crescendo, all the while blending their melodic voices with the rhythmic movement. According to the program, they sang in the Kapel language from Liberia. Bishop noted that the performers weren't all African. There were whites, Hispanics, Asians, and others of mixed races. Yet if he closed his eyes, he would have sworn that the performers were all African.

The show lasted only about fifteen minutes, and the performers parted in the middle as they exited to the left and to the right. As the stage lights came up, a spotlight pointed stage center. Out from behind a dark curtain came Sarday, wearing ceremonial robes that could have been worn by a tribal chief.

In a deep, resonant voice that echoed off of the walls, Sarday began to speak.

"I would like to welcome the members of the chamber of commerce to my humble home. I know that many scoff at what we do here at our school. Please, you are all welcome to attend any of our classes. We only ask that each of you opens your mind to the ancient teachings and rich culture of the continent of Africa.

"We want to be a contributing member of the community. During our seminars, attendees stay in your motels and make purchases at your stores. Although our full-time acolytes must live in the slave quarters, much of the money from our school goes directly into the community. We do not operate as a non-profit organization, and therefore each year the city taxes our thirty million dollars in revenue. Of course, the school also pays property taxes.

"But, enough of the speeches, please join me at the main house for a time of refreshments and friendly conservation," he concluded, smiling and bowing slightly to the audience.

The dancers came out from behind the stage and mingled with the visitors, gesturing and encouraging the guests to follow them out of the pavilion and up the brick pathway that led to the old mansion.

No one who had ever been on the plantation property in the past could believe what they now saw right before their eyes. The old house had been restored to its past glory and beyond.

Instead of weeds and overgrown bushes, the grounds had been graded and artistically landscaped. The manicured grass formed patches of green between rose beds, sculpted shrubs, and delicate bedding plants. A large, flowing fountain rose from the center circle, its waters running in rivulets to a dozen pools in the foreground.

On the left side of the gardens an outdoor feast awaited the visitors. Tables were decorated in brightly colored fabric. Each featured a floral arrangement composed of exotic blooms. Hors d' oeuvres – open-faced sandwiches, sliced cheeses, tropical fruit, skewered pieces of roasted meats and more – were all set out for the taking.

"Holy shit, he's really putting on the dog," Grossman whispered.

Bishop slipped into his social event mode, walking around, gripping and grinning to people he knew.

Once he had filled up with his late lunch and early dinner, his attention shifted to the wide porch that ran along the front of the old building. It, too, had been transformed since this Sarday had moved in. The house itself was open to visitors, and Bishop joined a small group near the front doors to take an inside tour.

Bishop wasn't a bit dismayed to discover that Trisha would again be his tour guide. He smiled inwardly as he admitted to himself that he enjoyed watching her move about in the flimsy gown.

As they entered the front room, it seemed like he was stepping back into the nineteenth century. Trisha rambled on about the antiques and the restoration done on the house. Bishop wandered toward the kitchen. No old stuff here. The kitchen was ultra modern. The only thing that had not changed was the door leading to the basement.

The door reminded him of that day two years ago when he had first met Sarday in the ruins of the old building. He had found Mary Jane McDonald, Sarday and Jalah in the dark basement.

MJ – always the professional realtor – had apparently led them into the basement while she was trying to sell the neglected property. Bishop recalled the look of terror in her eyes when he directed the beam of his flashlight right at her at the bottom of the stairs. MJ seemed to stutter as she explained how her own light had slipped out of her hand. Of course, he could understand her freaking out in a musty cellar with those two characters. That same day the plantation was sold to Sarday.

"Gosh," he thought sadly, "it's been almost a year and a half since MJ died."

Alone in the kitchen, Bishop stepped toward the wooden door to the basement. He lifted the latch and pulled on the door.

"What the hell?" he said, perhaps too loudly. Instead of an opening, he found a heavy, steel door just like on a vault. He reached out and touched the door. He jerked back suddenly, cradling his right hand in his left. That door was freezing cold. So cold, that his fingers almost stuck to the metal. He closed the wooden door and rejoined the group in the front room.

Weird, he thought. Really weird. What's down there anyway? Some sort of giant freezer?

12

At the University of Virginia, it was unusual to play a varsity soccer game at one o'clock in the afternoon, but this was different. It was homecoming weekend.

THE TOP DOGS IN THE ALUMNI ASSOCIATION ASKED FOR THE SCHEDULE change. The football game was at night, and, with the afternoon soccer match, visitors would have two sporting options on the same day. It was smart to give the Virginia Cavalier alumni what they wanted, and the athletic department was more than happy to comply.

The university would use the opportunity to showcase its winning soccer team and show off Klockner Stadium, a world-class soccer facility. Funding for the complex came from Klockner-Pentaplast, a German-owned industrial conglomerate. The firm had built a large plastic film manufacturing plant in Gordonsville just outside of Charlottesville. The company had donated several million dollars to the University of Virginia specifically to build the soccer stadium.

The university hosted NCAA tournament games, United States Soccer Federation events and served as the training site for the Olympic soccer teams. It had weight rooms, classrooms, training rooms, men's and women's locker rooms and offices – all on a par with the football facility at Scott Stadium.

No one could ask for a better day to be outside. Virginia had enjoyed a classic Indian summer. The early October day promised temperatures in the mid-seventies. Fans lined up early. All of stadium's nearly eight thousand seats were already gone, most sold to alumni. Students stood in the end zones or sat on the grass on the hillside. When the first whistle blew, more than twelve thousand fans had turned out to watch the Cavaliers take on their archrivals, the Hokies from Virginia Tech.

No other varsity team had done as well as the university's men's soccer team. In the last two years, the men had compiled a thirty-game win streak. Thousands of soccer fans had come out to support the team, yet even this game's attendance paled in comparison to the sixty-one thousand fans that would crowd into Scott Stadium that evening to watch the homecoming football game.

Although the university's soccer team had made headway in attracting fans, football was still was on top. Today's game, with all its promotion as a homecoming event, could mean that soccer could take another step forward in its rising popularity.

This match-up proved to be the Cavaliers' toughest challenge in a long time. In the first forty-five minutes, neither team had scored. During the fifteen-minute intermission, Coach Jack Bronson quickly went over second-half strategy.

The coach had already told the team that the stats were daunting, yet he had confidence that his men would come out ahead. The Hokies were good, no doubt about it. This season, they had averaged 2.48 goals per game. Scouting reports indicated that their offense was flawless. The scouts claimed that their goalkeeper was as good as Tim Martin. That, in itself, said a lot.

Martin had all the attributes to make him the perfect goalie. He stood six foot, five inches tall, ran fast and was smart and alert enough to read the opposition's moves. Holding a black belt in karate, his martial arts training easily made him a master in blocking goals.

Finally, thirty-two minutes into the second half, the Cavaliers scored the first goal of the game. Eddie Dixon's corner kick was head-butted into the Hokies' net by Mickey Surewood. Thirteen minutes remained in regular time.

Martin couldn't remember a tougher game. He had lost count of the number of goal attempts he had stopped. Then there was the Hokies Number 17, a striker about Martin's size. He was one of the five forwards whose job it was to remain close to the Cavaliers' goal. When the action got hot, this guy used his feet, elbows and upper body to take out opponents. He was slick and stealthy, getting away with more than his fair share of questionable moves. The referee had thrown only one yellow card against the guy.

He's already done damage. Just before the intermission, Martin had taken an elbow in the ribs so hard that it still hurt each time he tried to catch his breath. He had staggered backwards, and everything had faded to gray. Martin's thinking got fuzzy.

For a while, he thought that just he and this guy were alone on the field. The temperature seemed to drop below the freezing point, and Martin couldn't stop shivering. His vision was out of whack. He blinked his eyes and rubbed his scalp. He looked up and saw Number 17 change before his eyes. Instead of facing another college athlete, Martin saw Number 17 become something not quite human. The thing wearing that number seventeen grinned and stared down at him.

Again, Martin felt confused and disoriented. He shook his head from side to side and found himself back in the game. Number 17 was nowhere in sight. During the intermission, Martin's head finally cleared, and he entirely forgot about the strange incident.

During the second half, Martin felt fine, and his team held onto the lead. Now, as the seconds ticked down to the finish, the Hokies began moving the ball into the strike zone. Then a disaster occurred. Four players got tangled up, and two Cavaliers went down in front of the goal. Martin saw the ball head into the penalty area, and he took a flying dive to stop it.

He grabbed the ball and rolled to the right. Once again, his vision blurred, and he felt dizzy.

Suddenly the creature wearing Number 17 stepped within two feet of his midsection. Martin could see a sharp, cloven hoof coming down toward his gut. From his prostrate position, he shot out his right foot and tangled with creature's leg. It went down, rolling and twisting on the field.

Whistles blew. All action stopped. Players froze in place. The Hokies' medical crew hauled out a stretcher. Martin stood and watched as Number 17, who looked like a normal, but battered, human being, was carted off the field.

Martin felt confused and all alone. No one looked at him nor spoke a single word.

Play resumed. Again, Martin couldn't recall any details of that incident. The play clock ticked off the time left to the final whistle. The Cavaliers' victory was within reach.

With less than a minute to play, the referee called for a corner kick against the Cavaliers. Everyone in the stadium got to his or her feet. An eerie silence replaced the wild cheers. It had been a corner kick that had given the Cavaliers the game's only goal. Could the Hokies pull off the same trick and take the game into overtime?

Martin positioned himself in front of the goal. The kick was off. The ball sailed through the air. Heads turned; all eyes followed its trajectory. A Hokies player leaped into the air, his head connected with the ball. Martin saw it coming. The ball was too far to the right. He would not be able to reach it. With all his strength, he launched his body sideways, arms outstretched. With his entire body airborne, his hands caught the flying ball, pulling it out of the air. He crashed to the ground with the ball in his grip.

He never heard the final whistle, but he knew it was over. The victory was theirs. His teammates lifted him to his feet and hoisted him on their shoulders. The roar of cheers echoed inside the stadium and across the surrounding hills. Martin breathed a sigh of relief as streams of sweat ran down his face, mingling with his tears.

While the crowd pushed its way out of the stadium, Rodney Moran thumbed through the images on his Nikon digital camera. *The Richmond Tribune* had sent him out to cover the football game. He had left plenty early and the traffic hadn't been as bad as he had expected.

What the heck? Might as well take in the end of the soccer game. If the press credentials would work for the football game, they would likely get him on the sidelines of the soccer match.

He had snapped a series of shots as the goaltender dived for the ball and saved the day for the Cavaliers. His camera had caught the young athlete mid-air as his fingertips reached for the ball. This photo would be on the first page of the sports section. Moran had taken some good photos in his career, but this was one of his very best. It would likely be an award-winner.

As for the teams, the difference between a winning and losing team's locker room is like night and day. The losers, the Hokies, walked slowly down the corridor, heads hung low on their way into the visitors' locker room. No one said a word; there was nothing to say.

Robbie Swanson, Number 17, leaned back into the pillows that had raised him to a sitting position on the training table. A light blue ice pack was strapped to his right knee. A couple of guys had patted his shoulder on their way to the showers, but no one said anything. It would be a quiet bus ride back to Blacksburg.

It was a different scene in the home team's locker room. The winners, the Cavaliers, had run off the field, laughing and joking. Soccer balls bounced from elbows to arms to heads and back again. Some snapped white terrycloth towels on their buddies' backsides. Others splashed bottles of sports drink on the heads of coaches, visitors and anyone lucky enough to participate in the pandemonium.

Martin finally wound his way through the crowd to his locker. He removed his cleats, shin guards and uniform. He slipped on a pair of sweats and running shoes. He planned to shower and get dressed back at the dorm. It was a little over a mile from Klockner Stadium to Dunnington House.

"You coming with us to O Hill to get something to eat?" asked Dixon. The dining hall back on campus was their traditional, after-game hangout. The pizza was always good, and the price was always right.

"I'm going back to the room to shower, then I'll join you," Martin answered.

"See you there," said his roommate as he playfully punched Martin on the arm.

Martin was on his way out of the dressing room when Jim Dugar, the assistant coach, tapped him on the arm.

"Coach wants to see you in his office," said Dugar.

Martin nodded and about-faced to turn right into the hallway that led to Jack Bronson's office. Bronson sat behind his desk, his large hands clenched together behind his head. He rocked slowly back and forth in his black leather chair.

Bronson was one of Martin's lifetime heroes. For him, as for many other young men, Bronson had become like a second father.

In the locked trophy case, Bronson kept one of his most precious possessions – a gold medal from the London Summer Olympics. He'd been on the staff of the US team when they took the gold. Martin remembered how excited he'd been when he found out that Bronson had been hired at the university. The coach had transformed the school's excellent team into a superior team. The Cavaliers were considered a powerhouse in NCAA soccer.

"You wanted to see me, Coach?" asked Martin.

"Come in, and close the door," he said without expression. "Sit down."

Martin was a little confused. Bronson didn't look at him; he just stared at his desk. Finally, he spoke.

"Why'd you do it?" the coach asked.

"What?" asked Martin, puzzled at the question.

"Why did you take out Swanson?"

"Who's Swanson?" asked Martin.

Robbie Swanson, Number 17 on the Hokies. I talked to their coach. Swanson will need surgery; he might never play soccer again," said Bronson, now visibly angry.

"Coach, I didn't," Martin said. His hands began to shake, and he began to feel that familiar confusion overcome him.

"Stop! Don't you lie to me! It's bad enough without that!" yelled Bronson.

Martin felt his heart begin to race. He had difficulty breathing. The room began to close in on him.

"Because, because he was evil," mumbled Martin.

"Evil? What in hell are you talking about? All right, the kid was an asshole. I saw him bullying players. I saw him cheating. But that doesn't give you the right to seriously injure another athlete," said Bronson, shaking his head.

Martin was barely hearing the coach's words.

Questions ran through his mind. *Why did I say "evil"? What did I see on the playing field? What have I done?*

"Are you listening to me, Martin?"

"Yes, sir."

"If I could prove you did this, you would be off the team. But I can't and the alumni would burn my ass if I pulled you without even a protest from the other team."

Bronson shook his head.

"Martin, you were the best goaltender I have ever seen. I was going to recommend you for the Olympics. Now, I won't. I will not have someone with your attitude representing the United States of America.

"Go on, get out of my office, and close the door on your way out."

Martin wasn't sure he could stand up. His face felt hot. It must be burning red. He slowly walked to the door. As he started to close the door, Bronson had a final comment.

"Tim, I should be mad at you. Unfortunately, I am more hurt than mad. And I am mighty mad," he said, swiveling the chair and turning his back. "Now, get out."

13

*The University of Virginia may have won, but
Tim Martin wasn't celebrating.*

THE COACH'S DOOR CLOSED SECURELY BEHIND HIM, AND MARTIN
stepped out into the south hallway. He paused at the water fountain
and took a long drink. He leaned his back against the wall, exhausted –
physically, mentally and emotionally. All he knew was that he had to get
away from this horror of a day.

Somehow he found the energy to run. He burst out the side doors,
sprinted past Lannigan Field, and ran, ran, ran. Finally, he stopped, his
chest heaving and his heartbeat thundering. He leaned forward, hunched
over, and braced his hands on his knees. It took him a few minutes to get
his bearings. This must be Ivy Road, he thought. Soon he found himself
in the lobby of Dunnington House.

In the elevator, he punched the "three" button on the panel. When
the doors opened, he took a dozen long strides down the empty hallway
to his room. He fumbled for his key and finally got inside. Exhausted, he
turned and fell in his chair, gasping for air. He stared up at the ceiling as
his mind raced through everything that had happened that terrible day.

First, he was angry, damn-blasted mad. Then his mood switched to
unbearable sadness. He tried to dry his eyes with his fists, but the moisture continued to well up and turn to tears. After the alternating bouts of
anger and sorrow, came the shame, unparalleled, unstoppable shame. He
tried to pinpoint where it hurt the most. It wasn't the loss of a spot on
the Olympic team. Maybe it was just his overwhelming failure to reach

his dreams. Maybe it was the certainty that he would lose the respect of friends and family.

What was wrong with him? Was he losing his mind? If he closed his eyes he could still see the thing, not human, standing on the turf wearing Number 17.

He hadn't felt this way for a long time – for six years to be exact. Why did the images of the brutal attack flood back into his mind? He recalled the stunned sensation of finding his mother and his dog, King, lying in pools of blood. His mother recovered, but his faithful King didn't. He recalled the pressure of his index finger pulling back on the trigger and the blasts that killed two thugs. Martin had killed two men. Since that day, he couldn't cry. Sure, a tear of joy or pain or fear sometimes hit, but never with the intensity of that dark day in Africa.

He'd been through a series of hellish times in his life. Who else knew that bottomless sorrow when the girl he loved rejected him for someone else? Who else could have kept his cool when he had been held captive in a dismal cell? Who else suffered like he did when his gramps clutched his chest, fell forward, and died in his grandson's arms?

And once again he came back to the shame of the day. Hot tears rolled freely down his cheeks as he sobbed. He let it go and cried until no more tears would come.

Somehow this release made him feel better.

He got to his feet, stripped naked and stepped into the shower stall, turning the water on as hot as he could bear. For a good twenty minutes, the hot water rushed over his body. Then he turned the water all the way cold, holding his breath as the near-freezing water left him shivering. He turned off the faucet, stepped out and began toweling off.

He stopped and listened when he thought he heard someone knocking at the apartment door. He loosely wrapped the towel around his waist, held it closed with his left hand, and sprinted to the door. He pulled the door wide open.

He couldn't believe what was standing before him – here was the most beautiful woman he had ever seen. She was tall. Martin, at his imposing height, seldom had ever seen a woman he could look at almost eye-to-eye. Her skin was a light brown, but people would call her a black woman. Her eyes were hazel, not brown. Her short hair fell in waves. She was thin, svelte even, but not skinny. She had on designer jeans and a brown T-shirt. Her breasts, Martin noticed, were small and well formed. He couldn't see any evidence that she wore a bra, quite to the contrary. This woman could make the cover of the swimsuit issue.

While Martin checked her out, she couldn't help but notice that this hunk of man framed in the doorway. He wore nothing but a loosely draped towel.

"Oops, wrong room. I was looking for Eddie Dixon."

"This is his room, but he's not here," said Martin. "I'm his roommate."

"Do you know where he is?"

"Yeah, if you give me a minute to get dressed, I'll go with you," Martin said as he turned to pick up his discarded clothes. "I'm supposed to meet him at the O-Hill dining hall. Have a seat."

Martin scooped up his jeans, a T-shirt and his running shoes. He went back to the bathroom and closed the door. As he dressed, he glanced in the mirror.

Eddie never told me about her, he thought.

In a matter of minutes, they left the room and took the elevator to the lobby. In the enclosed space, Martin could smell the faint scent of her perfume. His heartbeat quickened. He tried not to stare, but it was impossible not to admire this magnificent woman.

Outside, it was still warm. The October evening would be cool, but for now, T-shirts were just fine.

"Have you known Eddie very long?" Martin asked.

"All my life," she responded.

Huh? Must have been high school sweethearts, Martin thought, but didn't dare say it out loud. "So, you're from Washington, D.C. too?"

"Yes, I go to Howard University. I came down to watch Eddie play in the soccer game. So, you're the goalie?"

"Yes," answered Martin. He was glad that she didn't ask more about that day's events. Maybe she already knew what had happened. He felt a moment of embarrassment.

He quickly changed the subject. "Do you play soccer?" he asked.

"No, I'm on a basketball scholarship."

Martin figured as much, once again admiring the graceful way her body moved. He began to imagine those long legs wrapped around him. Then he stifled the thought. This was Eddie's girlfriend.

"I'm surprised you room with a black guy," she said, throwing Martin for a loop.

"What did you say?" he asked.

"You know, don't you get a lot of bullshit for living with a black guy?"

Martin wondered if she was some kind of an activist, but he hid his surprise.

"No." he answered. "Eddie and I are good friends, and I don't care what other people think."

Not true, Martin thought. He did care what other people thought. Her question brought back the sinking feeling he got when he thought about the scene in the coach's office only a few hours earlier.

They walked side-by-side into the dining hall. Martin pointed ahead to where members of the soccer team sat at their regular table, scarfing down pizza. Eddie stood up and flashed a broad smile.

"Hi, Tim. I see you've already met Sam."

"Sam?" Martin asked.

"For Samantha," she said, reaching out to Eddie, who threw his arms around her.

Martin felt a tad bit of jealousy. What could she see in Eddie? He was a good five inches shorter than Sam.

Eddie pulled out a chair for her and tapped on the back of the one next to it for Martin. Everyone kept at the pizza while talking about the game. Martin wished they would talk about something else, but with a big win like that, the game was bound to be the main topic.

Martin's attention wandered away from soccer and settled on this fabulous specimen of femininity sitting right beside him. He picked up some of the chatter between the two.

"Then what did Mom do?" asked Eddie.

Samantha laughed. "You know how Mom is, she insisted on paying for everyone."

Something was crazy here, Martin thought, watching their interaction.

"You have the same mother?" he blurted out before thinking.

They both laughed again.

"Same mother, same father. Yeah, we're twins," said Eddie, watching Martin for a reaction.

"Twins?"

"Well, not identical twins," laughed Eddie. "For some reason, Sam got all the tall genes, and I got all the short genes."

"You're not joking, are you?"

"Of course not."

"But you never mentioned you were Eddie's sister," said Martin.

"Didn't I?" responded Samantha as she winked at him.

All Martin could do was smile back.

14

*At the newspaper office on Broad Street, Marty Noonan scanned
the proof sheet of ads for Wednesday's paper.*

IT LOOKED LIKE THE FIVE-PERCENT INCREASE IN ADVERTISING WAS HOLDING
steady. *The Johnsonville News,* with its circulation of nine thousand,
provided the only local news in town. Noonan's salary depended on
advertising. If this kept up, the publisher might finally cough up a pay
raise for his hard-working editor – at least Noonan hoped he would. Even
the local school bus drivers made more money than he did and worked far
fewer hours. Any increase would help pay the bills.

Shannon O'Kelly, the advertising manager, poked her head in the
door.

"You have a visitor."

"Who?" asked Noonan. She handed him a business card. He glanced
briefly at the card. It read "Dr. George Nah Sarday."

"Shit!" Noonan said and took a deep breath. "Tell him I'm on the
phone. As soon as I finish the call, I'll see him."

"The phone?" asked Shannon. Noonan clearly wasn't on the phone.

"Just tell him I'll be there as soon as I get off the phone," he growled.

"Right," she said as she closed the door.

Noonan immediately stood up, cleared his desk, set a chair beside
the desk, ran his fingers through his hair and straightened his tie. He was
worried. The paper had just gone out. He had written a rather scathing
editorial about Sarday's so-called school. He really had considered removing the bit about the school being the next Jonestown, that infamous

place in South America where a weirdo cult committed mass suicide. Maybe Sarday's followers would be the latest bunch of loonie-tunes lining up to drink poisoned Kool-Aid.

Maybe this guy wanted to take the paper to court, charge him with libel, or find some way to kill free expression in Johnsonville. But Noonan had gone on that chamber of commerce get-together about a month ago. He knew he wasn't alone. He had heard the undercurrent of complaints from the business people. He had every right to add his two cents to the mix.

He started for the door, but stopped before opening it. He turned back to the desk and picked up his brass nameplate. He ran his right shirt cuff over the metal to wipe off any dust or fingerprints. It read, "Martin S. Noonan, Editor." He approached the office door once again, took a deep breath, and stepped into the waiting area.

Sarday was sitting quietly, legs crossed, reading the latest edition. He looked up when he heard Noonan's door open. Sarday stood, pausing to give Noonan ample time to take in his commanding stature and admire his light gray suit, silk shirt and expensive tie. Noonan didn't even own a suit. He made do with a sports coat and Dockers when he had to dress up. Sarday's suit probably cost more than Noonan made in a month.

"How may I help you, Dr. Sarday?" he asked.

"Mr. Noonan, I would like to discuss your editorial." Noonan felt his pulse quicken. But Sarday smiled and seemed congenial enough.

"Of course, would you like to come into my office and have a seat?"

Sarday closed the door behind him and sat in the chair near the desk. Noonan eased himself into his own chair and prepared for the assault.

Sarday smiled, and then spoke slowly.

"Obviously, you are not a believer in our school."

"No, sir, I am afraid that I just do not believe in what you do," said Noonan.

"But why would you discredit us? If the school were a Jewish synagogue, a Buddhist temple or a mosque, would you write such disparaging remarks?"

"Well, no, but those are established religions."

"Well, our religion is older than all those other religions," said Sarday.

"Sir, I attempted to interview you before I wrote the piece, but your office said you did no interviews. If I had a better understanding of what you did, I could write a new editorial."

Sarday smiled, "Mr. Noonan that is why I am in your office. I want to tell you about Dacari Mucomba, and I believe that once you learn what we have to offer, you will even want to join."

Fat chance, he thought, but he held his tongue.

"Go ahead, Mr. Noonan, ask the hard questions."

"Very well, Dr. Sarday, you claim that you channel the spirit of a guy you call Dacari Mucomba. What is he, some kind of ancient warrior?"

"Oh, my, no," said Sarday, his voice smooth and even. "Dacari Mucomba is not a warrior. He is not even human. He is a being of great power. His kind has existed since the dawn of time."

"What do you mean 'not human'?" asked Noonan. "What is he, a devil or an angel?

"They are neither," answered Sarday.

"They? You mean there are more than one?"

"Of course, but I only communicate with the one called Dacari Mucomba."

That was enough, Noonan thought. This guy is definitely a nut case. He paused long enough to scribble a few notes on his tablet. Then he looked up and asked, "If there are a number of these creatures, how come no one has ever heard of them?"

"Oh, but that's not true," explained Sarday. "In ancient Egypt, Seteh, the god of the desert, storms, darkness and chaos, and Apep, whose existence was believed from the time of the Middle Kingdom, were both these beings. Then in West Africa, the Tien who my people call water spirits, are really these beings. Throughout your recorded history, these beings are found in folklore of all nations."

"Can these beings die?" frowned Noonan.

"Of course, all creatures die, but they live for a very long time."

"Like how long?" asked Noonan.

"For thousands of years," said Sarday, smiling broadly and spreading his arms out wide.

Noonan looked up from his notes and shook his head.

"All right, Dr. Sarday, so far, the only thing I believe is that you are pulling my leg."

"Oh, no, Mr. Noonan. What I tell you is only the truth."

"Let's try a different approach," sighed Noonan. "Why the old Johnson plantation?"

"It is the perfect place to focus the power of these beings," replied Sarday. "The ley line that begins southeast of Washington D.C. and ends in Danville, Virginia, passes right through the property."

"The ley line?" Noonan asked, puzzled by the term.

"The Earth is a large magnetic engine. Ley lines are areas on the surface of the planet where these magnetic forces can open doorways to other worlds. A ley line passes through Stonehenge in England. The great pyramid of Giza in Egypt is on a ley line. Mount Rainier in the state of Washington is on a ley line. In my country of Liberia, the ancient village of Zigda is located on a ley line."

None of that made any sense at all to Noonan. He decided to drop that topic and move on to another question.

"On the chamber of commerce visit to the plantation, some young folks gave us a tour. They called themselves acolytes. Are they students?" asked Noonan.

"Much more than students," said Sarday. "The forty acolytes are all young adults who were lost to society. They lived on the streets, were into drugs, prostitution and had no family. I have given each of them a new life. Now they give their very essence in the service to the school."

"So they aren't students?" asked Noonan.

"No, the students are men and women who realize that I can give them great wealth and power through Dacari Mucomba."

"I understand that you charge a hundred grand to become one of your students. Is that true?" asked Noonan.

"Yes, that is a start," said Sarday.

"A start? You mean you charge more?"

"Of course, for some who wish to become followers, I charge millions."

"Why in the world would anyone give you that kind of money?" asked Noonan, amazed by Sarday's statement.

"Why? For immortality, wealth beyond one's dreams, and power over our fellow men," said Sarday.

"You're kidding me," said Noonan.

"Of course not," laughed Sarday.

"But immortality, that's impossible. How?" asked Noonan.

"Why did you say you were a Christian in your editorial? Don't you believe in eternal life?" asked Sarday.

"Yes, I do, but by immortality. You're talking about never dying," said Noonan.

"All right, I might be exaggerating a little," said Sarday. He looked down and smiled before continuing. "But if you could live for a thousand years in perfect health, would you pay for that opportunity?"

"I guess so," said Noonan. "What about power and wealth?"

"Mr. Noonan, imagine being able to control another person by using the power of your mind to stop them in their tracks, to make them do your bidding. What would that be worth? And, what if you could have the power to have all the wealth you could ever want? Would you pay for that?" asked Sarday.

"Of course, but that isn't possible," said Noonan, shaking his head from side-to-side for emphasis.

"I disagree," said Sarday. "For years, it has been proven that by using our minds, we can change the outcome of an event. Let me give you an example. Do you have a quarter?"

Noonan reached into desk drawer, fumbled around in a small plastic container and pulled out a quarter.

"What is the probability of the quarter coming up heads?" asked Sarday.

"Fifty-fifty," said Noonan.

"So what are the odds of the quarter coming up heads ten times in a row?"

"Pretty low I guess," answered Noonan.

"All right, I want you to flip the quarter, and let it drop on the desk. We will do it ten times. Heads will come up ten times in a row."

Noonan flipped the coin. It struck the desk, rolled and landed heads. He flipped the quarter eight more times. Each time, it came up heads.

"Wait a minute," said Noonan. "What if I switch quarters, will it still come up heads?"

"How many quarters do you have in your desk?" asked Sarday.

Noonan searched in his change box. He had seven more.

"Throw all eight into the air at the same time," said Sarday.

Noonan flipped them up, allowing all eight to fall on the desk. When they stopped rolling, he looked down at the eight quarters. Each one had come up heads.

"Wow, that was some trick," said Noonan.

"No trick," said Sarday. "Now a much greater test. Write down these numbers: 3, 7, 19, 22, 48 and 78."

Noonan wrote the numbers in his notebook.

"What am I supposed to do with these?" asked Noonan.

Sarday looked at his watch.

"It is five o'clock. The state lottery closes for tonight's drawing at six. Go across the street to the shopette and select those numbers for tonight's drawing."

Sarday suddenly stood.

"I must go," he said. "It has been nice talking to you, Martin Steven Noonan." Before he left, Sarday turned back, smiled broadly and made his final statement. "Mr. Noonan, my fee for you to become a student of Dacari Mucomba is one hundred thousand dollars."

Noonan stared at the door for a full ten minutes before he got up and walked out.

Shannon hadn't gotten anything done while Sarday was in the office. When Noonan came out, she looked up anxiously.

"Are we going to be sued?"

"I don't think so," said Noonan. "I'm going home for the night. Lock up when you're through."

15

In his apartment, Noonan stared at the TV. It was just another of those boring, lonely nights.

HIS ONLY COMPANY WAS THE BEACHED BLOND WEATHER GIRL WITH the big boobs. She had just told him there was a fifty percent chance of rain tonight. Since he could hear the water running down the gutters outside, she had only been off by fifty percent.

Must be nice, he thought. At least in her job, she didn't get fired even if she was wrong. Not like newspapering. Everyone is out to get those "damn journalists" any time they disagree with what you write.

Just another pity party at Marty's pad, he thought.

He shifted his feet to an empty spot on the coffee table. His shoes shared the cluttered tabletop with out-of-date magazines, rumpled newspapers, a half-eaten pepperoni pizza, and four hand-compressed beer cans. He clasped his fifth beer, raised it to his lips and guzzled the brew until the can was empty.

"What a dump!" he said to no one but himself. The cramped, one-bedroom apartment was too small to hold his second-hand furniture, beat-up books, dirty laundry and overflowing garbage and recycling bins. His ex-wife had been right after all; she had always nagged him about being a slob.

"Well, screw you!" he said. She had taken everything he had; he could damn well live in a mess if he wanted to.

That spooky Sarday episode popped into his mind again. He had to laugh out loud at that phony huckster. For a mere hundred grand, Sarday had said that Noonan could join his so-called religion. Hell, he could barely pay his rent. His credit cards were maxed out. What a joke!

More TV ads droned on louder and longer than the news itself. Noonan had to pee. He was about to get up and go when he heard the announcer say, "Are you ready for the Virginia Lottery's Pick Six?"

That hyper guy must have had ADD as a kid, and it stuck with him, thought Noonan. He could delay his trip to the bathroom, but not for long.

"Tonight's jackpot is four million dollars. Will there be a lucky winner?" Then the announcer spun the wheel and the little white balls bounced around.

Noonan reached into his pants pocket and pulled out the wrinkled lottery ticket. What an idiot he had been to waste a buck on the stupid ticket, especially after that trick Sarday had pulled with the quarters. Every time he had ever bought a lottery ticket, he had lost. When he lost this time, he would really burn Sarday in next week's editorial. By God, he'd drive the black son-of-a-bitch out of Johnsonville.

The first number rolled into the slot. "Seven!" screamed the announcer. The second number came down, "Forty-eight!" The third, "Nineteen!"

Noonan held his breath.

The fourth number, "Twenty-two!"

Noonan squeezed his eyes shut and pounded his fists on his knees. "Let the next one be a three," he whispered.

"Three!" yelled the announcer.

Now Noonan began chanting, "78, 78, 78. Let it be 78."

The balls dropped; time stood still. It stopped. Noonan couldn't watch.

He heard the announcer make the final call.

"Seventy-eight! Tonight's winning numbers are 3, 7, 19, 22, 48, and 78."

"Oh, my God!" Noonan sobbed. "Oh, my God! I can't believe it! I won! I won four million dollars!"

He laughed uncontrollably. He really couldn't believe it.

16

For Tim Martin, Christmas had been a bust.

HE WOULD BE RELIEVED WHEN THE WHOLE CHRISTMAS HOLIDAY WAS finally over. When he was a kid, he'd loved visiting his grandparents in Newburgh, New York. But just six months earlier, Grandpa Martin had passed away suddenly. Grandma had tried her best to put on a brave face, but too often, Martin saw her eyes well up with tears.

Martin didn't even have his parents there to ease the pain. Dad couldn't get leave to come back from Hawaii. That left him to cope with aunts, uncles and a pack of little cousins. Grandma had begged him to stay through New Year's, but Martin had already planned to spend a few days in Silver Springs, Maryland, with Eddie and his folks. It was time to hit the road.

"Here, Tim," Grandma said. "This might hold you over until you get to your roommate's place." She held out the shoebox, loosely tied with Christmas ribbon. He knew without even looking that Grandma had put together survival food: ham sandwiches, fresh veggies, a couple cans of Diet Coke and a bag of chocolate chip cookies. Those were the standard going-away goodies she always fixed for him when he drove off. Martin lifted up a corner and took a whiff of the fresh chocolate smell. He and Gramps had always enjoyed their "cookie time" together for as long as Martin could remember. He gave Grandma a warm hug, a kiss on the cheek and added an additional hug before heading off on the six-hour road trip to Maryland.

Back in the Navigator, he planned to travel south on the Palisades Interstate Parkway, to the New Jersey Turnpike, then 95 to 695. He headed west on the 695 Beltway toward Eddie's place. The power under the hood, the smooth road, and the simple sense of once again being on his own gave him a temporary high.

Although Christmas was bad, it wasn't any worse than the rest of the semester. From day one, the entire semester sucked. Martin had maintained an outward appearance that everything was OK. But each day, he felt himself sinking deeper and deeper into a funk. Call it depression, call it anger, call it embarrassment – whatever it was – wasn't good. His grades had gone into a free-fall. He counted the days until the semester would end. He was just done with the college scene. Most seniors had been sending out resumes, scheduling job interviews or applying for graduate school. Not so for him. His future was set in concrete.

Since he had gone to college on a ROTC scholarship, he was committed to spending the next five years as an infantry officer. One week after graduation, he would report to the Infantry Officer Basic Course, followed by Airborne training, the Ranger course and then on to an assignment with the 82nd Airborne Division at Fort Bragg, North Carolina.

As recently as five months ago, Martin would have said he was excited about his future. Now, the army, like the rest of his life, was just a matter of going through a series of meaningless steps. It was just putting in an appearance and nothing more.

Sometimes he couldn't believe the changes in his thinking. Sometimes this new Martin was downright frightening. Since that soccer game in October, he just did what he had to do, not what he wanted to do. During the rest of the season, he kept his position as the team's goaltender and helped the Cavaliers win the NCAA national championship. He'd been one of the seniors to be formally recognized for the achievement by the college president. Most young men would have been thrilled at the honor. Martin felt nothing.

His relationship with Coach Bronson had gone from bad to worse. They were like a married couple who knew their relationship had failed, but who stayed together for the sake of the kids. They'd pass each other on the field without even making eye contact. Martin's self-esteem totally tanked when it was announced that Bronson would take a two-year leave of absence to coach the U.S. Men's Soccer team for the coming Olympics. Bronson would go for the gold; Martin would not.

Soccer was no longer part of Martin's life. Nothing seemed a part of his life.

He yawned, "Maybe I should stop for coffee," he said out loud. He didn't. He was on the road. Nothing short of being low on gas or really needing to pee would stop him now. Yet, he had to admit, he was tired.

He got no release from his ongoing depression, even at night. He couldn't sleep. He was plagued by bad dreams – nightmares – that jolted him awake and kept him wide-eyed for hours. The first episode began shortly after his vision of the thing on the soccer field. The same terror had come back another ten times. It was always the same. Martin would find himself struggling in total darkness. He couldn't breathe. He would be at the bottom of a deep, dark well. Above him, the pressure of hundreds of feet of water held him down. He would struggle to swim out of the darkness, but would feel icy, cold fingers pull him down deeper and deeper. His lungs would be on the verge of bursting, and he would wake up soaked in sweat. His breathing would still be labored. Several minutes would pass until he could finally catch his breath.

The last night of terror happened at Grandma Martin's house. The next day, his ankle hurt and he found himself rubbing the place where the hand had grabbed it. Even now he reached forward and ran his hand down his lower leg toward the gas pedal and back up again, trying to ease the phantom pain.

Same dream, each time, no different.

Martin dared to mention his ongoing depression to the team doctor when he had a routine physical. The doctor shrugged it off, chalking it up to "senior blues." He said it wasn't uncommon for students to feel anxious or depressed so close to graduation. It was the end of the college years, and the beginning of real life on the outside.

He pulled off at a gas exit, found a low price, and filled up. Standing up was good. Already his back ached from sitting in the same position for so long. He topped off the tank, pressed and turned the gas cap, got back behind the wheel and pulled into a parking spot. After using the restroom, he bought a large black coffee and slipped back into the car.

OK, now I'm jazzed again, he told himself. The chilly air and strong coffee had revitalized him. Now that New Year's Day was coming, Martin resolved to take a more positive outlook on life. He told himself that a healthy twenty-two year old man shouldn't be depressed. After all, he had his whole life ahead of him. Perhaps the next four days would turn things around. Going to Eddie's place would be a good starting point – besides, Eddie's sister, Samantha, would be there.

Just thinking about that dark goddess made him feel good. Strange, that terrible day on the field was also that wonderful day when he first met Sam. He could close his eyes and recall the first time he saw her standing at his door. Although they had only spoken a few words and he had been with her for less than an hour, he wanted to see her again and again.

"Good old Eddie," he said, smiling and nodding his head while tapping the steering wheel. It was Eddie who had suggested that Tim spend a few days with the Dixons over the holidays. They had been sitting with Eddie's parents at the soccer banquet when Eddie asked if Tim would like to visit. Both parents had seemed genuinely pleased with the idea.

His thoughts went back Samantha. She looked like her mother, but had her dad's height. Her mother stood maybe five ten and actually had blond hair. Apparently, one of Eddie and Samantha's grandparents had been white. Their dad was as black as any Liberian he had met when his dad was stationed in Africa.

Martin exited the Beltway onto Highway 97 North. He took the Hewitt Avenue Exit and turned into a strip mall and pulled into a parking space in front of an expensive boutique.

This wasn't uncharted territory for him. His parents had bought a home in McLean, Virginia, when they returned from Africa. He lived there during his last three years of high school, Mom stayed there while Dad was commanding an Infantry Brigade in Iraq, and they were still in McLean when Dad got orders for Hawaii. He was familiar with the

Hermitage Park area because his high school team had played a soccer game with a private high school in Wheaton, Maryland. It was a pretty classy area. Most of the upscale homes were located in gated areas where entry was limited. He figured he'd have to call first in order to get in.

He thumbed through his contacts and called the Dixons on his cell. On the third ring, a woman with a Spanish accent answered.

"Dixon residence," said the woman. "How may I help you?"

"This is Tim Martin. May I speak to Eddie Dixon?"

"One moment, please." Martin waited less than a minute.

"Tim, where are you, man?"

"In the mall off Hewitt Avenue."

"Great, take Hewitt to Layhill Road, turn left on Attwood Road. You'll go about one mile, then take a left on Townline Road. Take the next right on Killmier Road. Follow the road to its end. I'll tell the guard at the gate that you're on the way," said Eddie. "See you in about fifteen minutes."

Martin followed Eddie's directions. He passed multi-million dollar homes. He knew Eddie's dad was a big-time defense attorney. Business must be good to live in this neighborhood.

Once on Killmier, the houses were even more impressive. It looked like they were sitting on at least ten-acre sites. Horses grazed in pastures along the road. The distance between homes grew even longer.

The paved road had been freshly plowed from a recent snowstorm. In the distance, the rolling hills were white with snow. Small oak groves dotted the wide pastures. White railed fences paralleled the road, almost disappearing in the snow. The road curved. An imposing stone wall at least seven feet tall began along the shoulder. The road finally ended at a wrought iron gate.

Martin saw a man approach his car. The guy was wearing dark pants, boots, a short-waisted leather jacket, and a black baseball cap. He walked to the center of the road and held up one hand signaling Martin to stop. A nine-millimeter Glock was strapped to his hip and a logo above his nametag read "Anderson Security."

Martin wondered if he had somehow taken a wrong turn. Granted, Eddie's directions were a bit complicated. This must be a really exclusive development, he thought. Most neighborhoods don't have an armed guard at the gate.

Martin rolled down the window. A blast of 26-degree air reminded him that it was really cold outside.

"I'm here to visit the Dixons," he said. "Do I have the right place?"

"Name?" asked the guard.

"Tim Martin."

"Driver's license?"

Martin pulled out his wallet and showed the man his license. The man checked the picture on the license and looked at his clipboard.

"Go ahead."

"Which house is the Dixons?"

"Just follow the road," the guard said.

"OK, thanks," Martin said, just a little irked. He closed the window, pulled through the gate and started up a hill. "Well, he didn't say I had the wrong place," mumbled Martin. "So, I must have the right place."

He figured the homes must have the owner's names on the mailboxes, so he slowed down in case he'd have to stop to look. At the top of the hill, he put on the brakes. "Holy shit!" he exclaimed as he looked down into a valley.

Below him in the valley stood a single, two-story mansion. That was the only word he could use; it was clearly a mansion. The walls were gray granite, and the roof was slate. On the left stood a huge garage, large enough to hold at least six cars. Next to the house was a smaller house, also two stories tall. To the right were stables and in the field next to the stables, three dark brown horses stood side-by-side staring blankly as the Navigator drew near.

Martin saw a lighted tennis court adjacent to the house. The circular driveway could accommodate dozens of vehicles. A flight of stone steps at least twenty feet wide led up to the expansive front porch that ran all along the front of the house. Impressive double oak doors, each four feet wide and at least nine feet high, marked the formal entry. The house looked old, perhaps built in the thirties. Tim could see a large array of solar panels in a nearby field. He guessed that the house might have been updated with state-of-the-art technology.

He slowly drove down the hill and pulled up in front of the house. He stepped out of the car onto the dry pavement. He was just about to close the driver's door when he saw the front door open suddenly. Eddie ran down the steps, whooping a Cavalier greeting to his friend.

"Hey, man, great to see you!" he yelled.

"You too, Eddie."

"How was the trip?"

"Not bad, a little snow in Newark, but it wasn't sticking," Martin said.

"Well, come on in. We can get your bags later."

They walked into a house that the King of England would have found comfortable. Martin noticed the oak paneled walls and the thick oriental rugs on the hardwood floors. A grand stairway with an oak banister led to the upper floor. He couldn't recall ever having been inside a house like this one. He had to remind himself to close his mouth and not let his jaw drop open in amazement.

A short, round Latina woman in a maid's uniform reached out to take Martin's jacket.

"Your coat, sir," she said in a whisper.

At first, Martin didn't react to her request. When he realized that she was waiting for him to do something, he figured out what she wanted and slipped off his coat.

Just walking down the wide hallway was a parade of wonders. Each room they passed was artfully decorated and filled with only the highest quality furniture. He was amazed that he had roomed with Eddie for half the school year, but had never suspected that he would have lived in a place like this. He'd met Eddie's parents twice and his sister, Samantha, only once. He never had a clue that the family was so well off.

Now, at least, he understood what Eddie meant when he said there'd be no problem with him spending a few days with them. Before they left for winter break, Eddie had mentioned that his grandparents would be visiting from France. Martin repeatedly asked Eddie if there was room for one more, but Eddie had laughed it off and insisted that he come. Now he understood what Eddie meant.

Eddie must have picked up on Martin's reaction to the opulence.

"Don't worry, Tim," he said. "We've lived here for ten years, and I still have a problem dealing with this house."

"Why in the world were you living in a dorm?" Tim asked.

"Well, I really didn't have any choice. Dad told both Sam and me that we had to experience the same hardships as the other students," Eddie answered.

Martin was especially amazed at the size and quality of the library. The large room featured several comfortable reading areas, each with overstuffed chairs, brass reading lights, and thick area rugs. In one corner, he noticed a heavy oak desk. Its highly polished surface likely measured six by eight feet. Behind it, he heard the steady ticking of a tall grandfather clock encased in a dark wood.

Four adults were having coffee at a low oak table. Martin immediately recognized Eddie's parents. The other couple was older, perhaps in their seventies. The older gentleman was black with snow-white, closely cropped hair. Martin detected a military bearing. The woman was white, thin and fine-boned. Her blond hair was streaked with tones of gray. When she looked up at Martin, he thought he saw Samantha's eyes.

Question answered, Martin said to himself. This distinguished-looking couple must be the grandparents. Now he knew where Samantha and her mother had inherited their light skin.

After the introductions, he and Eddie pulled up two wooden library chairs and joined the group. They started out with small talk about the weather, sports, and the differences between France and the United States.

The grandfather, Howard Nichols, asked Martin what he intended to do after graduation. Martin told him about his military obligation.

"So just why did you decide to get into ROTC?" Nichols asked.

"Well, the military is kind of a tradition in our family," Martin answered. "My father's in the army and so was my grandfather."

"Hmm," Nichols said. "I'm curious. What was your grandfather's name?"

"William Martin," he replied.

"Not Major General William Henry Martin?"

"Yes, sir."

"That proves once again that it's a small world," Nichols said. "I knew your grandfather. We were in the same section at the War College in 1988. He was an officer in the Corps of Engineers; I was an Infantry officer.

"By the way, I read in the alumni bulletin that Martin passed away this summer," he told him. "I was so sorry to hear that."

"Thank you," Martin said quietly. "It was quite a jolt to the entire family."

Martin learned that Nichols was now a retired colonel. His wife and Martin's grandmother had also known each other at the War College.

"Small world, indeed," Nichols said once again.

Martin's attention shifted to Eddie's father who hadn't participated in the conversation. The man had his arms crossed in front of him. His welcoming smile had changed to a frown. Maybe he was tired of army talk. Maybe he thought Martin was just another self-centered, starry-eye kid. Maybe he was talking too much.

Martin was about to try to turn the conversation to another topic when Eddie's mother did it for him.

"Eddie," she said, ignoring her husband's demeanor, "why don't you show Tim his room? Let's give him time to clean up before dinner."

"Sure thing, Mom," Eddie said as he stood up and grinned at his friend. "Come on, Tim. Let's see if we can find our way around this place."

17

Tim rolled over and opened first one eye and then the other.

"Nine a.m.? How could it be nine o'clock in the morning?" he asked himself when he could focus well enough to read the time display on the clock radio. He had slept straight through the night without dreaming. It was the best sleep he'd had in months.

Rays of sunlight streamed between the wooden slats covering the large double windows. He stretched his arms and legs and yawned. He sat up on the edge of the bed, stood, and went to the window. He adjusted the shutters to get a better look outside. Despite the sunshine breaking between the clouds, a delicate, light snow was falling. He yawned again, put his hands on his hips and stretched backwards, side to side, and forward once again.

"This is going to one great day," he said, recalling his resolution to ditch the depression and to look on the brighter side.

Finally awake, he remembered coming up to the guest room and crashing, but he hadn't taken a good look at his accommodations.

"Hell, yes!" he exclaimed as he gazed around the spacious room. This could be a super expensive room in an exclusive hotel.

The enormous room was really sweet. He knew enough to recognize a Tiffany lamp and a colonial writing desk. He figured most of the furniture was that light-colored Danish Modern stuff. That king-size bed sure didn't come from a mattress outlet, and the slick sheets and puffy comforter were top quality. The room even had a little sitting area – a sofa, two side chairs and a wide coffee table. The tech stuff was good too – a forty-two-inch flat screen HD-TV and an Apple laptop. He fired up the computer just to see if it was connected wirelessly, and, sure enough, he was online right away.

Tim looked down the wide hallway that ended in a walk-in closet. To the left, he admired the huge bathroom with slate flooring, granite counter tops, mirror-covered walls, double sinks, a jetted tub and a walk-in shower.

And this was just a guest room; the family's rooms were likely just as swanky or better. Martin figured that if he picked up the phone, he could have ordered room service.

So far, he felt very welcome. At dinner the night before, Eddie's family sat down together in the dining room. The main course was chateaubriand with béarnaise sauce, prepared by the family's French chef. A maid had brought serving platters to the table and then stood at attention by the kitchen door.

Eddie sat to Tim's right. When the main dish was served, Tim's eyes widened. Eddie, noticing the reaction, kicked his lower leg.

"Hey, buddy," he whispered, stifling a laugh. "Don't worry. That's really just beefsteak, and that stuff on top is made from wine. Want me to tell them that you want catsup?"

Tim glared back, drew in his breath, and shook his head at his friend. Eddie smiled and asked his dad to pass the potatoes.

When they finished their meal, they moved into the family room for coffee and tiramisu. On the way there, Tim noticed another, larger dining room to the left of the kitchen with a long, polished wood table that could easily seat twenty people. Above it hung an elaborate cut-glass chandelier.

Although Tim had been amazed at Eddie's home, he was deeply disappointed to learn that Samantha had her own apartment in Washington, D.C. She hadn't been there for dinner, and Tim didn't want to risk comments if he asked where she was.

Soon after dessert, the two young men retired to the game room. The room was as big as a three-car garage. It had a hardwood bar that ran all along the narrow side of the room. Behind it, rows and rows of every imaginable kind of liquor were lined up in front of a mirror-covered wall. Game tables, a huge television, couches and easy chairs made the place look more like a hotel lounge than a private home. Along the far end, a regulation pool table sat in an alcove.

The two headed right for the green felt. They soon were tied, each having won two games. Tim was about to run the table when he thought he heard a familiar voice. The cue slipped in his hand, Tim looked up, and the eight ball plunked into a pocket. He had lost his cool. And, no wonder, there again, right before his very eyes, stood Samantha.

"Hi, you guys!" she said. "Got room for another player?" Although she spoke to both of them, she only looked at Tim.

"S-s-sure!" he stuttered. Once again, Eddie kicked Tim's shin and laughed.

Sam wore a chocolate brown cashmere sweater that showcased her shapely breasts. She had on black wool slacks and calf-high leather boots in a dark brown. Her long hair was pulled back at the nape of her neck and held in place by an oval, tortoise shell barrette.

Tim handed her a cue, allowing his fingers to briefly caress her hand. She smiled right at him, positioned the cue, and made a bumper shot that sank three balls. The three of them shot pool for another hour then sat side-by-side on the sofa playing video games until almost three o'clock in the morning.

That was last night, and today would be a new day. Tim resolved to shake this depression for good. No more lying around in bed. He stripped to his Jockey briefs and headed for the bathroom. He stepped into the shower and was immediately blasted by warm water coming from half a dozen showerheads. There was enough room in there for four people to shower at once. Of course, that was too many, but showering with one other – Samantha – would be just right. Just imagining her standing naked in front of him resulted in an automatic physical response. He turned the water to cold.

After the shower, he shaved, brushed his teeth, dressed, and walked downstairs to the kitchen. One of the employees directed him to the sun porch where Eddie and Samantha were having breakfast.

He found a large, glass-enclosed room. White rattan chairs and tables were casually placed around a large freshwater pool. As he passed by, he dipped his fingers into the water and startled a dozen koi. The large, colorful fish must have figured they were going to be fed, thought Tim. Tropical plants with bright red and yellow flowers filled in the perimeter, and ten-foot high palms made up the background. Artificial lighting and the warmth coming from nearly invisible sunlamps created a feeling of perpetual summer. Yet beyond the thick glass windows, a flurry of tiny snowflakes reminded him that winter was far from over.

Sam saw Tim coming before he noticed her sitting with her brother across the room. She watched him descend the three steps to the slate terrace and run his fingers through the fishpond. For her, this young man was beginning to become a major dilemma. If she closed her eyes, she could remember the first time she ever saw him, half-naked with a towel tied loosely around his waist. She smiled, recalling his fantastic upper body, and she suspected that the same held true for his lower regions. She loved being able to look almost straight across at this tall young man. Last night convinced her that he was smart, quite good looking, and fun to be around. And she also knew that he was infatuated with her.

Men are so simple, she thought. They would swear that they weren't looking at a woman's boobs, butt or legs. They could stand right in front of a woman and undress her with their eyes, thinking they were being so subtle. Well, it works both ways, she told herself. Only difference is that a woman could do the same with a guy, but much more discreetly. She smiled and sized up Tim Martin, who didn't have a clue as to what she was thinking.

But there was no denying that this black-white thing could be a problem. Tim didn't seem racist. He didn't have a problem rooming with Eddie, and he seemed totally comfortable around their parents. But a relationship was another issue.

Sam's unique ethnicity had been a lifelong battle for her. She had inherited Grandma Nichols' hazel eyes, her skin was lighter than her mother's, and her hair was brown and straight. She was too different to pass for white and didn't want to. Yet she wasn't really black either.

Even some of her black friends treated her oddly. She had wondered why Grandpa had ever married a French woman because their descendants would forever have to deal with their mixed ethnic roots. The family's wealth had bought admission to an exclusive high school, but one almost totally white. She had dated some white guys and had even slept with one.

It would always be the same. The doting mothers would ask the standard question: What will the family think? Even the black guys wanted really dark-skinned women or totally white blond women.

Was Tim just wondering what it would be like to caress a brown breast or sleep with someone "exotic"? Could he be comfortable around a bunch of black men his age with no whites around? She doubted it. She suspected that most guys would cut and run from such a situation.

Well, there was one way to find out. She'd invite Tim and Eddie to the New Year's Eve bash at The Cave. The Cave was an all-black bar near Howard University that catered primarily to the black students. Probably fewer than five whites dared to come into the bar in any given year.

She smiled as Tim walked up and found her staring at him.

"Hi," she said.

"Hi," he said. "I guess I slept in."

"Not by much," she responded. "We just got here ourselves."

They ate breakfast together and chatted comfortably just like they did the night before. Sam explained that she had things to do during the day in town with her mother, but asked if they'd like to join her and some friends for a New Year's Eve party at The Cave. She briefly felt bad setting Tim up; he had seemed genuinely excited at the invitation.

What the heck, she told herself. It was better to put him to the test now rather than getting involved and being disappointed later. If she had to place a bet, she'd say that this would turn out like her other relationships with men – a total bust.

18

New Year's Eve would be spent in D.C.

THE GUYS TOOK A TAXI FROM EDDIE'S HOUSE INTO THE CITY. ANYONE out on New Year's Eve in D.C. was better off without a car. A friend of Eddie's who went to Howard had said they could crash at his place after the party. They didn't have to be back to the house until two o'clock in the afternoon for the family's New Year's dinner. Both of them were ready to party!

The taxi dropped them off about eight o'clock in front of an older building in the city's commercial area, a couple of blocks from Howard University. The street was lined with shops on street level and apartments on the upper floors. Most businesses catered to the college crowd. Tim watched as the taxi passed by pizza places, bookstores, coffee shops, and at least six bars. Crowds of young people were in a hurry to get wherever they were going.

"Wow, where's everyone going?" Tim asked Eddie. "Looks like everyone's out and about."

"Yeah, it's definitely got the party atmosphere," Eddie answered.

The taxi dropped them off on a street corner. Eddie paid the cab fare and tip then led Tim around the corner and down an alley. Normally, Tim might have been a little anxious to be in a strange place hurrying down a dark alley, but he was with Eddie, and they were headed to wherever Samantha was going to be. For that, he could survive anything.

Eddie came to a halt about halfway down the alley. At first, Tim couldn't figure out why they stopped. They stood in front of a heavy steel door. Above the doorway, Tim saw a dim neon sign. The six-inch yellow tubing spelled out "The Cave." Tim had to trust that Eddie knew what he was doing when he rang a doorbell on a rusty metal plate. Seconds later, someone inside pulled the door open. Tim ran his left hand along the door for balance as they stepped inside the dark reception area.

Two large black men blocked the entry, but Eddie didn't hesitate. No words were spoken. Eddie reached into his jacket pocket and pulled out two tickets.

"Driver's license?" asked the taller man. They both opened their wallets to show their licenses. The man nodded to his partner; both these guys were over twenty-one. Eddie and Tim figured they'd passed the entrance exam and started to step inside.

"Hey, hold it!" demanded the second man, thicker and more muscular than the first. He put his heavy hand on Tim's sleeve, but stared at Eddie. "He's going in, too?"

"Sure," Eddie said. "Why not?"

The man shrugged and lifted his hand. "Because we don't get many like him, that's why." Then he pointed downward, indicating that the two were free to pass.

They went into a room about the size of an average living room. Tim had to pause to study the elaborate décor. The entire room had been converted into a simulated cave. Fiberglass had been molded to simulate walls of an underground cavern. All the surfaces walls, ceiling and floor looked as if they were made of irregularly shaped stone. On one wall, Tim could make out an elevator. On the opposite side, the walls narrowed to form a dark tunnel.

Wooden benches lined the walls in what he figured was the foyer or entry room. Couples sat closely side-by-side, apparently waiting for their names to be called. Once summoned, a hostess would lead them into the tunnel. Tim could hear the hip-hop music blasting from inside. He followed Eddie up to the podium.

"Are you with a party or by yourselves?" asked a well-built young woman who managed the seating.

"Samantha Dixon party," Eddie answered.

The woman turned to a hostess and asked them to follow her.

"Please hold the handrail," the hostess said as she turned to make certain the two were behind her. Probably a good idea, thought Tim, as the tunnel turned into a dimly lit stairway leading to a lower level.

"This is so cool!" he shouted to Eddie over the loud, pounding music.

The entire basement area had been converted into a stone grotto. It had several levels for open seating. The bar along the far wall was crowded and noisy. In the front, a live band was playing, and the dance floor was filled to capacity with couples gyrating to the beat. Tim could make out a number of smaller, private party rooms off to the side. He figured there were maybe two hundred people already there in party mode.

He couldn't have heard Eddie say anything even if he wanted to. He just followed obediently, saying, "Excuse me," and "Pardon me," as he threaded his way to a private room not far from the band. Finally, they followed the hostess into a smaller room. Tim didn't count, but he guessed that thirty or so people had already arrived. The small tables were littered with bottles, glasses and plates of partially eaten chicken wings, pizza crusts and scattered French fries.

Everyone stopped talking and stared as the two of them entered the room.

Tim nearly laughed out loud when he realized he was the only white guy in the room, and likely the only white guy in the entire establishment. The only reason he had to laugh was because it brought back the classic scene from "Star Wars" where the aliens fell silent as the good guys walked into their bar. Come to think of it, Tim thought, since no one else laughed with him that maybe it wasn't so funny after all.

"Sam!" Tim shouted over the silence when he saw Samantha sitting at the far end of the table. "Hey, Sam!"

While Tim beamed with enthusiasm, Sam shuddered with embarrassment. She felt absolutely horrible. She never should have invited him; he would feel so out of place.

She rushed up to him. "I'm sorry, I'm so sorry," she repeated. "I'm sorry. This isn't a place you would enjoy."

"No, no," he reassured her. "I think it's cool. Come on, introduce me to your friends."

"You're sure you're OK with this?"

"Sure," said Tim, "introduce me to your friends."

Sam shrugged and hooked arms with him. She made the rounds. Everyone settled back into the routine, laughing and talking.

Sam turned around and realized that she had missed one introduction. She led Tim to a dark young man who wore a tie-dyed shirt. Tim could see evidence of tribal scaring on the man's chest, partially visible near the V-neck collar.

"Tim, this is Andy Sayah. He's from Liberia," Sam said.

Much to her surprise, Tim said something to Andy that she couldn't understand. She looked at Tim, seeking an explanation. But he didn't respond to her. Instead, he listened intently as Andy spoke directly to him in the same language.

The two men laughed out loud together and then shook hands, popping fingers as in the traditional Liberian greeting.

Andy turned toward Samantha and other nearby partygoers. He beamed as if he had just met the most famous person in the world.

"He's da one," Andy announced, smiling broadly. "I saw him and his maw and pa. They come through my village with President Moray and Minister Weah. I be only eleven years. He was not big like now. He be younger then and skinny. But everyone say he walk with the spirit of the leopard. He be the young boy, Tim, who was friends with the greatest witch doctor in all Liberia!"

Samantha, like all the others within hearing distance, didn't know what to make of Andy's outburst. Some looked askance at him, unsure if he had just gone off his rocker. Their concern turned to relief as they looked at Tim who was grinning as if he'd just found his long-lost brother.

Samantha stood dumbfounded, trying to make sense of Andy's babble. It was clear that Andy believed that Tim was someone special. Besides, she wondered, how in the world was it possible that he could speak Liberian?

Tim shook hands again with Andy and patted him on the back as he and Samantha moved on.

"What was that all about?" Sam asked.

"It's no big deal," Tim said. "I guess when my folks and I were upcountry in Liberia, we must have passed through his village or something."

"Oh, that's right," nodded Samantha. "Eddie did say that you and your folks lived in Liberia for a while, but I assumed you lived in the capital city."

"We did for part of the time, but we also spent some time in the interior."

Samantha had a whole new outlook on this Tim Martin. He was interesting in more ways than one. The two of them passed the evening together. They moved from group to group, but finally sat down alone together at a small table in the back of the room. Sam didn't notice that Reggie Wilson had been observing them for the past hour. Reggie wasn't happy about what he saw. Tim and Samantha had been talking exclusively to one another, clearly engaged in deep conversation. From time to time, one or the other would burst out laughing.

What a bummer! Reggie thought. He had been hustling Sam for the past two months and believed he had been making headway. He had figured that New Year's Eve would be the perfect time to make his move. He had planned to score big time tonight. But now this white asshole shows up and moves right in. Samantha was so involved that she didn't even know that he was watching them carry on like that.

Just as Reggie was about to bust up the little love fest, Tim stood up and walked out of the room. Reggie hesitated. Should he move in on Samantha now, or should he have a little man-to-man talk with this Martin guy?

Reggie nudged his buddy, Leon, who was sitting next to him.

"What's up, man?" asked Leon.

"Come on, I want to talk to that Martin guy."

They both got up and followed Tim as he walked past the band. He looked up, searching for the sign to the restroom. He kept on walking down a short hallway, unaware that he was being followed. When he entered the restroom, he was surprised to find that the cave theme didn't extend to the facilities. This place looked like something from fifty years ago – walls and floors covered with white tile, overhead fluorescents, eight urinals along one wall, and six commodes along the other.

Two guys were in the restroom when Tim first entered. They turned and stared at him.

Nothing like being the only white guy in an all-black bar, he thought. He walked to a urinal and relieved himself. Finished, he zipped his fly, turned and walked to one of the sinks.

Now alone in the restroom, he washed his hands and punched the button on the hand dryer. He saw Reggie walk in. Tim looked up and nodded. Reggie frowned at him first and then walked up right up to him.

"I'm on the Olympic boxing team. I plan to win the gold in the heavyweight division," Reggie said, looking Tim right in the eyes.

"Congratulations," Tim said as he rubbed his hands together.

"The reason I'm telling you this, motherfucker, is so you can make the right decision."

"Decision?" asked Tim.

"That's right, I want you to get your white ass outta here right now. You're not welcome, asshole."

"Look, I don't want any trouble," Tim said calmly as he turned and faced Reggie. He took advantage of the moment to size up his adversary. He was maybe two inches taller than Reggie, but Reggie was thirty pounds heavier and had budging biceps.

Tim thought he'd try to figure out what Reggie's problem was. He didn't have to wait long.

"Samantha Dixon is my woman, and I don't take kindly for some honkey taking up her time."

"Your woman?" asked Tim.

"What's the matter, motherfucker, are you deaf? I've been courting her for two months, and tonight I'll get into her pants."

Tim felt his blood pressure rise. He flexed his fists and looked Reggie directly in the eyes.

"If you've been trying to get into her pants for two months and haven't, then she isn't your woman," Tim said coolly.

"You're dead, you white piece of shit!" Reggie charged forward and swung a roundhouse punch. He moved fast, and Tim wasn't quick enough to side step his move. The blow struck his right shoulder, sending him flying backwards against the wall. It felt like he had been hit with a baseball bat. He had not expected Reggie to react so violently. Reggie charged again, and, even with Tim's experience in the martial arts, he was having a tough time defending himself.

At the same time, his brain was running full tilt. He didn't need this. First of all, getting into a fight in an all-black bar, or any bar, would only lead to disaster. Second, this Reggie guy was Samantha's friend. If Tim were lucky enough to take him out, she might not appreciate him beating up her friend. That could end any chance he had of getting to know her better.

Finally, if either he or Reggie ended up bloodied, the police would be called and he, or Reggie, or both of them could find themselves spending New Year's Day in jail. All this was going through Tim's mind, as he danced around the restroom, avoiding the full impact of Reggie's lightning fists. It was a technique he had learned in Dojo when the opponent has you outmatched.

Tim used this stalling technique to study his opponent. Reggie's agitation seemed to inhibit, rather than enhance, his effectiveness. Beads of sweat dotted his forehead. His eyes darted from side to side as he followed Tim's moves. He took phantom punches, yet never took clear aim. His anger neared the boiling point.

"Hold still, you chicken shit!" Reggie shouted.

Yeah, right, thought Tim. Why don't I just stand here and let you beat the crap out of me? He knew that in hand-to-hand combat, opportunities occur, and, if you have the skills, you can take advantage of your opponent's mistakes.

Reggie charged, forgetting all about boxing. He just wanted to grab Tim, wrestle him to the floor, and then pound the crap out of him. Reggie's mistake was assuming that Tim hadn't had any training in karate or judo. Reggie suddenly found himself face down on the tile floor, his right arm pulled up behind his back with Tim's knee jammed into his kidney. He held Reggie's right arm by the wrist, then jabbed his left thumb into the nerves above Reggie's right elbow. Tim watched as pain shot through Reggie's body. Reggie gasped for air. He couldn't move, and he feared his bladder would let loose.

"Are you really on the US Olympic boxing team?" asked Tim.

"Yes," gasped Reggie.

"Listen very carefully. I make one twist, and your arm will snap. If I do that, your career in the Olympics is over. Do you understand?"

"Yes," sobbed Reggie.

"All right then, I am going to let you up. Then we are going back to the party. If you even make a threatening move towards me, the only Olympics you'll be participating in will be the Para-Olympics."

Tim released his hold, got up and walked to the door. He stopped and looked back. Reggie still sat on the floor, hunched over, rubbing his arm. His friend, Leon, leaned on the wall outside the restroom. Tim nodded to him as he walked down the hallway and stepped up to the bar. He ordered two drinks and headed back to Samantha.

Leon watched Tim disappear into the crowd. The bathroom door opened suddenly, and Reggie walked right up to Leon.

"Let's get the fuck outta here," he said.

"What do mean 'outta here'?" Leon asked. "Like somewhere else?"

"Yeah, yeah, that's what I mean – somewhere else," Reggie said, his temper rising again.

"You taking the Dixon chick with you?" asked Leon.

"Fuck her! Fuck Martin! Fuck this party! Let's go!" Reggie demanded. As they walked out into the alley, Reggie flexed his fingers again. The feeling had just begun to return.

Meanwhile, Tim sat down next to Samantha and slid his chair close to her.

"You were gone quite awhile," she said.

"Bar was busy," he said.

They continued to enjoy the evening, dancing closely and talking softly. Sooner than they expected, the bar manager announced that it was five minutes to midnight. People began to get up and exit the room.

"Where's everybody going?" asked Tim.

"Out on the street!" Sam shouted, tugging on his arm. "We'll celebrate out there. Come on, Tim. Come on!"

Sam grabbed Tim's hand, dragging him along behind her as they wound their way through the mob rushing to the street. Once outside, they joined the countdown to the final seconds: "Ten, nine, eight … three, two, ONE! Happy New Year!"

The crowd became one rowdy being – swaying, shouting and celebrating the end of everything old and the promise of everything new.

A string of firecrackers popped to the left, leaving puffs of white smoke and the lingering odor of gunpowder. A trio of impromptu vocalists stood on a dumpster and belted out "Auld Lang Syne."

Beer cans and champagne bottles came out of nowhere. Some were passed from one set of lips to another and yet another. Some bottles fizzed and sprayed the crowd with the sweet scent of alcohol. All around, couples pressed together, caught up in the magic of midnight.

Someone stumbled behind them, propelling Samantha into Tim's arms. They both hesitated, staring into each other's eyes. Sam reached up, wrapped her arms around his chest and rested her head on his neck. He pulled her closer, encircling her shoulders in a full embrace, all the while caressing her back with his fingertips. She could feel his heart beating. He felt the softness of her breasts against him and pulled her even closer.

Their lips touched lightly at first, but soon their kiss became something far more meaningful. Neither had ever before experienced anything as deep and powerful. For Sam, it seemed like fireworks suddenly exploded inside her. For Tim, the moment created a hunger for more. He pushed his tongue deep inside her open mouth, and she responded with a moan and a sigh.

The crowd faded away, and they became the only two souls on Earth. They pulled apart, held each other at arms' length and searched each other's face for answers to their questions.

"Let's go for a walk," Tim said, reaching for her hand. As they broke from the group, he noticed Eddie standing with a group of young men on a street corner. He nodded at Eddie as they passed by. Eddie grinned and returned the nod with a wink and a smile.

The two strolled along the streets of Washington hand-in-hand for fifteen minutes without speaking. Sam knew the area better than he did, so he let her lead the way. They turned a corner to a side street. The commercial area lay far behind. They entered a residential neighborhood with three-story brownstone apartment houses lining the streets. Now and again they could see the twinkle of Christmas lights inside the cozy homes.

"This way," whispered Sam, pointing to an older building on the right.

She led him up a half dozen concrete steps to a walkway leading to a wide porch. She opened one side of the doublewide front door. Straight ahead, Tim could see a row of apartments along each side of a narrow hallway. Sam turned directly to the left and bolted up the inside staircase to the second floor.

At 2A she stopped, pulled a key from her jeans pocket, and unlocked the apartment door. Once they were inside, she hit a light switch and closed the door firmly behind her. She backed up to the apartment door, her breathing coming in short bursts.

Tim's eyes adjusted to the brightness of the overhead light. They were in a living room furnished with older, second-hand furniture. It was neat, he noticed, obviously a woman's apartment.

"Welcome to our apartment," she said.

Tim looked around again, searching for the other part of "our."

Sam laughed softly and smiled. "My roommate is spending the holidays with her folks in Florida. I'm here alone."

Tim's smile widened, and he took two giant steps toward her. He braced his hands against the door, corralling her between his outstretched arms. He leaned forward and brushed his lips against hers. She reached up and pulled him closer. He dropped his right hand to her breast and began to massage it softly as he moved against her, his hips pressing rhythmically against hers.

He hesitated when Sam lightly pushed back on his shoulder.

Oh, God, Tim thought. He couldn't stop now.

He sighed when he discovered that Sam's hand had moved downward to his crotch.

"Oh, God, yes!" he said. "Oh, yes!"

"Happy New Year!" Sam said.

"And a very Happy New Year to you, too," he said as she reached for his hand and led him into her bedroom.

She closed the door behind them.

19

A blue Capital cab pulled to the curb next to the brownstone
at noon on New Year's Day.

The driver, Kasheik Alzera, quickly sized up the couple. He knew from experience that one couldn't be too careful in this part of D.C.

The man was tall, well over six feet. The woman nearly matched his height. He was a young white man; she was a light-skinned black. This was generally considered a black area, and seeing a white man in this neighborhood was unusual.

The man's arm was around the woman's waist. This open display of a sexual nature still sickened him. The infidels did things in the open that would never be tolerated back home. Here, they have no shame. But what can a devout man do? One has to find food for his family. He must try to ignore the evil in this country.

He opened the back door of his cab and the two slid onto the seat. They sat too close together, their bodies touching. The woman told him to take them to an address in Wheaton, Maryland. Alzera nodded his approval. This meant it would be a good fare and that pleased him.

He headed north to the Maryland border. He frequently checked the rearview mirror to monitor the couple's behavior. They were young, likely in their twenties.

The woman was beautiful for a mixed race person. She could have been a queen in the days of ancient Egypt. A woman should be veiled, he thought. Only a husband should see a woman's face and only in private. Here in America, brazen women did not hide their faces. Alzera could gaze openly at their beauty without fear of reprisal from the women's families. Although he knew that his furtive viewing was strictly forbidden, it pleased him to watch her talking so intimately with a man.

Just who was this woman? What was she doing with that young man? He often played a guessing game about his passengers. The man must be the son of a wealthy family. Many rich people lived in Wheaton. Perhaps this mongrel of a woman earned her living on the streets. Yes, she could be a prostitute. But, no, how could that be if the man was taking her to his parents' home? He could only imagine the great mansion where the young man lived in luxury.

He forced himself to turn his thoughts from the couple and concentrate on his driving. When he exited the Beltway onto Highway 97, the woman – not the man – was telling him where turn. Men should not take orders from women. He shook his head in disgust.

He followed a winding road past large, expensive homes. Finally, the houses gave way to open fields with no houses at all. For a moment, Kasheik worried. Perhaps this young couple planned to steal his cash and leave his battered body in a remote ditch.

A stonewall ran along one side of the narrow roadway. It followed the curving hills for more than a half-mile. Finally, Kasheik came to an iron gate, about seven feet tall. Both sides of the gate stood open.

A man in dark pants, boots, a short-waisted leather jacket, and a black cap walked into the center of the road. He held up one hand, signaling Kasheik to stop. A nine-millimeter pistol was strapped to the man's hip. Kasheik felt a moment of terror, just as if he were back at one of the infamous palaces in Iraq.

The woman rolled down the back window.

"Happy New Year, Greg!" she said to the guard.

"Same to you, Miss Dixon. Everyone's already here."

The guard waved the taxi through the gate.

Kasheik followed the road after leaving the gate. He crested a small hill and looked down in the valley at a magnificent, two-story mansion. Its walls were gray granite, the roof was slate, and to the left of the house stood a six-car garage and a carriage house. He saw horses, stables and tennis courts.

"Oh, look! There's Mom and Dad, greeting the guests!" said the young woman to her companion. A tall black man and a short black woman stood by the massive front doors.

"This is *your* house?" blurted Kasheik.

"My folks' house," said Sam.

Alzera shook his head in disbelief. He would have quite a story to tell his wife about the magnificent mansion owned by black people.

"I thought you said that this was a little family gathering?" Tim whispered to Sam as she paid the driver and got out of the cab.

"It's just Daddy's law partners, their families and some of my cousins, aunts and uncles – just fifty or sixty people," answered Samantha.

As they walked toward the entrance, Eddie bounded down the stairs like an excited puppy.

"Hi, Sis, you look a little tired. Didn't you get enough sleep?"

Samantha frowned at her twin brother and seethed as only a sibling can do. But Eddie just winked and smiled knowingly at Tim.

The three, not exactly ready to immerse themselves in a crowd of friends and relatives, walked around to the back entrance. Eddie bolted ahead while Tim and Samantha held hands as they walked slowly beside a tall fence. An evergreen hedge hid the narrow road to the service area at the back of the house. Tim took advantage of the moment alone to kiss Samantha full on the lips.

He just happened to look up at the porch as they continued on the pathway. He could see Sam's father speaking quietly to an older white man and a woman who appeared to be his wife. He assumed that the man was likely one of the partners in the law firm.

Sam's father turned and glared down at the couple. Tim blushed and scurried along to catch up with Eddie.

Oh, God, he wondered. Is it that obvious that he and Sam had become lovers?

It was shaping up to be one long afternoon.

20

In Gbarnga, Liberia, it was hot and muggy, as usual.

MUSTAFA SAYEH SHUDDERED AND LOOKED DOWN. HE PRETENDED TO ignore the skinny white man when he saw him drive up in the red Range Rover. He didn't want the man to see the fear in his eyes. This white man was called "The Gray Ghost," and Sayeh feared the power of the supernatural.

It was still early, only nine o'clock in the morning, and it was already too hot. Sayeh sat at a wooden table outside the shop. He was aware of the movement of the old soldier, although he never took his eyes from the bowl in front of him. He knew that the man had come to the Country Chop Shop for more than just food.

The man stepped out of the hard-driven vehicle in his typical garb – a white T-shirt, faded blue jeans and worn desert combat boots. Sayeh knew better than to be fooled by the man's appearance.

A first glance, he looked old. Both his closely shorn hair and his bush-like eyebrows were a chalky white. The dark, sun-tanned skin disguised his heritage; he was much darker than most white men who came to Africa. He was probably in his early sixties, although no one seemed to know for sure. Nevertheless, he was far from feeble. The muscles in his thin arms stood out like thick elastic bands.

Sayeh, and most other native men, would be cautious in dealing with him. The dark eyes and the brooding expression made many men think twice before confronting him. A jagged scar ran down his left cheek. "Ghost" seemed to fit him, although it was not his real name.

"May I help you, boss?" asked the proprietor when the man walked up to the counter. The white man ordered a bowl of country chop and a local beer. To the proprietor's surprise, the man spoke fluent Kapel, the local native language.

He paid three Liberian dollars for the bowl of chop, the native dish of boiled rice topped with a spicy soup made from palm butter, meat and vegetables. The price included a warm bottle of beer. The white man waited for his food and then walked out of the shop and sat down at the table next to the Liberian.

"What's happening, Mus?" the white man asked.

"Not much, AB. You say you need a guide."

Mustafa did not look directly at the white man. He feared this man as much as he had feared Charles Taylor during the years when Taylor ruled Liberia and later left the country broken and bloody.

The old man came into his line of business during the civil war. That's when he began buying and selling African art. In the war, soldiers over-ran villages, raping and looting. When they wanted money, the drunken soldiers would bring him old masks and artifacts in exchange for money, booze or bullets.

"I need someone to take me to the lost ruins along the Saint Paul River west of Saint Paulsville," said A.B. Lynden, the old man's true name.

"No one goes near the lost ruins, AB. Not even during the wars did we ever go near the ruins," answered Mustafa, his dark eyes flashing a glint of fear.

"Of course, they didn't," laughed Lynden. "They would have had to walk through the jungles. Besides, there were no women to fuck."

"Powerful spirits guard it. Even the Poro do not enter the bush around the ruins," whined Mustafa.

"Well, you and I are going to do it today," Lynden said, gulping down the last of the beer. "Come on, get in the Rover."

Lynden walked briskly toward the Range Rover; Mustafa lagged behind.

"When you get me there, you will be $5,000 richer," Lynden called back over his shoulder.

Mustafa hesitated. It was always better to seem unwilling to do a job in hopes of getting more money. But Lynden had stopped talking, and $5,000 was a lot of money.

"For that kind of money, you have a deal," Mustafa agreed as he climbed into the passenger seat. Lynden started the engine, dropped the Rover into first gear and pulled out.

They headed north towards Gbalatoah, the small town on the south bank of the Saint Paul River. Mustafa fumbled with the controls on the door, searching for the button to roll up the window.

"Leave the window down," growled Lynden.

"Doesn't this car have air conditioning, AB?" Mustafa asked.

"Of course," said Lynden, "but I don't like air conditioning. Leave the window down."

They drove in silence. Even after all these years, Lynden took pleasure in driving on the laterite roads in Liberia's interior. He'd been in the country so long, he considered himself a Liberian. And, indeed, he felt like one.

His life ran parallel to the history of Liberia. He knew this country better than any other, including the U.S.A. He could recite the line of dictators, presidents and outright criminals who had been in power in Liberia.

No one could get away with driving this fast and rough in America, he thought. He punched the gas and swerved to miss the big potholes, but bounced through the ruts and smaller holes as if they weren't even there.

Lynden was born in 1962 at the mission hospital at ELWA, short for "Ever-lasting Love Winning Africa." ELWA was the call sign of the Christian radio station run by the Sudan Interior Missions. It broadcast a Christian message to most of West Africa, using transmitters located just outside of Monrovia.

AB's father fixed generators, and his mother worked as a nurse in the hospital. They were both from Seattle, Washington, and had been called to mission work in Africa after they were married. Arthur Broderick Lynden and his younger sister were both born at ELWA. The family had served in Africa for almost two decades.

Conditions in Liberia took a turn for the worse when Master Sergeant Samuel K. Doe overthrew the standing government in Liberia, killing President Tolbert. Young Lynden was a senior at the American Cooperative School in Monrovia during the upheaval. Following the bloody coup, the family left Liberia and settled in Seattle.

Lynden enrolled at the University of Washington. But college wasn't in the cards for him. He flunked out during the first quarter and enlisted in the army. He got a free ride to play soldier in the first Gulf War. Lynden decided that the army wasn't his thing either. In 1992, he found himself unemployed. No one wanted to hire a used-up infantry staff sergeant.

Liberia still called him. After Doe was killed, Lynden returned to Liberia. The CIA had an opening for a guy who was fluent in the native language. He became a contract employee working as an agent for the U.S. government. All that stuff was supposed to be secret. To cover his real job, Lynden became an exporter of African art. He and Charles Taylor, the new president, had become friends. The connections helped Lynden polish his knack for finding rare African masks. He found that he could make a good profit at selling the artifacts to investors.

But in-country conditions went from bad to horrible. Taylor's thugs pillaged the country, killing tens of thousands of their countrymen, and that included plenty of women and children, too. The civil war raged on and on. Lynden always seemed to find a way to survive – and profit – from his knowledge of the people and their history.

Finally, things leveled off. Sierleaf became president, and the nation finally began to get back on its feet. Twelve years later, Dowling's regime took over, and the country once again slipped back into anarchy. Despite all the unrest, Lynden had truly found his calling. He was making his fortune and loving every minute of it. Things had smoothed out, and Lynden was on a roll. Now since Charles Moray had come to power, the nation had once again begun to prosper.

Lynden's net worth was about to take an upswing if he could take advantage of the good times ahead. Maybe he'd retire and buy a mansion somewhere by the seashore.

He turned off the main road and headed down a rough, narrow road leading into the jungle. The Rover hit a foot-high ridge on the right. Mustafa gripped the door handle and closed his eyes.

Lynden had become well known and almost respected among natives and ex-patriots for his knowledge of the country. Just yesterday his office had been a barstool in the lounge of the Ducar Hotel. He wasn't sure how long he'd been sitting there, but it was a good way to meet prospective clients. He'd ordered his third, maybe fourth drink, swiveled around to survey the rich customers. Anything could happen if he kept his eyes and ears open.

He had been a bit startled to find that a heavy, middle-aged German had settled in next to him at the bar. The man was already talking without so much as a brief hello.

"Have you ever heard of the Lost City on the Saint Paul?" asked Herman Gustaff, who specialized in buying African art for wealthy Europeans. He had looked like he knew something that Lynden had missed.

"Yeah, sure. The Kpelle tell stories of sacred ruins deep in the unexplored forests north of the Saint Paul," said Lynden, who wasn't keen on being told something that he already knew. "But they're all just stories. Besides, there are no roads or access to that area. The triple canopy forest would hide any ruins even if they were real. A guy could hunt for years and years and never find the place, even if he was standing just ten feet from it."

"I have a client who knows the exact location of the site. He wants someone to acquire a statue that is located there," said Gustaff, believing every single word that came out of his own mouth.

"Sounds like a wild goose chase to me," scoffed Lynden.

"Maybe so, but my client says he has GPS coordinates that pinpoint the exact spot. He has an accurate drawing of the statue. He's willing to pay a substantial amount to whoever finds and delivers the statue to him."

Lynden had liked the ring of the words "substantial amount."

"Like how much?" asked Lynden, who always appreciated a good offer.

"Well, what would you think of $50,000 up front to pay for the search and another $150,000 if you actually find and deliver the artifact?"

Now Lynden's attitude had taken a sudden upward turn. That much cash certainly sounded appealing, even if he was sent out on a crazy, wild goose hunt.

"For that kind of money, I'd kill my own mother," Lynden had said with a grin. "You've got a deal."

To his astonishment, Gustaff had reached into the inside pocket of his jacket and pulled out a thick manila envelope. Inside were five hundred $100 bills and the directions to the lost city.

Later, as he was preparing for the search, Lynden pulled up Liberia on Google Earth. He punched in the coordinates given by the client.

To the south of the river was Lewis Town. Like all these villages, it appeared as a reddish-yellow spot in the virgin forest along the riverbank. The clearings were created by the slash and burn method that took out the jungle to create farmland. The area north of the river appeared to be a sea of dark green. The jungle remained nearly untouched. The coordinates indicated a spot to the south of a rock outcropping about two miles from the river.

Lynden had been methodical in his planning for the trip. He knew just the man who could help him. That was Mustafa Sayeh.

He had first met Mustafa fifteen years earlier. Mustafa had been a captain in Taylor's militia. He had been born in the nearby town of Belefaunai. He had once told Lynden about a ceremonial clearing deep in the jungles to the West of Saint Paulsville, on the north side of the river. It was Mustafa who had first told him that there was treasure – gold and diamonds – hidden in the area. Lynden thought if there was treasure, the famous ruins might be nearby. But this was the time of the bloody siege on Gbarnga, and Lynden hadn't been interested in traipsing through jungles, possibly filled with Prince Johnson's soldiers.

Mustafa had freely recited the local lore. Supposedly, the ruins were from a tribe of light-skinned people who traveled by boat up the Saint Paul River eons ago. They built a city of stone, but the ancestors of the

Kpelle destroyed it. There was even some crazy stuff about demons and men in the same body called *endosyms* that had ruled the ancient city.

They'd been on the road for almost two hours. After they had left Gbarnga, they passed through the town of Gbalatoah, crossed the bridge and entered the village of Saint Paulsville. Mustafa pointed to a winding trail just barely wide enough for the Rover. The road was so neglected that Lynden had to put the Rover into low range four-wheel drive. They crawled along, passing a number of rice and cassava farms. After approximately six miles, they ran out of road.

"From here, we walk," said Lynden as he pulled out a rucksack. He handed it to Mustafa. "For $5,000, you can carry this," Lynden continued, fastening a canteen on his belt. He handed Mustafa a machete and took a second one for himself.

Initially the trail was easy to negotiate. Then they came to an overgrown raffia barrier, the classic Poro warning that a sacred bush was ahead. The uninitiated could not enter or the dark spirits would kill them. The trail had all but disappeared.

They stepped carefully around the barrier and began to pick their way along the path. Several times they had to use the machetes to cut their way through the thick brush. Twice they reached forks in the road. Lynden nodded to Mustafa who seemed to know which fork to take.

About three o'clock they crested a hill. Below, they could see a small valley. The forest had once been cleared of all growth. But now, small trees and underbrush were again claiming the area.

Lynden thought he could make out the remains of a circular stockade in the center of a clearing. Its walls had originally been constructed of six-inch saplings. The few that remained reached more than twelve feet in height. However, not many remained, and most of the walls had collapsed. Lynden figured the stockade measured about two hundred feet in diameter. As he further scanned the land below, he thought he could make out a large, circular mud dwelling. Its thatched roof had collapsed years ago.

Lynden wondered what could have caused the people to desert this large a compound. He figured that some cataclysmic event must have occurred. One clue to the mystery might be within the stockade itself. He could see a depression in the ground at the middle of the enclosure. The earth had collapsed inward, leaving a deep hole. He couldn't even wager a guess as to the depth from his current position at the top of the hill.

"Are these the ruins?" asked Lynden.

"No, AB, the ruins are over that rock hill down by the river. There is nothing left but square blocks of stone on the ground."

"What's the purpose of the stockade?" asked Lynden.

Mustafa seemed reluctant to answer.

"It is an evil place. No one dares go down into the valley. We must skirt around the side of the hill and reach the river before dark."

Lynden couldn't believe Mustafa would be afraid of the dark. This Mustafa wasn't the type to be frightened by something as trivial as this so-called evil. He had seen Mustafa charge at three men, each holding an automatic weapon. Mustafa had rushed at them, slicing madly with his machete and leaving them chopped to bloody pieces.

"That's OK," said Lynden. "Show me how we go around the hill. You lead the way." Mustafa seemed relieved.

"Follow me," he said, veering off to the left and allowing a good distance between them and the stockade. They began to descend the hill, carefully choosing their footing.

Mustafa moved ahead without looking back to check Lynden's progress. The gap between the two men gradually widened. Mustafa didn't see Lynden reach into his back pocket and pull out a snub-nosed .38 special with a two-inch barrel.

Lynden stopped abruptly. He lifted his arm and pointed the pistol at the back of Mustafa's head.

He pulled the trigger.

The shot echoed off the nearby hills. A flock of birds screeched as it took flight from the surrounding trees. The hollow-point round exploded in Mustafa's head, spraying brain tissue and bits of bone in a wide radius around the intact, but twitching, body. Within seconds, the movement stopped. Lynden approached the corpse, rolling it over with his boot, and removed the rucksack. He kicked it again, and the body tumbled downhill and came to rest in the thick undergrowth.

Lynden placed the revolver back in his rear pocket and headed down to inspect the clearing. When he got to the ruins of the hut, he pulled out his GPS and took a reading. The hut was right on. It matched up with the exact coordinates given in the directions.

Now Lynden was close enough to check out the hole. He neared the edge and peered down into the darkness. It appeared as if an underground tunnel had collapsed. Perhaps the coordinates indicated an underground location. It made sense. If the treasures were out in the open, they'd have been discovered by now.

Lynden moved to the perimeter of the stockade, tossed down the rucksack, and stretched his arms while moving his head from side to side. He felt tired. It had been a long hike and an eventful day. It would soon be dark, and he'd have to wait until morning to conduct a more detailed search.

He was about to sit down on a flat boulder near the wall when he was startled by a wild ruckus and rapid flapping of bats' wings that poured out of a cleft in the hillside near the rock outcropping.

"Bats, lots of bats," he said. Thousands of bats dived and swirled in the cloudless sky. "Must be a cave up there. Must be a really big cave," he reasoned. "Perhaps it would connect with a tunnel under the hut."

He yawned and stretched again. He reached for the rucksack and pulled out a poncho. He spread it out next to the wall of the old hut. He sat down, leaned his back against the wall and closed his eyes.

21

Deep in the Liberian forest, Lynden would begin the final leg on his path to great wealth.

AT FIRST LIGHT, LYNDEN ROLLED UP THE PONCHO, PULLED THE rucksack over his shoulders and started hiking toward the cleft in the rock. Last night he'd seen thousands of bats fly out of that opening. He was eager to find out if this was yet another clue to locating the lost treasure.

It took almost an hour to reach the hole in the rocks. He dropped the rucksack and pulled out two high-intensity LED lights. Each light had twenty-four bulbs, powered by three double AA batteries. They could operate up to twelve hours on a single charge. The powerful lights were lightweight and provided superior lighting. He quietly congratulated himself on being well prepared for the search.

The cleft was wide and high enough for him to walk right in. It appeared that someone had enlarged the natural opening. He could see chisel marks on the rocks at the entrance. It took a few minutes for his eyes to adjust to the bright sunlight. He felt the air cool as he stepped into the darkness.

After walking about fifteen feet, he entered a natural limestone chamber. He flashed a light upward. Suspended heads-down from the ceiling hung countless sleeping bats. He flashed his light downward and covered his nose. The floor was knee-deep with bat guano. He gingerly skirted the bat shit by stepping from stone to stone along the edge of the wall.

Pointing his light forward, he could see an opening to the right. It also looked as if it had been enlarged hundreds of years before. He cautiously made his way along the edge of a tunnel that began to slope downward. He followed it for nearly a hundred yards until it opened into yet another limestone cavern. It was too large for the LED lights to reveal its interior. Above him, Lynden saw stalactites hanging like icicles from the ceiling. He paused to listen to a constant drip-drip of water.

Lynden had been in limestone caves before, and this one seemed typical. In some places he had to crawl on his hands and knees to get through a narrow passage. Elsewhere, the caverns were so expansive that his lights couldn't reach the top. Some tunnels branched off either to the right or left, but Lynden stayed on the path that looked more worn. He passed by several pools of crystal clear water, taking extra care not to slip.

He paused by a coral-red outcropping and reached out to touch it. The toe of his boot came in contact with a circular object, about eight inches in diameter. He bent over and picked up what looked like a brass disk. It was shaped like a large doughnut, but had small, protruding bumps on its surface. Lynden held it and estimated that it weighed as much as five pounds.

The disk wasn't anything new to Lynden, either. He had sold similar objects to collectors. In the art world, they called these Tiens or "water spirits." Most came from Sierra Leone or Liberia. They were formed from bronze, using an old casting method. They were often found along riverbanks.

Even the experts were stumped when they were asked how old these were or who had made them. No one knew. The current inhabitants of West Africa didn't use them. Their origin remained unknown.

As he continued deeper into the cavern, he discovered more of the brass objects along the trail. They weren't uniform in size. They varied from only a few ounces to perhaps thirty pounds.

He pushed farther into the cavern, finally coming to another narrow passage. He lowered his head and crawled several hundred feet until he could see a larger, smooth-walled chamber.

"Shit!" Lynden shouted.

In front of him he saw an incredible cache of stored objects including brass spears, wooden crates, large golden plates, a wooden throne inlaid with precious gems, and two large wooden statues. All the surrounding walls were decorated with hieroglyphics and multi-colored drawings. It all reminded Lynden of what explorers must have seen when they entered the treasure chambers of Egyptian tombs.

Lynden didn't claim to be an archeologist, but he'd been around ancient treasures enough to know that this place surpassed many other discoveries of ancient Egyptian art. He passed his light over dozens of objects that could bring in millions of dollars on the open market.

Along the walls he could see primitive drawings. One scene depicted an open valley. Groves of trees spotted the verdant, rolling hills. Flocks of sheep and goats grazed in open pastures. In the center of the scene, he could make out a large stone statue. It looked like the Great Sphinx from Egypt. But it couldn't be. The pyramids were located on open, arid land, not on fertile pastures.

The next drawing showed men bowing in front of two horned creatures. One was tall; the other was short and dwarf-like, perhaps only three feet tall. The creatures appeared to be arguing. Lynden thought that the two creatures were very similar to the one in the drawing of the wooden statue.

The next drawing showed the taller creature leading a group of men toward the Sphinx. The following drawings seemed to depict the smaller creature leading another group out of the valley. Other pictures showed people in the act of making human sacrifices.

One lined drawing looked like a crude map. Lynden thought it formed what could be the Mediterranean Sea and the western coast of Africa. Arrows and simple drawings of ships seemed to indicate a route to West Africa by sea. A portion of the map could be the Saint Paul River. Perhaps the people who had lived here had come from Egypt by boat up the river.

Other drawings showed men dressed in Egyptian costumes. They seemed to be greeting naked black men. Some of the men were tied and bound together. Piles of the bronze disks, the water spirits, were stacked nearby. The Tien could have been used as money. Perhaps the Egyptians were trading the bronze pieces for slaves.

In another drawing, men were building a great city. Black slaves worked on temples. In all the pictures, the dwarf-like, horned creature appeared to be directing the Egyptian priests. Another map showed a road leading from the city into a valley. The next drawing was of the inside of a cavern and the construction of another temple and an amphitheater.

"So, the stories of an ancient city were true," mumbled Lynden.

The final group of drawings differed from the first ones. They were more crudely drawn than the others. Black men were attacking the Egyptians with spears. The city was in flames. Egyptians were blocking the entrances to the caverns with stones.

"These fuckers have been killing each other since the dawn of time," Lynden said. Then he laughed out loud. "So true, so true," he said, shaking his head.

He spent an hour searching for the old wooden statue with no luck. He located a doorway leading out of the chamber. It was filled with broken rocks, likely from a cave-in. This could have been the part of the tunnel that had collapsed in the stockade. At the far end of the chamber he could see a doorway carved in the rock wall. Two wooden statues of the man-demons also known as *endosyms*, each almost ten feet tall, stood on either side of the passage.

As he stepped through the door, he felt a sudden gush of air. He moved forward and pointed the light around the tunnel. He looked down in time to spot a trip wire. Thank God, he had a strong light. A simple flashlight wouldn't have revealed the wire. Within the next hundred feet, he found two more trip wires. He stepped carefully over each one.

He continued cautiously down the tunnel. Ahead, he saw light. The farther he went, the brighter it became. Finally, he stepped into the largest chamber yet. He would call it a grand chamber, hundreds of feet in diameter. It reminded him of a Roman amphitheater. Rows of benches faced a granite temple, framed by marble columns.

He wondered how this magnificent structure could ever have ever been built. He couldn't even guess at the number of hours it must have taken to complete. The place was so large that it was difficult to see from one side to the other.

The people who had built it must have chanced upon a truly unique feature – the chamber was illuminated with phosphorescent light. Lynden reached out to touch the tunnel wall. When he pulled his hand away, his fingers glowed. Apparently some kind of light-producing algae grew inside the cavern.

He moved farther into the amphitheater. For the first time, he noticed something on the benches. Thousands of round objects had been placed side-by-side. He moved down a rock pathway toward the center section. When he neared the first row, he stopped. The objects on the benches were human heads. He leaned down and directed his light at one to examine it more closely. It still had shrunken, dried flesh and strands of hair. The farther down he went, the older the heads seemed to be – more like skulls with no flesh or hair.

He couldn't help but marvel at the cruelty of man against man all throughout the ages. There truly wasn't anything new under the sun. Weapons had changed, but men were all basically the same. Whoever did this was just as bad as the guys he ran around with during the seventeen years of civil war.

Finally, he saw what he had come for – standing on a granite block at the center of the temple was the wooden statue. He moved carefully down the steps leading to the temple. He crawled up on a marble platform, then stood up and approached the statue.

It was exactly as he had imagined. It stood about three feet tall. It depicted a naked male body. One leg was missing and a metal shaft had been added to stabilize it. It had a dwarf-like body. Its head was disproportionately large. Two horns protruded from either side of the head. The face had heavy eye ridges as one would see in a Neanderthal. Huge buckteeth stuck out from its smiling lips. The eyes had a certain glow, probably a reflection of the phosphorescence. Yet they were distinct – there were no pupils. For a second, Lynden felt a chill move over his body, but it quickly passed.

Although Lynden was the son of missionaries, he had never caught their religious fervor. He had lost what little belief he'd had in God long ago. Now, the only spirits he held in high regard were the Devil himself and the hundred proof spirits that came in bottles. None of these ancient spirits would have any impact at all on him.

"But," he chuckled, "some of that hundred proof would sure taste good right now!"

He pulled a collapsed nylon duffle bag out of the rucksack, walked over and gently picked up the statue. He tossed it lightly it in his hand to get an idea of its weight. It weighed next to nothing. He eased it into the duffle bag, zipped the bag, and turned to retrace his steps out of the cavern.

22

Back in Monrovia, AB Lynden downed his final beer, got up and dropped a ten-dollar tip on the table.

HE HAD EATEN A LATE-NIGHT MEAL IN THE SINKOR RESTAURANT two blocks from his rented apartment.

Everything had gone smoothly, and Lynden was pleased with his day's work. He had already shipped the statue through the American Embassy's post office in Monrovia. One of his CIA contacts had agreed to handle the shipping. All he had done was to place the statue in a wooden footlocker. He didn't even have to pay duty because it was identified as African art.

It would arrive at JFK tomorrow. UPS would take it to its final destination in Johnsonville, Virginia. Once it arrived, he would be sent a bank draft for $150,000.

Couldn't be any easier than that, he thought. He had never felt more confident. Things promised to get even better. All his dreams would soon come true.

The coming bank draft was insignificant compared to the fortune he would make when he started selling the artifacts he had found in the chamber. The value of those would surpass that of the treasure found in King Tut's tomb. And, even better, Lynden didn't have to share. Only he knew where the treasure was located. Only he knew the vast array of relics that were hidden there.

He yawned and looked at his watch. It was eleven o'clock. He stepped out into the warm tropical night. Once the sun went down in the rural villages, people disappeared into their huts. Here in Monrovia, the night streets were crowded with noisy people going from place to place, laughing, singing and enjoying life. Monrovians perked up in the evenings when the temperature dropped and ocean breezes came inland. The city even smelled better at night. He breathed in the delightful odors of charcoal mingling with the grilling of meats and vegetables.

He turned to the right and walked to the dead-end street where he lived. The side streets weren't as crowded as the main avenue. One man briefly caught his attention – a young Liberian was coming his way. The man looked to be in his early twenties. He wore a ragged white T-shirt and tan pants. Lynden even noticed his worn tennis shoes. He had probably come in from the interior and was trying to find a job in the big city. They made quick eye contact, but Lynden looked away, ignoring him.

When the man was two feet from Lynden, he suddenly rushed at him with lightning speed. Lynden tried to react, but sixty years and five beers were no match for youth and speed.

The eight-inch blade of the survival knife penetrated AB's left side, just under the ribs. The blade was thrust upward reaching into the left lung and heart.

As the assailant extracted the bloody knife, Lynden's heart exploded in his chest. Lynden dropped to his knees. The last thing he saw was the even, white teeth of the smiling young man. The man quickly pulled Lynden's wallet out of his back pocket, checked to see if anyone had seen what had happened, ran as fast as he could to the main street, and disappeared into the night.

It was just another robbery that had gone too far.

Arthur B. Lynden would never tell a soul about the ancient ruins, the hidden treasure, and the true story of the *endosyms*.

23

*Ziggy Roberts moved his head and shoulders to the heavy
drumbeat reverberating through the custom speakers in the silver
Lexus convertible.*

HE HAD THE TOP DOWN, EVEN THOUGH IT WAS A COOL SIXTY DEGREES
this early in the morning. He'd been asked to stop by Johnsonville City
Hall and pick up the approved permits for the fence around the school.

What a deal he had. Two years ago, he was a black ex-con, flipping
burgers at McDonald's in Charlottesville. Now, he was one of the elite
guards at the school. Half the guards were black; the other half, white. In
prison, they would have been at each other's throats. Now, they all served
Dr. Sarday.

That was the other funny thing. Obviously, Sarday was the greatest
scam artist he had ever met. He drew rich guys from all over the place to
his channeling of some dead dude from Egypt.

What a crock of bullshit! His job required him to stand by the doors
to the pavilion, to ensure that the uninvited were excluded. On several
occasions he had even handled inside duty.

Sarday would come out in those fancy African robes with a funny
little hat on his head. He looked like an ass, but he would speak to the
clowns in the audience, and they would be mesmerized. He was charging
three grand for a weekend session, and those folks were so stupid that
they came back for seconds and thirds. It made no difference to Ziggy; he
was pulling down ten grand a month to look tough.

The whine of a siren finally caught his attention. He looked out the rear view mirror and saw the flashing red and blue lights. He glanced at his speed in the heads-up display on the windshield. It showed fifty miles per hour. Great, that's all he needed.

He pulled over to the right, and the patrol car came up behind him. Ziggy patted the 40 mm Glock in the shoulder holster under his leather jacket. Funny, you never get over the desire to blow away a cop when you're pulled over. But he didn't need to worry; he worked for Sarday.

He reached over and pulled the registration papers out of the glove compartment. The car was registered to the School for West African Spiritual Studies Enterprise, Incorporated.

Ziggy watched in the rear view mirror as the cop got out of the cruiser and walked toward the Lexus. This cop was a young black, maybe in his early thirties. He looked at the nametag on the cop's uniform.

"Good morning, Officer Johnson, is there a problem?"

"Sir, I clocked you at fifty in a thirty-five mile an hour zone. May I see your driver's license, proof of insurance and registration?"

After he handed him the documents, the cop walked back to his cruiser while Ziggy sat twiddling his thumbs. He couldn't stand this part. He hated waiting.

He was still waiting when he saw an unmarked black cruiser pull up in front of the Lexus. It was a white dude wearing jeans. Ziggy recognized him immediately. It was the town's chief of police. Brian Bishop got out of the car and walked toward the Lexus. He paused by the drivers door long enough to get a good look at the man.

"Good morning," said Bishop.

"Morning, officer," said Ziggy, gazing absently at the dashboard.

Bishop continued walking back to the police cruiser.

"Morning, Jimmy," said Bishop.

"Morning, Chief."

"What have you got going on here?" Bishop asked.

"Speeding. No wants or warrants on the vehicle. The school place owns it."

"Did you run the driver?"

"Just doing it, Chief," Johnson answered. As soon as he had gotten the words out of his mouth, the data popped up on the screen.

Bishop leaned in the window and smiled. "Looks like it's Ziggy No-Middle-Initial Roberts. Did ten years in the state for armed robbery."

"Come on, Jimmy, get out of the car," signaled Bishop.

"But…but, Chief," Johnson argued, "I haven't finished writing the ticket!"

"Forget the ticket," said Bishop. "And, by the way, I want you behind me as a back-up – with your weapon in your hand."

"Weapon, Chief?"

"Yeah, that's what I said. Your weapon," Bishop replied as he started walking up to the Lexus.

"Mr. Roberts, step out of the car," Bishop ordered.

"What?" Ziggy asked.

"I said, step out of the car."

Ziggy looked up at Bishop and then back at Johnson. He could see that Johnson had a Glock in his hand. Even Bishop rested his hand on his holster. Ziggy shrugged his shoulders, opened the door and slowly got out of the car.

"Both hands on your head," Bishop said. He reached around Roberts, pulled open his jacket and removed the pistol.

"Saw the holster when I spoke to him," said Bishop to Johnson. Then the chief pulled Roberts' right hand behind his back, then his left, and cuffed him. He turned him around.

"You're under arrest," Bishop said firmly.

"You're making a big mistake," Roberts growled.

"Take him down to the station and book him for violation of the Virginia Penal Code 263, a felon in possession of a handgun," Bishop told his officer.

Johnson cupped Ziggy's elbow and directed him to the patrol car. He opened the back door and shoved him into the back seat.

As the door was closing, Roberts yelled, "You stupid cops, you're through! You have no idea what you have done!"

Unfazed, Bishop laughed, walked to the Lexus and climbed into the driver's seat. He turned the key to "on" and pushed the button for the convertible top. The electric motor hummed as the top rolled up. Bishop secured the latches, rolled up the windows, stepped out and pushed the "lock door" button on the key fob. He tossed the keys to Johnson.

"When you get him back to the station, let him call the school, and they can send someone to pick up this car."

"Yes, sir, Chief," said Johnson.

The rest of the day went routinely for Bishop. It was a little past two o'clock when Bishop got a call from the dispatcher.

"Chief, the mayor wants to see you as soon as possible."

"Thanks, Shannon, I'm on my way," said he said as he turned the cruiser around and headed to into town.

It didn't take Bishop long to get to city hall. He skipped the elevator and climbed one flight of stairs to the mayor's office. He told the receptionist that he was there to see the mayor.

Harvey Bradley poked his head out his office door before the receptionist could announce Bishop's arrival.

"Come in, and close the door, Bishop," the mayor said.

Bradley's gruffness and the fact that he didn't say "chief" caused a quick chill to run down Bishop's back. Something was wrong. Before, the mayor always referred to him as "Brian" or "Chief Bishop."

Bishop entered the office and pulled the door closed behind him. When he sat down, he couldn't believe that this was the same man as he had seen a little more than a month ago. The running nickname for Bradley had always been "Mr. Dumpy." No one called him that to his face, but everyone agreed the name fit him well. Bradley always looked as if he had slept in his suit. His shoulders slumped forward, and he stooped when he walked. Although he said he was five feet, nine inches tall, he looked shorter. Even his voice was less than authoritive. He always spoke softly, almost in a whisper. If Bradley hadn't been a Johnson on his mother's side, he probably never would have been elected as mayor.

But today was different. There he stood in a tailored suit that must have cost more than a month's salary. He had on a crisp, white shirt and a silk tie. Gold cuff links were fashionably visible under his coat sleeves. He stood ramrod straight, making him appear taller than ever before. He looked as if he had shed twenty pounds of fat. But, the most significant change was the man's very presence. His eyes literally bore into Bishop as he flexed his civic power.

"God damn it, Bishop. This is the last straw!" Bradley shouted.

"What are you talking about, Harvey?" Bishop asked, puzzled by the mayor's appearance and change in attitude.

"It's Mayor Bradley, you twit. What did you think you were doing this morning when you arrested Dr. Sarday's security chief?"

"Wait a minute now. The guy I arrested was a felon. He served ten years for armed robbery. He was carrying a concealed weapon. That's against the law, Mr. Mayor," Bishop snapped.

"Bishop, Mr. Roberts has a permit to carry that weapon within the city limits. He has a written permit from me personally."

"You can't do that. It's against the law," Bishop replied.

"Like hell I can't!" Bradley said, his anger flaring. "Furthermore, you'd better remember that I hired you, and I can fire you!"

"What for? Doing my job?" Bishop shouted back.

"No, for being a drunk. I knew I shouldn't have hired a passed-over army major. You have been nothing but an incompetent ass since the day you were hired. Last year when you got in that fight in Richmond during the law enforcement convention is just one example of your incompetence," shouted the mayor.

"That was just a misunderstanding," Bishop said.

"Misunderstand, my ass. You were drunk in a bar. What do you think? That we are stupid? Every social event you attend, within two hours, you're the life of the party, and Ann ends up driving you home. I wouldn't be surprised if I did a blood alcohol test right now that you would be under the influence. Unless you want to hand me your badge and gun right now, you'd better get your butt over to the jail and release Mr. Roberts. I can't believe you would embarrass this town and offend Dr. Sarday," said Bradley.

Bishop was left totally speechless. He could feel his face turning red. He stood up, turned around, and walked to the door. He was reaching for the door handle when Bradley fired one more insult.

"Bishop, I'm putting you on a plan of improvement. You stay away from Dr. Sarday and his staff. One more screw up, and you're gone!"

24

The fight with Bradley had left Bishop listless and confused.

HE HAD NO CHOICE NOW. HE WALKED INTO THE MAIN OFFICE. HE saw Officer Johnson standing next to Shannon's desk. The two of them were paging through a stack of reports.

"Johnson, go release Ziggy Roberts from the holding tank, take him back to his car, give him back his gun and tell him he is free to go," Bishop said without so much as a hello to either of them.

"But, Chief, I thought…"

Bishop interrupted before Johnson finished his sentence. "Just do it, and I mean right now!" he demanded.

Bishop walked into his office, slamming the door behind him so hard that one of his award certificates crashed to the floor, shattering the glass and breaking the frame. Bishop collapsed into his chair and stared blankly at the closed door.

He felt ashamed, embarrassed and frightened – all at the same time. The whole incident reminded him of when he was thirteen and his mother had found the Hustler magazines hidden in the back of his dresser. He knew she knew what he was doing while looking at the magazines, and it was as if she caught him in the act.

He had never been so intimidated in his adult life until today. He should have quit on the spot, but they couldn't afford their house and car payments on just Ann's salary. How could he face their friends if he was fired? What did Mayor Bradley mean that he was a drunk? He wasn't a drunk. He could handle his booze better than anyone he knew.

Bishop was breathing so hard that he thought he was going to have a heart attack. He opened the bottom drawer of his desk, fumbled around behind the files, and pulled out a half-full pint of Jim Beam. He unscrewed the cap and took a long swig.

"To calm my nerves," he whispered. "To calm my nerves."

25

They'd spent the day in Charlottesville.

TIM AND SAMANTHA WALKED HAND-IN-HAND AS THEY LEFT THE Cineplex 17 Theater. They strolled through the mall, sometimes stopping to gaze in store windows. They talked about the movie they'd just seen and agreed that it had amazing action and special effects. They weren't in any hurry to get home. Just being together was enough.

"Hungry?" asked Samantha.

"Always!" Tim said, looking like he had an appetite for something more.

"For food, silly," Sam said, knowing full well what he wanted.

"Sure, for that too," he replied with a grin.

"How about a pizza?" she asked, steering them into Pizza Hut.

They pulled their chairs close together and studied a menu. They agreed on a large pan pizza with mushrooms, pepperoni and green peppers. For drinks, they both asked for draft root beer.

Tim draped his left arm around her shoulders while she rested her hands on the table. His right hand covered both of her hands. He rubbed his thumb over her long fingers. They talked about everything and about nothing. The world could have stopped spinning, and they wouldn't have noticed.

"Your order, sir," the waitress said as she set down the hot pizza. "More root beer?"

"No, thanks," Samantha said, smiling at Tim. "What we have is just right."

They were working on the second half of the pizza when boisterous laughter erupted from a table on their right. Two beefy young men dragged out chairs, scraping them along the floor and bumping them together to position them at their table.

"Beefy" was sure right. Tim guessed each one of them weighed more than three hundred and fifty pounds. Their UV football jerseys had high numbers, indicating that they were linemen. Even though they looked heavy, they were fit and well conditioned without an extra ounce of fat on their bodies. Their muscled arms were bigger than an average man's thigh. It was obvious they spent more time pumping iron than they did studying.

Unfortunately, they were not only loud, they also appeared to be drunk. Their obnoxious banter included a string of obscenities. Both Tim and Samantha stopped talking, and Tim pushed the pizza pan to the center of the table.

The two men began to talk even louder than before. One stared at Samantha and then turned to his buddy with a grin.

"You know, Gary, I smell something black."

Both Tim and Samantha froze. Neither of them knew which one of the men had made the remark, but it didn't really matter. Samantha knew they were talking about her. She looked at Tim, but his face had turned pale, and he stared down at his empty hands.

Tim clenched his fists. His muscles tightened. He was losing it once again. He fought to maintain his equilibrium. He didn't want a replay of the incident on the soccer field. He saw the evil that had poured from the young man's inner being. Tim opened his hands and rubbed his knees. Not here, not in front of Samantha, not now.

Samantha seethed. She was on the verge of picking up a chair and slamming it down on either one of the bastards.

"Let's get out of here," whispered Tim. He grabbed her arm as he rushed her to the door. She could hear the assholes laughing at them as they hurried out the door.

Neither of them spoke as they walked toward the parking garage, each consumed by their own thoughts.

It had happened again, thought Tim. That incident on the soccer field hadn't been a fluke after all. When the football player wearing the number 78 jersey had said, "I smell something black," just like the soccer player, he had been transformed into a demon.

The incident in the restaurant made him want to kill both of them with his bare hands. He didn't know what might have happened had they stayed there any longer. He still felt himself shaking. Just what was happening to him?

Sam's thoughts were far different. She was deeply hurt by the man's crude remark. She had already been having problems in dealing with her relationship with Tim. It was bad, even at home. She first noticed that something was up when they had returned to the house on New Year's Day. They had slept together the night before at her apartment. When they got to her parents' house, her father spent the remainder of the day glaring at Tim.

She had no idea how her father knew what had happened that night. He never said anything, but Samantha was sure that he knew. Was he unhappy that Tim was white? So what? Her own mother was half white, and Grandma was all white. Maybe her dad was just upset because someone was sleeping with his daughter. His ability to figure things out was one reason he was such a successful attorney.

She recalled that in February her father had asked if she was still seeing "that Martin boy." She'd almost snapped back to say that he was a man, not a boy. But she simply said, "Yes."

Tonight she faced another dilemma. Tim appeared to have been frightened by the two drunks. Instead of confronting them, he had literally run out of the Pizza Hut. She thought he was actually shaking with fear. Sure, they were drunk. Sure, they were huge, muscular men. If he had swung at them, he could have ended up in the hospital. Nevertheless, she didn't know what to think. Could she love a man who wouldn't stand up for her?

She remembered back in high school when she had dated a big football player. He could have confronted these two, but he was a total jerk on a date. He spent most of his time admiring his own physique in the mirror in a movie theater as they waited in line. He would probably have walked up to those two guys and gotten involved in a discussion of what type of weight-lifting equipment produces the biggest muscles.

Still, Tim's fear bothered her.

26

Just five miles from JFK International, the massive UPS
warehouse took up acres of land.

IT SERVED THE CITY OF NEW YORK. IT SERVED AS A DISTRIBUTION
center for parcels received and those shipped via international and
domestic flights. It also handled overland truck shipments.

The wooden crate the size of an old army footlocker had arrived from
Monrovia, Liberia the day before. The US Customs office had x-rayed it
and checked it for explosives. The customs declaration indicated that the
crate contained antique African art.

The operator watched the image on the screen as the box rolled down
the conveyer belt. It contained a number of wooden items including
something that looked like a large spoon, a drum, small statues, several
bowls, and a larger statue sandwiched in between the smaller items. It
looked similar to other crates that had been sent to African art dealers in Manhattan. Nothing seemed out of place. The operator stamped
it "Cleared." He glanced at the address. It was to go to Johnsonville,
Virginia. He used a second stamp to send it to its next stop.

Reginald Walton stifled a yawn. It was only two o'clock in the morning, and he had another four hours to go on his shift. He was on his lunch
break, and, as he did each working night, he wandered aimlessly around
the warehouse.

Reggie wasn't a heavyweight. He was just twenty-two years old,
stood five feet, ten inches tall, and weighed in at one hundred forty
pounds. He had a chalky complexion, dotted with pimples. His greasy,

black hair hung unevenly. Reggie participated in the recreational use of crack cocaine. He frequently forgot to shower. His co-workers sighed with relief that he had never come into the break room. Otherwise, they just ignored him.

No one would ever call Reggie a health nut, and he sure didn't roam around the place just for the exercise. Instead, he was on the prowl, looking for items to steal. He needed fast cash to buy drugs. He was pissed about the tracer codes on the labels. The only way to successfully take something was to slice open a package, remove one or two items, and tape the box back together again. That made it difficult for inspectors to figure out exactly where an item had disappeared.

When he saw the wooden crate from Monrovia, Liberia, he knew that he'd hit the jackpot. The customs tag indicated that it contained antique African art. It would be easy to open the crate, take out one or two small objects, and seal it back up again. No one would be the wiser. He could slip the items into the inside pocket in his jacket. When it was quitting time, he would walk right out the door and get in his car.

He reached in his pocket and took out his Leatherman multipurpose pliers. He popped out the screwdriver and began to loosen a screw on the box lid. When the first screw was loose enough to turn manually, he worked it with his thumb and forefinger. Then he lifted it up to examine it more closely.

"Son of a bitch!" he cursed. The damn screw was dripping with blood. The sharp edge of the screw had cut deeply into both his thumb and his forefinger. He shook his hand. A glob of blood flew through the air, striking the crate with a splat.

"What the fuck?" Reggie gasped. Something was wrong with him. He felt dizzy and disoriented. He reached down and placed his bloodied hand on the crate in order to steady himself. A bolt of pain shot up his arm. It threw him backwards, and he landed on the concrete floor. He raised his head and stared at the crate. He thought he saw the crate begin to shimmy.

He slowly picked himself up and waited until his mind cleared. He looked around for the Leatherman, found it, and grabbed it. He jammed it into his pants pocket and scurried down the aisle. He cradled his hand and arm close to his body in an attempt to stop the bleeding and lessen the pain.

"Fuck!" he said under his breath. "I've got to lay off the goddamn drugs!"

27

Johnsonville Plantation's renovated mansion could have fooled
almost anyone.

ON THE SURFACE, IT LOOKED AS IF IT HAD BEEN PLUCKED OUT OF 1862 and set down in the twenty-first century. But underneath, it was as technologically sophisticated as anyone could imagine.

The decorators had been ordered to restore the mansion as closely as possible to what it had been in Nathanial Johnson's day. They could spend whatever was necessary to do the job. All four floors had been furnished with the finest antiques. The restoration crew had combed the state in their search for just the right pieces. They had even discovered some of the original furniture stored in one of the plantation's outbuildings.

A suite of offices on the third floor served as the school's headquarters. Dr. George Sarday's office, the largest and most luxurious, overlooked the mansion's main entrance. From his windows he could see the comings and goings of students and guests.

Sarday was particularly pleased with his desk, an oversized Federalist piece, likely crafted in the early nineteenth century. Local historians said the desk was an original one, probably commissioned by old man Johnson himself. Their assumptions were confirmed when workers had discovered false bottoms in four of its large drawers.

Inside were a dozen dusty and dog-eared record books. The pages were filled with meticulous pen and ink columns tallying the day-to-day business of the plantation. When the handwriting had been compared to official documents in county records, it was confirmed that Johnson himself had maintained the books. Particularly interesting had been his careful listing of slave names, prices paid, dates sold, births, deaths and marriages. Since most of the records kept by plantation owners had been burned, lost or destroyed, Johnson's work would have been considered an historical treasure. Of course, that's only if Sarday had permitted them to be released.

The tables had certainly been turned, thought Sarday. Here he was, a black man from Liberia, and now the supreme master of the plantation. He looked across the broad surface of his desk and smiled at the white man, Mayor Harvey Bradley, the great, great grandson of the old slave owner.

Bradley might have considered himself as Sarday's friend and social equal, but that was far from the truth. Sarday detested the weak creature that fouled his office. But, for his plan to succeed, the entire town of Johnsonville had to come under the control of the *endosyms*.

The power must first be focused here at the plantation before spreading all across the nation. True believers would then pass the word from city to city and then from state to state. After a ten thousand year hiatus, the *endosyms* would rise to their greatest grandeur yet.

"I can't believe what a change has taken place in my life. Your teachings have made me a new man," Bradley said.

Sarday looked up and stared at the mayor. He hadn't been listening closely to this man's inane chatter. He heard only the phrase "your teachings."

"Not my teachings," Sarday explained. "You owe your new vitality to Dacari Mucomba.

"Of course, Harvey, this is just the beginning. The first step is enlightenment. Then from the many who receive my message, few will be selected.

Those few will serve Dacari Mucomba. Those few will know its truth. Those few will know and speak its name. And, those few will receive power and wealth beyond the imagination of mortal man," Sarday said, speaking slowly and in monotone. His deliberate repetition worked to hypnotize the ignorant beings.

"I just know I will be one of the chosen," Bradley said, convinced of his own worth. "But when will this happen?"

"Patience, my dear friend," replied Sarday. "I have received word that the key to the final ceremony for Dacari Mucomba is en route to the school as we speak. Once it arrives, those who are worthy will be selected to participate in the second phase of the transformation."

Now it was Bradley's turn to lose concentration. Sarday's words had nearly lulled him to sleep. Suddenly, he looked down at his watch and rose to his feet.

"Oh, my, I must leave right now. Tonight is the city council meeting," he said.

"Let me accompany you to your car," Sarday said. This man, the mayor, could be a crucial player in recruiting others. They walked down the wide staircase to the foyer.

"Don't forget, Harvey," Sarday continued while patting the man lightly on the shoulder. "We need more members. It would be exceptionally helpful if you can bring ten new candidates to our session next weekend."

"Not a problem," Bradley responded. He figured he was related to half the population of Johnsonville. It would be easy to get family members to come.

As Bradley drove away, Sarday surveyed the plantation's grounds from the wide front porch. Everything was unfolding as he had known it would. Soon, he would have complete sovereignty over these simple fools. This time, nothing would stop him from taking total control.

Soon, very soon, blood would flow in the sacrificial chamber.

28

Michelle was having a bad night.

SHE HAD TOSSED AND TURNED ALL NIGHT, SOMEWHERE BETWEEN awake and asleep. She was exhausted, but too uncomfortable to sleep deeply in the stifling heat. Her breathing came in starts and stops. Her arms and legs felt too heavy to move. She opened both eyes as wide as she could, but saw only darkness.

What had happened? Where was she?

Suddenly, fear clutched her heart. Her gauze-wrapped body was lying in a casket. It had been left outside in the sweltering sunlight. Then six men carried the box to the gravesite. They began lowering it into the red dirt. She tried to scream, but no sound came from her lips. She willed her legs to move. She kicked out with all her strength.

With a thud, she landed on the floor tangled in her bed sheet.

Michelle groggily got to her feet, reached up and switched on the lamp beside the bed. Mr. P sat on the floor beside her. He looked at her, his tail swishing back and forth.

"I know, cat," she said. "I fell out of dah dang bed."

Her face was beaded in perspiration, and her cotton nightgown soaked in sweat. She hadn't been this hot for a good forty years, not since them hot flashes quit. She used both of her gnarled hands to pull the nightgown over her head and let it drop to the floor. Strange, she didn't feel any cooler, even if she was nearly naked.

What in the world did Willie do? Did he turn the heat up instead of down?

She'd better go check on that thermostat. She padded over to the bedroom door, opened it, and stepped into the hallway.

Now what?

She was totally blinded by a bright light. She covered her eyes with her fists and gave herself a minute or two to adjust before peeking out between her fingers.

"Lordy, lordy!" she exclaimed. Mr. P let out a low growl, as he stood at attention near her ankle. "We ain't in Johnsonville no more, Mr. P."

Just the two of them, Michelle and her cat, stood in an African village.

I'm having a dream, she thought. It's got to be a dream since I am standing here naked except for a pair of white Depends underpants. My old titties are hanging down for everyone to see.

If it was just a dream, how could it be so real? The village was nestled on a stretch of low-lying land, bisected by a river. Above it loomed rugged mountains, covered by impenetrable forests.

People must live here in the village, Michelle reasoned. Natural thatch served as roofing for their huts. No rusty scrap metal marred the landscape. Well-tended farms with herds of healthy goats and orderly rows of vegetable crops fanned out from the village.

Despite the tranquil appearance, not a single person could be seen, yet it appeared that they had been there just recently. Thin clouds of smoke rose from cooking fires behind the huts. The smell of burning charcoal mixed with the odor of roasted meat and vegetables.

It was mid-day and the sun was directly overhead. Michelle felt the heat warming her head and shoulders. She dared to walk toward one of the huts. The cat, Mr. P, followed close behind.

"Hello, anyone here?" she asked, poking her head inside the doorway.

No one answered. She checked several other huts with the same results. As she walked toward the west side of the town, she felt a sharp pain in her foot.

"Ouch!" she exclaimed. She stood on one leg and pulled a thorn from her right heel. "I thought a person couldn't feel pain in dreams," she said to the cat.

Once again on her two feet, she continued searching for the people who lived in the village. She ducked into several more doorways as she hobbled along the red laterite path.

Suddenly Mr. P burst ahead of her, rounded the corner of a hut and disappeared. She followed after him as swiftly as she could.

"Mercy me, mercy me!" she screamed, suddenly stopping in her tracks.

Fewer than twenty-five feet in front of her stood a massive leopard, its sides moving in and out as it panted, and its green-gold eyes glaring right at her.

Mr. P was walking directly toward the fearsome beast.

"Mr. P, stop! You come back here, cat. He gonna kill you and eat you all up!"

She covered her eyes with her hands to avoid the horrifying sight of her cat being devoured by the leopard. She waited for the scream of the death kill or the horrifying growl of the huge beast. She kept waiting. When she heard no sound, she lifted one hand just a little and peeked out.

"What?" she asked out loud.

The leopard sat calmly on its haunches. Mr. P. sat by its side. Both cats looked to their right. Michelle's gaze followed theirs.

An old man sat on a dried log. Barefoot and shirtless, he wore nothing more than a loincloth made of animal hide. He was mostly bald with the exception of a narrow fringe of white hair at the back of his head. He smiled and beckoned to Michelle.

"You, you, come. Please, sit by me," he called.

Michelle ventured a few steps forward before reconsidering the move. She had nothing on but her Depends. Dream or no dream, modesty had always been important to her. She splayed her gnarled hands over her breasts. The old man looked up and flat-out laughed.

"Old woman, neither you or me would know what to do with those," he said, shaking his head from side to side.

"You dirty old man! I saw you staring at my titties," she said while shaking her finger at him. Nevertheless, she dropped her hands to her sides and sat down beside him. "Where am I?" she demanded.

"Why, you're home," he said, surprised by her ridiculous question.

"Home?" she asked again, still puzzled.

"This is where your mother's mother was born," he said. "She was a great *zo*, and then the slavers come and took her to the island where your momma was born."

"And who be you?" Michelle asked.

"Why, I am Chea Geebe, the greatest *zo* in all of Liberia — 'cept for your mama's mama."

"How did I get here?" she asked.

"As we near the time when we no longer habit our bodies, it is easier for us to leave for brief periods," the old man said with a knowing smile.

Michelle shivered, recalling that terrible night when she returned to the old slave quarters. What she had seen there had struck terror throughout her very being.

"Why am I here?" she asked.

"Because of the *endosym*," he answered.

"The *endosym*?" she asked.

"Yes, you met him that morning by the slave quarters."

"You mean Sarday?" Michelle asked.

"This is not just the man Sarday. It is far more evil, and you and everyone you love are in great danger," answered Geebe.

"Danger?" asked Michelle.

"Yes, the *endosym* captures men's souls. He must be stopped."

"How?" she asked.

"You must find Tim!" said Geebe.

"Tim?" she asked.

"Tim Martin," he said. "Show him the statue. He is the only one who can stop the *endosym*."

"I don't know any Tim Martin," lamented Michelle.

"You must find him," urged Chea. "Our time is up. You must go."

"Go?" she asked.

Suddenly it was dark again. When she regained her composure, she found herself once again sitting on the bedroom floor. Mr. P sat beside her, awaiting her next move.

What a strange dream, she thought.

She rose to walk to her dresser to get a clean nightgown. The very first step brought her to an abrupt stop. She couldn't step down hard on her right foot without it hurting. She collapsed on a chair and lifted her foot to get a better look at her right heel.

"Oh, my!" she exclaimed. The bottoms of her feet were covered with red powder. She saw the small puncture wound where she had stepped on the thorn.

"Mr. P," she said. "We gotta find that Tim Martin."

29

A visit to Shantytown was in Bishop's plans for the day.

THE PAST THREE WEEKS HAD BEEN TROUBLING FOR BRIAN AND ANN
Bishop. Heading out to follow up on a possible crime would help him get
his mind off his troubles.

The chief still felt like he was walking around in a fog. Ever since that
run-in with Mayor Bradley, he couldn't stop replaying their angry con-
frontation. He had a creeping feeling that the axe might fall. He could be
terminated at a moment's notice.

He pulled a cinnamon Pop-Tart out of the toaster, poured a cup of
coffee and stirred in two heaping tablespoons of sugar. He frowned as he
walked over to the side cupboard and reached up to the very top shelf
to pull out a partial bottle of Jim Beam from behind a cereal box. He
twisted off the top and poured an ounce, or maybe a little more, into his
cup. He moved the teaspoon slowly back and forth before sampling his
morning brew.

And Ann's problem didn't help either. At least when he worried
about her, he couldn't dwell on the mayor's accusations.

Just last night Ann had come home from school yet again very upset.
Two weeks earlier one of the eighth-graders at Johnsonville Junior High
had disappeared. Despite an exhaustive search, no one had found a scrap
of evidence that could lead to his whereabouts.

Kevin Williams had told his mother he was going to hang out in
their back yard until dinnertime. When she went out to call him in, he
was gone. She called her neighbor, and they had knocked on doors and

combed the neighborhood. She'd been nearly hysterical when she called the police. The woman at the station told her that the police couldn't do anything until someone had been missing for more than forty-eight hours.

Two days later, Kevin was still missing. Police filed a missing person's report, and detectives interviewed neighbors and Kevin's friends. There was no sign of foul play, no ransom notes and no custody issues.

Kevin was a fairly average thirteen-year-old. He hadn't been a standout, but he hadn't been a troublemaker either. Just yesterday the case was suspended, and Kevin had been listed as a runaway.

Brian had tried to explain to Ann that teenage kids went missing all the time. Usually, they turned up somewhere. He didn't tell her that Johnsonville had a history of far more runaways than towns of similar size. He had run a search and found that five kids had gone missing within the last six years. Even more disturbing was that now, counting Kevin, two had disappeared in the last three months.

Ann had told him that all five had been black kids.

"If they'd all been white, the search would still be going on, and it wouldn't stop due to such lame excuses!" she complained.

Brian agreed to personally conduct his own investigation. Reviewing the case would give him something to do and help him get his mind off his own problems. This very morning he intended to talk to Kevin's mother.

First, he stopped at the station and asked his secretary to send him all the missing persons files from the past year. He thought he'd wait before digging into the older cases. The other missing person was an eighteen year-old black kid named Randy Parker. He had managed to accumulate a five-page juvenile record. The department had speculated that he had moved on to the streets of Richmond to sell drugs.

Kevin's missing person's report was clean. He had no juvenile record. But that didn't mean that Kevin didn't just get tired of school, and he had decided to hit the road.

From the office, Bishop drove out to Shantytown and followed his GPS to the Williams' house. It was fairly typical of the cheaply constructed homes in Shantytown. Bishop noted that the grass in the front yard needed to be mowed. He also saw a ten-speed bike chained to the front door.

When he knocked, an attractive black woman in her early twenties came to the door.

"Is your mother in?" Bishop asked, showing his police ID.

"My momma don't live here," she said. "I'm Shona Williams. Have you found my boy Kevin?"

It took a moment for Bishop to recover. This young woman was the mother of a thirteen-year-old? She must have been twelve when Kevin was born.

"Not yet, Mrs. Williams. I'm Chief Bishop. My wife, I mean, Principal Bishop, asked me to follow up on Kevin. May I come in?"

"Oh, yes, please, and it's Miss. I ain't never been married."

Bishop scanned the living room. Although the furniture was obviously second, or third-hand, it was all neat and clean. The walls had fresh paint. The kitchen counter was clear of unwashed dishes. The faint order of Pine Sol added a fresh scent to the home. Bishop had learned time and time again during his career that a lot could be learned about the occupant from the condition of the home.

"Can I offer you something to drink, Chief?" she asked.

"No, thank you, ma'am," Bishop answered. "Miss Williams, I know you have gone over this with the other officers during the investigation of your son's disappearance, but it would be helpful if you could answer a few questions for me."

"Please, Chief, call me Shona."

For the next quarter hour, Bishop asked a series of questions about the case and what the police had done.

"You said in your statement that Kevin had gone out to the garage after school. Did he do this often?" asked Bishop.

"Oh, yes, Chief. It was his special place. He worked on his models and even watched TV."

"May I take a look in the garage?" asked Bishop.

"Of course, here's the key. It's out back."

Bishop stepped out into the back yard. It was unfenced and sloped downward toward Johnson Creek that served as the back boundary. The garage was on the left. It was a single car, wood-framed building with a pull-down door. Two ruts ran along the side of the house out to the street. A smaller, padlocked side door faced the back yard. The garage had no windows.

He inserted the key in the padlock, opened the door and looked inside. It was too dark to see much of anything. He ran his fingers along the wall until his hand touched a light switch.

When the overhead fluorescent shop lights flickered on, he could see that the walls and ceilings had been painted with flat white latex. A threadbare gray carpet covered most of the cement floor. On the far wall, he saw a workbench scattered with a few tools. Three shabby overstuffed chairs formed a sitting area. An old, thirty-two inch television with a DVD player sat on a wooden box in front of the chairs. On top of the TV was a digital analog converter and a pair of ancient rabbit ears.

A half dozen narrow planks had been hung against the wall to create display shelves for a number of model cars, planes and boats. Although the models were crudely put together, Bishop was impressed at the number of hours it must have taken to do the work. He also noted a heavy cardboard box that served as a makeshift coffee table. Dog-eared magazines on subjects including cars, sports and naked women were scattered on top.

Bishop thought it was an ideal teenage hideaway. Any thirteen-year-old boy would love this place.

According to the mother's statement, the day Kevin disappeared she had called him in for dinner, but he hadn't answered her. She had gone out to the garage, found the door open, the lights on, and the television blaring. Nothing seemed out of place. She had told investigators that sometimes Kevin would walk along the creek. The police had searched outside, but hadn't found anything. The slow-moving water was less than eighteen inches deep. There were no signs of foul play anywhere. Even Kevin's friends had been at a loss to explain his disappearance.

"Where are you, Kevin?" whispered Bishop.

He shut off the lights on his way out and locked the door behind him. He turned right when he came to a worn path that ran along the house side of the creek. He followed it along past the back yards of several homes.

The first person he saw was an older black man who was raking up grass cuttings. Bishop waved and walked up to talk with him.

"Sir, I'm Chief Bishop, Johnsonville police," he said, flashing his ID.

"I know, Chief. I seen you before. I'm Raffer Johnson."

Bishop asked him to tell him what he could about the missing boy. The man said he hadn't seen anything unusual the evening Kevin had disappeared. He knew the boy and said that he was well liked and got along well with his mother.

Johnson didn't have anything more to say, so Bishop turned around and headed back to the creek. He hadn't gone far when he noticed a dilapidated wooden footbridge that spanned the creek. He turned back to Johnson.

"Mr. Johnson, where does that bridge go?"

"It's the path to the old Negro cemetery," said Raffer. "But you can't go there any more."

"Why?" asked Bishop.

"When that African man bought the old Johnson plantation, he put up that big old fence. Now you can't go there no more."

"Thanks," Bishop said.

He decided to cross the bridge and follow it as far as it would go. The path was fairly wide and the ground beneath it was hard as pavement. It wandered through a grove of tall oaks. In less than a mile, he came to the chain link fence that surrounded the school. He scratched his head, momentarily bewildered. He hadn't realized that Shantytown was so close to the old Johnson plantation.

He paused to study the area around the fence. When he had gone to Sarday's open house for the chamber of commerce, he had noticed the lines of fencing that ran along each side of the paved road.

According to Dick Raymond, who had been in charge of the city's construction permits, the fence was eighty percent complete. He anticipated it would be done within another two weeks.

Bishop studied the overall construction of the fencing. The outer fence was eight-feet tall topped with razor wire. The road was twelve feet wide and paved. The inside fence was eight-feet high, just like the outer fence, but it had no razor wire.

Something about the inside fence bothered him. He looked again.

"I'll be darned," exclaimed Bishop. The inside fence was attached to the posts with insulators. It was designed to be electrified. He pulled out his smartphone and snapped a picture. Why would Sarday need an electric fence? The only place he had seen such elaborate security was at a nuclear weapons storage area.

He heard the noise of an approaching vehicle. An ATV crested the hill, going along the paved road at about twenty miles per hour. Bishop stepped back into the underbrush in the shadow of a large oak. The ATV with two men inside sped by. Both men were dressed in black, military-style uniforms and carried assault rifles. He snapped a picture of the back of the vehicle as it proceeded down the hill.

God, would I ever love to catch Sarday and that asshole, Mayor Bradley, in some kind of illegal business, he thought. That would teach the mayor a thing or two.

But, right now his problem was Kevin Williams. He didn't think Kevin would have walked this far and gone to the trouble of climbing over the fence.

He wondered how far it was from the path to the new entrance to Sarday's school. He continued walking along the fence line. When he reached the top of the hill, he saw the new entrance to the school, less than four hundred yards from the path. That didn't prove anything, but it was interesting that someone from the school could walk less than a mile and a half to get to Shantytown.

It took Bishop about thirty minutes to walk back to the Williams house. He and the mother again sat down in the living room.

"Shona, I didn't see anything out of the ordinary. But I promise you I will keep the case open. You sure you two didn't have an argument that night?"

"No, Chief."

"What about his father?" asked Bishop.

"I don't know who he be," she answered.

"I don't understand," Bishop said.

"I was just twelve. They give me something, a drug, I guess. Then they all do it to me. No one in Shantytown say anything back then. I just be a poor dumb Negro girl. Then I find I be with baby. He must have been tall, is all I know. Kevin, he nearly six feet tall."

If he's that big, then no child molester would have snatched him, thought Bishop.

"Maybe he just wanted to get away," he offered.

"No, no," Shona said, shaking her head from side to side, on the verge of breaking out in tears. "He'd never go without this." She reached into a deep desk drawer and took out a tissue-wrapped object.

Bishop's hand automatically reached for his gun. He rested his hand on the butt of the pistol. When the woman unwrapped the paper, he realized that she was holding an artificial hand. Bishop could see the dark brown artificial skin and realistic fingernails. He could have sworn it was the real thing if it hadn't been for the straps hanging from the back. It was prosthesis.

"He doesn't have a left hand," Shona said. Bishop could see that the woman was about to cry again.

"Why didn't we have that in his description?" asked Bishop.

"I didn't think to mention it. The police asked for scars and tattoos," she said.

"What happened? How did he lose his hand?" asked Bishop.

"He was three years old. I was working at Burger King, flippin' burgers. Kevin stayed home with Momma. I come home one day, and he have a red spot on the back of his hand. The next day his hand is swollen and dark. We take him to Grandma Johnson, but she say her medicine not fix. We take him to the clinic. They send him to big hospital in Charlottesville. They could do nothing and had to cut off his hand. They say a brown spider bite him," said Shona.

"A brown recluse spider," Bishop muttered.

"Yeah, that what it be. When he was in first grade, his teacher, Mrs. Lewis, get Shriners to give him make-believe hand. As he gets bigger they replace hand.

"Two months ago they give him this," she continued. "It a magic hand. He can even pick up a glass with magic hand. He go nowhere without his magic hand," she sobbed.

Bishop rested his palm lightly on her shoulder.

"I'll keep looking for him, Shona."

Yet even as he said those words to reassure the mother, he knew that if a missing child hadn't been found after this long, the probability of finding him alive was very slim.

What in the world had happened to Kevin Williams?

He had no clue.

30

In the dormitory at UV, Samantha's fingertips traced an invisible, delicate line over Tim's chest, belly and lower body, stopping only to caress his most sensitive spots.

SHE FOLLOWED THE JOURNEY OF HER FINGERS WITH A STRING OF kisses, again stopping occasionally to tease and tantalize.

"Do you like this?" she asked, then giggled.

Tim breathed in deeply and exhaled slowly. He didn't answer. He couldn't answer.

"How about this? And this?" she asked, becoming more daring each time she asked.

"Hell, yes!" he answered.

He felt his heart racing, his patience nearly spent.

He couldn't stand the pent-up anticipation any longer. He felt like he was going to burst at any moment. He grabbed her forearms, held them over her head and rolled on top of her. She feigned shock as he rubbed against her. He grinned, but didn't finish the job.

"Let's see how you like being strung along, my pretty lady," he said, releasing her from his hold. He began to nuzzle her breasts then moved his fingers lightly along her inner thighs.

Samantha pretended to struggle, but she gave up and broke out laughing.

"OK, OK, you win!" she said, reaching out to touch him.

"OK, OK, I sure did, and so will you," he replied.

It wasn't the first time they both had won that weekend, but no one was keeping score. They couldn't count the number of times they'd made love.

Eddie, Tim's roommate and Samantha's twin brother, had gone home for the weekend, leaving the dorm room free for their lovemaking. Tim wondered what the other guys in the hall thought about their exceptionally long date. Although having girlfriends "sleep over" wasn't uncommon, Tim suspected the other guys would be green with envy.

On the other hand, maybe they didn't even know the room was occupied – Tim and Sam had hardly gone out.

Sam had made the hundred-mile drive from D.C. to Charlottesville on Friday night. She'd stopped at a deli and picked up sandwiches, beer and snacks. They'd called to order pizza on Saturday night. Tim had made a coffee and doughnut run on Sunday morning. The time had flown by, and Samantha would have to be on the road again soon.

"Sam, do you believe in love at first sight?" Tim asked.

"I didn't used to," she answered. "But maybe now I do," she admitted.

Sam felt just a little embarrassed by their almost insatiable appetite for each other. It had been tough trying to study and write papers while their minds were on each other. Once they rented a motel room midway between their schools. Often they had to make do with a few kisses on short visits. Sometimes they spent a couple hours in one of their cars, steaming up the windows and finding creative ways to please each other in the backseat.

During the week, they sent texts or spent hours talking on their cell phones, catching up with each other, making plans for their next time together, and talking about their dreams for the future. These two nights without interruption had been special.

Love like this was something new for each of them. They had begun to talk about making the relationship permanent. Yet, they were trying not to rush it; it had only been three months since New Year's Eve. They had realized right away that something special existed between them. Were they soul mates, destined to live out their lives together?

"Hey, move over," Tim said. He cupped her rounded rear with his hand. "You're hogging the bed!"

"No, I'm not. You are!" Samantha retaliated. She snuggled closer, daring him to make another move.

Moving wasn't easy. They were lying side-by-side on Tim's single bed. Neither of them was the petite type. Furthermore, college bunks certainly weren't intended for two tall and athletic students to use at the same time. However, they were both young, naked, and had spent the last two days having more sex than either of them had ever experienced before.

When Sam had begun packing up her things, both of them had fallen silent. Tim had propped up two pillows and watched her go back and forth between the room and the bathroom. It was Tim who had to stay; she would soon be on her way.

In the coming week, he would play back time and time again what they had done and said here. He had called her over to his bunk and laid his head against her shoulder.

"Hey, beautiful, how about it?" Tim had asked.

"Again?" she had asked, glancing at her watch. It was already four o'clock in the afternoon, and she had a long drive ahead of her.

Tim began caressing her back, moving his hand in a circular motion.

"Easy there, big boy, don't tell me you want to go another round," said Sam.

"Well, the mind is willing, but the spirit is a little weak," Tim admitted.

"Yeah, that spirit looks a little soft right now," Sam said, glancing down at his lap. She playfully pulled his hand off her back and brought it up to her lips.

"Tim, what happened to your finger?" she asked.

Half of Tim's little finger on his left hand was missing. It was not something too noticeable, but it was obvious that something had happened that resulted in a partial amputation of his finger.

Tim just lay back, pausing before answering.

"Wood shop," he told her.

"How?" she asked.

"I was cutting a board on the band saw, and my hand slipped," he said.

"Ouch, that must have hurt," she said, wincing.

"That's an understatement," he replied. Sam was quiet. He could see the concern in her eyes. "Hey, it's no big deal. You still love me even if I'm not perfect, don't you?" asked Tim.

"Of course, silly," she said. "Now, I really have to get going."

After she had gotten up, he sighed, fell back on he bed and stared at the ceiling. He didn't know why he had said that. He hadn't lost his finger in a wood shop accident. But, for the life of him, he couldn't remember what had really happened. He had the whole finger when his family went to Africa. He didn't have it when they came back home.

He remembered the attempted murder. Both Tim and his mother had come very close to dying. He remembered hiding in the village of Zigda. He remembered all the fighting. He remembered the deep friendships he'd made in Africa. But he was totally unable to recall what had happened to his finger.

He had a moment of fear compounded by anxiety. Maybe he was getting senile. Maybe he was losing his mind. Twice he'd had weird periods in his thinking. Once it was that crazy thing that had happened during the soccer game. The second time the fuzzy thinking that had happened at Pizza Hut.

"Damn, damn, damn!" he said quietly, his elbows on his knees and his head in his hands. Finding Sam was the best thing that had ever happened to him. He should be looking ahead to their life together instead of slipping back into fear and confusion. Would she still love him if he ended up institutionalized?

After Sam had given him one last, lingering kiss and had gone out the door, Tim had tried to study, but he couldn't get his mind to work. That question about his finger had brought back that confused feeling. He piled his textbooks carelessly on his desk before he collapsed limply on the bed. He hadn't bothered to smooth out the rumpled blanket or rearrange the pillows.

He drifted off into a restless sleep, unable to shake his thoughts of a cold, dark cell.

31

JHS – that's Johnsonville High School to the uninitiated – wasn't such a bad place to be, but it wasn't cool to say that.

EVERYONE'S GOAL WAS TO ESCAPE. FOR THE SENIORS, THEY COULD barely stand spending one more stinkin' day trapped there. They'd rather be out making money to buy stuff, like real cars tricked out with good speakers, chrome rims and all that other good shit.

Sure, the old people in town liked to brag about how nice the school was, how it was getting bigger, had more kids, and how it had been drawn up by some architect place in Richmond. But they weren't forced to attend every stinkin' day. They didn't know what it was really like inside.

TJ squeezed the bottom of his catsup packet, the last one in the arsenal of ten that he had stuffed in his pocket when the lunch lady was making change for his buddy, Billy.

"Gotcha!" TJ bragged. The goal was to see how much of the red stuff you could get into the hole of the Coke can in the middle of the table. You'd lose points if you splattered it on someone's clothes or if you got caught by one of the on-guard teachers who hovered way too close.

The initials "TJ" didn't stand for anything. All throughout school he had been cross-examined by his teachers, who insisted that he must have a "real" name. The truth was that his parents couldn't think of any regular name to call their newborn son. Instead, they just gave him two initials. Since they ran Johnsonville Towing, they decided to name him TJ.

"Ya see," TJ explained to those snoopy teachers, "that's why I can't read – I'm Dis Lexic just like my parents!" The other kids knew that it was then their cue to laugh and get the teacher to waste time talking about something else instead of assigning them homework. It always worked.

Now tall, skinny and seventeen, TJ couldn't wait to be on his own. He pushed his light brown hair back off his forehead, then shook his head to get it to fall back again. He'd forgotten that his pimples didn't show as much if he used his bangs like a curtain.

Billy, that's Billy Joe Nelson, was the opposite of TJ. First, he had a real name, but Billy was just Billy, not short for William or whatever. Second, he was short and chunky. He wore his thick black hair in a crew cut. He'd had black whiskers since junior high, but didn't like shaving, so he didn't, not until his mother told him he had to. Unlike his buddies whose greatest aspirations were to make their careers at Wal-Mart or Piggly Wiggly, Billy was going on to junior college. Since his dad was the city's building inspector, he knew his parents wouldn't let him off easy. He didn't know what he was going to do there next year. "Do you think they have state playoffs for Coke catsup?" he'd asked his friends.

The third contestant in the Coke game, Johnny Butler, was the quiet one. He lived with his mother. No one knew much about his father or even if he ever had one. Johnny was just Johnny. He wore black-rimmed glasses. His mom bought clothes for him at the thrift store. If someone could have gotten hold of him, cleaned him up, bought him some real clothes and ditched those ugly glasses, he wouldn't have been bad looking at all.

The three had been friends ever since first grade. None of them did very well in school and could have cared less. They didn't do regular school stuff like go to games or dances or anything like that. Besides coming up with dumb ways to kill time during lunch, they had only two things in common – off-roading and mudding in 4WD trucks and a deep, abiding interest in sex. Unfortunately for all three of them, they'd never been able to score with any women. Their idea of a date with a girl was a Hustler magazine in the bathroom with the door locked.

Only ten minutes remained in third lunch. It was time to get down to business. Their mutual interest in seeing naked women was the primary topic for this Friday lunchtime huddle.

"You're sure we can sneak in?" asked TJ.

"Hey, man, trust me. My old man is the inspector for the project," said Billy Joe. "The fence on the north side of the school won't be all the way done until next week. Right now there is one of those contractor fences, tied together with wire. All it takes is a pair of wire cutters and snip, snip, we're in."

"Did you see how many cars were parked downtown at the motel? Those Dackeries, or whatever you call those idiots, must be planning one big event," said TJ, nodding his head enthusiastically.

"All I want to see is that tall, blonde chick that comes to town in that white robe. She's totally naked underneath," said Billy Joe, imagining what wonders might lurk inside that robe.

"I wonder if they have orgies," said TJ.

"Sure, you can hear the drums beat during those meetings, and that Sarday guy has a big open area lit up with floodlights. That's where they all get naked," said Billy Joe, confirming their wildest dreams.

"Come on, those are probably just stories," Johnny said.

"No, they're not. There are a lot of people in town that attend the seminars," argued TJ. "I heard that Miss Grant is one of them."

"I'd love to see her naked. My dick is hard during the entire hour of history class," said Billy Joe.

"Your dick is hard all the time," laughed Johnny.

"Fuck you," growled Billy Joe. Friends shouldn't joke about their friends' dicks.

"So what's the plan?" asked Johnny.

"We'll use my truck," explained TJ.

Both Billy Joe and Johnny perked up when they heard TJ volunteering his truck. Nobody had to sit right next to another guy because it was an extended cab with a back seat. Not only that, but TJ sometimes let one of them drive it.

"We can get around behind the school using the road through the old Smith farm," TJ continued. "We park the truck, walk down to the fence, cut the wire, sneak in, and go through the woods to the top of the hill. We can look down at the field next to the pavilion. It will be lighted, and we'll be in the dark."

"That's too far away. You can't see pussy that far away," whined Billy Joe.

"We'll bring binoculars, stupid," said TJ.

"I heard that they have guards that drive the perimeter road in ATVs during the ceremonies," said Johnny.

"Well, if they do, we hide in the woods, wait till they pass by, go down, cut open the fence, go inside, and temporarily tie the fence back together. It will be a piece of cake. Besides, they'll never expect someone to come in the back way," said TJ, taking charge.

"Damn, there's the bell for fourth period. I'll pick you guys up at eight. Tell your folks that we're going to the downtown cinema for the nine o'clock movie. Billy, tell your parents that we're staying at Johnny's house overnight. His mom works the graveyard shift at Jack in the Box, so she won't know what time we get in," said TJ. "Let's get this fuckin' school day over and get ready for fun."

This evening's entertainment promised to be drop-dead fabulous. They'd talk about it for the rest of their lives.

32

On the hill overlooking the pavilion, TJ had to congratulate himself on the success of the plan.

SO FAR, SO GOOD. THE THREE OF THEM HAD FOUND A PERFECT viewpoint, here under the oaks at the top of the hill. He checked his watch.

"Closing in on midnight," he whispered. "Looks like whatever is going on will happen right there in the pavilion."

The three looked like GI's from some old war movie. They stretched out as flat as they could and passed the binoculars from one to another, making periodic reports to the others.

"Looks like there's a goat tied to a stake," Billy Joe said when it was his turn to watch. "Nothing else there that I can make out. Just that grassy spot next to that stone platform. Good thing that they have some lights set up. Otherwise we couldn't see nothin'."

TJ wiped the sweat from his forehead. It was one hot night. He figured it had to be about eighty degrees now, even at midnight. He'd heard the weatherman say that a storm front would be heading in from the west sometime in the early morning. Then they had said there could be thunderstorms, the severe type, within the next twenty-four hours.

"Shit, it's hot," TJ said as he scanned the area. It was almost too hot to breathe.

"What a bummer," whispered Billy Joe. "Don't look like anything's gonna happen. Let's get the hell out of here. I'm tired, and it's too fuckin' hot."

"Shut up, Billy Joe," TJ said, adjusting the focus.

"Hey, look," Johnny said, pointing to the left of the pavilion. "Didn't that door just open?"

The three of them watched closely, not daring to say a word. They saw someone, probably a guy, step out of the door. He was dressed in a black robe, and his head was covered with a hood. Behind him, he saw some others, all wearing the same kind of outfit. They began to file out. TJ stopped counting when he got to twenty. He figured there were probably about sixty total, all wearing black.

"Shit, there's even more!" TJ said.

Now the people coming out wore brown robes. This group was larger than the black robe ones. Maybe two hundred came out. After them, a good forty young adults followed. The three teenagers froze in place as they watched in awe as the weirdos began to remove their robes.

"Holy shit," Billy Joe said, his voice about an octave higher than normal. "Holy shit, they're all naked under them robes!"

TJ punched Billy Joe in the arm.

"Shut up, you stupid idiot."

TJ re-focused the binos. He could see that the younger bunch took charge of the robes. They carried them back to the pavilion. All in all, TJ guessed about two hundred fifty or more, some men, some women, stood naked around the stone platform.

Johnny's heart pounded. He tried to breathe deeply so he could get more air. At first, seeing all those naked people together was kind of a turn-on. But then he began to feel a little embarrassed. It didn't seem right. It was like they were peeping Toms looking in somebody's windows.

When it was his turn to use the binoculars, Johnny thought he recognized several of the naked people. One was the mayor who stood with it all hanging out right there alongside some of the people on the city council. He recognized a couple of storeowners and even the minister of that brick church just off Main Street. Then he recognized Mr. Reynolds, his math teacher, standing next to Miss Barton, that new French teacher. He focused the binos again just to give his fingers something useful to do. To his surprise, he saw a couple of TV and movie personalities.

Johnny didn't need to see any more. He'd had enough. "Let's get out of here, and fast!" he whispered as loud as he dared.

TJ also wanted to go, but he was too curious to leave now.

"Wait one minute. I want to see what's going to happen next," he said.

The only person wearing anything at all was the original one in the black hooded robe. He stood next to the stone platform. Then two of the people in the brown robes stepped out of the shadows. They stopped when they reached the goat.

Suddenly, they wrestled the animal to the ground, tied its legs together, lifted it up and carried it to the stone platform. Another man in a brown robe brought in a large wooden bowl and laid it on the ground. By now, all the other people had formed a circle around the altar.

"What are they going to do to that goat?" asked Johnny nervously.

"Don't know," TJ replied. "Just watch, and we'll see."

The sound of drumbeats came from somewhere in the darkness beyond the floodlights. People began to chant in rhythm. The two men in the brown robes struggled to place the goat on the altar. Its head hung limply over the edge.

Now the black-hooded man moved to the right of the platform. He pulled out a long sword. He raised the blade high directly over the goat's neck. The drums and chanting reached a crescendo. Then the sounds came to an abrupt stop. The sword fell on the animal's slender neck, slicing cleanly through its spinal column. It cut through muscle and flesh, completely severing the goat's head from its body.

The head dropped into the wooden bowl. A fine red mist sprayed from the headless corpse. The goat's body convulsed; its legs still kicking. The arteries continued to spurt blood, powered by the still-beating heart.

TJ's hands had squeezed the binoculars so hard that they felt numb. To his right he heard a retching sound coming from Billy Joe's direction. He turned to see his friend vomiting green bile on the ground beside him. TJ dropped the binoculars and pressed one hand on his stomach and the other over his mouth to control his own urge to retch.

Then he heard a rumble coming up the valley from the west. Far off in the surrounding mountains, lightning flashed. The storm was closing in on them.

TJ jumped to his feet, turned, and ran through the dark woods, not once looking back to see if the others were behind him.

33

A strong storm hit Johnsonville early Saturday morning.

THE WINDS UPWARDS OF SIXTY MILES PER HOUR RIPPED THROUGH the valley. Lightning, hail, and heavy rain followed, leaving extensive damage everywhere. Several people reported seeing two funnel clouds touch the ground, but the twisters dissipated without causing any major damage. Police and fire crews scrambled to coordinate the efforts to restore order.

Power was out all over the region. Chief Bishop had called in reserve officers to direct traffic at major intersections where the stoplights were out. Inside city limits, line crews had the power up and running within six hours. The more rural areas around Johnsonville would have to wait longer to get their power back.

By Saturday afternoon, the sun came out. All around the area, people were outside, picking up branches, running chainsaws and clearing debris. For most residents, the storm was history, and people were getting back to business as usual.

"Chief, you'd better come listen to this," said the dispatcher.

A call had come in from a man who had been driving up the Old Quarry Road. He reported seeing the burning wreckage of a pick-up truck at the bottom of the quarry face.

"Probably an abandoned or stolen truck. Someone just lit it up and then pushed it over the cliff to get rid of it. But we'll check it out," Bishop said. The drive out there would give him an even better sense of the damage near the city limits.

After Bishop had looked down over the cliff, he returned to his car to make a call for assistance. He had a queasy feeling in his stomach. The vehicle was still smoldering, and he detected the smell of burning rubber.

He thought he detected another, more ominous odor. It reminded him of the smell that he had encountered when he arrived at an accident scene where there had been fatalities. It reminded him of the smell inside a demolished bunker after a brutal mortar attack. It reminded him of the smell of burning flesh.

When the recovery team got down to the truck, they found the remains of three badly burned bodies. It took them most of the day to conduct their investigation and bring up what remained of the three individuals who had perished. Unfortunately, the heavy rain had washed away much of the critical evidence.

Authorities were able to put two and two together when they learned that three high school boys had been reported missing earlier the same day. The wreckage of the truck matched the description given by one of the boy's parents. The charred VIN showed that the vehicle was registered to Gilbert Roberts. Roberts said that it was his son's truck.

Police speculated that the young men had been racing around in the storm. They likely had limited visibility and may have misjudged their location. The vehicle had accidentally gone off the cliff and into the quarry.

The cause of the fire was linked to the crash itself. Two metal five-gallon cans of gasoline had been stored inside the extended cab. They exploded when the vehicle fire heated them up. The heat was so intense that all three bodies were burned beyond recognition. The arms and feet were actually burned to ashes.

The county coroner was able to identify two of the bodies through dental records. They did a positive ID on Billy Joe Nelson and on Johnny Butler. The third individual had been seated in the back seat next to the gas cans. The coroner said that due to the intensity of the explosion, little was left to identify. Since the three boys were last seen together late Friday night and the truck had been registered to Mr. Roberts, the coroner concluded that the third body was that of TJ Roberts. It was simply a tragic accident. Case closed.

Had the coroner gone to the trouble of digging a little deeper, he would have discovered that the third body was missing its head. If he had taken a DNA sample, he would have found that the remains weren't those of TJ Roberts, but a black kid named Randy Parker. Parker had a five-page juvenile record and had run away from home six months earlier.

The real TJ Roberts sat curled up in the corner of a cold, dark cell, sobbing uncontrollably.

34

In his office in Washington, D.C., Senator Allan Carlson scrolled the cursor over his calendar, double checking to be sure the he was free on the second weekend of the coming month.

HE EVEN BUZZED THE FRONT OFFICE TO VERIFY THAT THERE WERE no commitments that hadn't yet been entered.

He had very important plans for his weekend in Johnsonville.

Life can sure lead us down unexpected pathways, he thought. One person fades out of my life, and two others come into it and change everything. He sighed with relief while running his fingers through the darkened strands of his remaining hair. He couldn't help but grin with unbridled schoolboy anticipation.

"Not bad for a sixty-four year-old," he said as he held his breath and puffed out his chest. He sucked in his protruding paunch and patted his belly. "A new life," he reflected. "A new, powerful, second chance at life."

No one could have ever denied that Senator Carlson was a true-blooded American man. He believed in his church, his family and in his country.

Since he was a mere boy, he had vowed that his faith was the cornerstone of his being. A staunch Southern Baptist, he went to church every Sunday, arriving at the last minute so that he could make a bit of an entrance smiling and nodding at other parishioners as he made his way to his accustomed pew near the front. Lately, while listening to his pastor's sermons, he'd found his mind wandering to his new life.

Carlson had also committed himself wholeheartedly to his family. Forty-five years ago he had married his childhood sweetheart, Judy. The couple had been blessed with three daughters. Over the years, his public life had taken a toll on the marriage. The couple had drifted apart. Judy stayed in their home in Charlottesville, while Carlson rented a luxurious condominium in D.C. He commuted as needed, finding more and more excuses to spend his time in the city. "Why not?" Carlson had asked himself. They hadn't shared a bed, or even a bedroom, for more than ten years. It wouldn't have mattered anyway. Carlson had been impotent for quite a while.

Carlson considered himself a real American. As the owner of a business, he fought to keep government out of his pockets. Carlson Chevrolet continued to prosper, and he took pride in being the third generation in his family to sell and service American-made automobiles. He worked hard for America and the Commonwealth of Virginia, serving nearly thirty years as a state senator.

His election to the U.S. Senate had been a fluke. The opposition party had run wild after it had swept the national elections, taking over the House, the Senate and the White House. The rival party had recklessly gone on a feeding frenzy, passing their pet projects regardless of cost. After two years of riding roughshod over Carlson's party, voters had been ready for a return to sanity. Carlson had ridden the wave of change. On a whim, he ran against the incumbent, a senior senator. With support of independent voters, Carlson won the election.

Yes, church, family and country formed the basis for everything he did – until now. Now he embraced a new belief, a new lover and a new worldview.

Carlson shoved his hands deep into his pants pockets as he stood looking out over the nation's capital from up high. He looked down at the crowded streets and stalled traffic. He turned around to admire the opulence of his office. He had retained much of the fine furniture of the man he'd replaced, and he liked what he saw. It was so unreal – he still couldn't believe that he was the junior senator from the Commonwealth of Virginia.

Nothing, absolutely nothing, could have prepared him for the cataclysmic changes in his life just a little more than six months earlier. That's when he first met Jill Ann Morrison.

"Ah, Jilly," he said out loud. "What you've done to me!"

As a U.S. senator, Carlson required a full-time staff. It was a bit of a shock at first. As a state senator, he'd gotten by with a much smaller staff. Some staffers worked for little or no pay as interns who earned college credit for the experience of serving a U.S. senator.

"Next," he had said, shuffling through a dozen or so of the pre-approved resumes. "Miss Morrison, Jill Ann Morrison?"

"Yes, sir," said the petite blonde. "I'm Jill."

At first, her school, the University of Virginia, had caught Carlson's eye. After all, UV was where he had earned his business degree. Graduates should stick together, he had reasoned.

"Ready, willing and able!" Jilly had said as she bounced her way up to his desk. She smiled broadly. Then she saluted.

Carlson looked up. She looked down. And they both broke out laughing.

"And why not?" Carlson said to himself. This young woman had a bubbly personality. She could add a little levity to the office. Besides that, he noted, she had a great ass.

He had hired her on the spot, and she proved herself to be an enthusiastic and competent worker. Carlson treated her like a daughter. After all, she was even younger than his youngest daughter. He often caught himself watching her as she worked. He loved to see her move from task to task. Sometimes he thought he saw her watching him with more than just professional curiosity.

She took to her work like a duck to water, often volunteering to work late. One evening, about four months into Carlson's term, only he and Jilly remained at their desks.

"Thanks, Jilly," he had told her. "If you hadn't put in extra effort, we wouldn't have wrapped up the preparation for this important bill. You made the difference."

"No problem, Senator Carlson," she responded. "I like working under you."

"Thanks, again," he said. "Hey, the least I can do is to offer to buy your dinner. No strings attached. OK?"

They spent three hours at a Georgetown restaurant. Both enjoyed a couple glasses of wine. He found himself laughing out loud, totally enjoying her company.

He soon discovered that Jilly was somewhat of a flake. She had all kinds of conspiracy theories, was a believer in horoscopes and Ouija boards, and had even dabbled in witchcraft. Carlson had scoffed about her weird beliefs, yet he found himself wanting to spend more time just listening to the sound of her voice.

Often he felt a bit foolish. Here he was – an old man infatuated by a free spirit. He suspected that she only agreed to dinner because of his status as a senator. There was nothing new about that, but as he listened to her chatter, he couldn't help but fantasize about getting her in bed. He knew he would fail in the sex department. That would mortify him, and she would find someone else.

One dinner led to another and yet another. Then one night she told him that she wanted to show him how the Ouija board worked. They had gone to her apartment. She opened a bottle of wine and poured two full glasses. They played with the letters, asking silly questions and got even sillier answers. When they were about to open a second bottle of wine, he leaned closer and kissed her on the lips.

She didn't resist. In fact, she crawled up on his lap and began to smother him with even deeper, more passionate kisses. The next thing he knew, they were both naked on her couch. He found himself more aroused than he had been in years. Yet when he attempted to complete the act, he suffered a total failure.

"No problem. You're just too tense," she said. She reached for her purse and pulled out two joints.

"Oh, no, we can't do this!" Carlson said, shocked at her suggestion. "I'm a U.S. senator!"

Jilly continued to insist, and he finally gave in, smoking only the second joint in his entire life. To his amazement, the drug resulted in great sex, better than any he could ever remember. He found himself spending a number of nights in Jilly's bed, always getting high before they made love. She was right, he thought, he'd just been too tense.

Sex was only part of their deepening relationship. Jilly had talked constantly about her involvement in New Age religion, Dacari Mucomba, and its leader, George Sarday. One weekend she had even convinced him to go to Johnsonville to meet Sarday himself.

For a Southern white businessman, a black African from Liberia should have been the last person on Earth that would change his life. Yet Sarday had totally mesmerized him. On the spot, Carlson had written a check for $100,000 to cover the cost of a private, weekend seminar.

The weekend was all that Carlson had hoped for and even more. He couldn't explain what happened during those two days. All he knew was that it was something mysterious and eye opening. Although he considered himself a man of faith, he had never had such a profound experience in all the years he had belonged to the Baptist church.

The ancient ceremony had been conducted in a strange language, one that entranced the audience with its highs and lows and captivating rhythm. White feathered chickens were sacrificed. The insane squawking and spurting of blood should have revolted him, but he was totally caught up in the tempo and mystical message of the ceremony. When the weekend was over, Carlson felt that he had become a new man.

As for sex, Carlson had been rejuvenated beyond his wildest dreams. No longer did he require a joint to get him ready for his sexual encounters with young Jilly. Indeed, their wild and frequent bouts of lovemaking would rival those of teenagers rutting behind the bleachers on a high school campus.

In all other matters, Carlson felt endowed with more strength and power than he had ever known before. His demeanor had changed. The sharpness of his thinking led to more precision in his speech. People began to listen more closely to the junior senator from Virginia.

Just three weeks ago, he and Jilly had been introduced to the more advanced teachings of Dacari Mucomba. He had been dressed in a coveted black robe; Jilly, a follower, had worn a brown one.

Carlson had risen to an even greater status after he had watched the sacrifice of a goat before the altar. As the severed head fell into the wooden bowl, Carlson had actually seen the goat's spirit rise from its body. At the same moment, Carlson felt a new, stronger power enter his being. He knew immediately that he was destined to become one of the most powerful men in the world.

Sarday had called to inform him that in the next ceremony, the true believers would meet the being, Dacari Mucomba, in the flesh. With that singular experience, those true believers would be one step closer to gaining total power over mankind.

Carlson was somewhat perplexed by Sarday's request that only he be allowed to attend the ceremony. Fortunately, Carlson had convinced him to permit Jilly to accompany him. Carlson was convinced that Jilly had been his soul mate in leading him to the bliss of worshipping Dacari Mucomba. Sarday had reluctantly agreed; Jilly would also attend the ceremony.

Now, on the second weekend of the next month, the two of them would be taking the next step toward immortality and power by their service to Dacari Mucomba.

35

In Hawaii, Tim's parents had arrived at the airport early.

BOTH HANK AND LINDSEY WERE LOOKING FORWARD TO SEEING HIM and meeting his two college pals.

"The plane lands in ten minutes," said Hank. He stood up, walked to the window and scanned the tarmac.

Lindsey joined her husband, reaching around his trim waist and tightening her hold.

"I didn't realize how much I've missed him," she said. "It's been eight months since we last saw him. In twenty-two years this is the longest we've ever been apart."

"We both have to realize that in three months, he'll be a college graduate. Then this will be a normal occurrence," he said.

"I know, Hank. I know," she replied. "It's just that we've been through so much as a family. It's hard for me to accept that a mother must let her son grow up and leave the nest."

Just two weeks ago, Tim had called his mother and to ask if it would be all right to bring two of his college friends along when he visited during spring break. Of course, it would be okay – if she could have her son home for a week, he could bring the whole soccer team!

She'd heard a lot about Eddie, his roommate. She had even seen photos of the young black man with Tim and his college friends. She couldn't remember anything about Sam, the other young man. Tim hadn't mentioned him in emails or occasional phone calls.

"United Flight 267 will disembark at Gate 37," a voice said over the loudspeaker.

The long wait at Honolulu International Airport was just about over. The announcement jolted them both into action.

"Let's meet them at the baggage claim," said Hank, setting off at a fast pace. By the time they reached the baggage area, passengers were already milling around, watching intently as the suitcases began to roll down the ramp. Lindsey felt her heart rate accelerate as she scanned the area, looking for her son.

Group after group of passengers had come and gone, yet she still couldn't spot Tim. She waited impatiently as the number of bags dwindled Even the crowd of passengers seemed to diminish. Maybe he missed the flight, she thought. If that actually happened, she wouldn't be able to contain her disappointment.

She turned around to check the main hallway once again. Then she saw him, standing so tall with his broad shoulders and that positive stance. My God, he so reminded her of Hank when she had first met him.

Right after she had reassured herself that it really was Tim coming toward her, he saw her and waved his arm. She started to run toward him and then realized it would embarrass him if his mother made too much of a scene. She forced herself to stand still and wait for him by the baggage carousel.

Lindsey squinted and recognized Eddie, Tim's roommate. It was quite a contrast to see the two walking side-by-side. Eddie was at least eight inches shorter than Tim. If she could see the two of them, why couldn't she pick out the other young man, Sam?

As they got closer she saw that Tim was talking to a tall, young, light-skinned black woman with almost blond hair. She was very attractive and the designer jeans and blouse she wore clearly didn't come from off the rack at Wal-Mart.

"Mom!" said Tim, rushing toward her. He wrapped his arms around her and lifted her off her feet.

"Dad, it's great to see you!" Tim said, seeing his father for the first time. He set his mother down carefully, kissing her lightly on the cheek. He turned to his father.

"You, too, son," said Hank. They wrapped each other in one, tight bear hug.

"Mom, Dad, this is Eddie Dixon, my roommate, and his sister, Sam, uh, I mean Samantha."

Lindsey had brought three leis to welcome each of them in the traditional Hawaiian way. First was Tim, then Eddie, and finally she gently placed the ring of pink flowers around Sam's neck.

Lindsey always considered herself a tall woman. She stood two inches shy of six feet. But Sam was perhaps six feet four inches tall in her heels. As she arranged the lei around Sam's neck, she felt her heart skip a beat as the two women's eyes met. She had a strong suspicion that this young woman was more than just another one of Tim's friends. Her mother's instinct was usually right on.

"Aloha and welcome to Hawaii," said Lindsey.

"Thank you, Mrs. Martin," said Sam.

"Please, call me Lindsey."

They located their bags, headed to the parking garage and piled the luggage into the back of the SUV. All three young people squeezed into the back seat, putting the short one, Eddie, in the middle.

Neither Eddie nor Sam had ever been to Hawaii before. Hank told them he'd take the long way home to show off Honolulu city. They drove out to Diamond Head, past Waikiki Beach and through the ritzy shopping district.

After the quick sightseeing tour, they drove to Hickam Air Force Base for lunch at the officers' club. During lunch the trio chattered about school, and Lindsey listened intently to find out more about Tim's roommate and his twin sister, Samantha. After lunch, they made the eighteen-mile drive to their quarters.

As the SUV cruised through the heavy traffic along H2 at fifty miles per hour, Lindsey explained that the 25th Infantry Division was stationed at Schofield Barracks, where Hank, a brigadier general, was the assistant division commander for operations.

Sam and Eddie listened to them talk about their home in Hawaii and Hank's job. Sam didn't know much about the military. Her grandfather had been a colonel in the corps of engineers, but with her dad being a lawyer, she knew far more about law than the military. It didn't seem like such a big deal. After all, Tim's dad was somebody's assistant.

Hawaii seemed a lot like Jamaica where the Dixons owned a villa. Honolulu reminded her of a larger, more modern version of Kingston. The beach at Waikiki was no different than the beaches in Jamaica, except for the much larger crowds. And, of course, instead of a large population of blacks, there were many Asians.

She wondered what the Martins' home looked like. She visualized a little, three-bedroom house with a white picket fence around the front yard. How strange it must be to live like that. If what she felt for Tim continued, would they end up in a three-bedroom house in the suburbs? Could she live like that?

The SUV slowed as Hank turned off the interstate on to a four-lane road at the entrance to Schofield Barracks. They pulled up to the main gate where armed soldiers waved the SUV forward. Lindsey turned around and asked the young people to hand her their driver's licenses. The guard saluted as Tim's dad handed the licenses out his window. The soldier checked the photos, comparing them to their faces, then returned the licenses. He saluted and said, "Tropic lightning, sir."

Tim's dad returned the salute and said, "Always ready, soldier."

As they drove on post, Sam saw that there were uniformed soldiers everywhere. It seemed like a city occupied by an army.

The passed clusters of the three-bedroom ramblers, just like the home she had imagined. They turned off into a residential area where the houses were larger. She saw large duplexes with double car garages. Farther in, the duplexes became single-family homes. The streets were lined with palm trees. All the lawns were neatly manicured. Tropical flowers were in bloom all around the homes. Occasionally, she saw playgrounds for young children. Finally, they turned into a cul-de-sac with just three homes.

General Martin pulled in the driveway of a large, white home on the left. "This is our quarters," Lindsey announced.

It certainly wasn't what Sam had expected. Sure, it wasn't like the mansion her dad owned, but it seemed rather imposing for a man who was only an assistant.

Now that's quite a home, Sam thought. Really quite a home.

36

In her house in Shantytown,
Michelle had worn herself to a frazzle.

She was frustrated by her attempts to find this Tim Martin man. She climbed into her bed, stretched out flat, and stared at the ceiling. Since her strange dream or vision or whatever it was when she had met Chea Geebe, she had tried to find that Tim Martin.

She had checked phone listings and asked around, but she could not find a black man with the name Tim Martin living in Johnsonville. She was afraid to tell Willie about her dream; he would ask too many questions. Since she didn't know how to use the computer to search for someone, she had resigned herself to give up and ask her grandson for help. She'd do it tomorrow. That would be soon enough.

What did Chea mean when he said that only Tim could save them? She knew how to drive out an evil spirit. The endosym would be no match for her abilities.

Mr. P was curled up alongside her, purring up a storm. She closed her eyes and listened to the deep rumble from the large gray cat's throat. Soon she fell into a sound sleep.

Within what seemed like only minutes, she was awakened by a deep growl coming from the cat. "Shush, cat!" whispered Michelle. The cat's growling continued, getting louder. "For crying out loud, cat, what has gotten into you?"

She sat up, threw her feet over the side of the bed, reached over, and turned on the bedside lamp.

Mr. P stood alert at the foot of the bed. His tail was three times its normal size, and his back arched. She couldn't understand what had happened to Mr. P. He was staring at the corner of the room. She followed his gaze. Her eyes widened when she saw the thing standing in the corner.

"Oh, sweet Jesus, help me!" she gasped. She must be going mad. She closed her eyes, then opened them. It was still there.

The thing was from one's worst nightmare. It stood no more than three feet in height. Its body was light gray. Overhanging brows, like those of a Neanderthal, shaded the blank eyeballs. Two horns protruded from the hairless scalp. It proudly thrust out its oversized male genitalia.

She heard it speak; its childlike voice evoked pure evil.

"What did he tell you, old woman?"

"Who?" gasped Michelle.

"The old zo," he squealed. "You will tell me, or I will kill your grandson and his wife. You will be forced to watch as I consume them."

The creature's horse-like face glared up at her as it bared its long yellow teeth. The red-veined eyeballs stared at her. Michelle could feel her heart pounding rapidly in her chest as she peered into the white orbs. They had no pupils.

"You don't scare me, you filthy demon," she whispered. She began to pray. "Our... our...," she sputtered. She tried once again. "Our Father who art in heaven..."

Finally, the familiar prayer rolled from her lips. Her breathing became less labored. She said it again. This time it came out even stronger and without hesitation. The rhythm of the words soothed her anxiety.

All the while, the creature stood by, watching. But Michelle was able to stare at the vile form without flinching, without retreating.

Annoyed by the litany, the demon emitted a high-pitched scream.

"You might stop me tonight, old woman, but soon, very soon, I will have the souls I need to destroy you and all you love in this world."

Michelle was jubilant at the thing's reaction.

"Sweet Jesus, drive this demon from my eyes!" she yelled. The thing covered its eyes with its talons. She squealed and said, "You just wait till I find Tim Martin, and then your ass is history."

Then the demon vanished. Only a funnel of gray dust whirled in the corner where it once stood.

She sat there triumphant. She had done it; she had driven the demon away.

She tried to catch her breath. For some reason, she couldn't seem to breathe. She tried again to bring in air. She began to panic. She stood up, staggered, knocking the lamp to the floor. She lurched forward, crashing into the wall, falling over backwards and landing on the floor with a thud. She felt a tingling numbness along her left side. Then a searing pain in her chest like someone was twisting a knife into her heart.

The bedroom door slammed against the wall as it opened. The overhead light came on, and Willie rushed into the room wearing only his boxer shorts.

"Grandma!" he cried. He knelt next to Michelle, trying to find a breath coming from the old body. "Jasmine, call 911. Tell them we need an ambulance. It's Grandma!"

Willie cradled the old woman in his arms. Tears ran down his cheeks. "Hang on, Grandma, the ambulance is on its way."

Michelle looked up at her grandson.

"Willie," she whispered, "get it out of the nightstand."

"What?" cried Willie.

"The nightstand," she gasped, barely able to lift her skinny arm and point her crooked finger at the bedside table.

Willie opened the drawer, all the while holding his grandmother in his arms. He saw her Bible and something wrapped in a towel. He reached for her Bible and held it up so she could see it.

"Not the Bible," she whispered.

He picked up the towel. There was something heavy inside. He held it up so she could see it.

"Yes, yes," she gasped.

A tightness again struck in her chest causing her to moan with intense pain. She saw a bright white light behind Willie. It seemed like they were in a long, dark tunnel and the light was waiting for her at the other end. She knew her time had come. She forced herself to come back. She must tell Willie what to do.

She turned her face toward him and forced herself to speak.

"Willie, you must find Tim Martin. Give it to Tim Martin."

"Who is Tim Martin?" asked Willie. "Grandma, who is Tim Martin?"

Michelle couldn't answer. She stared directly at her grandson, but there was no understanding in her eyes. Willie realized that she had stopped breathing. He held his grandmother's frail body in his arms as the medics rushed through the bedroom door.

As the medics worked to try to revive her, no one noticed the large, gray cat walking out the bedroom door, down the hallway, through the open front door, and into the night.

37

The first day of Tim's visit to Hawaii had come to an end.

LINDSEY HAD REMOVED HER MAKEUP, BRUSHED HER TEETH, SLIPPED on her short nightgown, and climbed into bed. Hank was already under the covers, engrossed in a novel.

Her mind still raced, re-playing the first day in a long time that she had her son with her under the same roof. She couldn't help but smile.

She had to make some last-minute changes in the sleeping arrangements. They had set up Tim's bedroom when they first moved to Hawaii, ready to accommodate Tim if he suddenly came to visit. She had placed his things as they were in Virginia. For this visit, she had planned to put the other two visitors in the guest bedroom with the twin beds, but then she discovered that Sam was female, actually a full-grown woman.

So Sam ended up in Tim's room, and Eddie and Tim were together in the guest bedroom. She suspected that Tim would have been perfectly happy to share his bedroom with Sam, but not in her house if they weren't married. Call her a prude, but that's the way she was.

"What do you think?" asked Hank.

"Think?" asked Lindsey.

"About Eddie's sister?"

"What about her?" asked Lindsey, waiting to hear what Hank had to say.

"You know, her and Tim. They seem pretty friendly."

"Yes, I guess you could say that," she said.

"So do you think he is sleeping with her?"

"Why, dear," she said, "I would have no idea."

"Well, I think he is," grumbled Hank.

"Honey, he's a grown man, and she's a beautiful woman."

"Yeah, but she's you know.... different."

"You mean that she's black?" asked Lindsey.

"Well, yeah, I guess that's it. He's never done that before."

"Honey, it's not the color of a person's skin that attracts them to another person," answered Lindsey.

"Well, it seems strange to me," he mumbled. "Would you be interested in a black man?" asked Hank.

"Of course not, dear, go to sleep."

Hank turned off his light. Lindsey could only lie there, pondering Hank's words.

She fell into a restless sleep, recalling their time in Africa. Was it only eight years ago? It seemed like only yesterday.

By now the fires had died down. Only glowing coals remained where flames had once blazed so intensely. People moved randomly to their huts. Lindsey chose her steps carefully in the darkness. Only dim lantern light illuminated the inside of her hut where she would be sleeping alone.

She kicked off her shoes, unbuttoned her shirt, took off her bra, and slipped out of her pants and underwear. Naked, she ran her hands over her breasts and then brought them to rest on her hips. Although no longer a young virgin, the night's fervor had left her strangely unsettled. Sleep wouldn't come easy.

The quiet, after all the night's pandemonium, should have calmed her. Instead, she stood still, almost as if she expected someone. For a moment, she thought she heard a slight movement outside her door. She turned. Behind her, stood Joe. Startled, she blurted out his name.

"Joe! Joe, what are you doing here?"

He didn't answer. She made no move to cover her nakedness. Instead, the two remained immobile, as if waiting or wanting the other to do or say something. Confused, Lindsey tried to sort out her emotions. Hank had been her only lover for more than sixteen years, yet she wanted Joe to see her like this.

The pulse of the drumbeat and the primitive pull of the sensual dance had captivated each of them. Neither spoke. Lindsey looked into his eyes. She thought she detected sorrow.

Suddenly, Joe turned and bolted out the door into the dark. Their moment was over.

Lindsey remembered those weeks when they hid in Zigda from the government forces that wanted them dead. Joe Weah, the chief's son, had saved them from certain death. They didn't know if Hank was even alive. During the time she spent with Joe, she was beginning to realize that she felt a strong physical attraction to this man.

Now Lindsey could see history repeating itself. Maybe Hank couldn't understand how Tim could be attracted to Samantha, but she knew first hand that the color of one's skin had nothing to do with the physical attraction between a man and a woman.

38

The visit to Hawaii would soon be over.

THE WEEK HAD FLOWN BY, AND TOMORROW THE THREE VISITORS would fly back to the mainland.

Sam and Eddie had enjoyed their visit. Sam had gotten acquainted with Tim's parents. His dad seemed somewhat distant, but his mom was warm and friendly. Sam had hoped to learn more about their time in Africa, but each time she thought she might find out a little more, someone had changed the subject.

"More coffee, Sam?" Lindsey asked. The two women relaxed on the lanai, enjoying the morning together. Sam had learned so much from Tim's mother. She had picked up some Hawaiian words and learned the names of many flowers and different foods.

"No, no thanks, Lindsey," Sam answered. Perhaps this would be a good time to ask what Africa was really like. "I was surprised to learn you all spent so much time in Africa. What was it like to live there?"

Lindsey hesitated. She poured her cup half full of coffee, added sweetener, and stirred her beverage slowly with a spoon.

"To tell the truth, it was a very trying time for all of us," Lindsey answered. "Say, what do you all have planned for today?"

Sam knew that once again, the topic of Africa would have to be put on hold.

"More tourist stuff," she replied. "Hawaii is so beautiful. There's just so much to see."

They'd done beaches and bars. Today would be their last chance to see the sights in the city. They had visited Kawaiahao church in downtown Honolulu, Ioani Palace, and, of course, the statue of King Kamehameha at the state judiciary building.

It didn't take long for Eddie and Tim to get bored by the tourist attractions.

"I know," said Tim. "Let's do Chinatown!"

They made their way to the colorful part of the city. Tim was just about to go into a shop when he spotted a sign with a dragon and a tiger as a part of the logo. The words read "Kenpo Karate."

"I wonder if that's the Dojo owned by my sensei's brother. It's supposed to be in Honolulu's Chinatown. Let's check it out."

They opened the door below the sign, climbed one flight of stairs and entered a large, open room. The floors were covered with tumbling mats. Floor to ceiling mirrors hung on the walls. About a dozen young men in their late teens or early twenties sat on the floor in a semi-circle. Two students sparred while a thick Asian man in his fifties supervised the match.

The sensei, Kim Jung Park, spotted the new arrivals. He told the students to continue the practice while he walked over to greet the visitors.

"May I help you?" he asked. He was surprised when the white man recited the Kenpo Creed in Korean.

"I come to you with empty hands. I have no weapons, but should I be forced to defend myself, my principles or my honor; should it be a matter of life or death, of right or wrong; then here are my weapons, my empty hands."

Kim laughed, "Ah-ha, you are a student of Kenpo."

"Yes, sensei. I studied under Chung Park in Alexandria, Virginia," answered Tim.

"My younger brother," said Kim. "How is he?"

"He was well when I studied with him last summer. My name is Tim Martin."

"I have heard of a Tim Martin. He was one of Chung's favorite students," said Kim Jung.

"I am embarrassed to say that it was I," said Tim bowing slightly.

"Oh, please, do you have a few moments for Kata? I would like to show my students Chung's techniques," asked Kim Jung.

Tim turned to Eddie and Sam. "Can you give me a few minutes?"

"Sure," they both answered at the same time.

Kim told Tim he would find a martial arts Gi in the dressing room. Tim returned a few minutes later wearing the traditional Gi, lightweight cotton pants and a loose-fitting jacket.

Around his waist, Tim had fastened a white belt, signifying a novice. Tim was a fifth degree black belt and was entitled to wear a black belt with a one-inch red stripe for the degree. Since he was a guest at the Dojo, he felt it more appropriate to wear the white belt.

"We have the honor of greeting Tim Martin, one of my brother's students. He will demonstrate the twelve steps of Kata.

Tim bowed to the students, did several stretching exercises, then began the steps of Kata starting with "Naihanchi Shodan." After twenty minutes, he finished with the twelfth, "Kata Niseishi." Sweating profusely, Tim finished with a bow to the students.

"Very good, Tim Martin. You have demonstrated the twelve Kata to perfection. Do the students have comments?"

A large Hawaiian, named Jimmy Kalulu, spoke up. "So the haole can dance, but can he spar?"

"Would you care to spar with Kalulu, Tim Martin?" asked Kim Jung.

"Sure, why not?" Tim answered.

What Tim did not know was that Kalulu was a member of an Hawaiian gang that terrorized Honolulu. They hated the whites. They blamed whites for polluting the islands.

In sparing practice, the opponents wear padding, similar to small boxing gloves, on their hands and feet. The two men faced each other and bowed.

"Begin," said Kim.

The two circled each other throwing punches and kicks, testing each other's weaknesses. Kalulu was a second-degree black belt and could deliver powerful blows. Unknown to his teacher, he used his knowledge of Kenpo to intimidate rival gang members and had killed two men with his hands and feet.

As the match progressed, Sam sat mesmerized. Since she had been dating Tim, she considered him somewhat of a wuss.

Yes, he was a good athlete, but she remembered the time when two white guys had made a remark about a white man dating a black woman. She particularly recalled those cruel words, "I smell something black." She had been offended and embarrassed. She had expected Tim to defend her honor.

Yet, instead of taking any action, Tim had seemed to freeze in place, almost sinking into a trance. Finally, he had suggested they just get up and go. At some level, Sam had been disappointed. Even if they had beaten him up, at least he would have demonstrated his love and respect.

As she watched him going through the Kata thing, it seemed like the two were dancers in a professional ballet. Tim moved fast, and, even to her inexperienced eyes, he looked really good. When the big, tattooed Hawaiian challenged him, she expected Tim to back down. Instead, Tim was making the guy look like a fool. Of course, they were wearing boxing gloves, so it was no big deal. Finally, the older man stopped the match.

Tim bowed, but the other man turned away. Tim had removed his gloves and was on his way back to the dressing room when the big man screamed and charged.

Tim had heard Kalulu's scream and was able to block a disabling blow with his arm. The man had struck with such force that he felt the blow reverberate through his entire body.

"No haole embarrasses me, asshole," growled Kalulu.

"Easy, man," said Tim as he blocked repeated blows.

Then something happened. Like in the soccer match in October, Kalulu changed before Tim's eyes. He was no longer a man, but some type of inhuman creature. Tim's manner also changed. Suddenly, he was fighting for his life against this creature.

He struck back with killing force. His fists became hammers. Blow after blow he drove against the creature until it fell to the ground. He drew back for the lethal assault that would end this thing's life.

Someone grabbed Tim's arm. He turned and drove his left fist into the second man's face. A forearm blocked his fist.

"Stop! Stop!" someone shouted.

Tim blinked. Sensei Park stood in front of him and secured both of Tim's hands. Tim was breathing heavily.

"Enough, both of you. The match is over!" said Kim.

Tim turned around to see Kalulu lying on the ground, blood streaming from his broken nose.

"Sorry, man," mumbled Tim, "I got carried away." Tim turned and walked toward the dressing room.

Kim Jung pulled Kalulu to his feet.

"I'll kill the bastard!" threatened Kalulu.

Kim Jung took one look at Kalulu.

"You are a fool. You are no match for the Martin boy. Had I not stopped him, the next blow he delivered would have ended your life. I have never experienced such 'Ki' in all my years of teaching. If you wish to continue to train in this Dojo, you will never go near or speak to Tim Martin again."

Tim, Eddie and Samantha walked out of Park's Dojo and back onto the streets of Chinatown.

"That was unbelievable. I have never seen anything that. I thought you were going to kill that guy," Eddie said, looking up at his friend with admiration.

"No, it was just part of the act. No big deal."

Sam glanced at Tim. She wasn't sure what had happened. She actually felt some fear in what she had seen in that Dojo.

She had witnessed something that was not part of the Tim she loved.

39

The Hawaiian vacation would end the next morning.

IN THE MEANTIME, TIM LAY ON HIS BACK, STARING AT THE CEILING fan. Eddie snored loudly in the twin bed next to him.

What was happening, wondered Tim. For the third time this year, he had gone crazy, seeing some kind of demon or something else sinister.

The first time had cost him a chance to play in the Olympics. The second time had been that demon episode in the pizza restaurant. The third time, today, he could have killed a man.

Tomorrow, they would be going back to school. They had to be at Honolulu airport by nine in the morning. They would have to get up by five o'clock. He closed his eyes and tried to sleep.

Surrounded by an indigo blue, the sun sat straight overhead. Tim and Sabo had pulled so far ahead of the other warriors that they would easily win the final phase of the competition – the race to the finish. Before they started, they had vowed to each other to clench hands as they crossed the finish line together. It would be a tie. Both would be honored as the greatest warriors in this contest with other young men from every nearby village.

The final turn was just ahead. They could see the village of Zigda in the valley below. All downhill now, they lengthened their stride. Both let out a scream of victory when they finally saw the taut line of yellow plastic, which marked the finish. Sabo laughed out loud as the two pushed themselves even harder. Just a little faster, Tim thought, and they could almost fly.

Ahead, just beyond the finish line, he could see people he knew in the waiting crowd. Mom and Dad, Joe Weah, all of his friends from school, and even the attaché families waved them on toward the finish. Nancy Matthews held up little Chrissie so she could see the oncoming runners. Chrissie giggled out loud, as babies often do.

Togba himself lifted a big black and white checkered flag. Now less than one hundred yards remained. Side by side, the two broke through the plastic tape at the same time. Tim lifted his arms above his head in a victory salute. Sabo beside him, Tim bent over to catch his breath.

First, it was complete silence. Then only darkness. Tim focused on his own breathing. A thick fog made it impossible to see clearly. Sabo stood beside him. He gripped Tim's left hand so tightly that it hurt. Sabo's hand seemed so cold. He imagined it was a frozen package of meat, not a part of Sabo's anatomy. He tried to form the words to tell Sabo not to squeeze so hard, but words wouldn't come. He turned his head to look at his friend, but Sabo had disappeared.

Instead, a midget, fewer than three feet tall, had taken Sabo's place. Its naked body was covered with a thin dusting of gray powder. Two pointed horns sprouted from the top of its oversized head.

Tim gasped and tried to make his body move, but he was frozen in place. The creature's horse-like face glared up at him as it bared its long yellow teeth. The red-veined eyeballs stared back. Tim forced himself to look into the white orbs. They had no pupils.

He opened his mouth, and his lips formed a scream, but no noise came out. He willed himself to pull away, but his weakness left him helpless. The creature laughed.

"Your soul will be mine!" it said in a childish whine.

It reached out its curved talons and guided Tim's hand toward its mouth. As if it were snapping a pretzel, it bit off the end of Tim's little finger.

A bolt of pain shot up his arm. Never before had he been in such agony. He heard himself shriek, coming from deep in his throat and from the depths of his lungs.

His tormenter only grinned more broadly, its black-forked tongue lapping Tim's blood from its white lips. It opened its mouth, revealing red liquid and tissue *from inside the dark cavity. It reached out and lifted the next finger, salivating as it readied itself for a second bite.*

It was just like the nature show on television. Wild dogs attacked a wildebeest. It struggled, rolling, kicking, as the dogs ate it alive. Tim had asked if the animal had felt any pain. His mother had told him that it hadn't. It would have gone into shock, desensitizing it from the sharp teeth that had ripped its failing body.

"Mom, you're wrong!" he screamed. "It hurts bad when you're being eaten alive."

But his mother didn't answer.

"Oh, God, oh, please," he cried. "Please, someone, help me!"

The creature's sharp teeth were just inches from Tim's next finger. Instead of biting, it stopped. It turned to look at someone or something behind Tim.

"Kill him!" the creature demanded.

The fog parted. Tim could now see the face and form of Junga Sayeh who held a pointed spear above him.

Tim shook his head. How could this be? Junga was dead. Tim was sure he was dead. He had seen the dark holes where the soldier's bullets had gone deep into the man's chest. Yet this Junga raised his muscled arm, preparing to follow the creature's demands.

Just then, a massive animal emerged from the shadows behind him. With one sweep of its powerful paw, a leopard knocked the spear from Junga's hand. It raked its razor-sharp claws across its victim's chest, exposing his bright red ribs. The animal lunged at the body, forcing it to the ground. Its teeth sank into Junga's throat, nearly severing the head from its body.

With a violent roar, the leopard turned toward the dwarf-creature whose face reflected its fear. It dropped Tim's hand and scuttled away on its stubby, bowed legs.

It didn't go quietly. Tim heard its final scream fade into the fog.

"You haven't won yet, Chea Geebe. I will have the boy's soul!"

Tim's chest heaved with uncontrollable sobbing. He held his mutilated left hand in his remaining good hand. He braced himself for the animal's inevitable attack. He closed his eyes, yet experienced an unusual calm.

Instead of claws, he felt the rough tongue of the huge cat, gently licking his bloodied hand. He gritted his teeth and awaited the pain. Rather than the crunch of the animal's jaws on his mutilated flesh, he heard a throaty purr. The cat's tongue had washed away the blood. It reminded Tim of his dog, King, and his friendly lick. Somehow, the cat's actions had served to diminish the pain. Now, he felt only a dull throb.

His attention shifted from the leopard to what he thought was the sound of a voice, although he wasn't aware of another presence.

"Tim, the endosym has taken only a small portion of your soul. You must continue to fight. The spirit of the leopard will help you, but you must ultimately win the battle by yourself. Here in the den of the endosym, do not eat or drink. If you fail to heed this warning, your soul will be lost."

The voice faded. The leopard stood, stretched and vanished in the mist.

"Wait! Wait, don't leave me alone!" Tim called out. The earth beneath him began to shake, and he felt pulled to another level of consciousness.

"I remember!" he shouted. "I remember. It wasn't a dream. It was real!" Tim exclaimed.

He opened his eyes and was blinded by the light.

"What the…?" He looked around. He was still lying on his back. But instead of his bed, he was lying on the ground in an African village.

"Zigda," he said, the village where he and his mother had hidden. He stood up. He was wearing his jockey shorts and nothing else. Yet, he was twenty-two, not fifteen, like in the dream.

"Well, well, young Tim. My, how you have grown!"

Tim whirled around. Standing in front of him was an ancient black man wearing only a leopard loincloth. Sitting to the right of the man was a large, male leopard. Resting in a wicker chair to the left of the wrinkled black man was an old black woman with a gray cat curled in her lap.

"Chea Geebe, is it really you?" asked Tim smiling.

"So now you remember old Chea. I have tried to bring you the warnings of the *endosym*, but you ignored my words."

"Was it you who made me see the demons in those men?" asked Tim.

"No, my son, your eyes saw the true inner spirit of those men, what they were willing to become, not what they are. I only helped you to see the inner man."

"I don't understand," said Tim.

"Tim, the *endosym* is back. You must stop him before it is too late," whispered Chea.

"I don't understand," Tim said again, confused.

"You are now the chosen one, the one who walks with the spirit of the leopard," responded the old man.

It was getting dark; the sun had already set.

"Wait!" cried Tim. "I still don't understand!"

Tim looked around. He was lying in his bed at his parents' house in Hawaii. He looked at the clock. It was 5:30 a.m. Eddie was still sleeping peacefully in the other twin bed. Tim didn't move. He was trying to gather his thoughts.

The dream had forced him to recall what had happened to his family in Liberia. It all happened six years earlier when he was just a teen-ager. He felt strangely unsettled, yet his memories had brought him closer to the reality of a terrible evil.

Now, it was a new day. He got up, headed for the bathroom where he showered, shaved, dressed and headed for the kitchen.

His dad sat at the table with both hands wrapped around his coffee cup. Tim poured his own coffee and sat down beside his father.

"Dad?"

"Yes, son?"

"Do you remember that leopard tooth we had in Liberia?" Tim asked.

"Sure, it's in the china cabinet in the den," answered Hank.

"Is it OK if I take it back to school with me?" asked Tim.

"Sure, it's yours."

"Thanks, Dad."

When Tim opened the cabinet, he found the leopard's tooth on the second shelf next to a small statue of a demon. The gold chain was gone. He remembered giving the chain to his mother to keep with her jewelry while they were packing for the move to Hawaii. It was now attached to its original leather cord.

Tim stuffed the necklace into his jeans pocket. Moments later, he pulled it out again. He placed the leather loop over his head and concealed the tooth under his T-shirt.

Tim walked out of the den smiling broadly and feeling better, stronger and more confident than he had felt in months.

40

The flight back to D.C. didn't turn
out as smoothly as they had hoped.

"Jeez," said Eddie. "This hour delay in taking off from Honolulu might make us miss that connecting flight from SF to Reagan. What do you think, Tim?"

"I think you're right," Tim said. "We'll just have to cross our fingers and hope we can get back home in time to make our first class on Monday morning."

Crossing fingers didn't work as well as Tim had hoped. They missed the flight out of San Francisco and had to hop on a red-eye to get to D.C. They got to Reagan at six in the morning.

Strangely, the inconvenience seemed to have had little or no effect on Tim. Eddie and Sam yawned and complained about sore backs, lack of good food and needing showers.

Tim had sailed right through the hassle. A real plus of the overnight flight was that Tim and Sam had a vacant seat in their row. They lifted the center armrests and snuggled together, stretching out their long legs toward the aisle. They covered themselves with airline blankets. When the cabin lights dimmed, they felt a bit more intimacy than if they had been on a crowded, daytime flight.

"Do you know how much I love you?" Tim had asked Samantha.

"No, why don't you tell me?" Sam replied.

"I wish I could show you right now," Tim said, running his hand under her sweater.

The weeklong stay in separate bedrooms had been difficult enough. Now they could only hope for a few quick kisses and caresses. The rest would have to wait until they could plan for a free weekend.

Tim was amazed at his own good spirits. No longer was he haunted by unknown demons. The dream about Chea Geebe had brought back all the repressed memories of what had happened in Liberia when he was just a teenager. He felt like he had been living in a fog. Maybe it was post-traumatic stress syndrome, he reasoned. He felt stronger now and more in control of his own life.

Once on the ground, all three got in high gear – they picked up their bags, rushed to the parking garage, and jumped into Tim's Explorer. They grabbed a quick breakfast at a drive-thru and dropped Sam off at her apartment.

On the way to the university, Tim drove in the fast lane as much as possible. When he got behind a slow vehicle, he moved in and out of traffic to make better time. He kept one eye on the rear view mirror. He patted his stealth radar detector that kept flashing green. Meanwhile, Eddie held tightly to the armrest and tried to keep calm. Tim's driving terrified him. He imagined them wiping out several times.

Tim made the trip to the dorm in record time. Eddie sighed with relief when they finally parked. Eddie's first class began in fewer than fifteen minutes. He rushed to the room, grabbed his backpack and headed for class.

Tim had a full hour before his class started. He took the luggage up to the room. He had time to take a quick shower. He had stopped to pick up the mail. He had just enough time to go through it quickly. He tossed the junk mail into the recycling bin.

One letter made him pause. It was a letter from Liberia. The return address was Captain Sabo Weah, Barclay Training Center, Monrovia, Liberia. Tim was pleased. It had been four months since he had last heard from Sabo.

Even though he was pressed for time, he ripped open the letter and began to read.

Greetings, little brother. I hope this letter finds you well.

Tim had to chuckle at his first line. Sabo was four years older. People unfamiliar with Liberia might find it strange for him to refer to Tim as a little brother. Tim knew different. The two of them had faced death together and had won. That created a bond that would last the rest of their lives.

Tim smiled as he held the letter. He had to know what Sabo had to say.

The children are growing taller each day. Judie sends her love. She is as beautiful as the day we were married. I find it hard to believe that she is the mother of our three boys.

Tim, I am sorry that I have not written sooner, but it has been a trying and sad time for our village. I wish I did not have to tell you this, but, sadly, your old friend, Chea Geebe, died last month.

Early one morning, Aunt Salmata found him sitting in the shade next to Togba's hut. She asked Chea if he would like a drink of water. When he didn't speak, she touched his shoulder. It was cold. He had died sometime during the night. He died right there, sitting on his stool next to the hut. No one knows how old Chea Geebe was. Some believe that he was more than one hundred.

The whole village mourned his death. Chiefs came from all around. The zoes from Zigda conducted special purification ceremonies for Chea, the greatest of all the zoes. Then on the third day after his passing, the ten highest members of the PORO carried his body deep into the sacred bush. Togba allowed me to accompany them to the place where Chea's body would be safe from evil while his spirit roamed the bush.

It was a place like I had never seen. It was a cave, hidden from view. Inside was the skeleton of a large leopard. Chea's body was placed next to the cat's skeleton. The leopard tooth that Chea had worn was placed on the leopard's skull. Strange, the skull was missing its two front fangs. Didn't Chea Geebe give your mother a leopard's tooth when we left the village?

Anyway, we left the cave, piling stones in the entrance so nothing could enter. It was a sad trip back to the village. Yet, the next morning, two of the elders claimed they had seen Chea Geebe sitting in his chair in the moonlight late at night. A large leopard sat on its haunches next to him.

Tim, I know that most white men would scoff at our beliefs, but you know that Chea Geebe, the greatest of all the zoes, still protects our village of Zigda.

The letter was signed simply, "Sabo." Tim brushed a tear from his cheek. He could envision the old, black man, thin and wrinkled, sitting with his back against the hut. He'd be barefoot and shirtless, wearing only khaki shorts. He remembered Chea's bald spot, fringed with snow-white hair. The two of them used to play checkers while Chea was on the job as their night watchman. People called him Everyday Walker because the house the Martins occupied once belonged to the Walkers.

Back then, they didn't know that Chea was a powerful witch doctor, called a *zo*. But now, Tim knew differently.

He remembered the day when they had to go into hiding in Zigda. The drums had announced that a powerful *zo* was coming. As the figure emerged from the jungle, the villagers huddled together and shook with fear. But Tim didn't share their anxiety. He could see that it was his old friend, Everyday Walker. Here in the village, he was known by his true name, Chea Geebe.

That night the village *zoes*, led by Chea Geebe, had conducted a ceremony that could have been performed at the dawn of time. The ritual saved the life of the chief's son, Joe Weah, Sabo's cousin.

Tim had to look at the letter again. One paragraph stood out.

"The leopard tooth that Chea had worn was placed on the leopard's skull. Strange, the skull was missing its two front fangs. Didn't Chea Geebe give your mother a leopard's tooth when we left the village?"

Tim reached under his shirt and removed the leopard tooth he wore on the leather cord around his neck. He held it in his hand. It felt warm to his touch, almost alive.

Just two nights earlier, he had a dream about Chea Geebe. The old man had been dead for more than a month. Why had he come back to him now?

The dream had been so vivid, and Chea's words so unsettling. The old *zo* had looked in Tim's eyes and spoke the words that could change Tim's life forever.

"Tim, you are now the chosen one, the one who walks with the spirit of the leopard."

"What's going on?" said Tim out loud. He didn't have time to come up with an answer his own question. He stuffed his laptop into the backpack and headed to class.

Yet, even as he rushed to class, he couldn't prevent Chea's words from running through his mind.

41

The Johnsonville Plantation was an excellent choice for the location of the school.

USUALLY SARDAY PAUSED OCCASIONALLY TO GAZE OUT THE LARGE windows of his second floor office and admire his work.

But today was different. He paced back and forth. He didn't stop even once to look out. Clearly, the man was thinking. Whatever he was thinking about had put him in a foul mood.

Oscar Jalah had no recourse but to watch the man walk to the left, turn, and walk to the right. He should have counted the number of round trips that Sarday had made. But it was too late now; he should have started sooner, but who could have guessed that the ritual would go on this long.

Shit, Jalah thought. He didn't dare say anything out loud. He knew that Sarday was annoyed and angry at something, but he didn't know what it could be. When Sarday was unhappy, Jalah preferred to be somewhere else.

Jalah resigned himself to the wait. He dug his heels into the thick carpet and pushed back farther in the overstuffed, leather chair. If Sarday chose to get lost in his thoughts, he could, too.

The man he knew as George Sarday had changed dramatically since the recent sacrifice of two young men to the dark spirit that Sarday called Dacari Mucomba. Jalah was now certain that Sarday had become an *endosym*.

The first sacrificial victim had been a black kid that the guards had picked up along the highway. The unfortunate soul had been hitchhiking. It was his mistake to accept the wrong ride. This boy's bloody demise had served to teach the new followers a crucial lesson in the teachings of Dacari Mucomba. His severed head was a vivid reminder of the power of evil.

The second sacrifice had been that tall, skinny white boy with the hair than came down over his eyes. He had been one of the three kids they had found snooping around the grounds. This boy had been lucky enough to have a few more days to live than his two companions.

Those two, along with the decapitated body of the black hitchhiker, had been incinerated in the pickup truck that had crashed off the cliff. After the black kid's headless body had been stuffed into the cab of the truck, a road flare tossed into the wreckage caused the vehicle to burst into flames at the bottom of the quarry. Jalah smiled. It was such a clever way to bring an end to three useless lives and to dispose of three bodies without causing suspicion. The police assumed the victims in the burned truck had been the three white high school kids.

He was anxious to observe the next sacrificial offering. It would be the young black boy who didn't have a left hand. That ritual was yet to come. Until then, he was kept in a cell in the cavern below the house ready for his death ritual.

Hell, he's still at it, Jalah thought. Sarday kept up his pacing.

Jalah had been with Sarday and others who worshipped the dark spirit since he was seventeen. He'd joined the rebels during the Liberian Civil War. Blood and violence had become a part of his life. He took pride in his unofficial title, the "Prince of Death." Even as a youth, Jalah had been a standout in the conflict. He had been selected to serve as an aide to a rogue officer in the Liberian army.

After the peace accord was signed, the officer, Julius Carpai, had slipped away to avoid prosecution. He was reinstated into the AFL (Armed Forces of Liberia) as a colonel. When President Dowling took over, Carpai became the nation's minister of defense. Jalah rose to the rank of major and served as the colonel's right-hand man.

Things went well for them for a while, but then the tables were turned once again. Sarday and Jalah were the only members of the cult to escape in the fall of Monrovia.

Damn lucky, Jalah thought. Now, here they were in America, the greatest nation in the world. Sarday had a plan that would make him so powerful that he would rule the entire country. It was impossible to know what Sarday's next move would be.

Jalah considered himself just a simple man. Like all Liberians, he believed in the spirits of the bush. He also knew that powerful men became even stronger through human sacrifice. The ceremony could evoke spirits that lived deep in the sacred bush. Those spirits would grant them power and wealth. For this reason, Jalah had no problem obeying Sarday's wishes. He knew that those who helped the *endosym* would reap the rewards of their deeds.

Even though he had spent years in Sarday's service, he still couldn't imagine what Sarday was planning next. Sarday had talked about a special ceremony where the curtain would be lifted between this world and the world of the dark spirits. This would require a special sacrifice of forty human souls.

Even stranger was Sarday's belief that other demons would pass through this curtain. They would establish more centers like this one in Johnsonville. This would be the beginning of the takeover of the United States by the *endosyms*.

It made no sense to Jalah. But, clearly, Sarday was more than just a mere man. Jalah could feel the power emanating from Sarday. All Jalah knew was that the next sacrifice would include those selected men and women who would rule the nation led by the *endosyms*.

Suddenly, Sarday stopped pacing and turned to Jalah.

"Oscar, I want you to kill Tim Martin."

Jalah sucked in a breath.

"Do you mean the Martin who helped Morray take back Liberia?"

"Yes, find out where the family lives and go and kill the son."

"But that was six years ago. How can I find them?" asked Oscar.

"Use the Internet," snarled Sarday. "The boy's father was an officer in the U.S. Army; it should be easy to find where they live. When you find them, kill the boy."

"Yes, sir," said Jalah. "I'll get right on it."

Finally released from Sarday's office, Jalah was confused. He frowned. Why would Sarday want to kill Martin?

In the next moment, his mood lifted. He laughed out loud. Just six years ago, Julius Carpai had sent him to murder both the Martin woman and her son. Finally, Jalah would get his chance to finish the job.

He'd do it one better yet – he'd kill the entire Martin family.

42

*It was as if the entire town of Johnsonville had turned out to
remember the old woman.*

AN OVERFLOW CROWD HAD GATHERED FOR MICHELLE JOHNSON'S
funeral. Inside the Calvary Baptist Church, the minister had asked people
to move closer together to allow the pews to accommodate as many as
possible. Outside, rows of folding chairs had been set up for others. People
still kept arriving, walking from blocks away where they parked their
cars. A speaker system, borrowed from the Methodist Church, allowed
those who were seated or standing outside to hear the service.

The funeral was into its second hour, and Johnsonville's chief of
police, Brian Bishop, needed to pee. He nudged his wife.

"How much longer do you think this will go on?" he whispered.

Ann smiled, figuring that her husband needed to take a break.

"I don't know. I've never been to a black funeral before," she answered
softly.

The choir was singing the fifth verse of "Amazing Grace." Bishop was
tone deaf, but even he knew that they were off-key, way off-key.

Movement seemed to help him get his mind off his bladder. He
crossed his legs and then uncrossed them. He turned his upper body to
the right and looked behind him. A number of white faces were inter-
spersed throughout the congregation.

For most of the whites, Bishop suspected that this was the first
time they had ever been in the all-black Baptist church. Bishop smiled

inwardly; heck, for many of them, this was likely the first time they'd been in any church since they were babies and had to get baptized.

Clearly, Grandma Johnson was a deeply loved woman in the community.

Finally, the service ended, and the congregation was dismissed, row-by-row, to pass by the open casket. They were instructed to exit through the side door and find their seats at the tables where the barbecue meal would be served. Willie had asked the Bishops to sit up front with the family. Ever since Bishop had found Willie a job with the grounds department after the incident in the black bar, Willie had always seemed beholding to him. Bishop didn't want to hurt Willie's feelings, so he had agreed. Now, he realized, they would be among the first to pass by the open casket.

Bishop put his hand lightly on Ann's back and followed her to the front. Grandma Johnson's body was lying in the casket, her arms folded over her shrunken body. She looked as if she had simply fallen asleep. Bishop took note of the white satin lining and the elaborate hardware on the silver metal casket.

God, this must be the Cadillac of all caskets, Bishop thought. It looked as if it had cost more than Willie's simple house in Shantytown.

Once outside, Bishop met Willie standing by the door. He grasped Willie's hand and expressed sympathy for his loss.

"Thanks for coming, Chief," Willie said, clearly moved by Bishop's presence.

Finally done with the social obligations, Bishop headed directly for the row of porta-potties that had been set up for the expected crowd. He felt a welcome relief.

He searched the crowd for Ann and saw her seated at one of the round tables. All the tables had been covered with white tablecloths. Small glass vases, each with a single red rose, had been placed in the center of the tables. He saw the Larsons and the Raymonds sitting beside Ann. He wound his way through the tables and joined them.

Everyone seemed to have been hungry. There was quite a feast. They finished their meals quickly, all the while telling stories and cracking jokes.

"Wow, every great black cook in town must have brought her favorite dish. I'm so full, I could just about burst," said Dick Raymond. "But I can't resist going back for another piece of that chocolate cake."

"Bring me just a teeny-tiny piece," said Dick's wife, Trudy. She held up her thumb and forefinger indicating a piece about an inch thick. "Or this big," she added. The distance between her thumb and forefinger had doubled.

Everyone broke out in laughter. Although it was a funeral, it felt good to be among friends and celebrating the life of such a beloved woman.

Moments later, Bishop felt a tap on his shoulder. It was Willie.

"Chief, sorry to bother you, but I wonder if I could speak to you for just a moment?

"Sure, Willie," Bishop answered. He excused himself and the two men stepped over to a large oak tree a short distance away from the noisy crowd.

"Chief, I need a favor. When Grandma died, she gave me this and wanted me to get it to Tim Martin," he said, handing Bishop a brown paper bag.

"Willie, I don't know a Tim Martin."

"Me neither, Chief," Willie replied. "But it was her dying wish."

"I suppose I can check our computer data base and see if the name Tim Martin comes up. Any idea as to his age or race?"

"I figure he must be black, Chief, but I don't know how old he be."

"What's in the bag, Willie?" asked Bishop, squeezing the bag, trying to identify the contents by its shape.

"It's a devil."

"A devil?" asked Bishop, puzzled.

"Well, a metal statue of one, I guess. I just peeked in, and it scared me," Willie said.

"All right, Willie, I'll see what I can do." Bishop took the bag and again told Willie how sorry he was to hear of his grandmother's passing. He walked back to the table and rejoined the others.

"What's in the bag, Brian?" asked Raymond.

"Would you believe, a statue of the devil? Willie wants me to find a man named Tim Martin. Seems it's his grandmother's dying wish that this Martin guy gets the statue," Bishop answered.

"Well, let's see it," asked Steve Larson, the Methodist minister.

Bishop reached in the bag, pulled out a towel-wrapped object, removed the towel, and set the small statue on the table.

Only ten inches tall, the statue was exquisitely carved. It was a representation of a man or something that resembled a man. Two horns sprouted from its large, balding head. The ears were long and pointed. Its face looked Egyptian, sporting the artificial beard, like those worn by the pharaohs. The creature had an old man's sunken chest, thin arms, and a potbelly. The bottom half was different. It had strong, muscular legs. Only a loincloth covered its genitals. Behind it was a long tail that stuck out and reached the ground. In one hand, it had an axe; the other held a spear. It wore some kind of a necklace around its neck.

"Wow, that is really different," said Raymond. "It looks like someone posed for the statue."

"Yeah, they had to search really hard to find someone with horns and a tail," joked his wife, Trudy.

"You know, it's not really a statue of the devil," said Larson. "At least not in the Christian sense. Remember, Lucifer was a fallen angel and had wings. Old drawings of the devil always showed wings."

Raymond examined the statue more closely.

"You know, this thing looks really old. It could be worth a fortune. The face looks Egyptian, but the axe it's holding could be from the Stone Age. See, it is a sharpened stone attached to a wooden handle, and the spear has knots in the shank. It's like it was carved thousands of years before the technology existed to make cast bronze statues using the lost wax method."

"What exactly is this lost wax method?" Bishop asked.

"The image is initially carved out of beeswax or another substance that melts easily. Then clay or a sand-cement mix is packed around the wax object. At the bottom of the statue, the sand or clay is scraped away. That exposes the wax at the base. Then the whole thing is buried in the ground upside down. The exposed portion stays level with the ground.

"A forge then melts a copper-zinc mix in a ladle. When the liquid metal is poured on the exposed wax, the wax melts. That drives the wax out, and the cavity fills up with the molten metal. When that metal cools and solidifies, the clay is broken off, and that turns the carved wax image into a bronze one.

"In some ways, it's the same principle as a Jell-O mold. The strange thing is that historically, this method of casting is about four thousand years old, yet this statue appears to be a Stone Age carving," Raymond explained.

Raymond's lengthy explanation caused the others to scratch their heads in wonder.

"Leave it to my engineer husband to overkill the subject," said Trudy, laughing along with the others.

"Jeez, Dick, how'd you know all that?" asked Bishop.

"Oh, I read a lot," said Raymond. "Just so happens I read about it just last week in the *National Geographic*. Didn't think I'd ever see an example of the real thing."

"Put it back in the bag, Brian!" shouted Larson.

Everyone turned and looked at the minister. His face was pale, and his hands shook.

"What's wrong?" asked Bishop.

Larson shuddered.

"There's nothing wrong. It's just not an appropriate thing to discuss at a funeral."

Bishop started to say something, but he had second thoughts. He just shrugged, rolled the statue back up in the towel, and put it in the paper bag. Everyone was quiet, unsure of what to say or do.

Finally, Trudy broke the silence.

"Wasn't that barbecued pork delicious?"

"Yes," answered Ann, a bit too quickly. "I would love to get that recipe."

The incident was quickly forgotten. Larson had regained his composure. Bishop felt like kicking himself. Of course, Larson would be upset. Any minister would have said that this devil talk was inappropriate for the occasion.

But, in most other matters, Larson was a rather laid-back, regular guy. Bishop thought that Larson had overreacted. He tucked the wrinkled paper bag under his arm.

The funeral over, the hard part was yet to come – finding Tim Martin.

43

The National Archives in Washington, D.C. had been easy to find.

PERHAPS HERE IN THE OLD BOOK SECTION, REVEREND LARSON COULD find the answers to his many questions.

He had gone through a personal hell in the last week, and his face showed it. He had dark circles under his eyes and his skin had taken on a sallow look as if he had gone for days with little food and insufficient sleep. Ever since the Johnson woman's funeral, he felt unsettled, unsure and unable to clear his head.

"Here are three of the missing pages believed to be from the Codex Gigas, Reverend Larson. Make sure you keep the white cotton gloves on when handling the pages," said the library clerk. The two of them sat at a worktable in a hermetically sealed room.

"Thank you, Miss Swanson," he replied. Even getting this far had caused him some anxious moments. He had been asked to get a letter from his bishop even to gain access to the documents. That, and a background security check, had taken several precious days.

"Let me know if you have any questions," she said. "I'll leave you here, but please be aware that I can see through the window, and your actions will be recorded on camera."

Larson took a slow, deep breath. All his deeply held beliefs would be under scrutiny as he dug deeper into the mystery of the statue.

Sunday's sermon had been a disaster. He couldn't stay on his topic, he lost his train of thought, and had to pause often and glance at his notes.

All he could think about was that statue. What had gone wrong with him? Why couldn't he shake this anxiety?

This summer, Larson would begin his twenty-third year as a Methodist minister. He had accepted Christ as his Lord and Savior when he was just seventeen. He had pledged to serve God for the rest of his life. He had walked with God every day. He had been blessed in the knowledge that Christ was real. All the assurances of his entire career had been based on his deeply held beliefs. Throughout his ministry, he had never experienced anything like this.

It had always been unquestionably simple for him. He had witnessed the power of prayer; he had seen God work His miracles. He prayed every day, asking Jesus to guide his way. Yet in all these years, God had never actually spoken to him. Not like God spoke with Moses on the mountain or like what happened to Saul on the road to Damascus.

But, that thing on the table had spoken to him, and it frightened him nearly to death.

At the funeral reception, he and his wife had joined the Bishops and the Raymonds. Everything had gone well until the police chief came back with a paper bag that Willie had given him. Somehow, that Michelle Johnson had gotten hold of a devil-like statue. He couldn't take his eyes off of it. He had sat frozen in his place, entranced by the mystery.

Suddenly, he had found himself inside a cave, surrounded by creatures that looked like the statue. The cave stretched as far as he could see. On the cave floor he could see what looked like thousands of bleached, white human skulls.

Was this a glimpse of hell? As suddenly as the vision came to him, it had suddenly left. He was sitting back at the table with the others, as if nothing, absolutely nothing, had happened.

For the last four days, he'd hardly left his office. He had spent every waking hour researching horned gods, man-beast creatures, demonology, mythology and witchcraft. He found that idea of a horned god seemed to cross many cultures and religions. The ancient Egyptians, Druids, Celtics, Romans, Greeks, Slavs, Wiccans, primitive cultures of America,

Africa and the Pacific, and almost every religion, all referred to a horned being with the power to affect men's lives.

In his own religious training, he had found it fascinating that the Devil, one of the most beautiful of God's angels, was often depicted in drawings as a horned being. In many drawings, it even had a tail, similar to the one on the statue. Depictions of a man with horns and a tail were even found in cave drawings dating back as far as thirty thousand years ago.

As far as Larson was concerned, all that evidence pointed to the fact that something real may very well have existed. What he feared even more was that it might still exist today.

His hands began to shake when he found a link to an article on the Codex Gigas, and the recent discovery of three of its eight missing pages. He couldn't believe his luck when he learned that the documents had been sent from Stockholm where the original book was stored at the National Library of Sweden. They were now on loan at The National Archives for further study by historians.

The Codex Gigas, known as the Devil's Bible, was shrouded in mystery. The words themselves translate into "Giant Book." It is believed to be one of history's largest books, measuring thirty-six inches tall, almost twenty inches wide, and a little short of nine inches thick. It took two strong men to lift the one-hundred-sixty-pound volume. Its nearly six hundred pages were said to have come from the hides of one hundred and sixty donkeys.

According to the legend, a monk was walled up alive in a cell for having committed a sinful deed. To avoid this punishment, he promised to write the world's largest book in a single day. Of course, that was impossible. Therefore, he called on the Devil for help. If one man alone had done the work, it would have taken him more than twenty years. Yet, experts who examined the script were convinced that a single man had written it.

Up to just recently, most scholars believed it was missing seven or eight pages. Some said that the pages were removed to hide an ancient secret. Finding just three of them was truly remarkable.

Most historians believed it was completed somewhere around 1229. Many scholars consider it one of the seven wonders of the Middle Ages. The Swedes keep close watch on it, insuring it for upwards of thirty million dollars.

Larson had always enjoyed studying history as well as languages. He had earned a minor in Latin in seminary, and, as a hobby, he enjoyed reading old Latin text. The pages sitting in front of him would require no translator.

He picked up the first page and began to read.

I was brought to this monastery when I was but eleven years. The monastery is built on a high cliff overlooking the river. It is built into the rock wall. The lowest level connects to a large cave where the monks who die rest until the resurrection.

I was taught to be a scribe and spent each day writing the word.

A year ago I was given the additional duty of going to the village twice a week to obtain eggs and cheese for the brothers. It was there that I fell into sin with a young wench. No one knew of my secret until Brother Bartholomew caught us fornicating. As was his duty, he notified the monsignor who judged me guilty of a grievous sin not only against the Brotherhood but also against our savior, Jesus.

My punishment was to be sealed in the catacombs until the Lord Jesus called the monsignor to his kingdom. I was taken to the lower level of the monastery. The great door to the catacombs was opened. I was told that every three days bread, cheese and water would be brought to me. I was also given my writing materials and sheets of beaten animal skin to write on. For the many years of imprisonment, I would be required to write about God to atone for my sins. I had no idea how long I would be imprisoned, but I knew that the monsignor could live for years or even decades.

The catacombs were inside a large room with walls of stone. The ceiling was as high as five men. At the top of the wall facing the river were two openings that allowed light into the catacombs. This room had a portal that led into the bowels of the Earth.

I was given no candle and passed through the portal only far enough to relieve myself of my body waste. I had a wooden bed, two fleeces and a large wooden table for my work. From the hour when the sun rose in the morning till sunset, the two openings provided light for me to write.

At night, it was so dark that I could see only a faint glow from the openings to the outside. Thirty days after I was placed in the catacombs I began to hear someone whispering. I believed the murmurs came from the dead monks whose bones rested in the cave.

I tried to shut out the sound, but each night I would hear it again. Then one day while I was doing my writing I felt that someone was looking over my shoulder. I turned quickly, but there was nothing to see. Two days later I saw movement in a corner. "Who's there?" I asked, but there was no answer. I was convinced that I was going mad. Then several days later, I saw a figure standing in the shadows. As I approached, the figure disappeared like a ghost. Two days later it reappeared.

I approached slowly, but this time the figure did not disappear. I approached and as the light from the windows moved with the sun, I could see it in the sunlight. I screamed, even though no one could hear me. Standing next to the wall was the Devil. He appeared to be without clothes and his skin was gray as in death. As I got closer, to my shock, I saw a tail coming from the base of the Devil's spine. He was naked. His private parts were that of a man. He had a tail, and there were horns coming out of his head. I knew I was going mad, and God had sent the Devil to torture me.

"Why do you torture me, Satan?" I asked.

He laughed and said, "I do not torture you. You torture yourself. I can grant you great power."

I laughed and said, "What can you do to help a poor man like myself?"

He said he would help me write the greatest book ever written. He explained that he was not the Devil, but a being that, with others like him, are hidden from our eyes through magic. They gain great power from the spirits of men who die by decapitation. As a man's head is removed from his body, these creatures consume the man's spirit, and their power becomes even more potent. To become more powerful yet, they must capture more souls. To do this, they grant mortal men great gifts to serve them. These creatures can live forever and can only be killed by one of their own.

But, on Earth, each of their bodies is not solid, but more like a cloud. Each must enter the chosen man as a host, and they will live together. They would be two beings in one body. He told me to touch his body, but I reached out, but my hand passed through the body as if it was passing through a ghost.

He then offered me the opportunity to leave this place by allowing him to enter my body. We were to become one. I had no choice; I knew I would go mad if I remained in the tomb, so I agreed.

He stepped forward. I felt fear in my heart. Then the strangest things began to occur. I could see well into the dark of the cavern, as if it were daylight. I could hear the sound of rats scurrying along the walls. I could hear the drip of water falling deep within the cave. Now I was no longer alone. I could have been sharing my cell with another monk. I knew myself, but I also knew the creature that lived within me.

I sat down at the table. My fingers flew across the page creating perfect letters; the words flowed out of our joint mind. I required no sleep, and the dark of night was no more. When food was brought on the third day, I had used up all the animal skins and ink.

As soon as the monsignor saw my works, he came to the catacombs. He told me that if I completed the great book, I would be set free, my sins atoned. All the skins and ink were provided me. In one half year, I completed the book.

These pages I hid in the cave to tell the true story.

When I was released, the creature that now lived within me promised me great riches. I would leave the monastery and persecute those who failed to follow the true religion. They would be dismembered and destroyed by fire. For each death, our joint being would grow stronger, richer and more powerful.

Larson could only stare at the last page. What had drawn him to the Codex Gigas in the first place was its half-meter drawing of a demon. It looked exactly like the statue.

These alleged missing pages told a terrifying story. He was convinced that it was true. Perhaps vampires, the living dead, were also men possessed by these beings. Perhaps they didn't actually drink blood, but lived from the essence of men's souls.

The statue was not only real, but it also seemed to channel a warning that these creatures truly exist.

Larson had to think about this. He remembered studying about how Christ dealt with demons. Larson had scoffed at the demon thing back then. What he was seeing now caused him to reconsider.

So, a man accepts the demon's offer, and he becomes something other than human, Larson concluded. From his biology class in college, the idea of one organism living in the body of another organism wasn't up for debate. The demon would be called an endosymbiont, a creature that lives in a host. The process itself was called endosymbiosis. Of course, in nature this usually occurs at the cellular level. But this seemed far more complicated.

Was that what the Bible meant when Christ drove the demons out of the man and they entered pigs? Larson wondered.

My, God, they were real, Larson thought, shocked by his own conclusion. Once a man accepts the demon, the new creature becomes, for lack of a better word, an endosym, a new creature – a very dangerous creature.

Larson pulled out his cell phone and dialed.

"Johnsonville Police Department, may I help you?" said the operator.

"This is Reverend Larson. Is Chief Bishop there?"

"One moment, please."

"Chief Bishop speaking."

"Brian, this is Steve Larson."

"Yes, Steve, how can I help you?"

"Do you still have that statue?"

"Yes, it's in my den at home. Why?" asked Bishop.

"Listen, I know this sounds crazy, but you must get rid of it. No, destroying it might be a better solution."

"I don't understand," Bishop said, surprised to be receiving orders from the minister.

"I think it is evil and dangerous. I know I am not making sense, but I swear, that thing is dangerous."

"All right, I'll see what can be done. Listen, Steve, you don't sound good. Maybe you need to see someone," said Bishop.

"No, I'll be all right," Larson said. "But, Brian, you need to get rid of that thing."

As soon as Larson ended the call, he placed his phone back in his pocket.

Then he bowed his head and began to pray.

44

The Charlottesville-Ablemarle Airport was busier than usual.

FEW PEOPLE WERE FORTUNATE ENOUGH TO WITNESS THE COMINGS and goings of the wealthy or well-known passengers who received special treatment when they flew in or out of the airport. Its general aviation side served the private jets. Normally, somewhere between four or five corporate jets and a number of smaller aircraft would be parked on the tarmac. Today, every slot was filled.

Richie Moore considered himself pretty lucky. He worked the passenger desk and frequently got to see the "beautiful people" up close. Today he was training a new girl, Joan Horton, who had been hired a couple of weeks ago to assist with the increasing number of passengers arriving by private jet.

He turned around to check out the action on the tarmac. A big Boeing 737 rolled to a stop next to a Leer jet. The 737 looked as big as a 747 jumbo jet compared to the all the corporate jets parked around it.

"Hey, Joan," said Moore, turning to his partner. "Are we having fun yet?"

"You bet we are," said Horton. "I've already seen at least a dozen limos drive up. Sure has been a busy day."

The ground crew rolled the stairway to the front door of the 737. The plane could carry one hundred twenty-five passengers, but today only nine people had exited the aircraft and walked toward the terminal.

As they got closer, Moore recognized the movie star couple who had adopted all those kids from Africa. Then there was that former action hero turned producer. He also recognized a blond singer, but he couldn't remember her name.

The big prize of today's group was Zack Trevor, one of Hollywood's most famous stars. He was the real thing. He had piloted the 737. Moore had heard a rumor that Trevor owned about a dozen of his own planes.

Trevor walked up to the counter.

"Good afternoon, Mr. Trevor," said Moore.

"Good afternoon," said Trevor, "I'll need the old girl refueled and ready for departure Monday morning."

"Not a problem, sir, we'll have it ready for you whenever you want it," responded Moore, flashing his best smile.

Moore took pride in his professional demeanor. It was required when working with this type of client. He was a bit surprised when Horton came up to the counter and stood beside him.

"Oh, Mr. Trevor," said Horton. "Uh, Mr. Trevor, may I have your autograph for my daughter?"

Moore cringed. Employees weren't supposed to harass the customers.

"Why, of course, dear," he answered. Trevor always tried to respond courteously to a fan, no matter how annoying some could be. "What's her name?"

"Joan," she responded quickly, hoping the star wouldn't read her nametag.

But she needn't have worried. Trevor's eyes looked downward as he scrawled some words on the back of an airline memo.

He wrote, "To Joan, from your friend, Zack Trevor." He pushed the paper back across the counter.

"Oh, thank you, Mr. Trevor! Have a wonderful day!" she called out to him. He had already turned and was listening to one of his aides who appeared to be telling him something important.

Moore concealed his irritation. When things calmed down, he needed to have a little chat with Miss Joan Horton. He walked over to the curbside door and held it open for even more of the well-heeled passengers who were heading toward two long, black limos.

Back at the desk, he leaned over to his partner.

"Joan, you don't have a daughter," he whispered.

"No, I don't," she said, blushing. She quickly changed the subject. "Oh, by the way, did you see Chuck Washburn, the producer? I thought he was dying of cancer."

"Well, he sure looked as healthy as a horse," replied Moore.

"I read in the tabloids that he had less than three months to live. Then he joined that cult over in Johnsonville. That cured him," she continued.

"Well, I don't believe anything in those tabloids, but I'll bet that every one of the people who are coming in today are heading for Johnsonville," Moore said. "I have no idea what that Sarday guy is selling, but the rich and famous sure are buying."

45

At Sarday's school, the ceremony would soon begin.

"MERLOT OR CHAMPAGNE?" ASKED THE DARK-SKINNED MAID HOLDING a tray of wine glasses.

JILLY MORRISON HAD BEEN TO MANY RECEPTIONS AS A MEMBER OF Senator Carlson's staff, but the maid's question had startled her. Jilly hadn't seen the young woman approach. She had been too engrossed in watching the crowd of well-dressed dignitaries laughing and drinking together. She had tried to stay inconspicuous and kept a low profile near the massive stone fireplace in Sarday's mansion.

"No, no thank you," she said quickly. She had already downed two glasses and had picked up a dozen or so of the small canapés from the sideboard. She figured that by eating some real food, the wine wouldn't have too much of an effect. It was abnormal for her to refuse a glass of free booze, but she'd been doing quite a few unusual things lately.

She had tried to count the number of people in the large room. Once she counted thirty-nine. Another time she counted forty-three.

"Screw it," she said out loud. It wouldn't matter to her anyway. Only forty people would be among the chosen ones who were to be elevated to the first tier of Dacari Mucomba. Maybe she had mistakenly counted Dr. Sarday or even herself when she tallied up the crowd. She figured she was unimportant; she wasn't included in the exclusive group. She was only a third tier server of Dacari Mucomba.

Being in the third tier was honor enough. At least she got in on Sarday's stories. That unknown being spoke only through Dr. Sarday. He told of a world composed of three tiers of power. The third tier was still above the common humans whose only purpose was to serve as slaves to the true believers. Jilly compared it to her work in D.C. That third level was like the congressional aides. The second tier was like the members of congress. The first tier were the true leaders, sitting only one step below Dacari Mucomba.

It wasn't entirely fair. She was the one who introduced Senator Allan Carlson to Dacari Mucomba. She had just assumed that they would be elevated together when the time came. Apparently, that wasn't the plan of the spirit entity. That disappointment was bad enough, but she was even more upset about what was happening to her.

The damn nightmares had kept haunting her, interrupting her sleep and even coming back to her during the day in spontaneous visions. She was no stranger to the occult. She had been dabbling in the spirit world since she was a teenager. She loved ghosts, demons and even the Devil himself. It had always been sort of a fun game. That sacrifice of the white-feathered chickens was gross, but not altogether that bad. The goat thing had begun to get to her. When its bloody head fell into the wooden bowl, she had almost vomited.

Even the senator had gone too far. He had seemed to change, as he got more deeply involved in the ancient religion. He was the one who insisted that she accompany him to tonight's ceremony. The last thing she wanted to see was another goat murder. She hadn't told anyone, but she had a sort of out-of-body experience during the goat head bit. When its head was chopped off and all the blood shot out, she had seen something really strange. She had experienced a flash vision of something kind of human and kind of not.

Whatever it was kept coming back to her in nightmares.

Shit, she thought. She wouldn't even be here tonight if it weren't for the senator insisting she come with him. At least she got a little good wine out of the evening. Even though the senator wanted her to be with him at the actual ceremony, Dr. Sarday had told her privately that she would have to stay upstairs in the library until the ceremony was over.

No goat blood for me tonight, she thought.

That was the job of a third-tier follower, just do as she was told. She understood her role. She had told Sarday that it would be no problem. Now only fifteen minutes remained until the ceremony was to start. Once again, she felt a creeping fear just like she had experienced in the nightmares and visions.

Drugs had always helped her overcome her weird feelings. She'd been using pot since ninth grade, but she had avoided the hard drugs. She had begun snorting cocaine when the bad dreams got to be too much. She had taken hundred-dollar bills out of the senator's money stash to pay for her habit. Even if he knew she'd been doing it, he hadn't said anything. Now she was a regular cocaine user. Just thinking about it reminded her that she needed a fix right then. She needed it bad.

Jilly moved toward one of the fancy bathrooms. She smiled politely as she moved through the crowd. She hoped no one would spot her and stop to talk. She didn't have time to talk.

Once inside the bathroom, she closed the door and twisted the lock. She put her purse on the tile counter and pulled out her compact. She admired the fine white powder inside the black plastic case. She took out two full pinches of powder and poured them in two parallel lines on the edge of the porcelain sink.

She took a crisp twenty-dollar bill from her wallet. She rolled the bill and leaned into the sink. Using the rolled twenty like a straw, she snorted in the powder by inserting the end of the roll in each nostril while plugging the other nostril with her finger.

Jilly carefully cleaned up the residue by running water and swirling it around the sink. Finally, she swabbed the sink's surface with dry paper towels. She patted her face with real face powder from another compact, touched up her blush and lipstick, and took one last look at herself in the mirror before she unlocked the door.

Snorting cocaine resulted in a slower high than mainlining the stuff with a needle directly into the bloodstream, but the high was there just the same, and she had really needed it right then.

She was startled as she turned into the hallway. Dr. Sarday must have followed her when she left the gathering.

"There you are, my dear," he said, taking her hand. "It is time for you to go upstairs."

Just the touch of his fingers seemed to affect her. She felt that she had no control over her own body. She couldn't recall climbing the stairs to the library. Sarday's words directed her every move. He led her to a large, leather easy chair in the corner.

"Jilly, you are now under my power. You will remain seated and not move again until you hear my voice."

She smiled passively, staring across the library at a framed landscape painting on the opposite wall. She felt warm and secure. She wanted nothing more than to sit and await his return.

46

The mansion's library was OK for a while – but not for long.

JILLY FOLLOWED SARDAY'S ORDERS, AT LEAST AT FIRST.

By now, the cocaine was coursing through her bloodstream, mixing with the alcohol and leaving her restless and confused. Her heart rate accelerated, and her breathing became somewhat irregular. She blinked her eyes rapidly and tried to force herself to breathe deeply.

She wondered where she was. She looked around, but nothing seemed familiar. Her mind was rattled. Damn, too much coke, she thought.

She tried standing and then plopped down again in the chair. She got up again immediately and walked rapidly around the room. Then she remembered the ceremony.

"Why couldn't I just watch?" she said out loud, shaking her head from side to side. "This isn't fair!"

Her anxiety level spiked. She had to be careful; someone may be watching her. For a moment, she thought she heard sounds coming from downstairs. She decided to go check.

Jilly stood at the top of the stairway, listening closely for Sarday's return. She leaned against the wall and took slow steps down the stairs, one step at a time. Everything was silent, except for the incessant ticking of the grandfather clock on the lower level. She tiptoed into the reception room. Used dishes and glassware were stacked on the coffee tables, but no one had come to pick them up.

She wandered around the first floor like a lost child. She cracked open the wide front door and peered out into the driveway. She saw long, black cars and the senator's Mercedes parked along the road.

"Where is everyone?" she shouted, but no one answered. Maybe she was alone. Maybe no one cared.

Suddenly thirsty, she burst into the huge kitchen, turned on the water full blast, and bent over and twisted her head so she could drink directly from the faucet. She wiped her mouth with the back of her hand, and then turned to leave. She stopped immediately. Right in front of her stood an open door.

"The basement," she said. "This must go to the basement."

She approached the door. To her surprise, behind the door was yet another one, an over-sized, heavy, vault-like door. She pushed, expecting it to be locked. But it wasn't. It swung inward. She stumbled. She had almost fallen headlong down the steps, but caught herself by grasping a handrail on the right.

She took two tentative steps down the stairs. In the darkness below, she could see a flickering light. Somehow, she felt drawn to it.

The drugs, they make me wobbly, she thought. Better take baby steps. She balanced herself with one hand and cautiously lowered herself, one step at a time. When she reached the bottom step, she paused to look around. She found herself in a large, open room. It had a concrete floor.

Small compartments lined the walls. Many contained lighted candles. So, that's where the flickering light had come from, she thought.

It was sufficient light to allow her to see neatly laid-out rows of stacked clothes. Clearly, this is where the group had removed and stored their garments. But she had no idea where the people had gone after they had disrobed.

As her eyes further adjusted to the dim light, she could see a part of the wall that looked different from the others. She walked to the wall and pressed her hands against it. She heard a rumbling sound as she pushed. The thick wall rotated, revealing a tunnel. She couldn't see its end. Again, compartments lined the tunnel walls. Every few yards, more candles lit the way.

A feeling of increased physical and mental strength surged through her. "I can do this," she whispered. "I can go on ahead."

The tunnel was constructed of concrete, and it sloped downward. She followed it until she reached a series of steps. She briefly hesitated. Then she re-gained her courage and followed the tunnel deeper and deeper into the Earth. Soon she discovered that it led to a natural limestone cavern. She stopped to take in the enormity of the cavern. It was then that she heard the familiar chanting coming from even deeper yet. The lighted candles marked the pathway toward the voices. Without the candles, she was sure she would lose her way.

She followed the candlelight for what seemed like a mile. The tunnel seemed to slant downward, going deeper and deeper. Finally, she saw a red glow. It appeared to come from something growing on the walls. It provided enough illumination to show her the way. She rounded a corner and gasped in astonishment – here before her was a gigantic limestone cave.

Limestone caves weren't new to her. As a teenager, she had accompanied her parents to Branson, Missouri. They had spent a day at Silver Dollar City. In the amusement park, she had taken a tour of Marvel Cave, the deepest and largest cave in the state of Missouri. That cave was big, but this one was at least three times as large.

She figured that the Cowboys Stadium in Dallas could fit inside the cavern with room to spare. She could detect some spots of the red growth on the ceiling high above her.

She remembered that the guide had said that caves like this were more than a million years old. This one was perhaps a thousand feet below the surface of those rolling hills to the southeast of Sarday's school. Certainly a cave of this size would have been marked on a map of the commonwealth, but she had never heard of it before. Perhaps it was still unknown to the general public.

Now she could see some people gathered in the distance. It looked like about forty people, perhaps those selected for the first tier. They were naked, kneeling before a stone altar.

Under normal circumstances, she might have been afraid, but the coke had given her unbridled courage. She walked fearlessly forward. With each step, more details became apparent. The altar was about four feet wide, maybe eight feet long and probably three feet high. She could make out the thick figure of George Sarday, wearing a monk-like black-hooded robe.

Two naked black men stood next to Sarday. She recognized one. It was that Oscar Jalah, Sarday's chief assistant. The other man was young, perhaps fifteen or sixteen. To the right of the men, she could see a stone wall. She had to squint her eyes and hold absolutely still to identify the objects on top of the wall. To her horror, she saw two human heads, one black and one white. Their vacant eyeballs seemed to focus directly on her.

"Fake stage props," she said to herself. Then she laughed, "Like salt and pepper shakers."

It was then she heard the drumbeat, like the sound of a human heart beating at one-second intervals. The drumbeat slowed and another man came forward, carrying an object about three feet tall. He gently placed the object on the ground directly in front of the altar. The man then placed a large wooden bowl at the foot of the object, equidistant between the object and the altar. Then the man moved to the right and stood next to Jalah and the teenager.

Jilly focused on the object. It appeared to be about three feet tall. The naked form was obviously male. She guessed it was very old. One leg was missing, and a metal shaft supported the body. The head was disproportionately large; yet, the body was like that of a dwarf. Two horns stuck out on either side of the head. The face had large eye ridges, like some prehistoric man. Large buckteeth poked out from the grinning mouth. The eyes were blank, with no pupils.

Jilly felt somewhat dizzy. Her head was spinning. She sat down on a large stone. If she was to figure out what was happening, she had to control her own body.

She looked up in time to see two men grab the teenager by the arms and escort him to the altar. After a brief hesitation and some prodding by the men, the young man climbed up to the altar and knelt facing the statue. Then he lay face down, staring into the eyes of the statue. The men pulled him forward by the armpits so that his head hung over the edge of the altar. For some reason, the teenager kept his head up and kept looking into the statue's eyes.

The chanting continued, louder than before. Dr. Sarday himself stepped forward to the right of the altar. From beneath his robes, he withdrew a sword just like the one he had used to behead the goat only two weeks earlier. The polished metal of the sharpened blade glistened in the red light. Sarday raised the sword high over his head. The drumbeat reached a crescendo that echoed off the cavern's walls and shook the ground beneath her. Then it suddenly ceased. The sword dropped toward the teenager's slender neck.

To Jilly, it all seemed to happen in slow motion. She wondered if the coke had affected her ability to judge time. The blade sliced the back of the young man's neck, severing the spinal column as if it were nothing more than soft butter. It continued to slice through the muscles and flesh and separated the head from the quivering body. The lifeless head fell forward. It seemed to float slowly toward the wooden bowl positioned at the statue's feet. It landed with a thump, like a ripened gourd thrown on a stone floor.

A spray of red mist shot from the headless corpse as the lungs expelled their remaining air, and the body contracted in massive shock. The arteries continued to pump blood from the heart. It continued its useless mission, unaware of the fatal trauma to its host. At first, the blood spurted well over three feet from the body, much of it showering the statue in red fluid. The statue's face continued to grin and leer at the teenager's decapitated body. The blood pressure dropped to zero, yet the vital liquid continued to drain from the body and pool on the altar floor before running in droplets down the edge of the platform.

Suddenly, static electricity arced throughout the cavern. Then Sarday, in his black robe, seemed to undergo a change. Instead of the man, she saw a horned creature standing above it all. It held the bloody sword in its claws.

Jilly had seen enough. She closed her eyes, trying to blank out the horror she had just witnessed. When she opened her eyes, she was once again back in the concrete tunnel.

"Good God!" she exclaimed. Was this for real or was it another nightmare?

She took one more intense look back at the gory scene. No, it was real, very real.

She ran back through the long tunnel until she finally reached the basement. Breathing heavily, she climbed the stairs and emerged once again in the kitchen.

The house remained as still and quiet as a tomb. She walked directly through the reception room, out the front door, down the steps and up to the driver's side of the senator's Mercedes. The keys were still in the ignition. She pumped the gas and peeled out of the driveway, spewing bits of gravel as she raced toward the gate. She slowed to a crawl when the guardhouse came into view.

"Good evening, Miss Morrison," said the guard.

"Hi," said Jilly, struggling to contain her fear. "Say, do you know if the Walgreens is open all night?"

"I believe so," answered the guard.

"Great! Senator Carlson feels like he's getting a cold and wants me to buy some decongestant. I'll be back in twenty minutes."

The guard pressed a hand-held control, and the heavy gate rolled open. She proceeded to exit the plantation grounds. Everything in her wanted to floorboard the vehicle and put the grotesque events far behind her. But she held her emotions in check. She drove slowly along the paved roadway. Once she reached the main highway, she punched the gas pedal to the floor and the sedan shot forward.

"Oh, my God! Oh, my God!" she sobbed, nearly out of control. The tears ran in streaks down her cheeks. This wasn't what she wanted. It was all just supposed to be fun. It had been cool to be involved with the senator, and she loved the mystery of Dacari Mucomba. But now her head was filled with the horror of all the blood and that evil thing by the altar.

She had to get away and get away fast. Her first thought was to drive all night and get home to the comfort of her mother's house. Her hands gripped the steering wheel; her knuckles turned white. The car rocketed down the road.

The crash happened so quickly. She had no time to react. The road had curved to the right. She tried to hit the brakes. The brake pedal went to the floor as the anti-lock braking system struggled to slow the vehicle.

The curve came up too fast. The car shot off the road and thundered through a field. She caught a brief glimpse of a large oak ahead of her. She screamed. The front bumper slammed into the tree. The air bags deployed.

Jelly lost consciousness. She was totally unaware whether she was dying or still clinging to life.

47

At Bishop's house the incessant ringing of the phone brought the
police chief out of a fitful sleep.

As HE REACHED FOR THE PHONE, HE LOOKED AT THE CLOCK. IT WAS
2:10 a.m.

"Hello?" Bishop muttered, as he fumbled for the light switch. He
put one hand over his eyes as he waited for his vision to adjust to the
sudden light.

"Chief, Jim Bradley here. We got a situation down here at the station."

"What's up, Officer Bradley?" Bishop asked.

"I've got a woman in the holding cell. She just drove a Mercedes into
a tree out on Old Quarry Road."

"Was she injured?" asked Bishop.

"Not really, the air bags gave her a couple of black eyes. She's stoned,
claimed she had snorted cocaine."

"Any ID?" asked Bishop.

"That's why I calling, Chief. She had no ID on her, but says she
works for Senator Carlson. I ran the plates, and the car's registered to the
senator."

"Well, go ahead and book her. We can talk to her tomorrow."

"Ah, Chief, there's something else. She claims someone was killed up
at that school."

"Sarday's school?" asked Bishop, suddenly alert. "I'll be right down."

Bishop rolled out of bed, grabbed his jeans and began to pull them
up to his waist.

Ann rolled over, still half asleep. "Any problem?" she asked.

"I don't know, I really don't know. I need to go down to the station." He pulled on his shirt and slipped his feet into his sneakers. He strapped on his Glock, grabbed his badge, and headed to the kitchen.

He needed a quick wake-up. He spooned a heaping tablespoon of instant coffee into mug and added water. Two minutes in the microwave should be enough, he figured. When the bell dinged, he reached for a potholder and carefully set the bubbling beverage on the counter.

"Whew, too hot," he mumbled. Maybe a cooler would help, he reasoned. He poured in a shot of Jim Beam. He added a touch more just for the heck of it.

It was still too hot to drink, but he'd be able to sip it on his way to town. He poured his special brew into an insulated cup and capped it with a lid.

As he drove to the station, he felt pleasantly alert and ready to ask questions about this alleged homicide. Someone killed at that school? Wouldn't he ever love to nail that Sarday on a murder charge. You betcha he would.

Bishop had expected to see Bradley's cruiser in the staff lot. He was surprised to see that it was gone. Perhaps Bradley had resumed his regular patrol. On weekday nights, usually only one man was on duty. Bishop reached for his keys and unlocked the door. Once inside, he headed directly for the holding cells.

Johnsonville didn't have a real jail. They got by with three holding cells, each with a bed, toilet and sink. People who were to be incarcerated for any length of time were transported to the Augusta County facility.

He unlocked the door that secured access to the holding cells. A young woman stood in the first cell. She didn't move, even when Bishop opened the door. She just stared at the wall.

"Miss, I'm Chief Bishop."

The woman screamed and backed up against the wall.

Wow, she must really be blown out of her mind, Bishop thought. He decided to do his questioning right there in the cell. Then she wouldn't try to run.

"Easy, Miss, I'm not going to hurt you."

"I've got to get out of here. He will kill me," she said, clearly panicked.

"Who will kill you?" Bishop asked.

"The Devil," she answered.

"The Devil?" asked Bishop.

"Yes, Dr. Sarday. He is the Devil. I saw him change tonight."

"Where did you see this happen?" asked Bishop.

"In the cavern," she answered.

"What cavern?"

"The one hidden under the house."

"Miss, I'm not sure I understand what you're saying," Bishop replied.

"It's Jilly. Jilly Morrison is my name."

"OK, Jilly, why don't you tell me what happened."

Bishop convinced the woman to sit still on the edge of the cot. He sat across from her on a stool. For the next twenty minutes the young woman rambled on about crazy cult things, chicken and goat sacrifices, and mystery spirits. Bishop listened half-heartedly. He had already decided that she was under the influence of some kind of hallucinogenic drug.

She got even weirder when she began talking about two human heads severed from their bodies, one of a white male and one of a black male. She also gave details of a human sacrifice she had allegedly witnessed.

By now, Bishop was certain that he had a real wacko at the station. He sighed. He'd give her one more chance.

"Could you describe the person who was killed?"

"He was young and black," she said. "Maybe fourteen or fifteen." Jilly's jaw was working on her knuckle. She stared out into the hallway, oblivious to the heavy bars that kept her inside. Bishop had the impression that she wasn't entirely aware of his presence.

"Were there any distinguishing marks on the man who was killed?"

"Well, his thing was pretty big," answered Jilly.

Bishop covered his forehead with his hand. Is this ever a waste of time, he thought.

She continued to chatter on and on. Bishop was just about to call it quits, but then she offered up a gem.

"He didn't have a hand," she said.

"What?" screamed Bishop. "What are you saying?"

"I said it was big," she said, frowning. "Well, it *was* big," she said again.

"No, what did you say about his hand?"

"Oh, yeah. His left hand was missing. It just ended at the wrist," she said.

"Kevin Williams…," said Bishop, his words trailing off as he remembered the boy's mother.

Jilly shook her head. "What? What do you mean?"

"I mean that his name was Kevin Williams," Bishop told her.

He stood up, ready to leave. Instead, he turned to the woman. "Jilly, I am going to get Judge Casey. Then I'm going to come back here. I want you to tell him this same story. Do you understand?"

"Yes, but I'm still afraid that Devil will get me," she answered, a look of anxiety crossing her face. She trembled with fear.

"No, Jilly, no he won't. You're safely locked in here," Bishop told her. "I'll be right back."

The chief rushed out the front door and jumped into his cruiser. He left two hundred-foot streaks of rubber as he accelerated out of the parking lot on his way to the judge's house.

He would need to get a search warrant to get on the school grounds. From the weapons he'd already seen there, he'd have to ask the county's SWAT team to serve the warrant.

Bishop punched the steering wheel with both hands. "Damn, damn," he said with a sigh. Sadly, he wouldn't be bringing Kevin Williams home alive. But he would nail that asshole Sarday. With any luck, he'd also make the mayor look like a fool.

When he got to Casey's house, he walked up to the front door and knocked hard. He glanced at his watch. It was 3:30 in the morning. The judge wasn't going to be happy about his early-morning visitor. Bishop could have waited if he had wanted to. But time was the enemy here. The longer he waited, the greater the chance would be that Sarday's men would dispose of the body and do all they could to hide any evidence.

Bishop saw a light come on in the living room. Then the porch light clicked on. Inside, someone pulled the drapes open slightly and peered out. Bishop waved at the window. He heard the dead bolt disengage. The door swung open.

"Chief Bishop, what the hell are you doing here at this hour?"

Judge Casey's red hair was mussed up. He had on a navy blue terry cloth robe tied loosely at his waist. He was a stocky man with a booming voice. He had a reputation as one of the toughest judges in the state. The cops loved him because they knew he was a man they could depend on to get the job done.

"Sir, I need a search warrant for a possible homicide at Sarday's compound," Bishop said.

"What happened?" asked the judge.

"Sir, I have a witness down at the station. You'll need to talk to her," Bishop explained.

"This better be good," growled Casey. "I'll get dressed and follow you down in my car."

Bishop returned to his car and waited. He checked his watch and continued to wait. He finished his cold coffee. A good forty minutes had elapsed. What in the hell is taking him so long, Bishop asked himself. Maybe he's taking a dump, he reasoned. It better have been one huge dump.

Finally, the garage door opened, and the judge backed his car into the driveway. Bishop led the way. He wanted to race back to the station and get on with the job, but he held the cruiser at the speed limit. When they reached the station, Bishop got out and unlocked the door. They walked into the office together.

"She's in the first holding cell," Bishop told him.

"Who is this person?" Casey asked.

"Her name is Jill Morrison. She's one of Senator Carlson's interns," Bishop said.

"Allan Carlson? You say you have one of Allan Carlson's interns in our jail?" he asked. "By God, Bishop, this had better be on the level, or I'll have your ass!"

"Sir, I assure you that once you hear her story, you'll understand how urgent this is," Bishop answered, hoping the judge would realize the seriousness of the allegations.

Bishop unlocked the door leading to the holding cells. The judge followed close behind.

"What the hell?" gasped Bishop. The cells, every single one of them, were empty.

"OK, Bishop, where is this Morrison woman?" the judge demanded. His face was turning nearly as red as his hair.

"Well, they must have moved her to the county jail," answered Bishop, his concern growing. "Uh, let me get Officer Bradley on the radio."

Bishop went out into the office and put in the call. "Base to Car 7, Base to Car 7. Over?"

"Base, this is 7."

"Jim, this is Chief Bishop. Did you take that woman from cell one into county?"

"What woman?" asked Bradley.

"That woman involved in the car wreck out on Old Quarry Road," Bishop said, getting irritated.

"Chief, there wasn't any car wreck out on Old Quarry Road tonight."

"Don't tell me that, Bradley!" Bishop yelled. "You called me at home and told me about the accident. You said you had a woman in the holding cell. I talked to her about an hour and a half ago right back there in that cell!"

"Chief, I never called you on the phone," Bradley said, speaking softly and slowly.

"Goddamn it, Bradley. You get over here right now," ordered Bishop.

"Chief, I can't do that. I'm backing up the county sheriff in a domestic hostage situation. I'm over in Cumberland, blocking off the road to the housing area. I've been here for three hours. Chief, I swear to God I never called you."

Bishop stood silently, holding the radio mike.

"Chief, are you still there?" asked Bradley.

Bishop turned to Judge Casey.

"Judge, I don't know what to say."

"Well, I know what to say," screamed Casey. He was so angry that he was nearly out of control. "You're through, Bishop. I don't know what kind of sick joke this is, but I can assure you that nobody gets me out of bed for crap like this. You've been drinking. I can smell it on your breath."

"I'm not drunk, Judge Casey. I'm telling you that someone has been killed at that school," argued Bishop.

"Well, in my opinion, someone doesn't reek of whiskey at three o'clock in the morning unless he's drunk!"

Casey turned and walked out of the police station, slamming the door as he left. Bishop was left standing by the desk, still holding the mike in his hand.

48

Alone at his desk at the station, Bishop was stymied.

"SHIT, I HAVE NO IDEA WHERE TO GO FROM HERE," BISHOP SAID OUT loud as he sat at his desk, staring at his computer screen.

It was three o'clock in the afternoon. His brain had gone completely blank. When Judge Casey had stormed out of the station in the early morning hours, Bishop's first thought was to drive out to the hostage crisis situation in Cumberland and drag Patrolman Jim Bradley out of his car and beat the holy shit out of the lying son of a bitch.

Not a good idea, he told himself. Instead, he got into his car and drove out to Old Quarry Road.

No surprise. He couldn't see a wrecked Mercedes anywhere. He got out of his car and walked slowly through the field, looking for evidence. If the car had really been there, he should be able to find something. He retraced his steps, this time taking particular care to check for damage to the oak trees. All of them had been hit at one time or another, but who knows when and by what. Bishop noted the ruts in the soft earth of the field. That didn't mean anything. Off-roaders liked to do wheelies in the grass.

Next, he drove out to the school and parked where he could observe the gate. He saw two uniformed guards. They seemed at ease. There appeared to be no need for additional security.

Then he heard his stomach rumble. He hadn't eaten since dinner the night before. You can't count spiked coffee as much of a meal. He abandoned his search and drove up to Jerry's for a late – really late – breakfast.

A flood of questions ran through his thoughts. Was he being set up? Was someone trying to play some sort of a sick joke on him? That Morrison woman was clearly upset. Sure, she was under the influence of drugs, but how on earth would she have ever known about Kevin's missing hand? Then, how in the world would she have been able to escape from that holding cell? Maybe Judge Casey himself was involved. Is that why he took so long to get dressed?

Bishop had called Ann before she left for work. He asked her to check phone messages on their caller ID. There should be a number listed from that call from Patrolman Bradley. One call had come in from an unlisted number. That couldn't prove that Bradley had made the call.

He wondered how he could verify that Jill Morrison had ever been taken in and locked in that holding cell.

His questions ceased momentarily. He had a chilling thought that maybe he had just dreamed that he had ever spoken with her.

The only things he could be certain of were that there had been a call to the house in the middle of the night. He did go into the station. And he did piss off Judge Casey – that clearly was no dream.

He asked for his bill and paid it with his credit card. He felt a little better now that he had eaten, at least physically. Mentally and emotionally, he was a tangle of nerves and scared shitless.

Let's take it one step at a time, he told himself. His professional training kicked in and gave him something positive to do.

Back at the office, Bishop wrote down everything he could remember from the early-morning incident. He listed the details of the interview with Jilly. He re-read it several times, adding more details as they came to mind. In a separate column, he wrote a list of facts based on the interview.

She had seen someone killed, beheaded by a sword. The description of the victim matched that of Kevin Williams. The incident took place in an underground cavern, accessed through a tunnel under the Johnson Plantation mansion. She saw two human heads, one of a white man and one of a black man. She claimed to be an employee in Senator Carlson's office.

Start at the top, taking the easy ones first, Bishop reminded himself. He put in a call to the senator's office in Washington, D.C. Yes, Jill

Morrison did work for the senator. Yes, Carlson was currently out of town in Charlottesville, a short drive from Johnsonville.

He called the Virginia Department of Natural Resources. Yes, there were underground caves in the area around Johnsonville, but they had no information about one near Johnsonville itself. However, the clerk had said, the commonwealth had at least four thousand known caves. Every so often, someone would report finding a new one. The only way that Bishop could prove that one existed was to search the actual plantation. It seemed unlikely that he'd be able to find the cavern, much less the body of Kevin Williams.

The Morrison woman had said she had seen two human heads. He gave that a little additional thought. One was Caucasian, she had told him. Were there any missing white men recently? He pulled up the missing persons report for the previous six months. He found nothing there.

He then remembered that terrible accident where three teenagers were killed in the truck fire about two months before. He put in a call to the county coroner's office and asked them to FAX the reports to him. He slowly went over the reports, checking line-by-line. The fire had been so intense that the coroner could only use dental records to make positive ID's. That had worked for two of the bodies. The third one had to be identified circumstantially.

Bishop wanted more details. He put in a call to the coroner himself. He was told that one victim had been so badly burned and the fire so intense that only part of the torso remained. Since the positive ID's were for Billy Joe Nelson and Johnny Butler, two of the victims, the third victim had been identified by process of elimination as TJ Roberts. No one took DNA samples. The case was closed.

Bishop rocked back in his chair and placed his hands behind his neck. He stared at the ceiling as if he could find the answers written high above his head. No luck. He stood up, hiked up his jeans and wandered to the break room and poured himself a cup of strong coffee.

The black juice got his mind going again. Could the third body have been mistakenly identified? Maybe TJ Roberts had been killed just like Kevin had been killed. Maybe it was his head that Jilly had seen. Maybe the torso had been that of Randy Parker, the black kid who had disappeared earlier in the year.

He shook his head. All this is just speculation, he told himself.

Bishop decided to take another approach. He sat back down at his computer and entered the name "George Nah Sarday" in the Google search box. He got thirty hits. He scrolled down to the list and found something written four years earlier in Liberia. It was a court document that included witness testimony from the trials held after the coup that overthrew President Dowling. The witness reported that a number of government employees allegedly had been involved in human sacrifices. One of those officials was a George Nah Sarday. Apparently, the new government didn't have enough evidence to extradite the bastard back to Liberia.

Another dead end, Bishop thought.

Without a doubt, a murder had been committed on the plantation. But Bishop had nothing solid to go on. If he could find Jill Morrison, then he'd have an actual witness. But it might be impossible to locate her. He was pretty sure that whoever got her out of the holding cell, cleaned up the car wreck, and bribed an officer would not allow her to live to tell her story.

His train of thought was interrupted by a knock on his office door.

"Yes," Bishop said.

The door opened slowly and the receptionist leaned in. "The mayor is here to see you, Chief," she said.

Oh, shit, Bishop thought. He guessed that the mayor had talked to the judge. That was just what he didn't need now.

He scooped up the reports and his notes and shoved it into a desk drawer. He shut down the computer. He figured that he would just tell the mayor that someone had tried to play a trick on him. He would apologize for getting Judge Casey involved. He wouldn't tell him of his suspicions about human sacrifices at Sarday's school – not until he had a hell of a lot more proof.

Bishop stood and had begun to walk around his desk to answer the door when it opened on its own. The mayor walked right in. Two "suits" followed immediately behind him. They looked and smelled like FBI.

"Good afternoon, Mayor," said Bishop.

"These men want to talk to you," said Bradley, without offering any sort of a greeting or stating the purpose of the visit.

"Chief Bishop, I'm Special Agent Anderson, and this is Special Agent Dunn," Anderson said as he flashed his badge and extended his hand. Bishop shook hands with both men.

"How can I help you, gentlemen?" he said. He glanced past them and saw Bradley still standing by the open door, smiling like a Cheshire cat.

"Chief, we're currently following up on a major drug bust at the University of Virginia. It involves millions of dollars and a flow of drugs from Mexico to D.C. It appears that a lot of the traffic is being funneled through smaller cities like Johnsonville," Anderson explained.

"I have had no indication of that going on here," answered Bishop.

"Well, the reason you haven't is because our informant said the police in Johnsonville are being paid off," chimed in Dunn.

Bishop hesitated, unable to believe the accusations he was hearing. He didn't say anything at first. Instead, his mind was racing. Sure, he thought. Jim Bradley is the mayor's nephew, and there's a very strong possibility that Sarday's involved with drug trafficking too.

Bishop hid his shocking conclusion. He kept his professional cool.

"So, did the informant provide a name?" Bishop asked.

"You," said Anderson, searching Bishop's face for a guilty reaction.

"What? What are you saying? Is this some kind of a joke?" he said, just about knocked off his feet with the enormity of the accusation.

"No, Chief, this is no joke," Anderson replied. "Our informant indicated that you are the point of contact here in Johnsonville."

"That's ridiculous, totally ridiculous!" Bishop said. "What kind of proof do you have?"

"Well, we have reason to believe that more than a quarter of a million dollars has been paid out to you by dealers."

"That's a laugh," Bishop said, glaring at the agent. "Other than our mutual funds and my wife's retirement fund through the commonwealth, we have less than ten thousand in our savings."

"Don't worry, Chief. We'll be checking that out," Anderson said.

"But we do need to ask you a few questions," Dunn said

"Go right ahead. I don't have anything to hide."

"First off, why did you order a special pursuit cruiser last year?" Dunn continued.

"I like fast cars," Bishop answered honestly.

"Did the city council give its approval?" Dunn asked.

"I guess so," answered Bishop. This time they might have tripped him up. He did slip that pursuit cruiser into the order package and hadn't told anybody. He did have a quick reply. "Well, having a special pursuit cruiser on the force doesn't make me a drug dealer."

"Well, maybe not," said Anderson with a grin. "But having an unmarked fast pursuit car seems strange for a small town police force."

Dunn looked at his notes. He wanted to be sure to be accurate in his questioning. "Now let's talk about your personal cars. You own four collectable cars, three Corvettes and a Sunbeam Tiger. They are insured for a total of a quarter of a million dollars."

"Wait a minute here," Bishop broke in. "I've owned two of those cars for more than twenty years."

"All right, Chief, that may be true, but right now, you are a person of interest in this investigation," Dunn said, closing his notebook.

"Another thing, Bishop," added Anderson, dropping a card with his name and contact numbers. "We will be going over your tax returns and other financial records. You are advised not to leave the country and you will report to us at the FBI regional office in Charlottesville any time you intend to leave Johnsonville."

Bishop was totally dumbfounded by this incredible turn of events.

"Bishop," said the mayor importantly, "as mayor, I am putting you on administrative leave until this matter is resolved. I want your badge, service weapon and the keys to the cruiser."

"Wait! You can't do that," argued Bishop.

"Yes, he can and should," interrupted Anderson.

"One more thing," said Dunn. "You will have no contact with any members of this or any other law enforcement agency during the course of this investigation. You will not discuss this action with anyone else with the exception of your attorney. Do you understand what I am saying?"

"Yes," Bishop answered.

"Should you violate this directive, you will be incarcerated," said Anderson.

Bishop dropped his badge and his Glock on the desk. He reached into his pocket and pulled out the keys to the cruiser. He dropped them on the desk and slid them next to the badge and gun.

"We can drive you home," Anderson volunteered.

"Never mind," Bishop said. "I can go over to the middle school and use my wife's car." Bishop had had enough. He stormed out of the office, walked quickly through the squad room and then out the side door. It seemed that everyone followed him with their accusing eyes as far as they could see. He picked up his pace as he headed west down Johnsonville Avenue to the middle school.

He couldn't help but wonder if all this were somehow connected to what had happened in the middle of the night. A feeling of dread passed through his mind. He stopped short of crossing the street. Instead, he turned left and headed toward First Federal Bank.

Bishop took a place in line and waited his turn to speak with the teller. He handed her his ID and a withdrawal slip.

"I'd like to withdraw three thousand dollars from my savings account," Bishop said, passing the paper under the window.

"How would you like that?" she asked.

"Hundred-dollar bills will be fine," he answered. "Oh, and one more thing: Could you let me know the remaining balance after the withdrawal?"

"Of course, sir," she answered. Then she counted out the three thousand and wrote the remaining balance on a piece of paper. Bishop put the money directly into his wallet, folded up the piece of paper and slid it into his pocket.

As soon as he was outside, he pulled the slip of paper from his pocket and unfolded it. "Oh, God, are we ever screwed!" he muttered.

The account balance read $357,208.15. Just a month ago, he and Ann had passed the ten thousand dollar mark. He had never had so much money in any kind of a bank account. Once the FBI checked his accounts, all their money would be frozen, and he'd be put under arrest.

What could he do now? His life was over.

49

Finding a secluded spot on the forty-acre grounds of the plantation hadn't been difficult.

IF ANYONE HAD BOTHERED TO ASK ANY OF THE THIRTY-NINE OTHER acolytes, they all would have agreed that Dwain was as gay as they come. Well, make that thirty-eight. Trisha knew different.

She was lying naked beside him on a wool blanket. They had spread it out under the leafy oak trees on the hillside overlooking the pavilion. Trisha could testify that this guy really liked sex with women. At least, he seemed to have been more than satisfied during the last half hour he had spent with her. Both of them had fallen into an exhausted slumber.

Since the nights had started to get warmer, this was the fourth time they had crept out of the dormitories, once the old slave quarters, and engaged in robust sex. Trisha was a great lay. She was as tall as he was, long-legged and had small, firm breasts. During sex, she would wrap her legs around his waist and dig her fingers into his back. Of course, the fact that Dr. Sarday strictly prohibited sexual relations between the acolytes made the romps even sweeter.

Once the lanterns were extinguished at eleven o'clock, Dwain and Trish would wait anxiously until one o'clock. Then each of them would sneak out of their respective dorms and meet behind the latrines. Under cover of darkness, they would climb the hill, making their path through the low shrubs and find their special place overlooking the pavilion.

During the day, the acolytes were given the freedom to wander around the compound at will. Dwain had discovered a small clearing hidden in the leafy woods where they could be hidden from view. As long as she didn't moan with too much pleasure, Dwain was confident they wouldn't be disturbed. Tonight's full moon allowed Dwain to more fully appreciate the beautiful young body beside him.

They lay side-by-side, recovering from a particularly athletic coupling. It gave him a chance to think about where he was and what he was doing with his life. He wasn't totally convinced he liked this acolyte thing, but it beat the living conditions he used to have. He'd put in almost a year now. Like other acolytes, he didn't have a last name anymore. No one did. When they came to this school, they were instructed to forget their past lives.

That was totally fine with Dwain. His past life wasn't anything to brag about. When he was just twelve years old, his mother, a single parent, died of cancer. The state, in its infinite wisdom, had placed him at the Boys' Ranch, a Catholic-run home for boys with no next of kin.

He hadn't been on the ranch for more than a week when an old priest came into his room and climbed into bed with him. The first time the old man did it to him, Dwain wanted to die. Later, the priest had broken down in tears and begged Dwain's forgiveness. The next night the son of a bitch came back for more. The next day, Dwain walked out of Boys' Ranch and never looked back.

For five years he had lived on the streets, finding food in trashcans behind supermarkets and fast food joints. Sometimes he had to resort to stealing just to survive. At some point, he had figured out that some old farts had an appetite for young, light-skinned black kids. Even as a teenager, Dwain had looked younger than his actual age. These old dudes would pay well for the quality service he provided.

It was a dangerous life, and some of the dirty old men were sadistic in what they did to him. One time, a john had seriously hurt him. While the guy slept, Dwain had picked up a table lamp and beat the guy to death. He had ripped off the guy's wallet. That didn't last long. He had to use his cash to pay off the bill for his own treatment in the emergency room. His injuries kept him "unemployed" for four months. That's when he really perfected his talents for petty theft.

Last year, when he was seventeen, Dr. Sarday found him. Actually, Dr. Sarday was a pretty good customer. He had paid him for sex, then gave him a thousand bucks and told him that he could leave his life on the streets and find harmony at The School for West African Spiritual Studies as an acolyte.

Dwain didn't want to face more time on the streets. Joining Sarday's little business made it an easy decision. Sarday had a mesmerizing impact on so many of them. But now, over the last few months, Dwain wasn't sure that becoming a member of Dacari Mucomba was all that it was cracked up to be.

"Dwain, we need to get back," whispered Trisha. Dwain reached over and pinched a nipple.

"Sure you don't want to do it again?" he asked smiling.

She giggled. "There are more nights, and we don't want to wear it out."

She stood up and picked up her white gown and let it slip over her head. Dwain sighed, pulled on his own gown, stepped into his sneakers, and rolled up the blanket.

They headed back, walking hand in hand. Dwain came to a sudden stop.

"What's that?" he asked.

"What's what?" asked Trish.

"Shush! Listen!" he said.

They heard someone scream. Then there was shouting. More screaming.

"Come on, let's see what's going on," Dwain said. They moved cautiously through the trees, staying in the shadows wherever possible.

"What the hell?" remarked Dwain.

A group of people stood closely together on the lawn in front of the main house. The moonlight allowed Dwain and Trish to see that they were all acolytes, all people they knew. A dozen guards surrounded them. Four of the guards held back German shepherd dogs that yapped and strained against their masters who fought to hold them back on heavy leather leashes. The acolytes cowered together, all looking scared and confused.

Suddenly, the double front doors opened and out stepped Dr. Sarday, a huge figure. He stopped momentarily in the framed doorway. A light from inside made the mere man look like a mythical figure, back lit from inside the imposing mansion.

He raised his right arm. Silence fell over the group. Even the dogs stood at attention and ceased barking.

"My children," he said. The voice had a strange effect on the crowd. Instead of coming from the man's lips, the words seemed to exist inside each of their heads. Even Dwain felt himself drawn to the man. But Sarday's voice trick didn't work for long on Dwain. Here they stood apart from the group. They were too far away to pick up on the communal impact. It seemed as if Sarday were trying to hypnotize them from across a wide street.

Sarday's melodic words rolled on.

"It will soon be time when you all will become one with Dacari Mucomba. You must now relax. You will follow each other as you begin your journey to the next phase in the release of your spirit. Come, my children, we go now to the chamber where you will prepare yourselves for the transformation."

Sarday turned and walked back inside the mansion. Meekly, the acolytes followed, one behind the other in single file.

Dwain blinked. The first urge he had to follow had completely vanished. He looked up to see Trisha emerge from the woods and walk toward the house to take her place in line. Dwain grabbed her arm and pulled her back.

"What happened?" she asked. She appeared confused.

"I don't know, but I don't like it," Dwain said as he dragged her back into the shelter of the trees.

For Dwain, the strange willingness he had experienced to follow Sarday had completely disappeared.

"Dwain," Trisha begged, "we need to go back. Dr. Sarday wants us to go with him!"

"No, it's you who doesn't understand. Think about it, Trish. Why did the guards drag everyone out? They could have just announced at dinner that we were to go into the house afterwards. Why would they need those dogs? We need to get out of here right now!" he insisted.

"How? There's a fence all around the place," said Trisha.

"I know," he replied, "but the inner fence is only six feet high with no razor wire on top. We can easily climb it. When I was out walking yesterday, I saw a place where a tree had fallen across the outside fence, crushing the razor wire. We can get over the fence right there. Come on, quick. Once they find that we're missing, they'll come after us."

They took off, heading back over the hill toward the south side of the property. They both were breathing heavily now. They had been jogging for about ten minutes.

"Hurry up!" said Dwain. They could hear the barking dogs draw closer and closer.

They broke into a run. They pushed through the woods and came out next to the fence line. It was easy to see. The moonlight made it stand out sharply. Dwain looked for the place where that tree had knocked down the fence.

"There!" he called to Trisha. "There!" he shouted, pointing ahead.

Just as his last words passed his lips, he glanced back and saw a large dog making a beeline towards them.

"Run! Just run, run," he panted. He knew that he would have no problem clearing the six-foot fence. He'd had plenty of experience running away from the cops when he was homeless.

When he reached the fence, he poked his fingers through the thick wire and grabbed tightly. As soon as his fingers came in contact with the metal fence, he saw a bright flash.

"What?" he said. But his mind wasn't able to process what had happened to him as the five thousand volts surged through him, bringing instant death.

His body fell to the ground, his flesh smoldering.

Trisha screamed and veered away from the fence, running as fast as she could. She dared to look back to see if she had escaped the dogs' gaping jaws. She was fast, but not fast enough.

The first dog on her closed its jaw around her right ankle, snapping the bone as she fell headlong into the grass. The others joined in their mad victory. Her screams echoed through the nearby hills and then ceased.

Then the only audible sounds were low growls and the ripping of tender flesh.

50

In his den at home in Johnsonville, the city's infamous chief of police struggled to open his eyes.

BISHOP HAD A SPLITTING HEADACHE. HE FELT LIKE HE WAS ABOUT TO barf his guts out.

"Where in the hell am I?"

He shouldn't have bothered to ask. He'd figure it out eventually. Maybe.

He finally managed to get both eyes to open simultaneously. He stared at the large, flat-screen TV. Although it didn't make any sound, he recognized one of his old buddies, that guy with the white hair from CNN. Almost every day, he and the guy had a TV date. Bishop knew who he was, but the guy had no idea that Bishop even existed.

"Oh, yeah, now I get it," he said. He was at home, sitting in his very own man cave.

He looked around the den as if it were the very first time he'd ever been there. He glanced at the wall on his right. He saw a row of photos taken during his career in the military police. Under the pictures, a display case held a slew of medals that he had earned during his twenty years of honorable service. On the left, he glanced over at his desk, piled high with unfiled papers. Not that they needed to be filed; most of them could just be shredded or tossed in the recycling. He'd do it when he got around to it.

The digital clock above the desk showed the time in red, fine-lined numbers – it was 3:15 a.m. He discovered that a ragged blue blanket had been placed over him. Ann must have covered him before she went to bed. He tried to put his feet up on the coffee table, but there wasn't enough room. Beside the remotes, junk mail, and old newspapers piled haphazardly on the table, one item occupied a place of honor. It was an empty bottle of scotch and a glass half full of dark liquid. Both sat at arm's reach, right in front of him.

That gave him a good idea. He reached for the glass and brought it unsteadily to his lips. He took a sip, just a tiny sip. He felt the warm alcohol run into his throat on its way to his gut. Then everything started to revolt inside his stomach.

"Not a good idea," he said as he staggered to the bathroom, a good fifteen paces from his chair. He felt a wave of dizziness come over him. He fell to his knees in front of the toilet and retched. A foul smelling liquid burned his throat and even came out his nose. He vomited until he had nothing left inside to throw up.

Weak and unsteady, he pulled himself up to the bathroom sink. He hung onto its edge until he felt strong enough to try to repair the damage. He wiped his face with a wet hand towel, popped three antacids and swallowed two aspirins. He held onto walls and furniture wherever he could to make his way back to the den. He flopped down in his recliner and held his hands over his eyes.

The money thing had really thrown him for a loop. He had no clue as to what had happened to their bank account. He must have been set up, but by whom and why? The savings account had more than $350,000 in it. Neither he nor Ann had made any deposits. Hell, they didn't have any money to deposit. Who would ever be able to gain access to the account? Who would have that kind of money to throw around?

Questions, questions, questions. All he had were questions – no answers. No answers at all. Bishop rubbed his eyes with his fists, trying to massage his brain into action, but it was all useless, futile and confusing.

The two FBI agents claimed that they had found a witness who would testify that Bishop had been involved in funneling the drugs through Johnsonville. That was just another blow in a string of trouble that had just about done him in.

He had been embarrassed when he had been relieved of his duties as chief of police. He was under investigation for drug dealing and racketeering. That was bad enough, but things had just continued to get worse.

Only two days after he'd been put on administrative leave, the local rag, *The Johnsonville Valley News*, ran a front-page story with the headline reading "Chief of Police Investigated for Dealing Drugs." The article stung, but Martin Noonan's editorial inside hurt even more. In it, Noonan wrote that as of day one when Bishop had first been hired, he had been convinced that the man was a crook. Noonan said he had been surprised that it had taken the higher-ups so long to nail him.

Now, a week into the mess, Ann had been told that the school board was reviewing her position as principal at the junior high. That group of do-gooders didn't want drugs mixing in with their precious pre-teens. Never mind her stellar record. Never mind that no charges had been filed. Whatever happened to "innocent until proven guilty"? To add insult to injury, that buffoon, the superintendant, had told her privately that it would look better on her resume if she resigned rather than be fired by the board.

Money continued to worry him. Their credit cards and bank accounts had been frozen, pending the outcome of the ongoing investigation. Ann couldn't even walk into a grocery store without people staring at her. Some even went out of their way to avoid contact with either of them. The only person who had even spoken to him during the last seven days was his good friend, Dick Raymond, the city engineer.

Even in Bishop's best moments, he could call up the images of that asshole mayor, Harvey Bradley, waving his index finger, accusing him of being nothing but a drunk. He blamed the city council for even hiring Bishop in the first place.

As much as Bradley disgusted him, Bishop had to admit that maybe he had a point. After all, he had been passed over when he thought he'd be promoted to lieutenant colonel. He'd been tactfully asked to retire. He knew that he had been an outstanding officer, but some of his efficiency reports lacked that "special wording" that would have moved him up to a higher grade. Oh, yeah, he remembered one more thing – that incident at the officers' club when he got carried away after one too many drinks.

Didn't everyone drink a little too much now and then? Was he really a drunk? He didn't think so. Sure, he used scotch to calm his nerves and help him unwind after a particularly stressful day. Besides that, he really liked the taste of scotch, and it made him feel good. OK, he had gone overboard in the last few days. Anyone would have, considering the circumstances.

Bishop's stomach had finally settled down. He shifted around the piles on the coffee table to make room for his feet. He stared blankly at the TV. All that vomiting had actually helped. Now he needed to rest and let that alcohol get out of his system. The other thing that always helped get his system back in sync was to go out for a run.

He stood up, now much more steady on his feet. He started to head for the bedroom to retrieve his running shorts and his running shoes. He stopped and reconsidered. He didn't want to wake Ann. She always got too upset when she thought he drank too much. Hell, he was already wearing an old pair of running shoes, his jeans and a T-shirt. He could just wear what he already had on. He took his wallet and keys out of his pockets and laid them on the coffee table. He tried to be quiet as he opened the front door and stepped out on the porch.

Even though it was late at night or early in the morning – he couldn't decide which – it was kind of nice outside. It was a comfortable fifty-five degrees, and the sky was dark, but clear. He noticed the stars that seemed unusually bright. He walked around the cul-de-sac and stopped to do a few stretches. Then he slowly began jogging to Cookingham Road.

The Bishop home was one of three on their road. It connected with Cookingham. It was two and a half miles to Steven's Chicken Farm. Bishop used this five-mile course year-round. On winter mornings, he ran in the dark. Parts of the route had streetlights that helped illuminate his path. The white center line showed up well, even on the darkest nights.

At first, he started off slow, increasing his pace after the first mile. When he got to the chicken farm, he turned around and began running faster yet. A half-mile from their house, Cookingham dropped down into the valley. Now, four and a half miles into it, he actually was feeling quite a bit better. He slowed his pace and decided to walk the last half-mile up the hill.

The silence of those pre-dawn hours seemed to lift his mood. He liked the smell of the fresh country air. He enjoyed listening to the morning sounds of crickets chirping and the occasional barking of dogs.

As Bishop crested the hill, he heard a vehicle coming slowly toward him. He was puzzled. He didn't see any car lights, but there was no doubt that a car or small truck was approaching. He stepped over to the shoulder and hid in the low brush. He watched as the car turned into Eastern Air Park, a small, private airfield down the road from his house. It stopped alongside one of the hangars. He heard doors open and close. He could make out two men. One wore dark slacks and a dark, maybe black, long-sleeved shirt. His shoes were also dark. He had a black ski mask pulled over his head. Bishop's heart seemed to skip a beat when he saw the man pull out a pistol with a silencer on it. He raised his right hand and pretended to shoot.

While the second man stayed with the car, the first one began walking uphill toward the street where Ann was still asleep in the unlocked house. If Bishop was going to do something, he figured he'd better do it quickly. But he was at a disadvantage – he was unarmed. Then he remembered the second man, leaning against the car.

Bishop cautiously crossed the road and sprinted toward the hangar. Staying in the shadows, he slowly moved up, one step at a time, to the other side of the car. When just six feet separated the two, Bishop jumped him, wrapping his right arm around the man's throat in a tight chokehold, cutting off the flow of blood to the man's brain. After a brief struggle, the man crumpled to the ground, unconscious.

The man had been dressed like the first guy, mostly in black. He wore a shoulder holster. Bishop pulled a .40-caliber Glock out of the man's holster. He pulled the slide back to verify that a round was chambered. Without a second to lose, Bishop raced toward his house.

Ann, he thought, my Ann's inside.

When he hit the driveway, he saw that his front door stood wide open. Maybe he was already too late. He moved silently onto the front porch, holding the gun in both hands, the standard police assault procedure. He stepped into the darkened living room. Their bedroom was to the right. He saw that the light spilled from the doorway.

"Where is he, bitch?" shouted the man.

Bishop froze. The man was inside his home, and he was threatening Ann.

"I don't know," sobbed Ann.

"All right, this is going to get nasty. I'm going to shoot you in the right knee. If I don't get the right answer, then I'll shoot the left knee."

"Please," she begged. "I don't know where he is!"

That was enough. Bishop stepped inside the bedroom. Just like he'd done in an FBI assault-training course at Quantico, he quickly sized up the situation. The glow from the overhead light made it all easy to see. Ann was lying on her back on the right side of the bed. The covers had been pulled off. She wore a blue nightgown.

The man in black stood over her, his face hidden by the ski mask. His left hand was positioned on Ann's throat; his right hand held the black automatic pistol, fitted with the long, gray silencer. He pressed the weapon against Ann's knee.

"Are you looking for me, asshole?" Bishop shouted, surprising the assailant. Bishop stood in the doorway, his hands gripping the gun he had taken from the man at the airport.

Harry Anderson had chalked up twenty-seven kills. From experience, he knew that he was better at this game than any of his victims had been. Even threatened by an armed man, most people will hesitate before pulling the trigger. That was just human nature. It isn't that easy to waste someone. He relied on that momentary hesitation to give him the advantage. When Bishop had shouted at him, he instantly knew that the threat had to be eliminated. With lightning reflexes, he brought the gun up, ready to fire.

This time, he was too late.

Bishop had plenty of training on the police combat course. That allowed him to instantly react. He had practiced taking the bad guy out. In twenty-five years of law enforcement, like ninety-nine percent of law enforcement officers, Bishop had never killed another man. But firing at mannequins or living flesh made no difference to him. He was ready.

He fired three shots. The blast was deafening each time he pulled the trigger. The first round hit the man just below the rib cage, spinning him to the right as the round passed through soft tissue and shattered the bay window. The second round struck him in the shoulder. The third round entered the left side of his chest and lodged in his heart. The force of the bullets drove him backwards against Ann's sewing table. Both the man and the sewing machine crashed to the carpet. As he fell, the man got off only one shot. It struck the ceiling, leaving a sizable hole in the sheetrock.

Bishop approached the body. He had seen enough dead men to know that this one was no longer a threat to anyone. He turned back to his wife. Ann hadn't moved. She stared at the ceiling, seemingly unaware of the presence of her husband. Many times, Bishop had seen victims withdraw into themselves to block the impact of the situation.

"Ann? Ann, honey," he said gently, holding her hand in his own. "It's Brian. Are you OK?"

She blinked and looked directly into her husband's eyes.

"Brian, I thought I was going to die," she whispered cautiously. In her mind, the man was still a threat.

"It's OK now," he reassured her. "Come on, you have got to get up and get dressed." He took her arm and helped her up from their bed. Placing his arm around her waist, he guided her into the bathroom. He found her panties, bra, jeans and a blouse. He set a pair of tennis shoes and socks on the counter. "Put these on," he said.

"What?" she asked.

"Put these clothes on. I'll be in the bedroom."

Without saying anything more, she began dressing, following his orders.

Bishop walked back into the bedroom and knelt next to the body. He searched the man's pockets and found no ID. In his front pocket, he found a folded piece of paper and three packets of a white substance. The packets looked like the typical cocaine hits. He dropped the packets on the floor and placed the piece of paper in his own pocket. Then he pulled off the ski mask.

"Holy shit!" he said, astonished by what he saw before him. The dead guy was one of the FBI agents who had come into the office last week. Then the other one, he reasoned, must also be an agent.

"Lock the bathroom door, and don't come out till I get back," he yelled to his wife.

He raced out the door and down the road toward the airport. As he reached the intersection, he looked toward the parking lot. The car was gone. The other guy must have come to.

Realizing that they had minutes before reinforcements arrived, he ran back to the house, dashed through the front door, and called out to Ann, telling her to get her purse. He ran into the den, moved the old icebox, and punched in his numbers on the wall safe. He grabbed their passports and the three thousand in cash that he kept for going to swap meets. He stuffed the passports and the cash in his briefcase. He was about to get Ann and get the hell out of there, when he noticed the statue sitting on the table beside his desk. Without thinking, he picked it up and crammed it into the briefcase.

No way he could leave without weapons. He needed to be prepared to defend himself and his wife. He opened his gun safe and took out his nine-millimeter Beretta and five loaded magazines. He put one magazine in the weapon and shoved the gun in the waistband of his pants.

He grabbed the twelve-gauge shotgun and a box of shells. He picked up the 40mm Glock that he had used to kill the SOB. He added his own baseball cap, sunglasses, and the small, portable police scanner that plugged into a car's cigarette lighter. He stuffed all but the shotgun into his briefcase and ran back into the bedroom.

Ann was still in the bathroom, staring in the mirror. She was fully dressed, but seemed disoriented.

"Did you get your purse?" he asked.

"No."

"Where is it?"

"In the kitchen."

"Come on," he took her hand and led her into the kitchen. He picked up the purse and handed it to her.

She paused when they stepped out onto the front porch.

"He is dead?" she asked.

"Yes," he answered.

"I'm glad," she said.

Bishop racked his brain, wondering what to do next. He had just killed an FBI agent. But this agent had no identification, wore latex gloves, and carried an automatic with a silencer. Then he speculated about the cocaine packets in the agent's pockets. "Christ, this seems like a classic set-up," he mumbled.

Both of them, he and Ann, would have been found shot to death in their home. Drugs would have been found in their possession. Bishop was already under investigation for dealing drugs. It would have been an open-and-shut case. He could see the headline now, "Drug Dealing Police Chief, Wife Found Dead, Killed by Mob."

Bishop reached for the keys to the car, and then he realized that they would never make it out of town in their own vehicle. These people would have connections with law enforcement. Maybe even the mayor had been in on it. They couldn't use credit cards or their cars. He had to think this over.

"Let's go," he said.

"Where?" Ann asked.

"For a walk," he replied.

It was still dark. Bishop checked his watch. It was 4:30 in the morning. It seemed like hours had passed, but it had actually been only a matter of minutes. They cut through the woods behind the house, following the tree line next to the road. It took them more than a half hour to reach Stillwater Lane. Only one car had driven by them, but they had hidden in the underbrush until it passed by. They turned up Stillwater. Bishop could see the sun beginning to rise in the east. It would be light soon.

They stopped in front of a large, gray two-story house. Bishop rang the doorbell. It took five minutes before a face appeared in the small window on the front door. They could hear a beeping as the alarm system was deactivated.

Dick Raymond opened the door.

"Brian, Ann what happened? What are you two doing here at this hour?" Raymond asked. Bishop could see Dick's wife, Trudy, come down the stairs behind him.

"Please, come in," Trudy said, pointing toward the living room.

Bishop stayed at the threshold. Ann stood at his side.

"I know this sounds strange, but we need your help, and I don't want you to ask us any questions. The less you know, the safer you will be," Bishop said. He could see the concern on their friends' faces. "All we need is to borrow a car," he continued.

"Sure," said Dick. "Let me go get the keys."

"Dick, make it the keys for the Kia," said Bishop.

"The Kia?" Dick asked. "Brian, you know that it's almost twenty years old."

"I know," Bishop answered. "I don't know when we will be able to get it back to you."

"All right, Brian, but at least let's sit down and figure out what's going on here. Tell us what we can do to help."

"Dick, I know that this sounds strange, but every minute we stand here puts your lives in danger."

They walked through the house to the garage. Dick handed over the keys to the old silver Kia Optima. Bishop sat behind the wheel, and Ann got in the passenger side. As Bishop started to close the door, Dick put his hand on his friend's arm.

"Brian, if you need anything at all – money, help, whatever – just call me."

"Guys, you've been a great help. I pray that one day I can explain all this to you. Thank you so very much."

Bishop backed the car out of driveway, dropped the transmission into drive, and drove away from the house. He looked back and saw Trudy and Dick standing in the doorway. He wondered if they would ever see the Raymonds again. He wondered if they would even live to see tomorrow.

"What do we do now?" Ann asked.

"I've got to find a place for you to hole up, and then I have to figure out what's happening."

They drove west toward the Richmond Highway. As they passed through Shantytown, Bishop finally came up with a solution to at least one of their problems. He turned left on Houser and then right on

Fairview. He pulled up in front a small white house with a wood fence. They got out and walked up the sidewalk to the front porch. The walkway was lined with rose bushes, and the lawn was neatly trimmed. It was still early, just 5:30 a.m., but the lights were on in the living room. In another half hour, the sun would be up.

Not finding a doorbell, Bishop knocked on the door. In no time at all, Willie Johnson's imposing body filled the space inside the doorframe. He stood six feet, ten inches tall and weighed at least four hundred pounds.

"Chief! What are you doing here?"

"Willie, can we come in?"

"Sure, Chief."

"Jasmine," Willie called. "We got company."

A small black woman no more than five feet tall walked in the room. They made a strange couple, Willie and Jasmine, yet Brian knew they were devoted to each other.

The house had belonged to Michelle Johnson, Willie's grandmother. Willie and Jasmine had lived with her, watching over and caring for her. When she died last month, they had inherited the house.

"Willie, can I pull the car around back?" Bishop asked.

"Sure, Chief," Willie said. "Mrs. Bishop, please come in," Willie said to Ann.

Bishop drove the Kia around back and parked it in the old garage. Fortunately, it fit inside with no problem. He closed up the garage, walked up to the back door and knocked.

Jasmine let him in. Bishop wasn't sure just what to tell the two of them. He had planned to make up a story, but he wasn't sure he could come up with anything as bizarre as what was really happening. He decided just to tell the truth. He gave them the complete story, leaving nothing out. Both Willie and Jasmine had listened intently as Bishop related the strange events. The only thing that he omitted was the part about being under the influence late last night before all the drama began.

The story jogged his memory. He remembered the piece of paper he had pulled out of the agent's pocket. He reached in his pocket, pulled it out and unfolded it. It was a photocopy of a picture that had appeared in the sports section of the *Sunday Richmond Tribune*. He checked the date. It had been in the paper five months earlier.

He was confused. Why would the agent have a soccer picture that old in his pocket?

Bishop studied it and read the caption. "In the playoffs, University of Virginia goalie Tim Martin saves the day, holding off Virginia Tech, 1-0. The win moves UV even closer to the national championship."

"Willie, do you remember when you asked me to find a Tim Martin for your grandmother?"

"Sure, Chief. You said there was no record of anyone by that name living here in the county."

"Well, I think I just found him," Bishop said, glancing down at the folded paper in his hand.

"Willie, I need to lay low until tonight," he continued. "Could Ann stay here for a few days? I have to drive up to UV and see if I can find this Tim Martin. I'm beginning to get the feeling that somehow this whole thing has something to do with that darn statue you gave me."

51

*The University of Virginia administrative offices probably
wouldn't open until eight o'clock.*

HE HAD TIME TO KILL. HE PULLED THE KIA INTO A SPEEDY MART,
picked up a quart of beer and a beef burrito. It was six o'clock in the
morning. He walked back to the car, ate the burrito, and drank the beer.

He had put on the baseball cap and the sunglasses. He didn't know
if he even needed to disguise himself. As far as he could tell, no one had
been looking for him. He had been listening to a talk news radio station
out of Charlottesville on the drive from Willie's house.

It had been two days since he had killed that FBI agent. He hadn't
heard anything about a homicide at their house in Johnsonville. He'd
monitored the police scanner and hadn't heard anything about a dead FBI
agent or a rogue chief of police who was wanted for questioning. He concluded that he could forget the hat and glasses when he got on campus.

Yesterday he and Ann had just hidden out at Willie's house in
Shantytown. He had given Willie and Jasmine money to buy them some
clothes and toiletries. Jasmine had shopped at a thrift store. Both he and
Ann had been impressed with her purchases. The price was right and
everything fit.

Willie had gone to work as usual. The Bishops had stayed inside
watching TV. Nothing was on the news about any dead FBI agent or that
the police might be looking for them. Bishop wasn't sure how to take all
this. Was it good news or bad news? The good news was that the local
police weren't looking for them; the bad news was that the man's death

was being covered up. That could mean that some really bad guys wanted them dead, not just thrown in jail.

They slept in Grandma Johnson's bedroom. Brian had been surprised that Ann hadn't freaked out, considering that the old woman had died in the same room just three months earlier. She seemed to have recovered from the trauma of the assault. Strangely, the cat seemed to help. He thought that was kind of weird. Shortly after they'd gotten there, they heard a cat meowing at the back door. When Jasmine opened the door, a large gray cat with a noticeable limp walked right in the door, just like it owned the place.

Willie explained that the cat, named Mr. P, had belonged to Grandma Johnson. It had always stuck close to Grandma whenever possible. The day she died, the cat had disappeared. It had been gone for three months. When the cat came into the house, it had made a beeline for Ann and jumped up on her lap.

Ann had never really gotten into pets, and during their marriage, they never owned one. Yet while she spent the day just sitting watching TV, the cat refused to leave Ann's lap. Jasmine was astonished. She said that Mr. P would never go to anyone else but Grandma Johnson. The animal's possessive behavior had continued as they prepared to go to bed the night before. Brian had just pulled back the covers and started to climb into bed. Suddenly, the cat narrowed its eyes, let out a deep growl and hissed at him. Brian had tried to laugh it off, but the cat refused to stop. Finally, Ann gave it a try.

"That's all right, Mr. P," she said calmly. "He belongs up here beside me."

Neither of them could believe what happened next. The cat jumped off the bed and curled up on the floor at the foot of the bed. When Brian got up at four in the morning, the cat was still in the same place he'd been earlier. It seemed as if the creature was intent on guarding Ann.

Still trying to pass the time until the office opened, Bishop saw his briefcase on the seat next to him. He opened it and pulled out the newspaper picture of Tim Martin. He was still hoping to figure out how Martin fit into the situation.

Last night, he had questioned Willie again. Just what had Grandma Johnson told him about this Tim Martin? Willie told the story again, and it was just as crazy as it had seemed three months ago. Supposedly, this Tim Martin was a powerful man who could stop whatever was happening at Sarday's school. She had only told Willie to show Tim Martin the statue, and he would know what to do.

Bishop took another look at the picture. Martin was white, not black, as he had first suspected. He looked to be about twenty years old. Hell, it still didn't make any sense. But since this was the only lead he had, he would have to stick to it. If there had been any other plausible lead, he'd have taken it and written this one off as a wild goose chase.

He reached under the driver's seat, pulled out the Beretta and put it in the briefcase along with the statue. He closed the briefcase, started the Kia, and pulled out of the parking lot.

As he crossed the bridge over the river on Highway 29, he rolled down his window and picked up the Glock he had taken from the other FBI agent. He tossed it in the river. Throwing away evidence ran contrary to all his training. However, since he had shot the man himself with this gun, he decided it was in his own best interest to ditch the weapon.

Finally on campus, he pulled into a UV parking garage. He slipped on his "new" sports coat, picked up the briefcase and headed toward Newcomb Hall.

"May I help you?" asked the elderly woman at the information desk.

"Yes, ma'am," he smiled, hoping his charm would help him get what he wanted. "My name is Brian Martin, and I am looking for my nephew, Tim Martin."

The woman scanned the directory before she answered.

"Sir, we are not allowed to give out room numbers, but I can provide his phone number. The phones over there against the wall may be used to make calls directly to dorm rooms."

"Thank you," Bishop said as he took the slip of paper with a phone number on it. Then he turned to the phones and used one to dial the number. It rang twice before someone answered.

"Tim and Eddie's massage parlor," said the voice on the other end.

"Is Tim Martin there?" Bishop asked.

"Tim, you're wanted on the phone!" yelled the guy on the phone. Bishop figured must be the roommate, Eddie. Bishop continued to hold the phone up to his ear.

"Hello?" answered man who must be Tim.

"Mr. Martin?" asked Bishop.

"Yes, who is this?"

"Mr. Martin, my name is Brian Bishop. I'm a reporter for *The Richmond Herald*. We are doing a follow-up on an article we ran about five months ago on UV's win over Tech. I was wondering if I could chat with you over a cup of coffee?"

"Yeah, I guess so. You want to meet at O-Hill?"

"O-Hill?" Bishop asked, unaware of any coffee shop called by that name.

"You know, the Observatory Hill dining hall over by Scott Stadium. How about ten o'clock at the Hoo Street Grill?"

"I'll see you at ten," agreed Bishop.

Since he had nothing better to do, Bishop wandered over to the dining hall and took a seat on the terrace of the Hoo Street Grill. The dining hall was a huge, modern facility, with seating for more than eleven hundred students and faculty. It had seven food stations. The grill station featured hamburgers, hot dogs and grilled sandwiches. People could choose between eating inside or outdoors.

Bishop was a good hour early. That would give him time to size up Martin when the kid arrived. He laid out the photo spread on the table and watched as people came up the steps that led to the food station.

At ten minutes to ten o'clock, Bishop spotted him. He wasn't a kid. Bishop figured that he stood taller than six foot four inches and weighed at least two hundred and thirty. He didn't have an ounce of excess fat. He had dark black hair and a good tan. He wore faded jeans, a blue T-shirt and running shoes without socks.

Bishop stood up as the young man approached.

"Mr. Martin?" he asked. "I'm Brian Bishop. Please have a seat. Would you like something? It's on the expense account," Bishop said with a laugh.

"A cheeseburger and a Diet Coke sound great, but we'll have to wait in line. They don't serve people at the tables."

They got in line, and Bishop paid for their meals. Martin was silent all the time they stood in line. Bishop, like all cops, took advantage of the wait to assess the young man. He thought something was bothering Martin. He seemed rather tightly wired. Bishop anticipated that he might have trouble getting information.

Once back at the table, Martin took a big bite of his burger. Still chewing, he looked at this reporter sitting across the table from him.

"What can I do for you, Mr. Bishop?" he asked.

Bishop took a deep breath and said, "I'm not a reporter."

"What?" Martin said a little too loudly. He spit out chunks of his burger in his haste to figure out what this guy really wanted. "Look, dickhead, if you are trying to sell me something, you can forget it right now." Martin slid back his chair and began to pick up his food.

Bishop held up his hand, a signal to wait a minute. "Hold it, kid," he said. "I'm a cop."

"Sure you are," Martin said with a sneer. "Show me some ID."

Bishop started to reach for his badge, then suddenly remembered he had relinquished it to the mayor. He decided to fake it. He pulled out his wallet and a card that certified his membership in the Virginia Police Chiefs' Association. It had his name and position written on it. Next to it was his military ID card, indicating that he was retired. He pulled it out, too.

Martin took a good look at both cards.

"You were in the army?" he asked.

"For twenty years. I was in the military police," Bishop said truthfully.

"My dad's in the army. He's stationed in Hawaii." The kid had calmed down, but he was still standing. Bishop was afraid he might leave before he could talk to him.

"What does your dad do?" Bishop asked.

"He's the assistant commander for the 25th Infantry Division," Martin said.

"Oh, a brigadier general," nodded Bishop. "I'm afraid he has a little more rank than I do. I retired as a major."

"I noticed that on your card," said Martin. "Why did you lie to me?"

"If you'll give me a minute, I'll tell you. Please sit down."

"All right," Martin replied. "But this had better be good."

Martin sat back down, but didn't look a bit happy about it.

Bishop laid the briefcase on the table and opened it. He took out the statue and set it down on the table. He expected little or no reaction. Even worse, he worried that the kid might take a swing at him, figuring he was some kind of a nut case.

But Martin's reaction astonished him. The young man stared at the statue, then he looked up and stared at Bishop.

"Where did you get my dad's statue? Who are you anyway?"

"What do you mean, 'your dad's statue'?" asked Bishop.

"It was in my dad's den in the house in Hawaii last month when I was there for spring break," Martin said.

"No way, kid!" said Bishop. "I've had this thing for more than three months."

"Where'd you get it?" Martin asked.

"It belonged to an old lady in Johnsonville where I'm the chief of police," Bishop answered.

"Where did she get it?" Martin asked.

"I really don't know. I think she found it in the old slave quarters on the Johnson Plantation."

Tim Martin's next statement nearly caused Bishop to pass out then and there.

"This old black lady, did she have a large, gray cat?" Martin asked.

"Yes, but how in the hell did you know that? Have you met her before?"

"Sort of," responded Martin. "You wouldn't understand."

"Look, kid, right now something weird is going on. If you told me that this was part of an alien abduction, I might believe it," Bishop said.

"What is this plantation?" asked Martin.

"Well, now it's called the School for West African Spiritual Studies. It's a New Age thing run by some quack named Sarday."

Now it was Tim Martin's turn to be amazed at what he was hearing.

Martin turned a deathly pale. "George Sarday?" he asked.

"Yup, that's the name. He goes by Dr. George Nah Sarday. He's got this guy, Oscar Jalah, with him. Both of them showed up at the same time. They have some sort of scam going that involves a lot of rich and influential people, including a U.S. senator," Bishop told him.

"It's not a scam. It's something far worse. You've got to stop them!" Martin said, clearly agitated.

"That might be a little difficult," said Bishop.

"Why? You're the police chief. Get a search warrant or something, find out what they're doing, and then stop them!"

"Well, kid, I *was* the police chief. Right now, I've got a small problem."

Bishop explained what had been happening. Tim listened thoughtfully. When Bishop finished, Martin had a question.

"Did you ever cross Sarday?"

"Yes, I guess you could say that. I believed he was involved in the disappearance of several teenagers. Then I had a run-in with one of his goons. The drug charges came up after Senator Carlson's squeeze showed up in my jail, babbling about human sacrifices at the school."

Tim stood up again and planted his fists squarely in front of him on the table. "We've got to do something. Come on, I need to go to my room and get some money."

The two walked back to the Alderman Road Residence Area. They had just started up the steps at Martin's dorm when two men stepped up and blocked their way.

"Tim Martin?" one asked. "FBI, we would like you to come with us."

Bishop first assumed that they'd come to bust him. Then he realized that these guys had no clue who he was. He couldn't believe that this was unrelated to what was going on back in Johnsonville.

One of the agents turned to Bishop.

"Sir, may I see some ID?"

Then Bishop made one of his quick decisions. He turned and started to walk away. The agent came after him. When the agent was within three feet of him, Bishop turned abruptly and swung the briefcase, striking the agent in the side of his head. The unexpected blow knocked him over backwards, and he fell to the ground.

The second agent pulled his gun, pointing it directly at Bishop.

"Freeze, motherfucker! Blink, and you're dead!" he shouted. "Drop that briefcase!"

Bishop reluctantly followed the man's orders. The other agent remained on the ground.

Without warning, Martin's foot lashed out, striking the agent's gun and sending it flying. Then the agent wheeled around, taking a martial arts defensive posture.

"You're dead!" growled the agent, kicking out his foot toward Martin.

The fight lasted just seconds. Bishop had never seen anyone move as fast as Martin had. The agent lay unconscious on the ground.

"Run!" yelled Martin. Bishop grabbed his briefcase, and both he and Martin dashed between the dorms and emerged on the playing field next to McCormick Road. An older SUV was parallel parked along the road.

"Get in!" shouted Martin, as he pulled the keys out of his pocket.

He started the SUV and pulled out, heading for Fountain Avenue. Within minutes, they were on I-64, heading west toward Richmond. Martin wove in and out of traffic, accelerating to more than eighty miles per hour.

"You might want to slow down. You know, the speed limit is just sixty," Bishop said.

"Screw the limit. Besides, I have built-in radar detection and suppression," grinned Martin.

"That's illegal. As a cop, I could arrest you for having prohibited electronics," Bishop said, acting as serious as he dared.

"Former cop," Martin said, correcting him. "You told me you had been relieved of your duties."

Without using a turn signal, Martin cut across three lanes of traffic and took the next exit. A driver in a red Toyota sedan honked his horn. Martin gave him the finger as he raced past him.

Good God, Bishop thought. This kid definitely has anger management problems.

He held his breath for a moment, trying to regain his control.

"By the way, where are we going?" asked Bishop.

"I need gas," Martin replied. "Oh, and we're headed for North Carolina."

Bishop held on to the armrest as Martin made a quick and unexpected right into a gas station. Martin jumped out, pulled out a credit card and began to twist off the gas cap.

"Wait!" yelled Bishop. "Don't use a credit card. They can trace you," he cautioned. "And if you're carrying a cell phone, pull the battery. Those phones come with a GPS. You can be tracked, even if your phone is off."

Martin pulled out his cell and took out the battery.

"Shit, I don't have any cash," Martin said, fumbling with his wallet.

"I do," said Bishop. "I'll go in and pay. You stay here and fill up. By the way, do you want anything to drink?"

"Diet Coke," Martin said.

"How much gas do you think you'll need?"

"Oh, probably about fifteen gallons," Martin replied.

Inside, Bishop told the clerk to add in a large Diet Coke and a six-pack of beer.

"That'll be six bucks a gallon for gas, plus the drinks, will make it $101," said the clerk. Bishop pulled out his wallet and paid the bill. He used the restroom and returned to the SUV.

He handed Martin his drink and twisted the cap on a beer. He took a long swig. He grabbed for his seatbelt as Martin entered the roadway, his tires squealing.

"Christ, kid, slow down. The last thing we need to do is to attract attention," warned Bishop.

Soon they were back on the interstate. Bishop had already put away one beer and opened his second.

Martin looked over at Bishop and made a quick assessment.

"What are you, anyway," he asked, "some kind of drunk?"

"Just thirsty," Bishop answered.

"Yeah, right. Two beers and it's only eleven o'clock in the morning."

"Look, kid, you just handle the driving. I'll worry about what I drink, and, by the way, keep the damn speed down. Do you want to get us killed?"

52

Reservations at one of D.C.'s
best restaurants had already been made.

DESPITE A RAGING HEADACHE, SAMANTHA HAD AGREED TO MEET HER father for lunch. That's not how she had intended to spend the day. She had only one morning class. The rest of the day was going to be spent studying and trying to get over the blasted headache.

Her dad had been in town for some legal thing with a congressman. That was in the morning. He had time for lunch with his daughter after he completed his business. It would just be the two of them.

"Here, let me help," said Sam's father, pulling out her chair at a corner table in one of Georgetown's fancy bistros.

Sam sighed.

As if I couldn't pull out my own chair, she thought. But Samantha knew better than to say that out loud. She had learned her manners, and she knew what her father expected.

After they both had ordered, they chatted about the weather, school and summer plans. They both admired the gourmet sandwiches they had selected. But soon they had just about exhausted all the easy topics.

"So, how is Martin?" her dad asked.

Here it comes, Sam thought. She suspected he had a hidden agenda. "Fine, just fine, Dad. Why do you ask?"

"Well, to put it bluntly, your mother and I were wondering if this is going to turn out to be something serious," he said.

Sam hesitated. Even she didn't know how it all would turn out.

"Daddy, I can't really say. I just don't know. All I know is that we get along really well and enjoy being together." She was sure that this broad statement wasn't going to satisfy her father. After all, he was an attorney. He knew how to get his witnesses to talk.

"You know, our families don't really run in the same circles," he said. He picked up his wedge of dill pickle and bit off the end.

"You mean that if Tim had been born rich, then it would all be OK?" she asked. She wasn't a lawyer, but she had the woman's talent for putting a man's feet to the fire, even if it was her own father.

Samantha's head began to pound. The headache had returned in full force.

The whole conversation was really beginning to irritate her. Here she was at twenty-one years old, and her father was acting as if she were some teenager going out on her first date.

"I'm not saying anything about how much money Tim has," her father said, defending his position. "I guess I'm just wondering about his plans for the future. You know that it's a different world out there. Good, high-paying jobs are hard to find. You're used to a fairly extravagant life-style, and I'm not sure that...."

Sam couldn't take much more. She interrupted him in mid-sentence, something she had never dared do before.

"Daddy, what's really bugging you? Is it that Tim's white and I'm not? Is that the problem? Do you think that being in a mixed marriage would affect his earning power?"

The pent-up anger surprised even her. She hoped that she hadn't said something that she would regret for the rest of her life. Yet she forged on.

"Mom's half white. Are you ashamed to be married to her? And, I'm a quarter white, so I suppose even I embarrass you with my light brown hair and lighter skin."

Sam didn't wait for his answers. Instead, she stood up, wadded up her linen napkin and tossed it on her plate. She stormed out of the restaurant, causing other customers to turn and wonder what had been going on between the tall, beautiful – and extremely angry – woman and the distinguished-looking middle-aged man.

When she reached her car, Sam sat and thought for a minute. She didn't know what to do or where to go. She decided to just drive. Maybe the act of moving through traffic would calm her nerves and help her sort out her emotions.

Before she knew it, she was heading toward Charlottesville and the University of Virginia. Twice she had decided to turn around. Twice she rejected the idea. Finally, she knew the answers to her questions could only come from a serious discussion with Tim. The longer they put off making a decision, the tougher it would be.

Mostly, she stayed in the fast lane. The power of the engine somehow soothed her. Her headache was still there, but it seemed to be diminishing. Her thoughts turned to Tim.

I've got to think logically, she told herself. What are the strengths in our relationship?

Without a doubt, the sex was great. If Daddy only knew what she and Tim did together, wouldn't he be shocked out of his mind. She smiled inwardly, remembering their last weekend together.

No, you can't judge an entire relationship on the quality of the sex life. She knew that, but, for the two of them, it wasn't just sex. It was true passion, real love and deep caring. She wasn't a clinical psychologist, but she believed that when two people were in a romantic relationship, they showed how much they cared for one another. Each partner would try to ensure that the other partner received the full benefits of the relationship. That's really what she and Tim had going on. She found the idea of sleeping with someone else unthinkable.

Sex aside, Sam could admit that there were other important things in a relationship. Would Tim's family accept her as his life partner? It was obvious that her own father hoped that they would call it quits.

What about children? Did Tim know that despite her light complexion, one of their children could be born as black as her brother Eddie? She had studied biology. The genes were there and could show up at any time.

And what about when they grew older, and sex was not the driving force in their relationship? Would he still love her?

Another issue came to mind – Tim's dark side. They hadn't even discussed it, but Sam knew there was something that he kept to himself, something that frightened her. There was tension, bottled up just below Tim's confident exterior. She had seen it when they were in Hawaii at the Dojo. Tim had been on the verge of killing that karate student. He would have done it, but the instructor intervened. Samantha shivered when she remembered the wild look in Tim's eyes.

Whatever..., she thought. She planned to have a serious talk with Tim. Tonight she'd either be making a lifelong commitment with Tim, or she'd be walking away. If they chose the first option, she might be the one proposing to him, not the other way around. So much for manners, she thought, feeling a deep-down happiness at the idea of proposing to him.

As she neared the campus, she tried calling Tim once again on his cell. She'd already tried three times. Each time a voice told her, "This phone is not in service." Again, she couldn't get through.

She found a parking space in front of the dorm. It was already nine-thirty at night. Both of them should be in their dorm room by now, she thought. She took the elevator to the third floor and walked down the hallway to room 321. She tried the door, but it was locked. That was strange; they never locked the door. She leaned her ear against the door. The TV was on really loud. That in itself was unusual; they hardly ever watched TV. She banged on the door. Maybe they just didn't hear her knock.

"Tim, Eddie? It's Sam. Let me in!" she called.

Still no answer. She pounded on the door with her fists.

"All right, guys, get your clothes on and answer the door!" she demanded. Again, no one answered.

Well, if they were out, she would just have to wait until they got back. Then, the first thing she would do is to turn off the damn TV. Then she remembered her own key. She dug through her purse and pulled out her keys. She found the one marked with the numbers 3-2-1 and inserted it in the lock. She opened the door.

"What the hell?" she shouted.

Sitting on a chair in the center of the room was her brother Eddie. He was gagged, and his hands were tied behind his back.

"Eddie? Eddie! What happened?" she screamed as she rushed to untie him.

No sooner than she had gone three steps, something struck her from behind. She flew forward and fell face-first onto the hard floor. The fall knocked the wind out of her. She struggled to stand, but found her arms pulled roughly behind her back. Handcuffs were fastened around her wrists.

She was jerked to her feet and shoved on the bed. When the room stopped spinning, she saw two men in dark suits standing over her.

The man with blond hair grabbed her purse and began digging through it. He passed her wallet to the dark-haired guy with the buzz cut. He thumbed through her cards and pulled out the driver's license.

"Huh, Samantha Dixon. You have the same last name as our Mr. Dixon over there," he said as he threw her wallet on the bed.

"He's my brother," Sam said. "What's this all about?"

"FBI," answered the blond guy. "We're looking for Timothy Martin. Do you know where he is?"

"He should be right here," she said. "Right here in his room."

Sam could hear a cell phone ringing. The blond man reached in his pocket and retrieved the phone. He flipped it open. Sam tried to concentrate on the conversation, although it was difficult – she could only hear one side.

"He got away with an older guy," the man said. "The old one took us out of action for a minute. By the time we recovered, they were gone. We've been going through his room.

"Oh, and we have another problem. There are two kids here in his room. What do you want us to do with them?" The man paused, listening to the instructions. "All right, we can do that," he answered.

"What did he say?" asked the dark-haired man.

"We're supposed to take them with us."

"OK, on your feet. You're going to be taken to the police station," said the dark-haired man. "Don't say anything to anybody," he ordered.

Sam and Eddie got to their feet. Each of them was escorted by one of the men. Once in the lobby, Eddie pretended to fall down, barely catching himself. He glanced at the night clerk, Don Carpenter. He was on the soccer team. He knew Eddie and his sister, Samantha. He knew that their dad was an attorney.

"What's going on here?" Carpenter asked. Whatever it was, it was serious.

"Police business," said the blond man. Both he and his partner flashed their badges at the clerk and kept on walking.

Sam and Eddie were shoved into the back seat of a silver Ford sedan.

"What *is* going on here?" Sam whispered to her brother. "Why are they looking for Tim?" She wondered if he had killed someone.

Before she could hear Eddie's answer, the blond guy had crawled into the seat beside her.

"Ouch!" Sam said as she felt a burning sensation in her right arm. The man held a hypodermic needle in his hand. He was smiling.

She felt a numbness take over her body. She began to fade away, but she had just enough time to reflect on their abduction.

These men aren't police. Something bad is happening, she thought. Something really bad.

Meanwhile, back in the lobby, Carpenter pulled out Eddie Dixon's emergency card. He dialed the father's number and waited nervously for an answer.

"Hello?" asked a woman with a Spanish accent.

"May I please speak with Mr. Dixon?" Carpenter asked.

"Who's calling?" she replied.

"My name is Donald Carpenter. I'm the night clerk here at Eddie Dixon's dorm."

"One moment, please," she said.

Carpenter held on to the phone for what seemed like an eternity.

"Hello?" said a man with a deep voice.

"Sir, is this Mr. Dixon?" Carpenter asked.

"Yes. Who are you?"

"Sir, I'm Donald Carpenter. I play soccer with your son, Edward. I also work here in the dorm as a night clerk," he said. Then he hesitated a moment before he spoke. "Sir, tonight the police arrested your son and your daughter."

"Is this some kind of sick joke?" Dixon shouted.

"No, sir. I just saw them leave the dorm with two policemen."

"That's impossible. I had lunch with my daughter today in D.C."

"Sir, I know all three of them. Tim, Eddie and I play soccer together."

"Tim Martin, I should have known. Was Martin arrested, too?" Dixon asked.

"Not that I know of. Just your son and daughter," Carpenter replied.

"OK, now just give me some information. What police department was it?" Dixon asked.

"Uh, sir, I don't know. They weren't in uniform," Carpenter answered, his voice beginning to shake.

"What? Not in uniform?"

"No, sir. They weren't in uniform. They were wearing regular suits."

"Well, how in the hell did you come to the conclusion that they were cops?" Dixon was getting more angry by the minute.

"They showed me their badges," Carpenter explained.

"What kind of badges?"

"I don't know," Carpenter said. He was almost in tears.

"Christ, what *do* you know?"

"I'm sorry, sir. I just run the night desk. All I know is that they had Sam and Eddie in handcuffs. They told me it was police business."

Dixon sighed. He wasn't getting anywhere with this guy.

"OK, can you tell me what kind of car they were driving?"

"I didn't see any car," answered Carpenter.

"Goddamn it, Carpenter," he said, about ready to give up on the clerk. "All right, you listen to me, Mr. Carpenter. I'll be right there at the dorm within two hours. This had better be true, or I'll kick your butt!"

Carpenter heard a click, and the phone went dead.

53

There are no secrets in Shantytown, so they always say.

ABOUT TEN O'CLOCK IN THE MORNING, COBY JONES, A MIDDLE school student who chose to skip school that day, was cutting through the alley. He saw Mrs. Bishop and Jasmine sitting on the Johnsons' back porch. Coby told his cousin Robbie, who told his mother, who told her sister, who told her boyfriend.

By three o'clock on the same day that Chief Bishop had first met Tim Martin, the word had spread that the junior high school principal, Mrs. Ann Bishop, also the police chief's wife, was staying at Willie Johnson's house.

The story got even more interesting when folks added in the rumor that the police chief had been fired, and no one knew where he was.

By five o'clock, Sarday knew where Mrs. Bishop was and sent four men to go get her.

At dinnertime, Ann, Willie and Jasmine were sitting at the kitchen table, preparing to eat their meal together.

The house was a Craftsman-style home built in the thirties. When Willie's grandfather, Henry Johnson, brought his new bride to Johnsonville, he had amassed a small fortune. That fact was quite remarkable, considering that Henry was a black man. But he had worked hard in steel construction in New York City. Salaries up North were better than those in Virginia. Henry had pinched pennies and saved up his money. He custom built the thousand square-foot house to accommodate his six-foot, eight-inch height. The ceilings were ten feet high, and the doorways had seven-foot tall openings.

His wife, Michelle, brought additional income to the marriage in her work as a mid-wife and healer. Soon, the third bedroom had been transformed into her medical office. Chairs were lined up in the living room, filled up with folks waiting to see the wise woman. As the years passed and the children grew up, the grandchildren came along. It was then that everyone began calling the old woman Grandma Johnson.

Grandma Johnson had been born in Haiti, and she had brought with her many of the legends from the people who lived there. Some referred to her as a "white" witch. That meant that she was considered a good witch. As long as anyone could remember, she always had a large, gray cat that came along with her wherever she went. Some said that her cat was her "familiar." That's the old term for a creature that could reach into the spirit world. The cat story stuck around for decades. Some people claimed that Mr. P was more than seventy years old. Of course, that couldn't have been true. There are always lots of gray cats everywhere. Grandma probably just replaced it several times over the years.

When Henry passed, her grandson Willie moved in to care for her. Truth be told, Grandma could have probably cared for herself, but she liked to have company around her. When Willie married Jasmine, she, too, became part of the family. When Grandma Johnson died just three months ago, the house and all her belongings transferred right across to Willie and Jasmine.

The two made a good pair. Willie consumed huge amounts of food, and Jasmine loved to cook. Meals were always simple, but tasty. Ann found that she was feeling more and more comfortable with each of them. Jasmine had just cut pieces of a key lime pie. Willie's slice was nearly half the pie; the two women were satisfied with two-inch pieces.

Ann gazed around the large, comfortable kitchen. The walls were covered with a bright yellow paint. The kitchen table, made of oak, was large enough to seat eight or more, depending on the size of the person. One chair at the end of the table was Willie's special chair, built to fit his huge frame. Even the table height had been jacked up four inches higher than a normal table so that Willie could get his knees under it. Both Ann and Jasmine sat on puffed-up pillows. Ann said that she felt like a little girl again. Except, when she was little, children had to sit on stacks of catalogs and phone books.

The linoleum floor was worn in spots, but was kept spotlessly clean. The single-bowl kitchen sink had been scrubbed so many times that some of the porcelain had rubbed off. Jasmine had sewn white, ruffled curtains for the kitchen windows. She made do with a thirty-year-old stove, bought on sale by Grandma Johnson at Sears. About five years ago, they'd spent a lot to get a big, double-door refrigerator. They faithfully kept paying their twenty-five dollars a month. That was as modern as it got. Jasmine didn't even have a dishwasher, unless you counted Willie, who sometimes stayed around to help clean up after meals. The dinnerware didn't care who washed it. The plates, bowls, cups and saucers all matched. That's how it was with Navy-surplus china, the thick dishes that had blue anchors painted on them. Despite the age of the house, it was clean and in good repair. Over the years, it had served them well.

Ann had finally gotten the two of them to call her by her first name. At first, it was "Mrs. Bishop," then "Missy Ann" or "Missy." She finally won them over when she started addressing them as "Mr. Johnson" and "Mrs. Johnson." Then she tried out "sir" and "madam." Finally they had both loosened up, and everyone seemed comfortable, chatting and laughing together.

Nevertheless, Ann was still on edge, worrying about her husband.

"Has the chief called?" Willie had just asked.

"No," Ann said, "but I didn't expect anything so soon."

"No one at the police station is talking about what happened," Willie said. "All the officers, even my cousin, sure are closed-lipped."

As they talked, Mr. P, who had been sitting by Ann's feet, began to growl and got up and raced into the living room. Then Ann heard another yowl from the cat that made her skin crawl.

"My God, what is he doing?" she asked.

Suddenly, the cat was back in the kitchen again, scratching at the back door.

Willie and Jasmine looked quickly at each other. Each stood up. Willie's chair overturned behind him, but he didn't stop to pick it up.

"Run!" he shouted. "Run out the back door!"

His huge hand clasped Ann's wrist. He pulled her to her feet.

"I need to get my purse," said Ann.

"No, no time for that! Run now!" yelled Willie. She saw fear in her friend's eyes as the three ran out the back door. It slammed hard behind them.

They crossed the back yard, went through the gate and headed down the alley. They cut through a yard littered with junk cars. A pit bull tied to a chain lunged toward them, only to be held back by the length of its tether. The dog's barking ceased abruptly when it saw the cat running alongside them. It stopped pulling on its chain and sat down on its haunches and watched them pass.

As they got deeper into Shantytown, the road had more potholes and the houses seemed to be even more dilapidated. The paint was cracked or peeling. Some weren't even painted at all, but patched together with discarded pieces of lumber. Most people wouldn't even call some of them houses, but just run-down shacks. Garbage, litter and pieces of rusty machinery took the place of grass, trees or flowers.

A few people sat in rickety chairs on porches built of salvaged lumber. Their eyes followed the three of them, but no one said a thing. By now, Ann was running out of steam. She was breathing hard; she wasn't used to such exertion. Fear was also taking its toll. She didn't know where they were going or who was chasing them. She had to trust in her friends to carry her along. They slowed to a more moderate pace, and Ann began to regain her strength. She noticed that they'd been passing fewer and fewer houses. The road had narrowed to a single lane, leading into the woods.

About a mile farther on, they came to a small stream. While wading across, Ann lost her footing and saw herself falling, only to be lifted to safety by a large, dark arm that wrapped around her waist. On the opposite bank, Willie pushed aside some low bushes. Ann realized that he had uncovered a hidden path.

They continued on for at least another mile. It was rough going. Sometimes the brush was so thick that Ann was sure she would fall behind, and the other two would lose sight of her. She thought that they had a good chance to get away from the danger. She was wrong.

As the trail curved around an old oak stump, three black men, each with an assault rifle, stepped out from the trees and barred their way.

"Just where do you think you're going, Willie Johnson?" asked a particularly tough-looking man.

Willie took a deep breath. The chase had begun to get the better of him, too.

"We got bad people coming, TL. We need to hide out here," he gasped.

"That ain't gonna happen, boy. You know better than to bring anyone back here."

TL, who seemed to be the leader, noticed Ann for the first time. Ann had been terrified when that man in the ski mask had threatened to kill her just two nights ago, but this man was far worse. She shook with fear as she looked at the six-foot, six-inch man with prison tattoos all over both arms and a jagged scar running from the corner of his right eye all the way down to his chin.

"You was dumb to bring that white woman here. She be dead now, man. She never leave alive!" TL said, throwing an evil look in Ann's direction.

But he was no match for what came next.

Suddenly, little Jasmine stepped forward and stood her ground right under the big man's nose. She poked her index finger in the man's belly.

"You shut that talk up, TL," she ordered.

"Jasmine, I don't care if you is my little sister. You otta know that no one comes up here and lives."

"Grandma Johnson says she comes up here and you protect her, TL!" screamed Jasmine, not backing down one inch.

"What's wrong wid you, girl? That old lady she been dead for like three months already."

"But *he* ain't dead," Jasmine insisted, motioning at the cat.

"He?" TL asked.

"Just you look at *her*!"

Ann cringed as TL's eyes looked her over from head to toe. It was the toe part that caused his eyes to grow as large as saucers.

Sitting comfortably by Ann's shoes was Mr. P. The big gray cat blinked its eyes and stared at TL. Ann was astonished to see the big man's demeanor undergo an unbelievable transformation. She saw fear in his eyes.

"Dem kinds of cats, they leave when the witch dies," said TL.

"No," responded Jasmine. "That cat he adopted her. He the one that warned us that evil was coming."

TL and his companions stared at the cat, shrugged their shoulders, and headed down the trail. Willie, Jasmine and Ann followed. Mr. P never left her side.

They'd only walked for about another ten minutes, when Willie came to a halt. Ann sighed with relief, hoping that he had decided to give them all a rest. She breathed in deeply, thinking that it would help her to revitalize herself. But instead of fresh air, Ann detected a powerful mix of odors somewhere between ammonia or ether, mixed with cat pee or even rotten eggs. She shook her head, trying to identify what may have caused the overpowering, foul smell.

Before, she had been certain that whatever evil pursued them wouldn't find them this deep in the woods. Now, she wasn't so sure. She leaned down and peeked under a leafy branch and saw the source of the noxious smells.

It was a meth lab, hidden in the trees and thick brush, protected by armed men and booby traps.

54

*By the time Tim Martin and Chief Brian Bishop got to the
Fayetteville exit, they had reached a level of cooperation.*

NEITHER OF THEM WOULD HAVE THOUGHT IT WOULD HAVE BEEN
possible just a few hours earlier.

Bishop had stopped calling Martin "kid," and Tim was actually calling Bishop by his first name. Sitting side-by-side in Tim's car for so
long had led to discussions about everything from politics to women.
Somehow, however, they'd avoided talking about the serious issue facing
them.

Tim followed the road signs to Fort Bragg. Just outside the main
gate, he turned onto Yadkin Road, and then took a right into one of the
older housing developments. The homes were forty to fifty years old, but
most of them seemed to be in pretty good shape. He pulled up to a one-
story brick ranch with a well-manicured lawn, flowerbeds and freshly
painted trim. An orange extended-cab Chevrolet Silverado 4x4 pickup
with a camper shell was parked in the driveway.

They both got out of the SUV and took a moment to stretch their
legs. They walked to the front door, and Tim rang the doorbell. It didn't
take long for the door to open.

A burly guy, at least six and a half feet tall, opened the door. Bishop
guessed that he was maybe in his seventies. At first, Bishop was a bit
taken back by the man's appearance. His head was polished, and he had
no eyelashes, making his eyes appear too small for his wide face. His
upper arms, thicker than most men's legs, bulged out of the sleeves in his

taut T-shirt. Like many older men, his gut spilled out over the top of his leather belt.

"Tim? Tim Martin, what in the world are you doing here?" he asked. Obviously, this man knew Martin and liked him.

"Tiny, I need your help," Tim said, as he was tightly embraced by his old buddy. "Oh, and this is Chief Brian Bishop," he added turning to Bishop. "And, Brian, this is Command Sergeant Major, retired, Wilbur G. Sprague. Tiny was my dad's senior non-commissioned officer when he commanded a Special Forces "A" Team."

"Chief? Like in fire chief?" Sprague asked.

"No, like police chief," Bishop said while reaching out to shake the man's hand. "I'm the chief of police in Johnsonville, Virginia."

"Well, don't just stand there, you two. Come on in and tell us what kind of trouble you've gotten yourself in, Tim Martin," Sprague said as he opened the door wider still and stepped aside to give them room to enter the house.

The house was exquisitely furnished in antiques, many with an Asian theme.

"Who's at the door, Tiny?" a woman asked from somewhere in the back of the home.

"It's Tim Martin," answered Sprague.

"Tim!" the woman screamed. A small, silver-haired Asian woman ran out from the kitchen. Then she threw her arms around Tim and began asking questions.

"How are you? How's your mother and father? What are you doing here?"

While Tim attempted to answer the barrage of questions, Bishop sized up the home and this very inquisitive woman. Although Mai Lee appeared to be in her mid-sixties, Bishop guessed that she had been a gorgeous woman in her youth. He couldn't help but compare the couple to another big-little relationship, that of Willie and Jasmine. He laughed inwardly. Why was it that very small women would marry very large men? He decided not to pursue his thinking on the issue.

Mai Lee glanced at the time on the regal grandfather clock in the corner.

"Oh, it's almost time for dinner. We eat, then we talk. No?" she asked.

"We don't want to impose on you," Tim said.

"You not imposing, Timothy. You get ready for dinner. We eat soon."

Tim looked at Bishop. They both shrugged their shoulders. Tim smiled at the woman. "I guess we have no choice, Brian. We'll have dinner before we talk."

"How about a drink before dinner?" asked Sprague.

The words were magic to Bishop's ears. God, could I ever use a drink, he thought. His answer came swiftly, perhaps too swiftly. "Double scotch on the rocks," he said, then hesitated before continuing. "That's if you have scotch."

"Does a dog have fleas?" Sprague asked, laughing at his own words. "And, Tim, how about you?"

"Just a Diet Coke," Tim replied.

Sprague returned a few minutes later and handed each man his drink. They rested in the comfortable living room and talked small talk. Bishop could see that Tim seemed to want to skip the little stuff and get right on to the issue at hand, but he resisted, talking instead about family.

"Dinner ready!" called Mai Lee from the dining room. Once they were seated, Mai Lee began delivering small white porcelain bowls, one after the other. The bowls contained finely chopped vegetables, delicate pink shrimp and steaming rice. Bishop was amazed. He'd eaten Chinese food before, but nothing like this. It offered a remarkable combination of flavor and texture. He couldn't believe that she could put on a spread like this, especially when she hadn't expected company for dinner.

The conversation turned to their time in Africa. Sprague and Tim told story after story, each one followed by hoots of laughter. From time to time, one or the other would pause to raise a fist and wipe a tear from his eye. Bishop was fascinated to see the two in action. It reminded him of two soldiers who were recalling their time together during war. It was strange coming from two men so far apart in age. Wouldn't Tim have been too young to serve in the military? Although some of the talk dealt with Tim's dad, much of it included Tim's own involvement.

After dinner, the table was cleared, and the men remained seated, waiting for dessert. The conversation turned to Sarday and his cohort, Jalah.

"Holy shit!" remarked Sprague. "You mean that son-of-a-bitch and that thug Oscar Jalah are right here in America, living in Virginia?"

"Tiny, if you are going to use that language, you go down in basement!" called Mai Lee from the kitchen.

The imposing man stood, rubbed his belly, and looked at each of his guests in turn.

"Gentlemen, would you like to join me downstairs? Maybe we can make some sense of this over a glass or two of brandy. We'll have our dessert later."

Bishop compared Sprague's basement to a small version of a museum of military memorabilia, yet it reflected the character of their host. It seemed solid, but comfortable.

On one wall, Bishop admired a large flat-screen TV. Brown leather chairs, one of them sized extra large, faced the screen. On the right, he admired the polished bar, tall stools, a deep sink and a well-stocked refrigerator. The walls, paneled in mahogany veneer, provided a backdrop for photos, plaques and certificates. A lighted display case contained trophies and smaller items. Bishop bent over to get a better look at its contents. He saw the Distinguished Service Cross, the nation's second highest award for valor.

The photos also drew Bishop's attention. One was of a captain, Sprague and members of the Special Forces "A" Team.

"That's my dad right there beside Tiny," Tim told him, as he pointed to a photo. "Hey, Brian, you need to check this one out," Tim continued, pointing at another picture.

This one had Sprague in dress blues. He was saluting a newly commissioned second lieutenant, one of the most stunning women Bishop had ever seen.

"And that's Ann Sprague, their youngest daughter," Tim said. Unlike her mother, Ann stood about six feet tall. He could see that Ann was a slender woman with raven black hair and ivory skin.

"Good name for a beautiful woman," Bishop said. "That's my wife's name, too."

Bishop reached up and ran his finger over a coin stuck to the picture frame. He had to grin. He knew the significance of the silver dollar stuck to the corner of the first photo's frame. The coin was the traditional gift given by a new second lieutenant to the first non-commissioned officer who saluted them. Ann had honored her father by giving him her silver dollar.

Another photo was of Ann's promotion ceremony when she made major.

Bishop's tour of the mementos was interrupted by the clank of glasses. Three brandy snifters stood at the ready in rigid formation. Sprague poured a half an inch of golden liquid in each – one for Tim, one for Bishop, and one for himself. His thick hand wrapped around his own as he raised his glass.

"To solving your problem!" he said.

"Here, here!" the others said in unison. All three raised their glasses and swallowed in one gulp. Tim looked as if he had been forced to drink bad medicine. Without speaking, each man set his empty glass on the bar.

All three sat back in the leather chairs. Sprague was ready to get down to business.

"OK, Tim, what's up? What brings you here? Are you in some kind of trouble?" asked Sprague. For the next twenty minutes both visitors told their stories. Sprague only nodded from time to time or asked simple questions.

When they finished, Sprague picked up a laptop computer from the coffee table.

"All right, Mr. Chief Bishop, you claim that the FBI is investigating you for drug dealing. You also say that you killed one of their agents. And you believe that they have frozen all your assets. Why don't we just take a look at what type of warrant is out on you?"

The computer beeped as it fired up. Sprague typed in a few words and waited.

"Strange," he said, frowning. He typed a few more words and looked again. This time, he waited about five minutes.

Then he added a few more words. Another screen popped up.

"What's your social security number?" he asked Bishop. Once that had been entered, he asked another question.

"What is the name of the bank where have your account? If possible, tell me your account number." Bishop had a blank check hidden in his wallet. He handed it to Sprague.

But Sprague wasn't done. He asked for all the credit card numbers.

"You know," laughed Bishop, "it feels kind of funny. Here I am giving a stranger, who I have known less than three hours, all my credit card numbers as well as my social security number. In most cases I would be concerned. But with everything frozen, I guess I could leave the information on a bar stool downtown and nothing could be done."

A few minutes later, Sprague tapped the return key. The laser printer on the desk sprang into action. The printer rolled out three pages. He picked them up and looked them over.

"Very interesting," he said. "I just accessed Homeland Security's master database. I have some good news as well as some bad news."

Bishop's jaw dropped.

"What? The master database? I can't access that, and I am the chief of police!"

"But I can," Sprague said, looking at Bishop with a wide grin. "I have close friends in very high places."

"OK, what's the verdict?" Bishop asked.

"Well, you aren't wanted by any law enforcement agencies. You are also not being investigated by the FBI or any other national law enforcement agency."

"Are you sure your information is accurate?" asked Bishop.

"Absolutely. Whoever these guys are, they ain't for real," Sprague said confidently.

"Now that's the good news," he continued. "The bad news that is someone very powerful has accessed your credit card accounts and canceled your cards. Your bank froze your accounts by order of the bank's president. It says you have $357,000 in your savings account, but you have to unfreeze the accounts to access the money. Apparently, they don't like you very much in your town, chief."

"Great," said Bishop, "I can turn this over to the state patrol or FBI, and let them find out what's going on."

"That's not going to work," said Sprague with a frown.

"Why not?" asked Bishop.

"Well, you have no evidence of anything going on. You claim that you have a witness who actually saw someone sacrificed at Sarday's so-called school, but she disappeared. You claim you killed some dude who was posing as an FBI agent, but I'll bet the body won't be found and that your house has been sterilized.

"Someone destroyed your credit, but tough shit," Sprague continued. "It would likely be impossible to trace the person who actually did the closures. You could go to your bank and demand that your accounts be unfrozen. They could apologize, open your accounts, and then whoever is doing this just waits until the time is right, and then 'bang,' you're dead. Since that drug set-up didn't work, I'd guess the next step is to kill you."

Tim had been listening closely to Sprague's analysis.

"Then how do you explain why they came after me?"

"Son, you know why. It's the same thing that happened in Liberia. It's here now, and you and I both know this is more than just some scam. Sarday has brought along something really bad. It is infecting the whole town of Johnsonville."

Tim scowled. He was about to ask more questions, when he was interrupted by Mai Lee screaming from the top of the stairs.

"Tiny, Tim's on TV," she yelled.

"What?" shouted Sprague.

"On TV, on CNN, turn it on!" she shouted.

Sprague grabbed the remote and punched in the CNN channel.

"Great, another string of ads," he said. Then he pressed the reverse on the TiVo to back up the picture. He stopped it and hit "play." The CNN news anchorman was speaking.

"Now, an update on our breaking story from the University of Virginia. The FBI has issued a nationwide search for Timothy Martin as a person of interest in the kidnapping of Samantha and Edward Dixon, the adult children of the noted defense attorney, Robert Dixon.

"Martin was last seen driving a dark blue 2011 Lincoln Navigator with a Virginia plate number ERT 132. If you see this vehicle, call 9-1-1.

"Martin is considered armed and dangerous. Within the next fifteen minutes, we expect a detailed report from the campus at the University of Virginia."

Tim immediately jumped to his feet.

"Come on, we have to go!" he shouted at Bishop. "They have Sam and Eddie!"

"Wait a minute!" Sprague said, laying both of his big hands on Tim's shoulders. "Let's not go off half cocked."

"You don't understand," Tim said, grabbing Sprague's wrists and trying to pull them down. "Sarday is going to kill them both. I've had dreams that something bad was going to happen."

"Christ, now the dreams!" Bishop said, hanging his head.

"Not so fast, Brian. I wouldn't discount Tim's dreams," Sprague said

"Right now, I need a drink," mumbled Bishop. He walked over to the bar, pulled down a bottle of scotch, grabbed a tall glass and filled it three-quarters full of the rich brown liquid.

"That's just what we need, for you to get drunk!" yelled Tim.

"Well, I might as well get drunk if I have to deal with your hot-headed behavior!"

Tim turned away from Sprague and took a threatening step toward Bishop.

"That's it!" said Sprague. He grabbed both men by the arms and pulled them over to the chairs.

"Tim, remember when I taught you to be a sniper? Do you remember the importance of patience, slow breathing and focus?"

"Sure, but this is different. I love Sam, and he's going to kill her."

"Well, I guarantee he *will* if you don't think through your options first."

Bishop took another drink of scotch.

"Right," he mumbled while shaking his head, "the kid was a sniper. When he was sixteen?"

"Actually fifteen," said Sprague. "He killed ten men. His longest shot was four hundred meters."

"I don't believe it for a minute," said Bishop. The alcohol was giving him more confidence to say whatever he was thinking.

"Well, believe it," growled Sprague, "and that's enough booze for you. You both have problems, and they are going to be resolved now.

"First, Tim, you go outside and move your SUV into the garage. I don't need the neighbors seeing it parked on the street. Then get back down here. We need to develop a plan."

Tim moved the SUV right away. When he got back to the basement, Sprague had already begun to gather the facts.

"All right, chief, I want you to tell me everything that has happened involving Sarday since the day he arrived in Johnsonville."

After Bishop finished talking, it was Tim's turn.

"All right, Tim, tell me about the dreams. Also, what's the deal with this Sam?"

The stories took more than an hour. Tim had a hard time sitting still.

When both men finished, Sprague frowned, folded his thick arms over his wide belly, and looked each of them directly in the eyes.

"It looks like we will be entering a heavily armed camp. We have no police back-up, so we will be on our own. I have a couple of friends who can help us out. They live right up here in the neighborhood. We'll also require some special tools and equipment."

He picked up the phone and made two calls. No one spoke. They all sat silently, watching CNN. Thirty minutes later, two men walked down the stairs.

Bishop hadn't been sure what to expect, but he was pretty sure it wasn't what he was seeing now. These weren't hard-charging special forces soldiers. He saw two sorry-looking old men with gray hair and bulging potbellies. Each one wore bifocals. He figured that they were long past their seventieth birthdays. Both men greeted Martin warmly, as if he were a long-lost grandson.

"Guys, let me introduce you to Chief Brian Bishop," said Sprague.

The first was Sergeant Major Mike Kellogg, retired. The second was Sergeant Major Bill Catfield, retired. Each man had put in more than thirty years in special operations, and each one had served an early tour with Delta Force.

Sprague brought them up to date. They began talking about what they should do. Tim still had trouble focusing. Several times he stood up and put his hands in his pants pockets and rocked on his heels. If he had his way, he would have jumped in his car and charged the front gate of Sarday's compound. Only Sprague's calm presence held him at bay. Finally, Sprague brought out a large sheet of butcher paper and taped it to the wall.

He plugged his computer cord into the TV. He punched up a code on the TV, then Johnsonville, Virginia and its ZIP code. They saw the name of the town scroll up.

"Google Earth?" Bishop asked.

"No, NIS computer database. The satellite took this picture today. They take images of the D.C. area every day. The radius includes half of Virginia and that takes in Johnsonville, too."

Sprague used the curser to bring in the school. The resolution was good enough to make out people on the ground.

"There must be something big going on. Look at all the cars. There must be hundreds of people," said Kellogg.

"These weekend events draw as many as six hundred followers," said Bishop.

"Christ, what do they do all weekend?" asked Catfield.

"Sarday channels some ancient being from Egypt that he calls Dacari Mucomba. All those people believe this being can gain them great wealth and power. They have all kinds of seminars. See that big building? That's called the pavilion. It's big enough so that six hundred can sleep on the floor. They also do things in those smaller buildings and in the woods. Sarday pulls in millions of dollars at these events," explained Bishop.

"So where would Tim's girl and her brother be held?" asked Sprague.

"Either in those white buildings over there or in the main house. The white buildings hold the acolytes, a bunch of young, twenty-something kids who are Sarday's followers. They sort of act as hosts," Bishop said.

"What about security?"

"They have armed guards who do regular patrols. An eight-foot chain link fence topped with razor wire surrounds the entire sixty acres. A paved road runs along the inside of the fence. Besides that, they have second fence. It's insulated and looks like it can be electrified," answered Bishop.

"Zoom in on that vehicle on the outside road," suggested Bishop. Sprague brought the vehicle into view. They could see three men in the vehicle. He zoomed even closer. The men wore military-style clothing. All three carried assault rifles.

They spent the next hour studying the property.

"I count twelve armed guards," said Kellogg. "Looks like there's a dog kennel with four German shepherds. Assume that they work in shifts, and those buildings next to that small parking lot are their barracks. That works out to up to thirty-six armed men on the grounds."

"I doubt if we can just walk up and ask where they're keeping Samantha and Eddie Dixon," Catfield said.

"All these civilians complicate the problem. Will they leave on Monday?" asked Sprague.

"We can't wait," Tim said. "Something bad is going to happen, and it's going to happen soon. I can just feel it."

"I think Tim is right," offered Kellogg. "But I just can't believe that six hundred everyday-Joe citizens are going to participate in human sacrifices."

"Don't bet on it. How many Joe citizens drank the Kool-Aid at Jonestown?" Tim asked. "If we're going to do it, then we do it tonight."

Sprague looked at his watch. It was four o'clock in the morning. "We'll infiltrate tonight at 2300 hours."

Tim jumped to his feet.

"We need to get on the road. We have to find a place to hide until dark," he said, finally relieved that there was something physical to do.

"We're not driving any farther than Fayetteville Airport," said Sprague.

"What's at the airport?" asked Bishop.

"A helicopter," said Sprague.

"Who's going to fly this helicopter?" asked Bishop.

"It's been taken care of," Sprague assured him. "With a helicopter, we can get close enough to this school so we can get in, rescue the Dixon kids, get out and back here before sunrise."

"Let's locate a place where we can land," said Sprague.

They scanned the area around the school.

"There!" Bishop suggested. "That's the Smith farm. It's abandoned, and we can land behind the barn. It's only a mile to the south fence of the school."

"All right, then we stay here until tonight. No one leaves my property," said Sprague.

"Wait a minute," said Bishop. "What are we going to use for weapons? Let me assure you, those thugs that Sarday has working for him are not going to welcome us with open arms."

"I think I have enough equipment to handle all contingencies," said Sprague, the corners of his mouth rising ever so slightly.

"Christ, said Bishop. "We need full SWAT equipment and tactical weapons, not a couple of shotguns and a pistol!"

Sprague leaned forward and picked up the TV's remote. He pointed it at the wall and pushed a series of buttons. Bishop could hear the faint whirr of a motor. The paneled walls slid open. Behind them was a thick steel door. He pointed the remote again. This time he fingered a different series of buttons. The heavy door swung inward, revealing a well-lit room.

"Right this way, folks," Sprague said.

The vault was about the same size as the den itself. Bishop shook his head in disbelief as he took in the array of weapons, stacks of boxed ammo and cases of plastic explosives. Sprague had enough weaponry to arm an entire infantry battalion. Bishop figured that there were close to one hundred camouflage tiger uniforms, fifty SWAT uniforms, racks of Kevlar vests, and one hundred boxes of tactical boots. All the weapons and equipment were stacked along the back wall.

"We'll need .40-caliber pistols with silencers, assault rifles, knives, SWAT uniforms and boots, ballistic vests, SWAT helmets with visors, camouflage sticks and ammo. We'll also need night-vision goggles, wire cutters, radios with Bluetooth earpieces and a few other goodies," said Sprague.

He moved to a rack loaded with pistols.

"This will work for your pistol. It's a 40-Cal Glock with a built-in laser sight and suppressor. As you lightly place your finger on the trigger, it activates the laser."

Sprague pointed the weapon toward the far wall. A light touch made a small red dot appear on the wall. He squeezed the trigger, and they heard a click as the hammer fell on the empty chamber.

"It's sighted to within one-half inch at one hundred fifty feet. Whatever the red dot marks is ground zero for the bullet that follows. The gun is threaded for the new aluminum alloy suppressor, much lighter than the old-fashioned ones. Only drawback is that they are good for only about three hundred rounds. But that won't be a problem for this operation. We'll also carry assault rifles and special ammo for the pistols."

He set a box of .40-caliber pistol ammo on the table.

"The ones with the red tips are the specials," Sprague said.

"What are the specials?" asked Bishop.

"I make them myself. I take a standard hollow point 150-grain bullet, drill out the tip, fill it with liquid mercury, and then melt lead over the top. They don't pass through the body – they fragment. Therefore, they won't wound a bystander. However, it tears apart the body it hits. The bullet literally explodes. Even a slight wound quickly becomes fatal. The liquid mercury contaminates the massive wound. They are designed for one purpose – to kill."

"My God, this stuff isn't legal. You'll go to jail if anyone finds out about this arsenal," Bishop said.

Sprague laughed out loud.

"No problem, Brian. I have an arms dealer's license. More important, my customers guarantee there is no problem."

"What customers?"

"Langley and Delta Force. All of these weapons are sterile. They can't be traced back to me or to the United States," answered Sprague.

Bishop shook his head, hardly able to contain his utter amazement.

"Tiny, Tim was sure right. This really is the place we needed to go for help."

55

Deep in the subterranean cavern,
Eddie tried to get Sam to wake up.

"SAM, SAM, CAN YOU HEAR ME?"

"Of course, I can hear you, Eddie. What are you doing here in my apartment?"

"Sam, come on, you've got to wake up!" Eddie put his hands on her shoulders and shook her, but Samantha just couldn't keep her eyes open.

She begged him to just let her sleep – just a little while longer. She didn't remember getting drunk, but she must have really tied one on. Her bed felt as hard as a rock. She didn't want to miss her first class, but she just wouldn't be able to make it.

"Eddie, go away," she groaned.

He tried shaking her again, but she rolled over and turned her face away.

"I told you to go away and just leave me alone," she said, beginning to get angry. She raised her arms to cover her ears.

Eddie persisted. Finally, she struggled to sit up.

She'd never felt quite like this before. Her throat was so dry that she had trouble swallowing. She tried to focus on something that actually stood still, but the room continued to spin. She recalled the night of her senior prom when she had guzzled an entire bottle of wine. She'd been sick for two days.

Sam blinked and gradually began to open her eyes. Everything seemed to be illuminated by a red light. She felt deathly cold. Even though she blinked, she couldn't focus her eyes.

"Oh, my God, I'm going blind!" she said, terrified by the thought. "My eyes, my eyes! Something is wrong. All I see is a red light!" she said, weeping.

"That's because there is nothing but the red light," her brother said.

"Where am I?" she cried, trembling.

"I-I don't know. I honestly don't know," Eddie told her.

Sam's head began to clear. She remembered being in Tim's dorm room, but he wasn't there. She remembered Eddie being gagged and bound. She remembered the FBI men. Then there was the car. They shoved her in the back seat. She had felt a prick in her upper arm. That man held a hypodermic needle. He was grinning.

This must be some kind of drug-induced dream, she thought. What else could it be?

"Would you like a drink of water?" asked a woman.

Now she could see a young black woman who offered a bottle of water. The woman was short; she probably stood fewer than five feet tall. Sam reached out for the water, unscrewed the cap and took a long drink. She stopped to take a deep breath and then raised the bottle to her lips again and took a second long drink.

Thirty or more people surrounded her. Some sat cross-legged on the floor. Others leaned against the walls or walked around aimlessly. Sam discovered that she wasn't lying on a bed, but on a thin rubber mat. Others were stretched out on similar mats. She could see their chests moving up and down in deep sleep. She shivered. It was cold and damp.

"Do you think you can stand up?" Eddie asked.

"I think so," answered Sam. Eddie reached out to give her a hand. "Gosh, it's so cold," Sam mumbled. She got to her feet, but still felt unsteady.

"Put this on. It will help keep you warm," Eddie said, handing her one of the white gowns. It was made of coarse, heavy cotton. Sam pulled it over her head. The sleeves were long; they reached her wrists and a little more. Gradually, she began to feel warmer.

"What's happening here, Eddie?"

"I don't know. It's really weird. These kids are really spaced out. You'll see for yourself what I mean when you talk to them."

"I've been awake about two hours. We're in some kind of cave. There is a bigger cave a little distance beyond those bars. I think someone means to keep us locked in here. Along the wall over there, I see cases of bottled water and boxes of food, granola bars and stuff like that. The chemical toilets are located at the back of the cave. It makes no sense to me," he said, baffled by the situation.

"Oh, and one more thing," he said. All these kids believe something big is going to happen."

"Hi, I see you're awake," said the same woman who'd given Sam the water. "My name is Amanda. You two must the Dwaine and Trisha's replacements."

"Replacements?" asked Sam.

"Oh, yes, Dr. Sarday said they needed forty acolytes to open the curtain and allow Dacari Mucomba to enter this world. When we first got here to the temple, Dwaine and Trish were left behind," the young woman smiled in a carefree, nonchalant way. "I'm so happy you have joined us. By the way, what's your name?"

"Samantha."

"That's a pretty name isn't it, Eddie? Oh! There's Bill. I need to talk to him," said Amanda as she wandered away.

"What on Earth is she talking about?"

"I have no idea, but you need to see what's outside," said Eddie. He helped her walk over to the bars that blocked the entrance. As Sam looked out beyond the cave, she couldn't believe her eyes. She saw an enormous, underground cavern. She couldn't see to the end of the cavern or see up high to the ceiling. Just like in the cave, the cavern seemed to be illuminated by the same red light.

"Where does the light come from?" she asked.

Eddie rubbed the wall with the palm of his hand. As he pulled his hand away, it also took on a red glow.

"What is it?" she asked.

"I don't know, but the walls are covered with it. It feels soft, like moss," said Eddie.

"What if it's radioactive? It might kill us," said Sam. A worried look crossed her face.

"Sam, this is bad, I think we are going to die or something even worse than that," answered Eddie, equally concerned.

Sam wondered if they were even on Earth anymore. It all seemed like a scene from a science fiction movie.

"We have to get out of here," she said. "And the sooner, the better!"

56

At Sprague's house in Fayetteville, they had done all they could do.
Nothing was left – except the waiting.

CHIEF BRIAN BISHOP HAD WANDERED OUTSIDE, KILLING SOME TIME before they all ate a light dinner. Soon they'd all be in open conflict against Sarday's goons.

Bishop shook his head. That Tiny Sprague was quite a guy. Who could have ever imagined that a private individual could be sitting on such an arsenal of modern warfare?

At first, Bishop couldn't believe that someone like Tiny and his buddies could be of any help at all. But these old guys had an incredible grasp of paramilitary operations. Furthermore, they truly believed that they could accomplish what they set out to do.

Now in the Spragues' back yard, he saw another side of the unique man and his talented wife. Bishop sat on a stone bench beside the koi pond. He could see a dozen or more large fish swimming lazily in the tranquil water beside him. One, the size of a small dog, kept looking up at him as it swam by then turned and swam by him again.

"You must be hungry, right, big boy?" he asked the fish. It didn't answer, but it didn't quit begging either.

The pond was well designed. It was maybe thirty feet across at its widest. At one end, a waterfall cascaded over a series of rock ledges. Several small birds splashed in the little pools. A fern grotto provided cover for whatever birds do when they wanted privacy. A large, gray squirrel hopped over a line of rocks, stopping often to see if it was being watched and scolding noisily when it noticed a stranger had invaded its sanctuary. Bishop found it hard to believe that he was in Fayetteville, North Carolina. If it wasn't for the six-foot high cedar fence that blocked the neighbors' views, he could have imagined that this secret wonderland could be in Hong Kong, where Mai Lee was born.

With the news that the FBI was not looking for him, Bishop should have felt relief, but now, he just felt depressed. He had a splitting headache and felt sick to his stomach.

He was prepared for war. He had been issued a state-of-the-art, black SWAT tactical response uniform that included classic, black nine-inch side-zip boots. Under his black T-shirt, he wore the ultra-lightweight, concealable ballistic vest. The Blackhawk-special operations H-gear shoulder harness would help distribute the weight of the gear, ammunition, and the .40-caliber Glock 22 ACC Evolution 40 suppressor package with seventeen-round magazines.

Never before in his military or police career had he used a weapon with a silencer. The suppressor was one and a quarter inch in diameter, ten inches long and constructed of aerospace-quality aluminum. The special Glock 22 pistol had an extended threaded barrel. Except for the barrel, the gun looked like an ordinary service weapon. It only took seconds to screw on the suppressor.

Earlier in the day, Bishop had fired several rounds through the suppressor to familiarize himself with the additional weight of the weapon compared to a normal pistol. It was easy to do even in a residential area, as long as it had a silencer.

To complete the uniform, Sprague had issued Black Global Armour's PASGT black lightweight ballistic helmets and light-enhancing goggles. The uniforms were stenciled in dark gray letters with the word "SWAT." On the right breast was a stenciled badge. He would appear to be a member of a police SWAT team.

That, of course, was Tiny Sprague's plan. They were going to drive to the Fayetteville Airport, go to the hangar where the helicopter was housed, load up the chopper, climb on board, and take off. Apparently somebody owed Sprague a really big favor. After all, they had given him permission to use the helicopter. Sprague's daughter, Ann, would fly them to Johnsonville. When the operation was over, she would fly them back to Fayetteville.

The whole rescue operation was adding to Bishop's depression. He understood that Tim Martin wanted to save his girlfriend and her brother from Sarday's cult. He was certain now that the woman, Jilly, had told the truth about witnessing a beheading. He'd read articles about people getting caught up in this type of thing. After all, that evil Charles Manson had convinced a number of young women to kill the actress Sharon Tate.

The aerial photo of the plantation indicated that close to six hundred people were inside. Could Sarday influence that many people to participate in human sacrifices? Of course, he reasoned, Adolph Hitler had been capable of duping an entire nation.

Bishop had no problem taking on that son-of-bitch Sarday, but to attack the entire school was something else. A real SWAT platoon and close air support were critical. Sure, those Jonestown followers had been crazy, but anyone who thought they could take on thirty armed men and six hundred civilians with only five men also belonged in the nuthouse.

They had spent all morning preparing for the assault. He had watched the three old men working with the weapons. They knew their craft. He watched them laughing and reliving old battles. My God, all three had fought in Vietnam. Bishop's own father had fought in Vietnam. They had to be his dad's age, all more than seventy. Sure, they were Special Forces, but they were old and out of shape.

In addition to their pistols, they were carrying M4A1 carbines with bayonet lug laser attachments. The M4A1 is the weapon of choice for the best SWAT units. It fires the same 5.56 round as the M-16 rifle. It has a thirty-round magazine and can fire single, three-round bursts or go on full automatic.

Catfield, who at times seemed to be going a little senile, insisted that he be allowed to carry the M4A1 carbine with the RIS-mounted M-203 grenade launcher and telescopic site. The M203 launcher mounted under the 5.56 carbine barrel was a single-shot weapon that fired low velocity rounds the size of a hand grenade. It had a range of one hundred fifty meters. The high explosive round had a kill radius similar to a fragmentation grenade.

Again Catfield, argued with the others. He wanted to carry fragmentation grenades. The others said that kind of firepower was unnecessary. They had agreed to carry flash-bang grenades but no fragmentation grenades. In a hostage rescue operation a frag grenade kills not only the bad guys, but also the good guys. Finally, the other men agreed that Catfield could have his M-203 with four high explosive M 203 grenade rounds, but no fragmentation grenades.

Tim was even more difficult than Catfield. The boy was clearly too hotheaded to follow orders and likely would get them all killed. Bishop understood the kid's motives. If Sarday were holding Ann, he would want to do the same thing. For that reason, he would have stepped back and let someone else go in. Once a soldier allows his emotions to take over, he is of no value to the team.

But the operation was only part of Bishop's depression. He, Brian Bishop, was the other part. He was his own biggest problem. When Sprague gave him his "no-drinking" orders, he'd put his glass down and hadn't touched a drop in the last twelve hours. Now all he could think about was getting a drink.

Sitting by the pond, he realized for the first time in his life that he really was addicted to booze. He thought back over his career and saw how booze had ruined his life. He realized that it was because of his drinking that Sarday had gained a foothold in Johnsonville to begin with. Now, he was going die with three old men and a kid. And, all that for nothing. The girl and her brother were probably already dead. Sadly, Bishop didn't care if he lived or died. Ann would be better off without him.

"Beautiful day isn't it?"

Bishop turned around. Sprague stood in front of him with a large glass of whiskey in his hand. He sat down beside Bishop.

"Son, this operation ain't gonna be easy."

"I know that," Bishop said, looking down at the water rippling in the pool. "Maybe we should just call it off and try to get the authorities involved."

"No," Sprague said. "I believe we must do this. But, I've been watching you. Your hands are shaking. I don't believe you're afraid, I believe you need a drink."

"You don't understand. I'm a drunk," Bishop said. "You don't need a drunk around, getting you all killed."

Sprague hung his head and hesitated before responding to Bishop's honest personal assessment. Little did Bishop know that Sprague understood only too well what addiction to alcohol could do to a man's life. He put his large hand on Bishop's shoulder before asking a serious question.

"Just when did you realize that you're an alcoholic?" Sprague asked.

"Today," Bishop admitted.

"Well, it was obvious to me when you first arrived yesterday. Of course, I'm a retired bartender. I know one when I see one," Sprague said.

"Unfortunately, today is not the day to go cold turkey. I hope you will make the decision to quit, but do it tomorrow. Alcohol is like any other drug. If you are dependent on it, when you quit, the withdrawal is hell."

"So, I want you to drink this glass of scotch, but do it slowly," Sprague said. "Otherwise, you *will* be worthless." He handed Brian the scotch. "Bring it with you. Dinner is on the table."

Sprague got up and walked toward the house.

Bishop stared at the glass beside him. He picked it up and wrapped both hands around it. Then he looked down at the big koi. He raised the glass slowly to his lips and took a sip of the golden liquid.

"This is my last drink, fish. I swear to God."

57

Locked behind iron bars, Sam and Eddie
tried to make sense of what was going on.

"WHAT ARE THEY DOING? JUST WHAT ARE THEY DOING OUT THERE?"

"I don't know, Sam, I really don't know," Eddie answered. He shook his head. Normally the calm one, Sam could tell that even he was overwhelmed by the horror of their capture.

They stood side-by-side looking through the iron gate. Each of them clenched the metal bars so tightly that their knuckles poked out like miniature mountain ranges along the backs of their hands. Sam had never felt her heart flutter like this. Drops of perspiration ran from her scalp and dampened her cheeks. Her breathing came in irregular gasps. She hung her head. They could do nothing but wait.

At eight o'clock things began to change. At first, they heard a drumbeat. One beat, two beats, three beats, each louder and closer together than the previous beats. Soon, a mysterious chanting mixed with the drumbeat. No words, just an eerie up and down, slower and faster, coming from everywhere, coming from nowhere.

"God, Eddie," Sam whispered nervously. "What's going to happen to us? Where are we? What are those people doing?"

Eddie shook his head again. Nothing made any sense. The weirdest part was the naked people. Whatever would convince hundreds of people to disrobe and stand in orderly rows inside an underground cavern?

For the first time, Sam noticed a stone slab in front of the crowd. It looked like a bench, flat and long, but without a backrest.

Not long ago, Sam had seen a documentary on the Travel Channel about African tribal music. There was chanting then. This chant seemed similar. But this wasn't Africa, or was it? She saw black faces in the crowd, but an equal number of white ones. Naked men and women stood shamelessly before them, oblivious to the obscene spectacle they made.

It was difficult to see what was happening from so far away. Not only was the distance a problem, but also the red light cast a disconcerting glow over the crowd. She squinted and stood as still as she could. Maybe if she really concentrated she would be able to make some sense of it all.

"Oh, this is so cool! So absolutely cool," said a young black woman who had wedged herself in between Sam and Eddie. "It's about time! We've been waiting so long for the ceremony to begin!"

Sam didn't like the way the woman had elbowed herself in between them. She needed Eddie's warmth and strength to keep her from falling apart. As his twin, she had always been able to count on Eddie's steady presence. She needed him more than ever right now.

As soon as Sam turned to say something, the woman had moved on, chattering excitedly. Sam tried to catch the gist of her talk, but none of it made any sense.

Then as suddenly as the drumbeat and chanting began, it abruptly stopped. Before, there had been noise, lots of noise. Now there was nothing, just complete silence.

Eddie nudged her. Without a word, he pointed a finger to the right of the crowd. Sam leaned down to see where he was pointing. She saw a line of people wearing black-hooded robes. The loose fabric enclosed their heads and hid their faces. They walked confidently in single file and formed a semi-circle facing the others. They blocked the slab from Sam's view.

The drum resumed, this time striking a single beat. Sam waited for a second beat, but it didn't come. Instead, the percussion from the first drumbeat echoed off the walls of the immense cavern. As the sound faded, nearly every participant fell to his or her knees. Only one black-robed figure remained standing.

"It's Dr. Sarday!" squealed a redheaded girl behind them.

"They'll be coming for us now!" someone else said.

"Isn't it wonderful?" asked a pimply-faced youth standing next to Eddie.

Sam knew they could wait no longer. They had to take matters into their own hands if they were going to survive this horror.

"Go over to the porta-potties," she whispered in Eddie's ear. "We're going to get in one and pull the door shut, but we won't latch it."

"Why?" Eddie asked. This was no time to use one of the portable toilets.

"Because if we hide in a porta-potty when they come for these crackpots, they might not notice how many actually go out. If the cell is empty and there are no red occupancy signs showing on the doors, we might just be able to sneak out of here once everybody gets involved in this ceremony. I don't think they'll lock the gate once the cell is empty."

Eddie nodded. For the first time, there was a plan – a glimmer of hope for the two of them. Their cellmates began to mill about in their crazed excitement, creating the perfect cover. Slowly, Sam and Eddie moved cautiously to the back of the cave. First Sam, then Eddie, stepped into the portable toilet, leaving the door partially open to indicate that it was unoccupied.

Then they waited. The sweet smell coming from the chemical toilet began to sicken Sam. She began to feel nauseous. She forced herself to think of something else. She wondered if anyone knew where they were. If they did, were they looking for them? She had no doubt that Tim would do everything possible to find them. But, how could he possibly do anything? She didn't even know if they were still in the United States.

Sam jumped, startled by the clank of the iron gate swinging open. She reached out and grabbed Eddie's hand. They both held their breath. Sam gasped and almost choked. She stifled a cough and held her breath again. Maybe her plan wouldn't work. Maybe one of those hooded guys would pull open the door and drag them out.

It seemed like they'd been trapped in the portable toilet for nearly an hour, but it probably had been only a matter of minutes, when the drumbeat resumed in earnest. They continued to wait. Finally, Sam pushed gently on the door. Just a few inches, she thought, just a little more. She opened it far enough to allow her a peek outside.

"Do you see anything?" Eddie asked.

"No, nothing," she answered. Bravely or foolishly, she opened the door even more. Finally, she gave it a stronger push, and it swung all the way open.

Just has she had hoped, the cave was empty, and the cell door had been left unlocked. They made their way slowly from the toilet, choosing their steps carefully as they moved toward the gate. They were alone.

"Now what?" Eddie whispered.

"Let's work our way over to those formations," Sam replied, keeping her voice as low as possible.

She pointed to their right where they could see a dark wall. The lower portion of the wall had none of the red, glowing matter. But it did have a number of limestone formations that could offer them partial cover. Sam figured that there might even be a tunnel leading to the outside.

Keeping low, they crept to the first outcropping. They scurried around behind it, concealed themselves, and peeked out cautiously at the crowd.

Something was up. Every person in the huge crowd, except the single dark-robed figure and the group of white-robed acolytes – just thirty-eight of them – knelt on the cave floor, their faces pressed into the dusty floor. The drumbeat had slowed. Two new figures in dark robes, stepped out in the open. They carried an object that was approximately three feet tall. They averted their eyes, as if it were too bright to view with the naked eye. They gently lowered it to the floor directly in front of the stone platform. A third individual stepped forward. This one held a large, wooden bowl. The bowl was placed about halfway between the object and the platform. All three individuals stepped back, bowed deeply, and pressed their faces into the earth.

From their vantage point, Sam and Eddie could only see the back of what appeared to be a statue. Its body was naked. It appeared to be very old. One leg was gone, and a metal shaft had replaced the missing leg. The head was disproportionally large. A small, dwarf-like body formed the bottom portion. Two horns stuck out from the top of the head.

Samantha couldn't take her eyes off the statue. She felt drawn to it. She recalled the feeling she got when she rode on a roller coaster – a slow incline and a sudden, deep descent, much like a free fall. Her heart felt like it was caught in her throat, pressured to remain fixed there during the rapid plummet down the rickety tracks.

An eerie glow began to surround the statue. Now, Samantha's arms felt as heavy as lead. She tried to look away, but the longer she focused on the statue, the more disoriented she became. Her heart raced as an intense fear enveloped her. Her breathing accelerated, and her temples throbbed. She must be hot, because she was sweating profusely. She must be cold, because her teeth were chattering.

The drumbeat intensified, exceeding one hundred beats per minute. The dark-robed individual turned toward the acolytes. He pointed at the nearest one. Without hesitation, she walked forward and stood directly in front of him.

"It's Amanda!" Sam whispered to Eddie.

Amanda reached down and pulled her white gown over her head. She unashamedly stood stark naked before the dark-robed figure.

Samantha knew she should be appalled at what she was witnessing, but she felt a strange lethargy come over her. She felt like she had sunk to the depths of an ocean, and the water weight pressed down, unrelenting, on her useless body. The scene before her seemed to be unfolding in slow motion, despite the increasing rhythm of the drum. The throbbing continued to the point of unbearable pain. She held her hands tightly over her ears to protect her eardrums from rupturing. She became captive to the scene, helplessly frozen, unable to move or avert her eyes.

Suddenly, the entire multitude in the cavern stood up in unison and faced the statue. They began to chant in rolling, melodic voices. As the chanting continued, the two individuals who had brought in the statue walked forward, took Amanda by her arms, and escorted her to the platform. The girl looked pitifully small next to the two robed figures. She stepped up on the stone platform and knelt, facing the statue. Then she reclined face down on the platform.

The two figures pulled Amanda's body forward so that her head hung over the edge of the altar. Amanda continued to hold up her head. She smiled as she looked in Samantha's direction. One of the figures stepped forward and stood to the right of the statue. From beneath the robe, the figure withdrew a long, silver sword. The polished metal reflected the red light as the individual lifted it overhead. The drumbeat reached a crescendo then stopped abruptly.

Samantha was transfixed by the young woman's unwavering smile. Then the blade fell rapidly, striking the back of Amanda's neck, slicing through the flesh, muscle and bone as if the slender neck were nothing more than jelly. The head fell forward, but it missed dropping into the wooden bowl. It landed on the cave floor before it rolled to a stop. The eyes continued to stare in Sam's direction as if seeking her approval for its random fall.

Red fluid from Amanda's headless corpse splattered the statue. The blood pressure in the headless corpse dropped to zero, yet the thick, dark liquid continued to drain out of the body and spilled down the front of the altar. The blood changed the red light to a bright, white glow. Sam saw the statue begin to grow larger. All around, the acolytes stood motionless.

"Oh, God, Eddie, no!" Samantha moaned.

The black-robed figure lifted the bloody sword and pointed it directly at their hiding place. Samantha froze, hoping against hope that she and her brother wouldn't be detected.

Then she heard a snicker that became insane laughter. The statue had come to life. In the statue's eyes, she could see the reflection of her own naked form lying on the stone slab.

"The two orbs of death," she said, her voice barely audible. She knew then that she was going to die. Her legs buckled. A paralysis overcame her body. She sobbed uncontrollably.

Then darkness – total darkness – closed over her. Now she was certain that there was no hope of escaping the horror. They were doomed to die here, lost forever in a subterranean hell.

58

At nine o'clock Sprague's Silverado was parked alongside Martin's
Explorer in the double garage.

BEHIND THE CLOSED DOORS, THE MEN BEGAN THE CAREFUL PROCESS
of loading the gear. Sprague held a clipboard and double-checked to be
certain they had it all.

"Wait! You wait!" shouted Mai Lee. "You gotta have your lunches."
Bishop took the large, brown paper bag from her and put it in the back
of the truck. "You be careful," she said.

"Thanks, Mai Lee," he said. What he said wasn't exactly what he was
thinking. Careful isn't in the game plan, he conceded. They were about
to undertake a paramilitary operation in the Commonwealth of Virginia.
In all likelihood, there would be casualties – on both sides.

It had taken forty-five minutes to load up. Martin, the youngest and
most fit man among them, squeezed into the bed of the truck and leaned
back against an ammo box. Bishop hesitated before closing the hatch on
the camper shell.

"Good luck, kid," he said to Martin, looking him directly in the eyes.

"You, too, chief – I mean Brian. You, too," grinned Martin.

Catfield held the passenger door open. Bishop climbed into the middle, straddling his boots over the hump on the floor. Catfield took the
outside position. Sprague, the driver, took up nearly half the space in the
front. Kellogg sat in the back of the extended cab.

"Ready, guys?" Sprague asked.

"Ready as we'll ever be," answered Kellogg.

The garage door rolled open. Sprague pressed the starter and the big, V-8 roared to life. They could hear the engine rumble as the exhaust shot out through the dual stainless steel pipes. The orange truck backed out slowly, turned right and headed down the curving pavement before getting onto the four-lane county road. In a matter of minutes, they'd be on Interstate 95.

Hell, Bishop thought, this is just like riding with Tim. Sprague was weaving in and out of traffic. Bishop looked over at the speedometer. Sprague was going fifty-five on a posted forty miles per hour, four-lane road. Bishop tried to ignore Sprague's flagrant infraction. The stores in the strip mall on the right flew past them. Up ahead, he saw the stoplight at the next intersection go from green to yellow. Sprague didn't even slow up. Instead of stopping, Sprague shoved the gas pedal to the floor while flashing a grin at his front-seat passengers. He obviously took great satisfaction in hearing the roar of the dual exhaust. Bishop watched the light turn red as they crossed through the intersection.

Bishop had been on the verge of issuing a warning to Sprague, when they all heard the roar of a siren.

"Shit!" Sprague mumbled as the red and blue flashing lights came on behind him. He pulled over into the parking lot of the strip mall.

"We're screwed," said Kellogg from the back seat.

For Bishop, it was a lesson in patrolling – now he knew how it felt to be pulled over by the cops when you were doing something you knew was wrong.

All the weapons were stowed in the back with Martin. That didn't make Bishop feel any better. Martin was so wired that he might do something rash.

Sprague must have had the same thought. He turned to Kellogg.

"Open the rear sliding window, Mike," he said. Tell Tim not to do anything stupid. Let him know that I can take care of this."

The four men sat in the cab and waited, watching the lights flash in the side mirrors. Bishop couldn't help but think about all the weapons sitting in the back of Sprague's truck. They carried more sophisticated weaponry with them than the Fayetteville Police had in their weapons rack back at the station.

Patrolman Stanley Crest ran the truck's plates through the computer, checking for wants and warrants. He had spotted the truck weaving in and out of traffic and was ready to pull the guy over for reckless driving. Then it had run the yellow caution light in the intersection. Crest had seen the light turn red while the truck was in the middle of the intersection.

That did it. He saw the shiny, twenty-inch chrome wheels and the custom exhaust. He was sure that some young paratrooper from Bragg was behind the wheel. Well, tonight this young stud would get two tickets – one for reckless driving and a second one for running a red light.

The computer chirped the answers. The owner was a Wilbur G. Sprague, local address near Bragg. No wants or warrants were listed for the vehicle. The patrolman stepped out of his car and walked up alongside the truck. He tried to get a look inside the camper shell, but the high-pressure sodium lights in the parking lot were so bright that it was impossible to get a look inside the back or even to check out the rear seat of the cab through its tinted windows.

Normally tinted windows made Patrolman Crest uncomfortable. There was no way to see if someone had a gun pointed at your head. The only saving grace was that the stop had been made in a lighted parking lot, not along some lonely country road.

He rested his hand on his service revolver as he stepped up to the driver's window. The window rolled down. Crest had expected to see a young guy with a high and tight airborne haircut. The kid was probably in his early twenties.

The driver had a short haircut all right. As a matter of fact, the driver had no hair at all. He could be a skinhead, but the rest of the description didn't match up. The driver was a huge, old guy, likely in his sixties.

Three men were crowded in the front seat. The man in the middle looked to be in his forties, and next to him was another senior citizen. He could also see the silhouette of a fourth man in the back seat. Crest felt his heart skip a beat, and his hand tightened on his revolver.

They all wore black. Crest thought he might be dealing with some white supremacists or paramilitary nuts. He kept his cool.

"Sir, your registration, proof of insurance and driver's license, please," Crest asked.

"Officer Crest," Sprague said, glancing at the cop's nametag as he handed him a laminated ID, "I suggest you call the phone number at the bottom of the ID."

Crest took the card back to his patrol car. He used his cell to dial the 1-800 number.

"Drug Enforcement Agency, Washington office," someone answered.

"Yes, this is Patrolman Stanley Crest from the Fayetteville, North Carolina, Police Department. I have a Wilbur Sprague here. The ID number is 1A7233645. I stopped him for a routine traffic violation."

"One moment, please," said a male voice. Crest remained on hold for a few minutes. Then the man responded. "The vehicle you stopped is on an active DEA operation. Your cooperation in allowing the vehicle to proceed would be greatly appreciated. Also, we request that you do not record this stop or mention this action to anyone else."

"Yes, sir," Crest said. He returned to the driver's window. This kind of federal action was new to him, but he didn't want to tangle with the Feds. "I'm sorry to have delayed you, Agent Sprague. Try to keep it down in traffic so you don't attract too much attention."

"Thank you, officer," Sprague answered. He smiled at the officer and re-started his truck. He pulled out of the parking lot and returned to the highway.

"What was that all about?" Bishop asked. He'd never heard of a special DEA card or phone number.

Sprague pulled out the card again and handed it to Bishop. It was a photo ID, identifying Sprague as a DEA agent. The 1-800 number appeared at the bottom.

"Is this legitimate?" Bishop asked.

"Heavens, no," responded Sprague. The number is to the duty officer at Delta Force. Each 1-800 number identifies the cover that the operative is using."

"Well, I'll be damned," Bishop said. "Whatever the case, keep it at the speed limit. We need at least to get to the airport alive."

Fifteen minutes later, they pulled on to Airport Road. They passed the terminal and pulled up to the guarded gate. Sprague flashed the same ID to the armed guard. He waved them through. They followed Control Tower Road to a sign indicating Hangar Road.

Ten large hangars stood in a row next to the general aviation ramp. The truck's headlights illuminated the sign for Hangar 7. Sprague stopped and turned off the ignition. He pressed a button inset on the left side of the glove box. He punched in a special code that activated the remote door-opening system. Cable drums mounted on the end of each shaft made soft, crunching sounds as the sixty-foot bi-fold aluminum door began a fourteen-foot lift.

When the door was up high enough, Sprague drove the truck inside. He quickly pressed the remote button to reverse the motor and close the hangar door. A sensor turned on the lighting system as soon as the first three feet of the truck entered the hangar. It energized twelve overhead high-pressure sodium fixtures. When the lights came up to full brightness, they revealed the interior. A soft clanking of the door latches indicated that the door behind them was closed and the hangar was secure.

A boxy-shaped MD 902 helicopter perched on a dolly in the center of the hangar. The helicopter was painted a flat black. It had no markings. Bishop chuckled to himself. He'd no longer ridicule the conspiracy theorists that talked about "black helicopters." Maybe those folks weren't totally paranoid after all.

Though diminutive in appearance, the helicopter's twelve-foot main rotor-to-ground clearance and overall length of thirty-four feet said otherwise. With its high blade clearance and lack of a conventional tail rotor, it was unnecessary to worry about losing one's head or stooping to approach a running helicopter.

The MD 902 had two direct-drive Pratt & Whitney Canada turbo shaft engines. Each engine was controlled with a single-channel control, rated at five hundred horsepower. The helicopter was single-pilot certified. It was full of navigation and communication goodies.

It had a maximum gross weight of sixty-five hundred pounds for internal payloads. That left a generous useful load of more than three thousand pounds. Fully loaded, the maximum speed was more than one hundred and fifty miles per hour. It could operate for three and a half hours and travel four hundred and fifty miles.

The helicopter had one of the industry's quietest rotors and anti-torque yaw control systems, a thirty-one gallon auxiliary fuel tank, exterior and interior night vision support, room for eight, including pilot and co-pilot. This spoke volumes about the ability and readiness of the machine to handle the night's work.

Bishop was awed by the power and capability of the helicopter. He tried to hide his amazement, but it wasn't easy.

"You're late, Daddy," said a female voice.

The men had scarcely gotten out of the truck when they heard – and saw – a woman walk toward them from a small office inside the hangar. She wore a Nomex one-piece flight suit. She had an aviator's shoulder harness that held a nine-mm Beretta automatic pistol.

At first glance, Bishop thought a man was approaching, but he soon found out just how wrong he had been. The woman was at least six foot tall. Her jet-black hair was cut in a bob, coming just below her ears. With jewel green eyes and tanned skin, the woman was incredibly gorgeous. She was far better looking than she appeared in any of the pictures back in Sprague's den.

It was Ann Sprague, now a lieutenant colonel. Bishop saw the name-tag, LTC Sprague, just under the master aviator wings. She also had master jump wings and a combat action badge. On her right shoulder was an 82nd Airborne Division combat patch.

"The traffic was bad," said Sprague, with a twinkle in his eye.

Ann laughed at her dad's comment, but then stopped short as she noticed Tim Martin.

"Oh, my God, Tim, how you've grown!" She turned to Martin, threw her arms around him and kissed him on the cheek. "If I hadn't changed your diapers when you were a baby, I would be dragging you directly to my apartment," she joked.

Martin's face turned beet red. The levity helped, considering that they would soon be walking into hell. Some or all of them might not be coming back alive.

After introducing the men, Sprague laid out the plan. Ann, who was stationed at the Pentagon, had obtained a satellite view of the plantation just that morning. The video indicated that at least six hundred people were on the grounds. They seemed to be engaged in routine activity.

It was obvious that the combat-wizened soldiers knew how to set up the mission. Ann assured them that the helicopter had been lightened as much as was practical. The passenger seats had been replaced by hold-down straps anchored to the cabin floor. A ground crew had taken off interior utility cabin trim, two cabin doors, passenger steps and the co-pilot's collective and cyclic sticks.

Ann had flown her own plane down from D.C. about three hours earlier. She was to take the men to Johnsonville and land them behind the barn on the old Smith farm. The flight would only take ninety-five minutes. Once on the ground, Ann would keep the helicopter ready for lift-off.

They all had state-of-the-art radios. After the two Dixon kids were rescued, Ann would fly them back to Fayetteville. If everything went as planned, six people would fly up and eight would fly back.

It sounded so simple, just like make-believe war games, but Bishop knew only too well that this was no game, and the odds were stacked against them. But he had been impressed by the positive attitude of these old soldiers. They almost made him believe they would be able to pull it off. Of course, all military leaders knew that you had to believe that the mission could be accomplished. If you didn't, you knew you had to step aside and let someone else take over.

Once the MD 902 was loaded with gear, all but Ann and Bishop were on board. Ann activated the motor to open the hangar door. She and Bishop hooked up a John Deere tractor to the helicopter dolly's tow bar ring. They pulled the helicopter out of the hangar and into a large space between hangars on the taxiway.

Ann stepped onto the dolly's deck and nimbly climbed into the pilot's seat. She fastened and adjusted her seat belt and shoulder harness, testing the harness's inertia reel lock. She put on her night-vision goggles and equipped flight helmet and fastened its chinstrap.

While Ann began going through her pre-start checks, Bishop blocked the dolly's wheels, unhooked the tractor, drove it back inside the hanger, and parked it next to the office. He switched off the office lights, walked over to the wall at the front of the hangar, and pushed the momentary contact button that signaled the doors to close and start the time delay to turn off the hangar's interior lights. As the door began its descent, he slipped out of the hangar and ran to the helicopter. It was perched on the dolly like a large, dangerous bird. Because he knew the terrain better than any of them, he climbed into the co-pilot's seat to help identify the landing zone.

"Well, Chief Bishop, I guess we're just about ready to take off," said Ann. "I've configured the intercom settings so that the three of us – Dad, you and I – can talk to each other and also monitor radio communications. Once you get that helmet on, we'll be on our way."

It had taken Bishop a little longer to get his seatbelt and shoulder harness adjusted. Ann passed him the NVG-equipped flight helmet. The three of them would be using the helicopter's intercom system for communications. Only Ann would be able to transmit outside with the radio.

"Ready, sir... uh, I mean, ma'am," Bishop said, using the helmet mike for the first time. "Let 'er rip!"

Bishop watched with a great deal of admiration, and maybe a little envy, as Ann Sprague skillfully continued her flight prep. He regretted that he had never taken flying lessons. Maybe after this was over, if he lived, and after he went on the wagon and got away from booze, he just might take up flying.

Ann turned on the battery and avionics master switches, giving life to the numerous instruments, lights and readouts, adjusted the interior and instrument light levels and set the altimeter to the field's elevation of one hundred eighty-nine feet above mean sea level. She switched on the anti-collision lights and fuel boost pumps and set the two engine switches to idle.

When she turned the rotary engine control switch, the engine igniter spark snapped. It was quickly followed by a soft whooshing sound as the engines came to life. They ramped up to a steady whine.

The sweet smell of jet-A exhaust from the building rotor down-wash circulated throughout the cabin. The aircraft began to vibrate. The mechanical beast came to life. Bishop felt a small rush of adrenalin as the engines accelerated and stabilized. Ann turned on the navigation lights, selected the radio frequencies she anticipated would be needed, and entered the coordinates for the route.

Ann looked back to make sure everyone was holding on to the floor straps. She set the engine switches to flight mode. She ran through additional checks until she was satisfied. She looked back at her passengers, gave them a thumbs-up and lifted off the dolly for a hover check. All systems were "in the green." She let her machine settle back on the dolly. Finally, she was certain that the aircraft was flight and mission-ready.

After receiving clearance from the control tower, she turned on the landing lights and lifted the collective pitch control, raising the helicopter to a three-foot hover. She pedal-turned the nose to a northerly direction, heading down the taxiway between the hangars.

"Let the games begin!" she said aloud.

She loved the dance of the five balls – the ballet of simultaneous control inputs to harness pitch, roll, yaw, climb and acceleration. An aircraft defies the laws of gravity. Some people even contend that flying defies the movements of the universe itself. A machine consisting of a gazillion moving parts, flying in close formation with other airborne beasts, beating the air into submission, and converting dollars into jet exhaust and noise. No doubt about it – Ann Sprague loved to fly.

The local time was now ten forty-five. She started the clock that would keep track of time en route. She turned the transponder from "standby" to "on" and began to climb while lowering the nose and accelerating.

The helicopter gently shuddered, and the airspeed increased to forty knots. She eased the nose up and began her climbing, left turn. She took up a heading to intercept her westbound course to her first waypoint, the town of Southern Pines, twenty-seven miles in the distance. They were running late. Because of the team's traffic delay on the way to the airport, they were going to be twenty minutes later than their planned arrival time.

Leveling off at one thousand feet, Ann established her cruise speed at one hundred thirty-two knots and completed the level-off and cruise checks. Weather reports indicated winds would be light and variable with unlimited visibility. At least they had no headwind to slow them down.

"We should be at the Smith farm landing zone in ninety-five minutes," she told her passengers over the intercom.

Bishop swore he'd never, ever forget the flight to the Smith farm near Johnsonville. He'd flown in choppers before, but he knew better than to use that nickname again around Ann. When he had first climbed in to the co-pilot's seat, she had asked him if he'd ever flown in a helicopter before.

"Yeah, a few times when I was in the army and a couple of times in police work," he'd said. "But I've never been in a chopper like this before."

"Helicopter," Ann had replied, correcting him. "I don't use that other word. I have too much respect for these rotary-winged aircraft."

Ann flashed him a smile, and Bishop knew he had been forgiven.

As they approached Southern Pines, she began the descent. When the altimeter indicated that the helicopter was five hundred feet above the ground, she leveled off. It was time for them to disappear. She turned off the transponder, navigation and anti-collision lights and dimmed the interior lights. Smith farm was one hour and twenty-three minutes ahead.

With the transponder off and flying so close to the ground, the aircraft would be lost in the ground clutter on radar screens. They had practically no discernable radar signature. The rotor system was one of the quietest in the business. No one on the ground would be able to hear them. The size and color of the machine made the helicopter about as stealthy as a non-military helicopter could get.

It was dark, and they were close to the ground. Flying this low and this fast, a sudden encounter with a hilltop or trees would be a disaster. The multi-function display showed a moving map, weather avoidance, and, most importantly, terrain avoidance and warning information.

Now it was time for them to implement the second part of the flight assurance plan. Ann switched the aircraft lighting from normal to the interior and exterior lighting configuration. They flipped down their helmet-mounted goggles, and the outside view took on a soft green glow. With ambient starlight, they could see the terrain clearly for miles.

So far, Bishop had been caught up in the excitement of the flight. But nothing so far could even compare to the last leg of their journey. They crossed over Interstate 81, eighteen miles from the landing zone. From that point on, the helicopter descended to a hundred feet above ground level. At two miles out from the landing zone, she descended to just above treetop level, with the skids just missing the foliage.

Flying in such close proximity to the terrain made any sound totally confusing to people on the ground. The noise would seem to be coming from all directions at once. A person would not know where to look for an aircraft. At one mile, she descended even more. She skillfully dodged between tall trees, keeping the rotor disk just above their tops while still maintaining the course.

Bishop had enjoyed Mai Lee's dinner, but he hadn't expected to see it come up this much later. He forced himself to concentrate on watching the terrain speed by. By sheer force, Bishop won the battle of the belly.

"Over there!" Bishop said, when he spotted the open fields of Smith farm. "Can you see the barn?"

The structure looked even more dilapidated at night than it did in the daylight. The roof sagged in the middle, the doors hung open, and the holes in the walls appeared black against the green background.

Ann made a rapid deceleration, leveling the helicopter as the skids softly touched ground. She immediately switched off the engines, applied the rotor brake, and brought the rotor system to a swift stop. As the engines spooled down into silence, all switches were turned off, and the shutdown sequence was complete.

Just one minute after touchdown, the helicopter sat silently on a hayfield near the plantation grounds. No one said a word. The next phase of the mission was about to begin.

59

On the ground near the plantation, the team stepped out of the
helicopter, some more gingerly than others.

THE OLDER MEN STOPPED FOR A MOMENT TO STRETCH THEIR LEGS
and take some deep breaths. The youngest, Tim Martin, laid his hand on
his weapon, squinted his eyes and scanned the horizon. For Martin, the
action couldn't start soon enough.

For all of them, the summer sounds and the quiet Virginia hills were
a welcome relief from the engine noise and the whirr of the blades. Just
like an athlete who sweats during a workout and cools down when it's
over, the helicopter made its own sounds of relief. The gyros finished
spinning. The hot metal clicked and snapped as it cooled. In the distance,
the team heard the croaking of frogs, the barking of a dog, and the chirping of crickets.

One sound they didn't hear was human noise. They were confident that the landing hadn't drawn any unwanted attention. Ann did
a post-flight inspection and prepared the aircraft for its return flight to
Fayetteville. Take-off would be quick. She would only have to hit the battery switch and start the engines. She would stay back with the big bird,
ready to fly at a moment's notice. She switched on her handheld radio so
she could monitor the team's transmissions.

The men unloaded the equipment, transferring it silently into the
barn. Once Bishop had his gear on, he stepped out of the barn for a
moment, just to be alone. This far out, the light pollution wasn't as bad
as near the towns and cities. The stars seemed brighter than usual. To the

south, he saw the floodlights from the school's ceremonial field, just two miles away. The compound's south fence ran only about a mile from the hayfield.

Bishop's eyes had become accustomed to the night. He could see shadows of the trees near the road. He suddenly froze. He thought he saw some movement near the old farmhouse. He dropped to his knees and put on the night-vision goggles. The house stood out at night just as well as if it were daylight. He focused on the area to the right of the house. He thought he saw a man peeking around the outside corner.

He pulled out his Glock and moved forward in a low crouch. He moved across the open space. Then it dawned on him that he should have thought to screw on the silencer. If he had to fire his gun, the sound would travel for miles. He didn't have time to do it now. Bishop hoped he'd be able to bluff his way through the encounter.

He slipped around the left side of the house. When he reached the back, he crouched down and looked around the corner. The goggles revealed a large man looking out from the house, apparently watching the barn. The man held a shotgun.

Bishop moved slowly toward the man, taking one slow step at a time. When he was fewer than three feet from the man, he whispered a warning.

"Freeze, asshole. If you even twitch, I'll blow your head off. Drop the shotgun! Now!" he ordered.

The man obeyed immediately. Then he turned around and stood face-to-face with Bishop. Both men stood deathly still. Bishop was the first to speak.

"Willie Johnson, what on earth are you doing out here?" Bishop asked.

"Don't shoot, mister. I ain't been doin' nuthin!" the man cried, his voice trembling.

"Willie! It's me, Chief Bishop!"

"Chief Bishop? Chief Bishop, it really be you? Did you come in that helicopter?" Johnson asked.

"Yes, Willie," Bishop answered.

"Oh, lordy me, chief. I thought I was dead. Chief, I think you made me pee in my pants," Willie mumbled, obviously embarrassed.

"Willie, what in God's name are you doing here at the old Smith farm?"

"We be hiding from them bad guys from the plantation. They come to our house. Try to get Miss Ann," answered Willie.

"Ann? My wife, Ann? What happened?" Bishop asked. Last he knew, he'd delivered his wife to Willie's house for safekeeping.

"She be OK. She and Jasmine and I been hiding in the farmhouse. Some of our kinfolk brung us food and water. It was way too dangerous to stay back at our own house," Willie said.

"Willie, are you telling me that Ann is here?" Bishop asked, astonished that Ann could be nearby.

"Yes, sir, chief. That I am," Willie said.

"Where are they?" asked Bishop, looking around the area.

"In the house. When we heard the noise, we thought them bad men were coming. Chief, I am so glad you're here. I be real scared," said Willie.

"Come on, Willie. I want to see my wife," Bishop said. Willie led him to the back door. It hung loosely by one hinge. Willie pulled on the door.

"Jasmine, Miss Ann, it's Chief Bishop," Willie called.

Almost before Willie could step out of the way, Ann Bishop rushed out of the door and threw her arms around her husband.

"Brian, thank God you're here! I've been so scared," she said as she pressed her face into his chest. She was almost overcome by uncontrollable sobbing.

Bishop ran his fingers through her hair. He loved her more at this moment than he had in years. He now realized how selfish he'd been to let alcohol take over his life. He whispered in her ear, "I love you. I love you so much."

It was too dark to see her face, but the warmth and softness of her body comforted him beyond belief. The days of anxiety had begun to take their toll.

But he knew the last few days hadn't been easy for Ann either. He stepped back to assess the strain she'd been under. Before he could ask her how she had been doing, Ann launched a barrage of questions.

"How did you get here?" she asked. "How did you find us? Why all the special weapons?"

"I think it's better if I show you, rather than try to tell you," he said with a grin. "Come on, all of you, there are several people in the barn that I want you to meet."

"I'll walk along with you if that's OK," said a deep voice from somewhere in the shadows.

All four jumped. Then they saw Tiny Sprague come out from the darkness behind them.

"I heard voices and figured you needed some help," said Sprague, with a wide smile that reassured them.

Willie reached out to shake Sprague's hand.

"You be almost as big as me," said Willie.

Sprague had to laugh. "There are very few men that can say that to me."

"Come on, enough talking," said Bishop. "We need to go to the barn."

They found the rest of the team spread out, their weapons pointed toward the unexpected visitors.

"It's OK," said Sprague. "These are some of the good guys."

They all moved into the shelter of the barn. They broke open several chemical lights that emitted a green glow that couldn't be seen from a distance.

Bishop introduced Willie, Jasmine and his wife to the rest of the group. There were some laughs when Ann met Ann. Willie gave the nicknames that identified them. One was Tall Ann Sprague, and the other Short Ann Bishop.

But even that was too long. They'd be called Tall Ann and Short Ann to keep it simple. Willie's homespun creativity brought everyone the smiles and laughter needed to relieve the building stress of the mission. Bishop wondered if it would be their last laugh, but he shook off the feeling, took a deep breath and picked up the pace. He introduced them all to Tim Martin.

"Willie, I found the man your grandmother wanted us to find," said Bishop. "When he saw the statue, he knew all about it," he explained.

Willie could only stare at this Tim Martin.

"Chief, that can't be right. He's too young to know Grandma, and he ain't black."

"Well, Willie, I am sure he's the one," said Bishop.

Martin hadn't said a word in the last few minutes. He didn't know what to say. He didn't remember any Grandma Johnson, and he'd never been to Johnsonville in his life.

A deep yowl startled everyone.

"Where'd that cat come from?" asked Catfield.

They all looked down. Sitting dead center in front of Martin was a large gray tomcat. It stared directly in Martin's face and let out another yowl.

"Be careful," said Catfield. "It might have rabies."

"He don't have no rabies," said Willie. "He be Grandma Johnson's cat. Now he be Miss Ann's cat. He saved us from the bad guys."

Martin's mouth dropped open as he looked more closely at the cat.

"I've seen that cat before," he said.

"That's not possible. You said you've never been here before," said Sprague.

"It wasn't here," said Martin. "It was in the village of Zigda in Liberia. He was sitting next to an old woman."

"Grandma Johnson ain't never been in Africa. When was this?" Willie asked.

"About a month ago," said Martin.

"That not be my grandma. She be dead then," said Willie.

"It was in a dream," answered Martin. "I know it sounds crazy, but I swear, I saw that cat in the dream."

"Well, he sure seems to know you," said Sprague. "But dreams aren't going to help us now. We have got to get into that school. Let's see if we can find your girlfriend and her brother and get them out of there."

Bishop had taken his wife outside the barn to explain what had happened since he had left her with Willie and Jasmine to go find Tim Martin.

"I don't understand," said Ann. He had told her that the real FBI was not looking for them, and all this had been some kind of frame-up involving Sarday and his cult.

Ann couldn't understand why the authorities couldn't handle it all. Despite Bishop's insistence that there wasn't good evidence, it still worried her.

Sprague interrupted them.

"Are you ready to go, Brian?"

"Sure, Tiny. Just a moment more," Bishop said, turning to his wife. "Listen, Ann, there is something I want to tell you – I have decided to stop drinking."

"Oh, Brian," she said, "I have been waiting to hear those words for years."

"I love you, Ann."

"I love you, too," she said.

They hugged each other tightly. Neither of them wanted to let go.

He then held her at arms' length. A more serious look came over his face.

"Honey, if something happens, and, I or we, don't come back, you get on that helicopter with Ann Sprague and fly directly to Fayetteville."

"Brian, nothing's going to happen. I don't want hear this," she said, tears welling up again in her eyes.

"Ann, I just don't feel real warm about this operation, but I have no choice. This is the only chance I have to prove that we're being framed. They want us dead and I refuse to lie down and let then put a bullet in my head like a rabid dog."

He bent down and kissed her on the lips, holding her tightly in his arms. This could be the last time he would ever embrace his wife.

60

The men were all ready. Bishop quickly grabbed his gear and joined the team.

THEY CLOSED THE BARN DOOR AND BEGAN THE TREK TOWARD THE compound.

They were soon close enough to the ceremonial field to see some illumination coming from the tall light poles that marked their destination.

"Thanks, Sarday, you old bastard," Bishop said aloud.

Sarday's lights gave just the right amount of brightness for the team to make its way toward the school. They couldn't get lost as long as they headed toward the lights. They followed the tree line due south of the Smith farm. The first half-mile was easy. Even though the fields had been untended for years, only clumps of dried grass, a few small scrub oaks and low bushes stood in their way. What Sarday's lights didn't reveal, the starlight did.

Martin followed close behind. He was totally committed to the mission. He had to do all in his power to save the woman he loved. If he had any doubt before, he had none now. The thought of losing Samantha tore him up inside. He had a sick feeling in his gut. He knew that Chief Bishop was convinced that Sam and Eddie were dead, and that they stood no chance at all of getting into the school and then getting everyone out alive.

Martin couldn't explain it to anyone, but he was certain that Bishop was wrong. He knew that both Sam and Eddie were alive. He also knew that they had to save them and save them quickly.

Six years ago he had been involved in a fight for his family's life in Africa. At age fifteen he felt none of the fear that now gnawed at his gut.

He recalled a magazine article he'd read years ago about child soldiers. Due to their immaturity, they didn't show much fear in battle. They were ruthless in attacking the enemy. After all, they didn't believe that death could come to them. The despots who ran the military took advantage of their "child weapons," and they took advantage of the children's reckless attitudes to spend their lives indiscriminately.

When Martin was fifteen, the experience in Liberia was mostly an adventure. He hadn't understood either the fear of death or possibility of injury. Now at twenty-two, he knew the dangers they faced and that someone he loved was in great danger.

He pushed aside a small oak, and he whispered a prayer, "Oh, God, I don't' know what I'll do if I lose Sam. Please help me save her."

"What the fuck? What in the hell is this shit?"

Martin heard someone thrashing about and screaming obscenities. They had reached the barbed wire fence at the edge of the Smith farm. Someone was tangled in the wire. As he came closer to the shouting, he realized that it was Catfield who was making all the noise. Martin pushed ahead, only to discover that Tiny Sprague had reached the man at the same time.

"Stop struggling, Bill. That barbed wire will tear you up," Sprague whispered, trying to keep the man calm.

"Goddamn it, Tiny. I didn't see the wire," cried Catfield.

"Just hold still," Sprague said firmly. "Tim, give me the wire cutters."

Martin reached into his utility vest and pulled out the cutters. Sprague quickly cut the wire, and then he unwrapped it carefully from Catfield's legs.

"You OK, Bill?" asked Sprague.

"Yeah, just a few scratches," said Catfield. "I guess the old eyes aren't what they used to be."

"Use the night-vision goggles. We'll probably all need them once we get into the heavier brush," said Sprague.

"All right, everybody, let's go!" said Bishop.

They headed into the dense woods. It was about one mile to the school's south perimeter. The going became more difficult. This late in the summer, the underbrush was heavy. They fought their way through wicked blackberry bushes and thick tanglefoot.

"We should have brought machetes," complained Catfield.

"Too late now," laughed Kellogg.

By the time they had gone only a half-mile, all three of the older men were breathing heavily and sweating profusely.

"Hold up a minute," said Sprague. He stopped, pulled out his canteen and took a drink. After a five-minute break, they began moving forward again.

It took them another thirty minutes to reach the fence line on the undeveloped side of the property. When the fence was built, the brush had been cleared in a thirty-foot swath. However, with the warm, wet summer, the grass, weeds and small trees were up to three feet tall.

They stood at the tree line, surveying the eight-foot chain link fence that was topped with coiled razor wire. With the night-vision goggles, they easily could see the road and the inside fence. Bishop indicated that the inner fence was insulated. Sprague had anticipated that problem.

"Once we breach the outer fence, I have a meter that will tell us if the inside fence is electrified. If it is, we will have to cut an opening with diagonal cutters using high voltage lineman's gloves. Our first step is to get through the outer fence. Obviously, us three old farts aren't about to scale this fence," said Sprague.

They walked along the edge of the clearing until they found a spot where shrubs had grown up next to one of metal poles. While the team waited, Martin moved carefully to the fence, knelt down, and began cutting the links to the right of the post. He cut a three-foot wide opening. He would now be able to pull up the fence and allow the team to crawl to the inner road. Once they were all through, the last man would wire the fence back in place. Unless someone walked right next to the fence, it would be difficult to see where it had been cut.

The big problem was the roving patrol that monitored the inner road. Martin worked quickly to cut the fence. Then he pulled it tightly and tied it back in place. He returned to the woods and waited for the patrol to pass. Six minutes later, an ATV carrying four armed men slowly drove by. Once it disappeared on the hill, Martin went back, opened the fence and crawled through. He again tied the fence closed and crossed the road to the electric fence. Fortunately, Sarday's men had not kept up with the growth of brush and small trees along the fence line. If needed, the team could benefit from the additional cover.

Martin pulled out the electric induction meter and held it about three feet from the fence. He pulled the trigger on the meter. The needle swung to the right, registering five thousand volts. The fence was really hot.

He pulled on the heavy insulated gloves, knelt down and cut the first link. As he inserted the cutters, he held his breath. Sprague had warned him not to allow the cutters to come in contact with his uniform or any part of his body. One mistake would be deadly.

Martin hesitated briefly. He thought through the instructions once again. He tugged on his gloves to assure that they were on tight. He slowly squeezed the compound-levered cutters and snipped the first wire.

There was no blinding flash of light. He felt no pain from an electrical surge. He continued to make careful cuts, concentrating on each individual link. He was so intent on doing the job cautiously, that he was startled when he heard Sprague's urgent call in his helmet earphones.

"Another vehicle is coming down the road!" Sprague warned him in a whisper.

They hadn't figured on a second patrol. A surge of adrenalin caused Martin's heart rate to accelerate. He didn't have time to get back to the team who waited anxiously outside the outer fence. Only one ATV had appeared on the aerial photos. It wouldn't have turned around and come back to this same spot, or would it? What should he do now? Where could he possibly go?

He threw himself to the ground, stretched his body as low as he could, and lay parallel to the electrified fence. The ground sloped slightly on both sides. His only hope was that the depression would obscure his shape from view. He was grateful that Sprague had issued the camouflage clothing.

Now, all he could do was to hope for the best.

61

Inside Sarday's compound, it was far from business as usual.

Oscar Jalah was confused. He didn't understand what George Sarday was doing. None of it made any sense. Then again, he knew that the *endosym* he served was no longer the old George Sarday. He looked like Sarday, he spoke like Sarday, but he was a now clearly a bush spirit in a man's body.

Jalah had no choice but to obey this being. He could feel its power, and he had seen how bloody and ruthless this George Sarday thing could be.

Only three days ago, Sarday had ordered the gruesome murder of his own men. The assassins were the seven security guards who had been on the front line at the ancient ceremony. Not all the guards had given their allegiance to Sarday. Many were only paid mercenaries, serving no master but their own greed. Although Sarday could easily win over those whose spirits were more gullible, these men had solely focused on blood money.

Only the seven guards in Sarday's inner circle – those who had truly fallen under the spell of the *endosym* – had been spared.

A total of twenty-three men would die that night, all murdered at Sarday's command.

It had not been a difficult assignment. The security force had been divided into two shifts, each pulling twelve hours. The first shift came on at noon; the second shift took over at midnight. The first shift of guards would assassinate the men on the second shift.

After the guards were killed, Jalah's next move would be to take out the eight additional security men, those who had accompanied the seven special followers. Within four hours, the eight had been silently murdered.

Jalah's seven men then went to the barracks where the other fifteen guards slept. They carried pistols with silencers. At four in the morning, they walked into the barracks and shot the three men who had been in the lounge watching TV. Then the men crept to the back rooms and killed the others who had been sleeping in their beds. The shattered bodies of those fifteen lay with the other eight.

Just tonight, Sarday told Jalah to have the remaining guards secure the entry gates with heavy chain and padlocks. He divided the men into two teams. Their mission was to patrol the perimeter in two ATVs.

None of it made any sense at all to Jalah, but his job was to carry out the *endosym's* orders. He wasn't there to think.

That reminded him that the next day he would gladly continue his quest to kill the Martin family. The men he had sent to the University of Virginia who posed as government agents had failed to capture the Martin kid. Fortunately, the *endosym* had been satisfied with abduction of Martin's roommate and sister who were imprisoned in the cavern. Tim Martin would die later.

Then Sarday had ordered the removal of that annoying chief of police who had been getting too close to finding out the truth about the school. Even that assignment hadn't been entirely successful, yet they had every expectation to kill that cop. It was just a matter of time until Bishop would also be dead.

But Jalah kept his thinking to himself. He didn't want to anger Sarday who seemed to know what he was doing. The demon that occupied his body had decreed that when dawn came, he would be so awesomely powerful that no creature would be able to stop him.

Whether Sarday was right or not didn't matter. Jalah had joined his men and ridden in the front seat of the ATV as it patrolled the perimeter. They had already been at it for more than three hours. Here it was, still hours until dawn, and Jalah could barely keep his eyes open.

As the vehicle rounded a curve on the inner road, Jalah felt a sudden chill. He sensed that someone was out there.

"Stop," yelled Jalah. The driver, Johansson, hit the brakes. Jalah stood up at his seat in the ATV and scanned the area. He listened carefully. He heard the clicking of cicadas, the hoot of a night owl, and the far-off whistle of a train. Nothing else.

He snapped on the one million candlepower portable floodlight and directed its beam along both sides of the fence line. He saw nothing out of place. He had first suspected something was amiss yards behind them.

"Back up!" he ordered. "Have your weapons ready!"

The ATV backed down the road while Jalah scanned the brush with the searchlight. He detected movement on his right.

"Stop!" he ordered. He quickly pointed the light in the direction of where he had seen movement. He caught a glimpse of the gray body of a medium-sized animal move deeper into the woods. Must be a possum or a cat, he thought.

"All right," said Jalah, "let's get going."

Johansson shifted gears, and the ATV pulled away.

Martin had kept his head down and his body motionless. He resisted the urge to look up and check to see what was happening. When the ATV finally drove off, he took a deep breath. When the ATV first backed up, he had considered making a run for it. It took every single drop of his willpower to stay still.

Now, with the ATV gone, he slowly got up, retrieved the cutters and insulated gloves, and resumed cutting the fence. He cut it upward another twelve inches, pulled it back from the post, and secured it with a bungee cord. The power continued to surge through the electric fence, but the opening would keep them safe and allow them enough room to crawl through.

He stood and signaled to the team in the woods.

They moved out of hiding, unhooked the opening in the outside fence and crawled through. Bishop, who was guarding the rear, stood by the fence. They had decided to keep it open until at least three of them were through the electric fence.

Sprague was the first to cross the road. Martin had already crawled through and waited on the other side. Sprague worked his way through the opening. Martin gripped the large man by the hands and helped guide him through. Martin held his breath as Sprague's big belly came within inches of the wire fence. If any part of his body had touched it, he would have been instantly electrocuted. But Sprague made it with two inches to spare.

Next came Mike Kellogg who slipped through with ease. That left Bill Catfield and Bishop. Bishop had closed and tied the cut fence so the breach wouldn't be visible.

"Bill, go on. I'll be right behind you," Bishop whispered.

"Roger," said Catfield, as he jogged across the paved road toward the fence. Catfield felt much better wearing the night-vision goggles. Although it was still blurry, he at least could see the fence. Just two weeks earlier, his eye doctor had told him that he had cataracts. He probably should have told Sprague, but, for some reason, it had slipped his mind.

It felt like the good old days as he jogged towards the fence. Not bad for a seventy-three-year-old, he thought. Martin watched as Catfield galloped across the road. But, for the life of him, he couldn't understand why the man would be jogging. What's wrong with just walking?

Martin was just about to tell him to slow down, but didn't get a chance to say anything at all. When Catfield stepped off the road, he lost his balance. His momentum carried him straight toward the electric fence. Martin, Sprague and Kellogg each froze in place. Bishop tried to reach out to Catfield before he got to the fence. He grabbed for Catfield, but fell short by a little more than a foot.

Catfield held his assault rifle at port arms. The additional weight of the M 203 grenade launcher helped propel him forward. He crashed into the fence, hitting with such force that he bounced off and fell backward.

Bishop fell to his knees, unable to avert his eyes from the man lying on the ground in front of him. He assumed the worst – Catfield had been electrocuted. A sick feeling passed over him.

Then Catfield moaned and struggled to his feet.

"Are you OK?" asked Bishop, astounded to see the man still alive.

"I think so," Catfield mumbled as he slowly stretched his legs. He took a tentative step. "Ouch," he said. "I think I twisted my ankle." He took a few more steps. His ankle hurt like hell, but he could walk.

"He's OK," said Bishop as the other men came to his side.

"What was the voltage reading on the fence?" Sprague asked Martin. Maybe Martin had been mistaken.

"I could swear it was five thousand volts," answered Martin.

"Let me take a look at the meter." Sprague aimed it at the fence. It read zero. "The power's off," he said, shaking his head in relief. He had been on the verge of losing a man who had been his friend for decades.

"Come on, everyone. Let's get through the fence before the power comes back on," Sprague ordered.

Once they were inside the plantation grounds, Martin fastened the fence back together. He had renewed respect for the insulated gloves. He imagined the power coming on at any moment.

Sprague rested his hand on Catfield's shoulder.

"You OK?" he asked.

"Sure, a little fall can't hurt me," said Catfield with a grin.

"All right, let's go," said Bishop, leading the way.

They moved off into the woods. Catfield gritted his teeth as he took one careful step after another, willing the pain out of his consciousness.

"Christ!" he said to himself. "This damn ankle feels like it's broken."

But, by God, he would walk on bone if he had to. There was no way he'd let his friends down. They needed each one of them to succeed in this mission.

They found a trail leading through the woods. It appeared to be heading to the top of the hill. Once they reached the top, they would be able to see the pavilion and the ceremonial field.

The team members made the slow climb to the top of the hill. They took a moment to rest and scope out the grounds. Bishop was the only one who had actually been on the site. That open house for the chamber of commerce had been worth his time. His professional training had given him the skills he needed to catalog hundreds of minute details. He was good at remembering things that most people would overlook.

They had all studied the satellite photos at Sprague's place. That made it easier to explain the scene that lay below them in the valley.

Bishop looked toward the west. No residual light appeared to be coming from the town of Johnsonville.

"This power outage looks like it's affecting the whole county. I wonder why those standby generators over by the pavilion didn't come on. They look large enough to provide power to electrify an entire city," said Bishop. "Something really powerful must have blown the transformers and knocked out power all around. Whatever happened must be causing the breakers on the back-up generators to kick off since they aren't running."

Bishop passed the night-vision binoculars back to Sprague.

"Did you see any activity?" asked Kellogg.

"Nope. No sign of movement, no lights, not even candlelight in a window," answered Bishop.

"It's almost two o'clock in the morning. Maybe everyone's asleep," Catfield speculated.

"Usually these ceremonies occur at night. Besides, all those cars are still parked over in the fields. Judging by the number of vehicles, I'd guess there are hundreds of people here. They are probably in the pavilion. I've been in there before. It can hold more than a thousand people," said Bishop.

"Well, sitting here on our butts isn't going to rescue Sam and Eddie," grumbled Martin, anxious to get on with the job.

"Tim's right. We have to move. Let's relocate down behind the old slave quarters where the acolytes are housed," Bishop said as he got to his feet and readjusted his equipment.

They began to move forward. Catfield stifled a groan as he took his first step forward. His ankle was killing him. When he took a second step, he almost went down. Taking up a rear position would help conceal his injury from the others. He hobbled slowly down the trail toward the old slave quarters.

They huddled together once they reached the building.

"Tiny, you, Bill and Mike take up good firing positions. Tim and I will see if we can find out where everyone is," Bishop said to Sprague.

"OK, sounds good. Leave your assault rifles with the back-up team. You'll travel lighter if you just carry the Glocks with the silencers," Sprague suggested.

They agreed. Martin and Bishop cautiously approached the old slave quarters. A search revealed no signs of life. But people had been there earlier and seemed to have left in a hurry. Clothing and personal items were strewn about randomly.

"It's clear here," Bishop said. "Next stop, the security buildings."

Bishop knew this would be the tricky part. If there were thirty guards, then half of them would be in the barracks still sleeping. The other half would be manning the gates and running security around the perimeter.

It took them almost ten minutes to reach the barracks. Again, there was no indication of life. Bishop couldn't see any lights coming from the windows. There should have been at least one night security light on the building. He assumed that the power had not yet been restored.

"Tim, stay here and cover me," said Bishop.

He ran in a crouching position to the side of the barracks. He slowly stood up and peered in a window. Even with the night-vision goggles, he couldn't see much. He moved to another window. He could make out dark shapes on the floor, but he couldn't detect any movement.

Bishop didn't want to enter the building, but he felt that he had no choice. He stepped up to the front door. With his pistol in his left hand, he crouched by the door, he reached up with his right hand, and he twisted the door handle. He pulled the door open just a few inches.

A sweet, sickening smell struck him immediately. He'd experienced that same odor before – it was the smell of death. Bishop remembered the same smell that had come from the car of an elderly man who had died of a heart attack. The car had been parked at the shopping mall. The man had been dead for several days before someone investigated, and they had discovered the body. By that time, the corpse had begun to reek. Even though the car was new, less than four months old, the insurance company had totaled it. There was no way that smell of physical decay could be removed from the interior. No one would want a car that smelled like death.

Bishop turned toward Martin and motioned to him to come closer.

"What did you find?" Martin asked in a whisper.

"I'm not sure. Come on. We have to check out the barracks," Bishop answered.

Martin held his pistol in his right hand.

"We won't need the guns," said Bishop.

"Why?" asked Martin.

"You'll see," said Bishop. Then he opened the door.

"God, what's that horrible smell?" gasped Martin, covering his nose.

"Death," said Bishop. "Try not to think of the smell. Just breathe slowly. If it gets to be too much for you, wait outside," suggested Bishop.

"I can handle it," said Martin. It wasn't easy. He felt on the verge of nausea, but vowed to overcome his urge to turn and run.

The two men pushed the door wide open and entered a living area with sofas, overstuffed chairs, card tables, and a large, flat screen TV. Bishop turned on a small LED light. With the night-vision goggles, the light easily illuminated the darkened space.

What they saw made no sense, no sense at all. Piled in the center of the room were the bodies of eight men. Each one wore dark, military-type clothing. It looked as if the bodies had been dragged from other rooms and stacked together in the large room. From the bloating and rigor mortis, Bishop guessed they had been dead for two to three days.

Bishop quickly examined several of the bodies. Each victim had been shot in the head. Another three were on the floor near the TV. Each of them wore a white T-shirt and fatigue pants. Bishop guessed that they had been watching television before they were shot.

"Why do you think they didn't fight back?" asked Martin.

"I'd wager a guess that they were all killed using weapons fitted with silencers. The guards on duty were likely shot by someone they knew," Bishop said.

Sleeping rooms were located at the back of the barracks. Four beds to a room and a total of ten rooms made it possible to accommodate up to forty men. Bishop had to correct his arithmetic when he realized that three of the rooms had only one bed, a desk and an easy chair. He figured these rooms might have been designated for team leaders. Then they found that half the rooms were empty.

In moving through the rooms, they discovered the bodies of an additional twelve men. Most had been shot as they slept. Several of the men may have been attempting to escape, judging from the position of their legs, one leg still in the bed and the other on the floor.

"What happened?" asked Martin. "Why would anyone want to kill so many guys at one time?"

"They were killed mid-shift, I think. It's like half the shift turned on itself, then they came back and killed the second shift while they were in bed. You had to have at least a half dozen shooters to take out this many men without a struggle. I count twenty-three dead. Obviously, we are no longer facing a thirty-man force, unless an outside bunch has tried to take over," Bishop told him. "Come on, let's get out of here."

Finally, they left the building. Moments after closing the main door behind them, Martin doubled over, clenching his stomach.

"I think I am going to be sick," Martin said, trying to control dry heaves.

"Think of something else, and it will go away," said Bishop. After a few moments, Martin straightened up and nodded at Bishop.

"All right, that leaves the pavilion," Bishop said. The whole situation was becoming more and more curious as they went along. He began to wonder if this whole set-up was like that Jonestown thing where many cult followers had swallowed the poisoned Kool-Aid.

As they cautiously opened one of the doors to the pavilion, Bishop came to a halt. He sniffed the inside air. He was relieved that he had not encountered that same sickening smell of death.

Inside the building, they entered the huge hall. Except for the emergency lights, it was totally dark inside. He remembered the little speech that Sarday had made at the open house in this same facility several months ago. So much had changed since then. He looked around as best he could. He remembered that there were emergency exit lights over the outside doors. Since they were battery operated, and the power hadn't been out more than three hours. They should still operate for some time.

Once they were reasonably sure the building was unoccupied. The emergency lights and the night-vision goggles revealed a bizarre sight. Lined up in neat rows, spaced about six feet apart was row after row of discarded clothing, both men's and women's garments – shoes, socks, bras, panties and underwear.

Martin reached down and lifted up a few items, including a pair of men's pants. He felt something bulky in the back pocket. He pulled out a man's wallet and opened it. It contained credit cards, a driver's license and several hundred dollars. He laid the wallet down carefully as close as possible to where he had found it.

"It looks like they weren't worried about someone stealing things," Martin said. "I still wonder where everyone went."

"Well, I've got a pretty good idea. Let's get back to the rest of the guys, and I'll tell you all where I think they are," Bishop said. They headed back to join the other three.

"So, you are telling us that six hundred naked people are inside that old house participating in some sort of ritual or ceremony?" asked Catfield.

"Not in the house," said Bishop. "Beneath the house. According to Jilly Morrison, a tunnel under the house leads to a large cavern. When I visited the old plantation house, I saw a steel, vault-like door in the kitchen. Behind it, there was a stairway leading down to the cellar. I am betting that you will find that this tunnel is located in the basement.

"Let's go to the house and see if we can locate Samantha and Eddie, and then get the hell out of here. With a little luck, we will find them in one of the rooms of the house itself. There is a good chance that armed guards are stationed in the house. We have to hit this quick, both front and rear.

"Tiny, Bill and I will take the front door. Kellogg and Martin will take the back door. We go in with silencers. If the doors are locked, kick them in. Try the door first, if it is unlocked, all the better. Less noise," explained Bishop.

Everyone had deferred to Bishop as the leader at this point. He knew the layout of Sarday's school and had met the major players. His police training would be invaluable.

"Let's go," said Bishop.

The team headed toward the old plantation house. They had spread out, keeping under the cover of the old oak trees that lined the main road up to the house. When they reached the front yard, Kellogg and Martin moved through the shrubs to reach the back of the house.

The throat mikes worked great for communication. Bishop took a second look at the old mansion through the night-vision goggles. Something wasn't right. It seemed so weird, the house appeared as old and dilapidated as the first day he saw it a number of years ago. He was sure that Sarday had fixed it up so that it looked as new as the day it was built. Sure, it was nighttime, but it seemed as if the house had aged once again. In some ways, it seemed like a living being, old and evil. Maybe his mind was just playing tricks on him.

"We're in place," said Martin over the COM system.

"Let's go," said Bishop.

"I'll take up the rear," said Catfield. "My ankle will slow you down."

They moved to the front steps. Bishop placed a foot on the first step. The wood creaked.

He was unaware of the thing under the step. It lifted its head when the step creaked. Its forked tongue tasted the scent of the man above. It was too big for food. The large copperhead eased itself to the ground while its body relaxed.

"Wait here behind me, Tiny," Bishop said. He walked across the porch alone. He had figured that Sprague's weight would make too much noise on the steps.

"Door's unlocked," Bishop said after he'd tried the knob.

"Back door, too," Martin responded.

"All right, let's go. Keep low as you enter. Be prepared for return fire. Shoot to kill. Go! Go! Go!" Bishop ordered. He pushed open the door. Sprague bounded heavily up the stairs behind him.

Holding the Glock in the standard police tactical position, using both hands, Bishop moved the weapon from left to right, searching for movement.

"Clear," he whispered into his voice mike. He moved into the next room. It took fewer than five minutes to determine that the entire house was unoccupied.

Martin felt total disappointment. Somehow, he had believed that they would find Sam and Eddie in a back room, sitting in chairs, their hands tied behind them.

All five gathered in the kitchen.

"That leaves the basement," said Bishop, as he walked over to the heavy door behind him and opened it. There was the inner steel door that he had encountered on his previous visit. He pushed on it slowly. It swung inward, revealing the stairway.

A light came up from the basement. They could smell candle wax.

"Stay here," said Bishop. "I'm going to check out the basement."

He slowly descended the stairs, at all times keeping his weapon pointed a few yards ahead of him. When he reached the bottom step, he found the basement totally empty. At the far end of the large room, he could see a light streaming out of an opening in the far wall. He walked over to the opening. Steps led down to another, lower level. Large candles placed on small alcoves along the wall gave off a low light. They had burned about halfway down.

"Come on down!" Bishop called while motioning to the others.

One by one, the team moved into the basement. The last one through was Catfield, who was limping badly.

"You want to stay here, Bill?" asked Bishop.

"No way," said Catfield. "I'm with you guys even if I have to crawl."

"Follow me," said Bishop, as he started down a second flight of stairs.

As he began the descent, his ears became plugged, similar to the way a passenger feels as a plane prepares to land. The pressure in his ears seemed to increase even more the farther down they went. He attributed the strange sensation to nerves. He was trying to keep his cool, but he knew that emotions can do strange things.

When they reached the bottom of the stairs, they could see a long, dark tunnel sloping downward. The tunnel was made of reinforced concrete. It was about ten feet wide and had at least an eight-foot ceiling. Candles provided what light there was inside the tunnel.

Bishop flipped up the night-vision goggles. It was bright enough in the tunnel to see without them. The team members followed Bishop.

They walked several hundred feet and came to another series of steps that dropped deeper into the earth. At the bottom of the stairs, they entered a natural limestone cavern.

In addition to the pressure in his ears, Bishop now heard a ringing sound.

"My ears are ringing," said Kellogg.

"Mine too," said Martin.

"It must be the pressure," said Bishop. "Mine feel like they are plugged." Then Bishop stopped talking. He turned around to Catfield who was directly behind him. "Listen. Do you hear that?" Bishop asked.

"What?" Catfield asked.

"Quiet!" Bishop said sharply.

Each man stopped in place. One by one, they nodded their heads. They all could hear what sounded like a chanting of human voices. Bishop thought it was still quite a distance from their current position. The lighted candles marked the pathway. Without their light or without flashlights, a person could get lost in the huge cavern.

As the team followed the candles, the chanting became louder and more distinct. They walked for what seemed to be almost a mile, always dropping deeper. Ahead, Bishop noticed a red glow. The farther they went, the more the cave's walls seemed to be emitting the red glow. He reached up and touched the side of the tunnel. When he removed his hand from the wall, he saw that it, too, had begun to glow red.

"It's phosphorescent algae," said Sprague. "It grows in some limestone caverns."

By now the chanting had grown much louder.

As they moved through the cavern, each man felt that something was amiss, yet no one told anyone else. Each of them was not aware that the others had also been affected. No one would have been able to clearly describe the sensation.

Bishop could have made a stab at describing how he felt. It was as if he had been trapped inside a deep well and that the water had begun to enter his mouth. He had a sensation of vertigo and nausea. Perhaps it was the flickering of the candles or the slight breeze flowing through the cavern.

Suddenly, Sprague tripped on the rocky, uneven cavern floor. His hand automatically went out to grab a rock that stuck out of the wall. When his hand was just an inch from the rock, a spark jumped from his hand to the rock.

"Ouch!" said Sprague. They all stopped.

"What happened?" asked Bishop.

"I tripped, and when I reached towards that rock, I got a shock," Sprague answered.

Bishop decided to try it for himself. He walked over to the outcropping and pointed a finger towards the rock. When he was within an inch of the rock, a blue spark jumped from his finger to the rock.

"It's static electricity," said Bishop. "Somehow, we're building up a charge. The rubber soles of our boots insulate us from the ground. My guess is that if we touch any part of the ground, this will happen."

Martin walked over to another stalagmite and stuck out his finger. There was a sharp crack as a spark jumped between the rock and his finger.

"Look at Mike's hair," said Catfield.

Kellogg wore his hair long and pulled it back in a ponytail. Instead of hanging down, the ponytail ran straight back, parallel to the ground.

"Just like a Van De Graaff generator," said Bishop.

"What's that?" asked Catfield.

"When I was in high school, my physics teacher had a machine that generated static electricity. It's called a Van de Graaff generator. If you put your hand on the aluminum ball at the top, your hair would stand on end," explained Bishop.

"Of course, that's only if you have hair," Sprague said, running his hand over his smooth head.

"Something is generating electricity down here. You can smell the ozone, like after lighting strikes. Maybe that's why I feel nauseous," said Kellogg.

"You're dizzy too?" asked Bishop.

"So am I," Martin said.

They suddenly found that all five of them were experiencing the same symptoms.

"Do you suppose there's some kind of poison in the air?" asked Kellogg.

"It's not bothering those people doing the chanting. Come on," said Martin, impatient to get to the source of the sounds.

"I don't like this," said Catfield.

"Neither do I," said Sprague, "but we've come this far, so let's catch up with Tim before he takes on six hundred naked people all by himself."

When they had gone another several hundred feet, they each found it difficult to keep up the pace. Although the ground appeared to be sloping downward, it felt like they were climbing a steep hill. All five were breathing heavily, but it was impacting the old men more than the younger ones.

"Slow down," said Sprague. "We can't keep up."

As he spoke, his voice sounded different. He had to repeat what he had said to get the attention of Bishop and Martin. The two of them turned around and stared. They seemed to be having problems standing up straight.

My God, Sprague thought. It's like we're all drunk. Then he realized that he wasn't thinking clearly either.

They pushed ahead, and finally caught up with the two in front.

"I wish we had brought protective masks. There must be some kind of gas in the air," Catfield complained.

"I don't think so. It's like it's in our heads. Listen to the chanting. I can hear it in my head," said Bishop.

"Come on," urged Catfield, "we need to turn back."

"All right, said Bishop, "We'll go around that corner. If we find nothing, we go back."

They moved slowly, but Kellogg then suddenly bent over and heaved up the contents of his stomach.

It's radiation poisoning, thought Bishop. We might be the walking dead. Yet, if that was the case, then they had nothing to lose. They would all be dead within seventy-two hours.

Sprague took Kellogg's arm and helped him to his feet. It seemed like it had taken forever to travel just a few feet. They rounded a corner and stood stock still. The cavern varied in width from ten feet to maybe fifty feet. Now they stood at the entrance of a gigantic cave, hundreds of feet across and a thousand feet below the rolling hills of western Virginia. This cave was several times larger than a football field. They looked up, but couldn't see the cave's ceiling.

The red glow of the algae was spread all over the walls. But now, the red glow was almost as bright as daylight. Furthermore, it seemed to pulsate, giving the illusion that they were inside a giant, breathing lung.

From where they stood, the floor of the cave was relatively smooth. It sloped downward for several hundred feet before leveling out into a flat area about three hundred feet in diameter.

They froze in place, in a state of shock at what they saw ahead – at least six hundred naked men and women of various sizes, ages and races – all standing at attention, facing toward something that was happening in the center of the cave. Up front, they could see a crowd. Each person was dressed in black.

Over to one side, there appeared to be a pile of headless mannequins. As the men stood silently, each of their confused minds tried to make sense of what they were witnessing. One of the figures lifted a sword. It flashed in a pulsating light. Then the sword came down, striking something hidden by the mass of humanity standing in front of them. After the sword dropped, the sound of a thud echoed throughout the cave. Then there was a crack of blue lightning that arced down, striking the ground near the figure with the sword.

As the bolt of electricity cracked, each man collapsed. Each one fell unconscious to the floor of the underground cavern.

62

Tim Martin thought he was in his bed in Virginia, but the nagging voice kept interrupting his sleep.

"GET UP, BOY! I SAID GET UP! TIME'S A WASTIN'," SAID THE OLD BLACK hag.

Martin curled up tightly in a fetal position. He wanted nothing more than to just be left alone. The warmth of a brilliant sun wrapped around him. He slept.

"Boy, if you don't get up right now, that girl you love and that brother of hers is both gonna die!" the squeaky voice came back at him again.

"Go away! Leave me alone!" Martin mumbled. "Just go away!"

The old woman was persistent. She kicked him hard on his upper leg. The gnarled toes of her bare foot jabbed into his thigh.

Finally, Martin opened his eyes. He recognized the place. He was back in the village of Zigda in Liberia. He was flat on the ground, breathing in the fine dust of African soil.

Just inches from his nose, he saw two skinny black legs. He raised his eyes to the woman's mid-section and stared straight into a pair of Depends panties. Further up yet, he saw two deflated breasts. They hung like two flat pancakes tipped with puckered black nipples. Farther up, he could see a wizened face, like the skin of a dried-up dark apple. The top of the head was thick with kinky white hair pulled back from the weathered face.

But the eyes stood out. They were bright and alive and angry.

Then he heard the meow of a cat. He turned to the creature, a large gray cat. It sat near the woman's right foot, its tail waving and twisting in annoyance.

"I see you're finally awake, boy. Are you listening to me?" demanded the old crone.

"What?" Martin said weakly.

"Boy, are you deaf? You need to get up and save your girl and her brother. I ain't got all day!" she screeched at his ear.

"It's a dream," murmured Martin. "I need to go back to sleep."

He closed his eyes again to blot out the insistence of the irritating witch and her damn cat.

Then the damn cat started licking his face with its coarse tongue.

"Go away, cat," grumbled Martin. He pushed the cat away with his hand. Suddenly, the cat jumped at him and bit at his finger. Its teeth sunk in deep enough to draw blood. "Ouch, damn it," he said as he shook his hand to soften the pain. Then he reached out again to take another swat at the little beast.

His sudden movement forced him to open his eyes. He could now assess his surroundings. That cat had jolted him back into consciousness.

"What?" he muttered.

He was in the cavern. The red light on the walls pulsated brightly. He could hear chanting. It all came back to him. He remembered the team, the tunnel and his mission to find Samantha. He climbed slowly back to his feet. All around him, he saw the men of his team, lying senseless on the rocky path. No one moved but him.

Something grabbed at his pants leg. He looked down, only to see the gray cat again. It pawed at his leg, yowled, and ran toward the mob of chanting, naked humanity. It paced back and forth, looked at Martin, and then moved forward a few feet.

Martin followed the creature as it walked purposefully toward the crowd. This was taking such a chance. Those people could turn on him at any moment.

When Martin reached the back of the crowd, he stopped dead in his tracks. For some reason, he felt the urge to reach out and actually touch the person in front of him. The man ignored his tentative movement. Martin grew bolder. He gently pushed the man aside, and the man stepped to the left, letting him pass. He followed the cat's path. Martin found that he could work his way deeper through the maze of bodies just by pushing them aside. Still, the cat led him on. He moved forward, seemingly unnoticed by the naked throng.

As he moved through the crowd, he realized that he no longer heard the ringing in his ears. The nausea and vertigo were gone. He finally elbowed his way through to the front row of naked bodies.

What he saw would be etched in his memory for the rest of his life.

Before him stood a stone altar like the one he had seen in the compound in Liberia. He and his friend Sabo had been held captive in a cell nearby. The altar was approximately four feet wide, eight feet long and three feet high. Standing in front of the altar was a black-hooded figure holding a sword in its right hand. More people in black robes with hoods stood near the altar. All their faces were hidden. It was impossible to tell if they were male or female.

Two of the hooded individuals lifted a man's headless corpse. They removed the body from the altar and stacked it on a pile of more headless, naked bodies of both men and women. One of the men slipped on the bloody floor and slid into a headless human form, his foot making contact with the gory stump of a man's neck. He stood up, his face maintaining its blank countenance.

At the far end of the altar Martin could see that the statue had been splashed with the blood of its victims. He knew immediately what the statue represented.

He could see the two horns protruding from the top of the head. The face had heavy ridges over the eyes like those of Neanderthal men. Huge buckteeth stuck out from its perpetually grinning mouth. The eyes were invisible due to the thick layers of human blood. But Martin knew that the eyes had no pupils, just white orbs. It was a statue of the dwarf-like demon that visited him in his recurring nightmares.

The sight of the decapitated bodies made Martin sick, but far worse was the pile of severed heads. A basket had been placed between the statue and the altar. It had quickly filled to overflowing. Some heads had fallen from the receptacle and had been rolled or kicked out of the way.

When he looked down, he saw the face of a young, black girl. Her expression was peaceful. Her eyes stared blankly. Her mouth was slightly open, almost forming a smile. How could she be so happy? After all, she had no body. All that remained was her severed head. The body had been hauled away.

The sight of the girl's head caused Martin to retch. He lowered himself to a sitting position and tried to clear his mind by taking deep breaths.

Suddenly, he felt a burning sensation against his upper chest. It hurt. He pulled at the Velcro straps on his protective vest. He reached inside his shirt. Then he remembered the necklace with the leopard's tooth. He hadn't taken it off since his spring break trip to Hawaii. He was about to rip it off to stop the burning pain. When his hand came in contact with the tooth itself, the pain suddenly vanished. The tooth felt cool to the touch.

Then he remembered the dream he had experienced when he was in Hawaii. He recalled exactly the words of the old man in his dream. The man had said, "You are now the chosen one, the one who walks with the spirit of the leopard."

Martin buttoned his shirt and fixed the Velcro tightly back in place. He willed his mind to close out the horror of the carnage. He scanned his surroundings.

To his right he noticed two people, a woman and a man. How could it be? Sam and Eddie stood only a few feet away, but he could tell by their faces that they were in a trance or under the influence of a powerful drug.

As Martin watched, one of the robed figures reached out for Samantha's hand.

"Oh, my God," Martin said. He realized that Sam, his Sam, was to be the next victim. "No!" he screamed as he lunged forward at the robed figure grasping Sam's hand. Martin rushed forward, ramming his bulk into the robed figure.

Its hood fell back. It was a woman who Martin recognized immediately. He had seen this actress in dozens of movies. Never before had her eyes looked so strange, so inhuman. She raised both hands and shoved

Martin backwards. He almost lost his footing but quickly regained his balance.

She roared like an angry beast and again charged forward. Martin quickly took up a defensive martial arts posture. She may have had super-human strength, but she lacked his skill. Martin easily outmaneuvered her. At first, he had been reluctant to strike a woman. This woman was a world-renown talent and an incredible beauty.

But none of that mattered now. She had Sam. His anger surged. She charged again, and he struck a savage blow to her perfect face. She had shown no mercy to the hapless victims. Despite her strength, she was nothing more than flesh and blood. His blow knocked her to the ground. She crumpled at his feet, motionless.

"Sam, come on! We have to get out of here!" Martin screamed. Yet Sam didn't move; she seemed unaware of Martin's presence.

He pulled Sam's arm, momentarily ignoring the other black-robed figures. He realized, almost too late, that he had neglected to prepare for the other, larger individuals who were coming toward him. These figures were most likely men. Martin knew that he was no match for their strength. The actress had demonstrated unbelievable force. He would unable to stop these men with just his bare hands. He pulled his pistol and fired at the first one. The .40-caliber round knocked the man backward, but he immediately got to his feet and prepared to charge once again.

"Super-human strength, but flesh and blood," Martin murmured.

This time he aimed at the dark hole under the hood where the face would be. With the laser sight on the Glock, anyone could be an expert. It was important to slowly squeeze the trigger while steadying the red dot on the target. He lifted the gun with both hands. This time the round struck the man's face. When he fell to the ground, he did not get up.

Martin looked down at the man's body lying still at his feet. He looked once again. The hood had fallen away from the face, revealing the bullet hole in the center of the forehead. The man looked strangely familiar. Allan Carlson? Martin asked himself. Could this be the senator?

Martin didn't have time to stop and stare. He swung the weapon to the right, firing at two more of the black-hooded men. With Martin's accurate headshots, both were thrown backward. They died before they hit the ground.

"Just a piece of cake!" Martin said out loud, laughing nervously.

Then something hit him with the impact of a speeding automobile. He was thrown more than fifteen feet, landing on his back. The force of the unexpected impact startled him. For several seconds, he didn't know for sure where he was.

A flash of steel came at him. Just in time, he rolled to the right. The blade of the silver sword struck the ground just inches from his shoulder. He scrambled to his feet and whirled around to face his attacker.

It was the *endosym* – George Sarday. Each human sacrifice had charged his being. His mental power was at its peak. He had total control of the humans in the cavern, except for this pesky man standing before him.

He lifted the sword to take a second swing. Martin ducked at the last moment. He felt the rush of air as the blade passed over his head. He regained control of the pistol and fired in Sarday's general direction, but the man moved quickly to the left. Martin had missed.

Then Sarday emitted a low growl, like that of a caged beast. He charged again. This time Martin was ready for him. He struck Sarday with a karate kick that should have knocked him off his feet. Instead, Martin's foot felt like it had come into contact with a brick wall. The blow had no effect at all.

Martin had to reassess his enemy. What he had been doing wasn't working. He scrambled away from this thing that was Sarday. But it moved more quickly than was humanly possible.

Once again, Sarday took a stance directly in front of Martin. He lifted the sword. It whistled as it sliced through the air. Martin fired three rounds point blank at him. The bullets struck Sarday's torso, yet he kept on coming. Martin backed away again, just barely avoiding a blow.

Martin felt his feet slipping on the loose gravel. His feet went out from under him. He fell backward, landing hard on his lower back. When he fell, he lost hold of the pistol. He looked up. Sarday stood over him, a broad grin stretched over his face. He lifted the sword, preparing to deliver the fatal blow.

"I'm sorry, Sam," Martin whispered. "I couldn't save you." Then he closed his eyes for the last time and said softly, "God, help me."

A scream like nothing he had ever heard before made Martin open his eyes. Sarday had dropped the sword. Both of his hands were up on his face. He continued to shriek. He tried to pull the attacker off his face. He grasped it and launched it forcefully into the crowd of naked worshippers.

Martin saw his opportunity. He dived for the sword and grasped it firmly in both hands. Sarday turned toward him, his face streaked with bloody lacerations.

The gray cat had ripped one eye out of its socket. Blinded on one side, Sarday failed to notice that Martin now had control of the weapon. Martin, on his knees, pointed the sword straight up at Sarday's torso.

The blade penetrated the soft tissue under Sarday's ribs. The sharp tip sliced through his innards. Sarday staggered backwards, grasping the handle in a futile attempt to pull it out of his open wound. His body struck the edge of the altar and fell to the side. Martin could then see the extent of the injury. The sword had passed completely through the man's midsection. The tip, and a good twelve inches of the blade, stuck out of the evil thing's back. Sarday blinked once. Then his eyes glazed over.

Martin backed up to the wall and used it to support his weight as he struggled to keep on his feet. He leaned forward, pressed his hands to his knees, and took several deep breaths.

Piercing screams interrupted his recovery. He looked up to see that Sam and Eddie had finally come back to their senses. They were looking at the carnage around them. Both of them continued to scream as if they had just awakened from a terrible nightmare.

"Sam!" called Martin. "Sam, it's OK!"

She turned toward Martin, tears of relief running down her cheeks.

"Tim, Tim, what are you doing here?"

"I've come for you," he said, as he pulled her into his arms.

The two clung together tightly, finally realizing that they had survived.

As Martin nestled his head in Sam's shoulder, he opened his eyes and looked forward. He could see for certain that Sarday was dead. He could breathe a sigh of relief because the man would never again commit such atrocities.

And Eddie was all right, too. He stood behind his sister, comforting her with a hand on her back. Martin reached out with his left hand and grasped Eddie's arm.

Martin looked around to see what else had happened in the cavern. The chanting had stopped. The remaining hooded figures and the naked followers were milling around, unsure of what to do.

"Let's get out of here," Martin said. He bent down, picked up his pistol, and grasped it in his hand. He didn't want to put it back in the holster. He had to be ready. No one knew for certain what Sarday's followers would do next.

Sam was finally aware of the white robe she wore. She reached down and grabbed the hem and pulled the garment over her head. She threw it on the cavern floor. Eddie followed her lead.

"Why were you wearing those things?" Martin asked.

"We were cold," Sam answered.

They walked into the crowd. As they passed, people stepped out of their way. Martin was glad they did. If they hadn't, he might have fired at them. He had no sympathy for any of these idiots.

These sick bastards just murdered a bunch of innocent people, he thought.

As they headed toward the exit, Martin saw that the rest of the team had recovered from their ordeal. They smiled and laughed, realizing all three of the young people were safe.

"I don't know what you did," said Sprague, "but, whatever it was, we owe you our thanks." The big man placed his hand on Martin's shoulder.

A crack of lightning and a roar of thunder caused them all to stop in place. A second, then a third bolt of lightning flashed through the dark interior of the cavern and struck the stone altar. Sharp pieces of rock flew through the air.

"What's happening?" asked Sam. Once again, she felt a wave of fear pass through her. She reached out to Martin. He held her close.

After the last blast of thunder, they heard a pitiful yowl.

"I don't believe it. I just don't believe it. That cat has to be dead," Martin said, as he looked down at the gray cat. "I saw Sarday throw it at least a hundred feet."

"I've heard that cats have been known to fall from ten-story buildings and then get up and walk away," Catfield offered.

"It looks like he wants us to follow him," Martin said.

Another five bolts of lightning lit up the cavern interior before striking the altar. Then a cold wind began to pass through the cave.

"Well, that cat's right," said Bishop, wrapping his arms around himself to try to stop from shivering. Each one turned, and, as a group, they ran back to the tunnel that had led away from the sunken chamber of horrors.

Catfield took up his position at the end of the line. He hesitated to watch the blue lightning strike the altar once again. He was about to turn and follow the others when he saw something strange. A dark circle appeared behind the altar. Then he shook his head. It wasn't a circle. It was more like the opening of a large, discharge pipe. It was at least twenty-five feet in diameter. He squinted to try to make sense of what he was seeing. A light opened up from inside, almost like a patch of blue sky.

"Damn these cataracts," he exclaimed. Whatever was inside the pipe-like thing wasn't coming in clearly.

Then Catfield remembered that he was holding his assault rifle with its six-power scope. That would help him figure out what he was seeing.

"Oh, hell," he cursed. "Which eye is the good one?" He had forgotten. First, he closed his right eye, and then he closed his left eye.

"Right one. Now why couldn't I remember that?" he said.

Even talking to himself didn't seem to help anymore. The words came out, but nothing seemed to stay in his brain for any length of time. Too often, things just didn't make sense.

Like right now, he thought, as he pointed the scope at the dark opening.

"Holy Mary, Mother of God," gasped Catfield.

Ten thousand years ago, the portal to the demon world had been opened. Now, the power of the Earth's magnetic field flowed through the ley line that passed beneath the cavern. It combined with the electrical drain from the power lines above. Together, focused by the release of mental energy from the deaths of thirty-eight young acolytes, the barrier between the Earth and the demon world had been breached. The invasion of the *endosyms* was about to begin.

He must be hallucinating. He looked again.

Three things, no not things, but demons, stepped out of the black, pipe-like opening. They were human and something else. Each one had two horns poking out from its large bald head. The ears were long and pointed. The bodies were human in shape except for the tails that came out of their back ends and trailed on the ground.

He could tell by their physical features that two were male and one was female. None had pubic hair. Two were shorter, perhaps younger. One seemed to take charge. He seemed older, with the sunken chest and potbelly of an aged man. His arms were thin, yet his legs were strong and muscular. He wore a golden chain around his neck. An amulet hung from it against his chest.

Catfield couldn't be sure he was actually seeing the creatures. He would never again be able to think clearly. Just six weeks ago his doctor had confirmed his worst fear – the tests were conclusive for dementia.

Late life had been hard on the old soldier. His wife, Cindy, had died from cancer just two years ago. They had no children. Except for some nieces and nephews, he had no one. He just had his old team members. They were the only ones who even gave a damn. Yet he hadn't told them about his diagnosis.

He checked out his disease on the Internet. He figured he knew more now than his doctors did, but he couldn't always remember what he had read. He seemed to recall that delusions could be part of the progress of the disease.

Clearly this was a delusion. He brought the scope up to his good eye again. The older creature stood over the Sarday's body. With both hands, it grasped the sword and withdrew it from the corpse. It then reached down and pulled Sarday to his feet.

That wasn't possible, Catfield thought. The man had a sword stuck completely through him. He had to be dead.

Yet Sarday seemed to defy logic. He reached out and took the sword from the creature's hand. He turned and grasped the sword in his right hand. He stared directly at Catfield.

"Kill them!" screeched a raspy voice. The words echoed in Catfield's head. All six hundred followers turned and began to approach him, the last man standing.

Catfield's heart began to beat rapidly inside his chest. He turned to run. Just then he heard a bone snap in his ankle. He sunk to the ground. An almost unbearable pain coursed through his leg and moved up through his body. He felt like he was going to pass out. He was trapped. There was no place to hide. He could see the naked, fearless crowd move toward him.

"This is crazy!" he said aloud, shaking his head in disbelief. Six hundred bare-naked people were closing in on him.

Catfield started laughing, crazy laughing.

Years ago, he had seen a documentary on HBO called "Naked World." A photographer had traveled throughout the world taking pictures of people in the buff. In Australia hundreds of people showed up – men and women, old and young, people of all races. Now, right here in front of him, hundreds of naked people were coming at him like friggin' zombies.

"My God," Catfield said, "I can't shoot naked people."

Catfield was a combat veteran of three wars. He'd killed in combat, but this was different. He just couldn't kill naked, defenseless people. But he had to stop them. Maybe he could just scare them.

He reached into his utility vest and withdrew a high explosive M203 grenade round and inserted it into the launcher. He aimed it at a forty-five degree angle. He pulled the trigger. An exploding round hitting the cavern roof was sure to get their undivided attention.

It took less than a second for the round to strike the ceiling, a good two hundred feet above their heads. It exploded with a bright flash. The sound reverberated throughout the cavern. Rocks, some as big as basket-balls, shook loose from the cavern walls and ceiling.

"Oh, shit!" Catfield gasped. "I'm sorry. I'm so sorry!" he cried.

He knew better. He should have thought it through before pulling the trigger. But, he reminded himself that he didn't have time to think. He should have lowered the weapon, causing the round to hit farther back. Now, an avalanche of broken rock fell heavily on the crowd. He saw a half dozen people go down. He felt overwhelming grief. His tears poured down his face. He wiped them away with the back of his hand.

He had expected to see the people scatter. They must be dazed, confused and in shock. Instead, they continued to advance. He saw an older woman come directly at him, blood flowing from a gash in her forehead. Others, injured but unstoppable, kept walking toward him.

First, he felt grief. Next, came uncertainty. Now, a total fear gripped him.

Never in his entire life had he felt fear like he did now. Before, in combat, he had known there was a possibility that he could die. But now, the fear was real – he knew he was going to die.

Catfield had been a Catholic all his life. He and Cindy had faithfully attended mass every Sunday. After Cindy died, he'd stopped going to church. At this moment in his life, he knew that he needed God more than ever. He fell to his knees and began to pray. He recited the Lord's Prayer. "Our Father who art in Heaven...," he began. Once he finished, he began it again.

He picked up his assault rifle and aimed it toward the advancing crowd. He closed his eyes and pulled the trigger. Rounds struck the first rank of people. They were just one hundred feet in front of him. He opened his eyes. At least ten people had fallen. Some stayed down, but others started to get up. This time, with his eyes wide open, he emptied the remaining rounds directly into the crowd.

He pulled the magazine from the rifle, reversed it, and inserted other full thirty-round magazine. The crowd was now within twenty feet. He put the weapon on full automatic and pulled the trigger until the gun had spent all its ammo.

Then he reached into his vest pocket and removed the fragmentation grenade that he had taken from Sprague's basement arsenal. He pulled the pin and held the grenade in his hand. He couldn't help but laugh as he remembered how Tiny Sprague had said that they didn't need grenades on this mission.

"Hell, yes!" he yelled. Sprague couldn't hear him now, but he was glad for his buddies that he had ignored the order.

The crowd was on him now, biting, scratching and clawing.

"God help me," he screamed. He broke loose, stood tall on his one good leg and released the handle on the grenade.

Then it exploded.

63

Jogging at a slow and steady pace through the passageway, the team, plus Sam and Eddie, made their way toward the mansion basement.

BISHOP'S MIND REPLAYED THE NIGHT'S EVENTS. EVEN IF HE TRIED, he couldn't stop the hellish scenes from flowing through his thoughts. The candles in the alcoves provided enough light to guide their way. It still would be a tough trek through the winding tunnel to the mansion's basement. Each of them yearned to breathe fresh air once again. They pressed on, anxious to escape the terror that had entrapped them.

"OK," Bishop whispered. No one could hear him. No one could see his lips move. His law enforcement training came back into play. Details made the difference.

First, they had entered a huge, underground cavern. Sarday and his followers were engaged in a ceremony that involved human sacrifice. Then each of the men on the team had passed out. The next thing he remembered was waking up. He recalled his astonishment at witnessing Tim Martin emerge from the crowd of naked people. Two people accompanied him. One was a stunning, black woman. The second was a shorter, black man.

Later, they found out that these two were the Dixon kids. Rescuing them had been their goal. He remembered being startled to discover that Martin's girlfriend was black. Even more incredible was that a big gray cat had been in the cavern with them. The only logical conclusion was that the animal had followed them from the old Smith farm.

Too many of the events simply didn't make sense. How could lightning bolts crash inside the cavern? He didn't know. All he knew was that it was spooky. Then Martin had insisted that he had killed Sarday. If that was true, then the people trying to kill him and his wife, Ann, were gone. He felt a sense of relief, but it was coupled with his ingrained skepticism.

Even now, as they ran from the cavern, the lightning continued to flash. Light flickered like in an old movie. Frames of reality were punctuated by brief periods of darkness.

"Maybe that's what it's all about," Bishop concluded. "Maybe this all didn't really happen. Maybe we're the victims of some elaborate hoax."

He stopped his speculation. "Facts, just facts," he reminded himself.

Yes, six hundred of Sarday's followers had been inside the cavern. He had seen them with his own eyes. He had seen their parked cars. He had seen their discarded clothing. Once the team got out of the cavern and back into the real world, they would contact the authorities. It would be up to them to enter the cave and round up the brainwashed believers. Their team will have already done its job.

"Thank God we're alive," he said. He'd soon be back with Ann, and the world would be good – even better – again.

"Kill them!" said a voice in his helmet earpiece. They'd only been traveling two or three minutes. The chilling voice stopped him. He had to find out what it meant.

"Kill them!"

"Who said that?" demanded Sprague.

"Is someone on our frequency?" asked Kellogg.

"Someone's going to kill us!" shouted Martin's girlfriend, Sam.

"How could you hear that voice?" Martin asked. "It came over our earpieces."

"No," said the brother, Eddie. "I heard it in my head."

"Me, too," Sam said. She was certain that she had heard it.

"That's not possible," Sprague said.

Just then, they stopped all their conjecture. They had heard a loud blast.

"What the hell was that?" Martin asked.

"Sounds like a grenade going off," Kellogg said. "Wait a minute, where's Bill?"

"I thought he was right behind us," Sprague answered. "His ankle was bothering him, so I figured he wouldn't be going as fast as the rest of us."

The roar of automatic weapons fire reverberated through the cavern.

"Come on!" yelled Sprague. "Bill's in trouble." Sprague ran toward the sound of the firing. A second automatic weapons burst caused him to pause.

"Slow down, Tiny. We need to know what we're getting into," Bishop yelled.

Sprague either didn't hear him or he chose to ignore him. He continued to jog toward the sound of the shooting.

"Sergeant major, you stop right now! That's an order!" Bishop barked. The military command caused Sprague to stop in his tracks. He waited for the others to catch up.

Now they heard the firing of an assault rifle on full automatic. It echoed through the cavern. Then they heard nothing at all for about five seconds.

"God, help me!" The team members recognized Catfield's voice.

Seven seconds later they heard a muffled explosion. It was the sound of a grenade going off from deep inside the cavern.

"Come on! Bill needs our help," Sprague shouted.

Bishop hesitated.

Catfield, the grenade, the explosion – Bishop feared that it was too late for Bill.

It wouldn't have mattered anyway. Now they could see a mob of naked people come around a bend in the tunnel. They approached at a steady pace; their faces reflected their determination to overtake the invaders.

Bishop grabbed Sprague's arm.

"Wait, Tiny," Bishop said calmly. "Bill doesn't need our help anymore. If we don't move now, we will all be dead."

"I'm going to kill those fucking bastards," yelled Sprague, as he aimed his assault rifle at the flow of advancing humanity.

"You might get the chance, Tiny," Bishop said. "But if we are going to fight, I want to be outside of this damn cave. We have a better chance in the woods. Besides, I'm not sure we have enough bullets to stop six hundred people, even if they are unarmed.

"Everybody, run for the basement right now!" ordered Bishop.

No one needed to hear the order twice. They took off running, heading back the way they had come.

Bishop had never before been as afraid.

"Keep together," he yelled. "Nobody falls back! Keep moving!"

At first, it was easy to stick together. But the return to the basement was all uphill. Within a mile, the elevation would increase by seven hundred feet. Sprague and Kellogg began to lag behind.

"Tim, you and Samantha go help Tiny. Eddie and I will help Mike. You carry their assault rifles. Give them a hand, and don't take any excuses!"

He glanced behind them. The mob maintained its steady pace, but they were gradually gaining on them. He prayed that they would reach the basement before they had to fight.

Just then, Sprague went down. The exertion was too much for the big man.

"Hold up, everyone!" Bishop called. Sprague had collapsed. He was gasping for air. Kellogg didn't look any better.

Were they going to make their stand right there? He turned to assess their progress. He could see the beginning of the concrete tunnel that led into the basement. If they could get into the tunnel, maybe they could slow down the mob. The tunnel was about twelve feet wide. They would be able to fire back toward the crowd, scaring them while they got the old men out.

Bishop quickly calculated the task ahead. He ordered Martin, Sam and Eddie to get Sprague on his feet. If necessary, they were to drag him into the tunnel. Bishop turned to Kellogg, took his rifle and threw the strap over his own shoulder.

He grabbed Kellogg by an arm.

"Move out, Mike, now!" he shouted.

They struggled toward the tunnel entrance. Bishop glanced behind him. The mob was gaining on them. It now had narrowed the gap to fewer than a hundred feet.

The tunnel was clearly within their grasp, but, somehow, they had to slow the mob's advance.

"Martin!" he yelled. "Come here!"

Martin joined Bishop. He carried two assault rifles, his own and Sprague's.

"Do you think that Tiny can walk with just Eddie's help?"

"I think so," said Martin.

"Samantha, you help Mike," Bishop ordered. "Keep going!"

Then he turned to Martin.

"Tim, you and I are going to have to slow them down," Bishop said.

Without a moment's hesitation, Bishop pulled his pistol, aimed at the mob, and opened fire.

But he missed. The followers were just beginning to enter the tunnel. The bullets passed over their heads. The crowd neither flinched nor paused.

"Shit!" Bishop shouted.

He holstered the pistol and took hold of the assault rifle. With Kellogg's rifle, he had two weapons. With the double magazines, he had one hundred twenty rounds. Martin also had the two weapons, plus another one hundred twenty rounds. Bishop recalled his thinking when they determined the content of their arsenal. He had no reason to believe that they needed more ammunition. They weren't going into Iraq. This was supposed to have been a simple rescue mission.

He did the mental math. If every round were a kill, they still would have hundreds pursuing them once they had expended all their ammo.

"Shoot for the head," Martin said to Bishop. "I had to kill several of them back in the cavern. They seemed impervious to pain."

This can't possibly be happening, thought Bishop.

He wasn't sure he could shoot unarmed men. In this case, he'd also have to shoot women. Then he remembered Bill Catfield's scream.

"You didn't see the bodies," said Martin, sensing Bishop's reluctance to shoot unarmed civilians. "They had beheaded dozens of kids. These things aren't human."

Now it was Martin, comforting and encouraging Bishop.

They both dropped to one knee. Bishop fired a few rounds above the mob's heads. They still didn't flinch. Their eyes were fixed stonily straight ahead.

Martin didn't waste a warning shot. He fired into the crowd and saw several people go down. Yet as each body fell, one behind simply took its place.

"Drop back!" ordered Bishop.

The two of them backed up, keeping their rifles trained at the oncoming crowd.

"Down again! Fire!" yelled Bishop.

This time, Bishop didn't stop to think. He took aim. As a head came into view, he pulled the trigger, and the assault rifle bucked against his shoulder. He found himself praying out loud. As he pulled the trigger, he muttered, "God, forgive me!"

If Bishop had his way, he would just give up and let them take him. But, another side of his brain kept forcing him to fire. Body after body fell. Both men flipped their magazines and kept firing, backing up, and firing again. The increasing pile of bodies slowed the crowd's advance. In the limited light, Bishop thought he recognized the faces of people he knew from Johnsonville. He prayed it was all only an illusion.

When his rifle clicked empty, he dropped it and began firing Kellogg's rifle. When its ammo was gone, he threw it down and yelled at Martin.

"Run! Run!" he shouted at the top of his lungs.

They both took off running. The delay had slowed the mob, but hundreds were still advancing. They had no more ammunition for the assault rifles. They reached the steps and emerged into the basement. The mob was at their heels. They met the others at the bottom of the stairs. They helped push Sprague and Kellogg up the stairway and into the mansion's kitchen.

Martin and Bishop stayed in place to hold back the mob and give the others time to get farther away. Martin made it into the kitchen. Bishop had reached the top step when he felt something grab at his ankle. It held with the strength of a vice. He turned to see Harvey Bradley, the mayor, clenching his ankle. Right behind him came another familiar face. It was Martin Noonan, editor of the town's newspaper.

It all seemed like a scene from his worst nightmare. Bradley grinned. Noonan's hands reached up toward him. Bishop imagined himself being pulled into the basement and being ripped apart.

A shot rang out. The mayor's eye disappeared. A second shot tore a hole in the center of Bradley's forehead. Finally, the man let loose of Bishop's leg and sank into the crowd behind him.

Bishop felt another set of hands grabbing at his shoulders. He almost fought back until he realized that Martin had reached under his armpits and yanked him onto the kitchen floor. Bishop and Martin together tried to pull the iron door closed, but too many fingers reached around the heavy door, preventing it from closing.

The fingers pried the door open enough to allow one man's head to peek around the edge. The door opened even more. Three shots rang out, one each from the pistols of Martin, Bishop and Sprague. Three bodies blocked the stairway. The two younger men kicked them back with their boots. Then Martin and Bishop continued to fire until their guns were emptied.

They pulled the door closed. Bishop turned the key and locked the door. He pulled out the key and shoved it in a pocket.

They all fell on the floor, gasping for air – fresh, clean, free air.

64

Finally safe inside the mansion kitchen, Bishop raised himself carefully to a sitting position and gazed at his exhausted teammates and the two Dixon kids.

NO ONE SPOKE. IT WAS ALL THEY COULD DO TO JUST BREATHE. Each person, totally exhausted, stretched out on the kitchen floor. Bishop was certain that they all had survived because he could see their chests rising and falling with each labored breath.

Thank God they had been able to secure the heavy door to the basement. He could hear people throwing themselves against the door. He didn't hear any voices. No one demanded to be let out. No one cried for help. All he heard was the constant banging against the other side of the door.

He still felt the gut-wrenching fear. He still nervously awaited another attack. He still saw Harvey Bradley staring up at him with a wild grin. The man continued to live in Bishop's mind, even with his blown-out eye and bullet-punctured forehead.

Bishop had no doubt that they had experienced something far more sinister than just one nutcase who had bewitched a gang of senseless followers. Whatever it was, Bishop was sure it was evil. It was an evil so unthinkably horrible that he and his team could never stop it by themselves. Sure, they might stall them, but this horror wouldn't just go away without some divine intervention. This was something far from the natural world.

They needed help, more than just man-made help. Years ago, the Bishops had been members of the Methodist church. He'd always believed in God. Somehow his spiritual life had been clouded by alcohol, and he had lost his way. He now was more certain than ever before that there was more than just a physical world. He couldn't overcome evil all by himself. He may be able to turn away from the booze, but he couldn't fight this supernatural evil without assistance from a force stronger than his alone.

Those things in the basement would eventually escape. It was just a matter of time. When they were released, he doubted that they could be stopped. For the first time in years, Bishop offered up a sincere prayer. He wasn't sure that he even knew how to talk to God anymore, but he had to give it a try.

He saw the others begin to stir. It was time to move.

"We've got to get out of here now!" Bishop said. "If they get out of the basement, we're dead meat!"

Sprague sat nearby, leaning his back against the kitchen wall.

"How are you doing, Tiny?" Bishop asked.

"I'm OK, Brian. I'm OK," Sprague said weakly.

Bishop knew that there was no way that the big guy would make it all the way back to the Smith farm. For that matter, they all would be pushing themselves beyond their limits.

"Tiny, I'm thinking we need to have your daughter fly over here and pick us up. I don't think any of us are in shape to hike the two miles back to the farm," Bishop said.

Sprague didn't answer. He simply pulled out the hand-held radio from his utility vest. He snapped it on and pressed the talk button.

"Black Widow, this is Big Daddy. Over."

"Go ahead, Big Daddy," Ann answered immediately.

"We need a lift. We'll be in the field south of the stream."

"Roger, Big Daddy. What should I do with the three musketeers?"

"Bring them along, Black Widow," Sprague answered.

"Roger, Big Daddy. Arrival 15 mike."

Bishop looked over at the old soldier. Light was poor in the kitchen. The sun still hadn't risen over the eastern hills. Nevertheless, Bishop could see that Big Daddy looked tired and haggard. It hadn't been an easy night for any of them. Fortunately, Sprague's mind was as sharp as ever as he clicked off the military code words.

"You told her to bring my wife, Willie and Jasmine?" Bishop asked.

"That I did," Sprague answered. "We all need to get out of this state ASAP. Ann will be landing in fifteen minutes."

"All right," responded Bishop. "Let's get out of here. We'll wait in the woods next to the field."

As they walked out the back door, Bishop had another question for Sprague.

"Why is your daughter's call sign Black Widow?"

"I don't know. That was her call sign in Iraq when she flew attack helicopters," Sprague answered.

"Is your daughter, Ann, married?"

"No," said Tiny. "Why?"

"Maybe she needs to change her call sign. It might be a deterrent to potential suitors," said Bishop.

He threw Sprague a genuine smile. He got another smile in return.

In the subterranean, limestone cavern 1,500 feet below the ground level of the plantation, a gathering was taking place that would change the world. The lightning continued to flash and the red algae pulsated as the static charges rippled through the air. The location was perfect for the focus of the energy required to keep the portal open to the other world.

Fifty million years earlier, the stage had been set for this event. At that time, dinosaurs roamed great swamps on this very site. Then the area changed. Earthquakes shook the ground. The Allegheny Mountains rose up through the earth's crust. The foothills, the site of the old Johnson plantation, were also born in this great upheaval.

The vegetation from the great swamps was buried in deep pockets under tons of rock. Millions of years later, it would be transformed into beds of coal. During the same event, large areas of limestone were rolled up between layers of granite. Beneath the cavern, the solid bedrock stretched all the way to the earth's mantle, providing the perfect conduit for the energy required to keep the portal open. The magnetic force along the ley line passing through the area was strong here – stronger than any other location on the North American continent. But it was a fragile balance. Next to the great cavern was a vein of coal. It was small, and of no commercial value.

A pocket of trapped methane gas had formed within the coal's vein.

Bishop checked his watch. It was almost five o'clock in the morning. The sun still hadn't risen from behind the hills, but it would soon. He could see the pink glow beginning in the east. Even now, he could make out the silhouettes of trees and the tops of the rolling hills. They trekked single file down the hill and waded across the small stream.

The cat protested. It paced along the steam's banks, seeming reluctant to get its feet wet. Bishop had to laugh. "And this was the same creature who dared to risk its life inside the limestone cavern?"

He bent over and picked it up. He was surprised at the cat's weight. It likely weighed more than twenty pounds. He felt along its ribs. It didn't carry any extra fat.

As they were crossing the stream, Sprague lost his footing and almost fell. Martin had been walking close to him. He reached out quickly, catching his arm and helping him steady himself. Although Sprague would never admit it, he was still suffering from their ordeal.

Once they crossed the stream, the cat had decided he'd had enough of the free ride. He struggled to be let loose. As soon as his feet touched the ground, he took off toward to woods at a full run.

"What's got into that cat?" asked Martin.

"Don't know," answered Bishop. "Must have seen a rabbit or something."

They walked towards the woods and soon settled down in a small clearing to wait for the helicopter.

For the first time, Bishop believed they were going to get out of all this alive. The roar of engines broke the morning silence as two ATV's raced over the hill headed directly at them. Within seconds, the two vehicles stopped on either side of the group. Eight men jumped out of the vehicles. Seven carried assault rifles. The eighth man was unarmed.

Both Bishop and Martin recognized the eighth man immediately. It was none other than Oscar Jalah. He smiled as he walked up to the team.

"So, you fought the good fight, but you cannot stop us," he said. "Your weapons are worthless. I have too much power!"

Something was amiss. Bishop knew that whoever or whatever was speaking was not Oscar Jalah. He didn't even sound like Jalah. As a matter of fact, he sounded like George Sarday. But Martin had said that he had killed Sarday. Bishop was puzzled; Tim Martin wasn't.

"Who are you?" Martin asked boldly. Bishop realized that Martin also knew that this man wasn't the Jalah he remembered.

"Why, I am the *endosym* that controls these humans," the man responded.

"*Endosym?*" Bishop asked.

"Yes, and you will all worship me and my brethren," he said. "For centuries, we have hidden among you, living off of your essence. But only one could pass through the curtain into your world before it closed. Tonight the curtain has been parted, and now my brethren are arriving. Soon, you all will be ours. We will rule, and you will be our slaves and your essence will sustain us."

"I'd rather die!" screamed Martin as he charged at Jalah.

Just as Martin lunged forward, a gray streak rushed out of the woods. Martin and the cat hit the man simultaneously.

"How dare you!" screamed Jalah. He fell over backward, with Martin and the gray cat on top of him. Jalah grabbed the cat and threw it violently into the underbrush.

The two men wrestled on the ground. Martin tried to pin Jalah, but Jalah quickly reversed the roles. Now he was on top. His long fingers ringed Martin's neck. Martin was caught by the man's body weight on his chest.

It was a natural, reflex action. From years of law enforcement training, Bishop withdrew his pistol and aimed it at Jalah's back. He pulled the trigger. The gun discharged. He pulled the trigger again, and yet another shot rang out. He pulled the trigger for a third time. Nothing. The gun was empty.

But Bishop saw that Jalah had ceased to struggle. He had fallen lifelessly on top of Martin. Bishop rushed over to the men and pulled Jalah's dead weight off Martin.

"Oh, God, no!" screamed Bishop. He could see blood all over his friend's chest. One of the rounds must have passed through Jalah's body and struck Martin. Bishop heard him moan. He dropped to his knees next to Martin, who was struggling to sit up.

"Don't, don't try to move!" Bishop said. "You've been shot!"

"No," Martin gasped. "It hit the protective vest."

Jalah didn't have such luck. One of the rounds had severed his spinal column just below the neck. He was dead.

All the while they had been dealing with Jalah, they'd ignored the seven men whose guns had been pointed at them. Bishop couldn't understand why they hadn't reacted when Jalah had been killed.

"They're just like puppets," said Martin, who had also wondered at their inaction. "Without the control of their leader, they just stand there."

Bishop stood and held out his hand to pull Martin to his feet. The others gathered around them. Sam threw her arms around Martin.

"I thought he was going to kill you!" she sobbed.

"He almost did," Martin told her. "If Brian hadn't shot him, I would be dead. Probably, we'd all be dead." Then he scratched his head. Something wasn't right here.

"Hey, Brian, I thought we were out of ammo."

"I thought so, too," Bishop answered. "But when you guys were shooting down the stairs, I was trying to close that door. There must have been two rounds left in my pistol."

Then Bishop walked over to one of the guards. He took his assault rifle. The man released the rifle without protest.

"Take their weapons. We don't need them to change their minds and shoot us," Bishop said.

The others collected the weapons. Without the *endosym* using Jalah's body to tell them what to do, the men were simply robots whose batteries had run down.

"Here comes the chopper!" shouted Kellogg. "Come on, let's get out of here before something else happens. I don't know about you guys, but I've had my fill of these loonies."

In the great cavern, a rumble reverberated off the walls. George Sarday and the three creatures standing next to the altar looked in the direction of the noise.

When Bill Catfield had fired the M203 grenade into the ceiling just prior to his death, the exploding round had dislodged several hunks of rock from the ceiling, causing little apparent damage.

In the last two million years, the steady drip of water had created the great cavern. The larger the cavern grew, the more fragile it became. Tons of rock pressed down from its high ceiling.

The initial crack was small, only a few feet. Within the last hour, the crack had been steadily increasing. It now was more than one hundred feet in length. Small pieces of the ceiling began to fall. Then a portion of the west wall slid almost three feet.

Ann Sprague brought the helicopter in and landed it gently on the grass. The sun was now up high enough for her to remove her night-vision goggles.

She shouted back at Willie, "Push that handle down and open the side door." The big, black man opened the door. She kept the turbines idling and the main blades slowly turning.

She watched them emerge from the woods. A tall, black woman and a shorter, black man had draped her father's arms over their shoulders and were helping him move toward the helicopter. Something must have happened. She did a head count. Where was Sergeant Major Catfield?

As a combat veteran, she knew what it meant when someone was missing. As a professional soldier, she tucked that thought in the back of her mind. She counted the members of the group coming across the field.

There were six of them. Add in the four on board, and the grand total was ten. The helicopter could carry eight people and two hundred twenty pounds of cargo. It was going to be close. She subtracted the weight of the fuel that had burned off. If they left some of the equipment behind, they should be able get off the ground all right.

Just then, the chopper shook violently.

"What the...?" she said as she peered out her window.

Her dad and the two black kids were on the ground. If there had been an explosion, she hadn't heard it go off. Then she noticed something irregular out of the corner of her eye. She blinked, hoping to clarify what she was seeing. A large fissure had opened in the ground to the right of the helicopter.

She felt another shudder.

"Tell them to hurry, Willie. Something is happening."

She didn't need to bother warning them. They were all rushing toward the helicopter. Running in right ahead of them was that gray cat. It was the first of the group to leap into the helicopter.

The ground suddenly shook, knocking the others to the ground. In a matter of seconds, they were back up on their feet, struggling to squeeze through the door. Directly in front of the helicopter, two large trees tumbled over. Their roots had been partially pulled from the ground.

Willie had been dragging the team toward the chopper. The big man was strong enough to get Sprague into the back. Willie, the last one in. "Strap yourselves to the floor hold downs," shouted Bishop over the roar of the engine.

Another fissure broke the ground in front of the chopper. Ann prepared to lift off. The aircraft shook and vibrated, but remained solidly on the ground.

"Oh, God. We're overloaded," she mumbled. "We can't take off!"

She was on the verge of panic. Her mind was raced. Her sense of unease was building.

Then she remembered a technique she had used and practiced with "Smooth Hal," one of her previous combat-tested instructors. She continued lifting the collective, demanding power that was exceeding the maximum torque and engine temperature limits. She gently and smoothly moved the cyclic forward, just to the point that the skids started to drag through the grass. Faster and faster, they slid – twenty feet, thirty feet, forty feet – and then translational lift.

The helicopter lumbered into the air, one foot up, then two feet up, climbing slowly but steadily with ever-increasing airspeed. Time seemed to stand still.

Not fast enough and not high enough. The top of the hill in front of the helicopter loomed just above them. The loss of lift resulting from a turn to the left or right would put them quickly into the side of the hill. They were going to plow straight into it. She ordered her passengers to brace for the crash that was surely coming.

Then the hill disappeared. The helicopter flew across a two hundred-foot depression as it continued to gain altitude. Ann gently lowered the collective until the torque and temps fell safely back within their maximum limits.

When the west wall of the cavern shifted, the ceiling above the great cavern began to sag. As it did, tremors reverberated through the rock strata. Fissures opened up.

Gravity finally overcame the weight of the ceiling and a quarter of a million tons of rock collapsed into the cavern. The three creatures dived for the portal to their world. George Sarday struggled to follow, but his wounds had weakened him. He fell short of the opening. It closed before his outstretched fingers, leaving him on the outside. He would continue to reside – dead or alive – in the human world.

As the walls were pulled inward, the granite rock separating the coal vein from the limestone cavern fractured and methane gas flowed into the connecting caves. Compression of the air forced the mixture of air and methane through the natural and man-made tunnels.

Powerful winds rushed through the concrete tunnel and passed over the bodies of Sarday's followers.

The wind knocked down the hundreds of survivors who had been milling about in the basement of the old plantation house. The wind was so strong that it snuffed out the candles that had lit the tunnels.

As the mixture of methane and air rushed into the basement, it became compressed. One candle in an alcove to the right of the entrance to the basement was still smoldering. As the compressed mixture reached the candle, the explosive gas ignited.

The chopper finally attained normal climb speed and rate of climb. Ann Sprague had just sighed with relief, and then she heard the blast. A shock wave struck the helicopter on its left side with sufficient force to roll it up into a ninety-degree bank. Everyone in the back was thrown to the side. They held on to the floor straps, certain they would crash.

"Thank God," whispered Ann. Everyone had held on.

Ann struggled to right the aircraft. Finally she got the helicopter leveled and into a normal climb.

"What was that, a small nuclear bomb?" asked Ann.

"Circle back towards the plantation," requested Bishop. "I want to see what happened."

At the University of Washington Seismic Center in Seattle, Washington, Dr. Fredrick Patterson put down his coffee cup and looked at the needle bouncing up and down on the cylinder of the seismometer.

"Well, I'll be damned," he said. "There was a 4.8 quake in Virginia three minutes ago. A very shallow one, less than five miles deep."

"What's the location?" asked Patterson's assistant.

"Just to the east of the town of Johnsonville, Virginia. I'll bet that shook up the town," he said.

Ann circled back over the plantation grounds. They all observed a large, black mushroom cloud rising above the fields.

God, maybe it was a nuclear bomb, Bishop thought.

But as they got even closer, it became apparent that although a significant explosion had occurred, it wasn't nuclear.

Spontaneous fires had broken out on the compound. The pavilion and the barracks were burning. In the very same spot where the Johnson mansion had stood for more than one hundred and seventy-five years, there was nothing – just a large, black hole in the ground.

The blast had been so large that pieces of burning debris had landed in downtown Johnsonville. Half of the town's residents had thought that World War III had just begun.

Ann looked down, amazed at the destruction.

"What do you think happened?" she asked Bishop.

"I think God answered my prayers," he said. He couldn't help but smile. "Let's go to Fayetteville."

As the helicopter flew east into the morning sun, the large copperhead slithered into the cool water of the stream. It would re-establish itself in greener pastures. It wasn't ready to die.

Its story would go on.

SIX MONTHS LATER

Suddenly alert, the gray cat on the porch knew Bishop was coming home even before the patrol car turned off the main road into the driveway.

THE CAT JUMPED OFF THE WICKER ROCKING CHAIR AND TROTTED down the sidewalk. Bishop got out of the car and slammed the door behind him. The cat ran up to greet him, rubbing against his pant leg and yowling to be petted.

"Yes, cat, I'm home," Bishop said as he bent down and stroked the cat's wide head. He opened the front door, and the cat walked right in beside him.

"I'm back," Bishop said.

"How'd it all go?" asked Ann, coming out of the kitchen.

"Not bad. Would you believe a surgeon has joined our AA group?"

"Well, that's good. You wouldn't want to have a drunken surgeon operating on you," she laughed as she wrapped her arms around his neck and kissed him on the cheek. He hugged her and returned the kiss.

"I want to show you something," he said.

He reached in his pocket and handed Ann the statement from their savings account. It read $7,622.15. The mysterious money was gone. All that remained was the money they had managed to put away by themselves.

"You did it!" she said.

"Yep," he replied.

"How did they take it?" asked Ann.

"Willie wants to give back the $175,000," he said. "And Kevin Williams' mother just cried. I told her that the $175,000 wouldn't bring back her son, but the money had been used to frame me, and now it might help bring a little good into her life."

"I'm glad we decided to do that with the money. Even though no one could figure out how it got deposited in our savings account, I would always feel that it would bring us nothing but bad luck," said Ann. "Dinner will be ready in ten minutes," she added.

"Oh, by the way," said Brian with a satisfied grin. "Guess who is the interim mayor?"

"Who?" asked Ann.

"Would you believe Dick Raymond? There were so many lost in the explosion that he was the only one left who was competent enough to do the job," he said. "Also, the *National Gazette* claims that the explosion at the school was the result of a flying saucer crashing into it," he said with a laugh.

The news media had treated the event as the story of the decade. By the time the first responders had arrived, the crater spanned a half-mile across. Burning gasses and debris still continued to rage unchecked. Authorities concluded that the smoldering veins of coal would make the immediate area uninhabitable for years to come.

No survivors were found nor were any bodies recovered. The rich and famous as well as the nameless souls who perished were mourned as the hapless victims of a natural disaster.

"Well, I like the story that it was a methane gas explosion that killed all those 'innocent' people. It's better for the families, friends and the community never to know what horrible things were done up there."

Ann turned to go back into the kitchen, when she remembered that she had some special information for him.

"Changing the subject," said Ann, "look what came in the mail today – a wedding invitation. Sam and Tim are getting married in June. It's in Hawaii."

"Great!" said Brian. "And we just gave away our savings."

"Not a problem," said Ann, "Samantha's parents enclosed round-trip airfare and free lodging in the invitation."

"We can't accept that," Brian said.

"Oh, yes, you can, Chief Bishop, and you'd better! I already bought my bathing suit," she said.

She reached her arms around his neck and leaned against him. Brian wrapped his arms tightly around her and pulled her closer.

"Maybe dinner will be a little late tonight?" she asked in a whisper.

He kissed her softly, rested his arm on her shoulder, and began to walk her toward the back of the house.

"No doubt about it," he answered with a laugh. "Dinner certainly will have to wait!"

Meet the most evil *endosym* on the planet
and get ready to run for your lives.
Book three coming in the summer of 2013.

THE CONQUEST OF EARTH BEGINS

ENDOSYM
BOOK THREE

THE ACADEMY

*RELIGIONS DEPICT DEMONS AS EVIL BEINGS. A MAN POSSESSED BY A DEMON
becomes an endosym: Two entities living in one humanoid body whose goal is to
become the "apex predator" of the planet.*

Hidden in the old tunnels beneath the United States Military
Academy is a creature that should be dead. A creature that was hanged in
1779. But it's hard to kill an *endosym*.

Its name is Duncan McDougal. In order for the conquest of Earth to
begin, first, the unborn child of Samantha and Tim Martin must die.

Hunted by the *endosyms*, Tim and Sam find a safe haven in the ancient
village of Zigda deep in the jungles of West Africa. There, they will learn
the secret as to why their unborn child may be the only human able to
stop the *endosyms*.

But the *endosyms* are not easy to stop. From the United States Military
Academy, to the New York City, and to the jungles of West Africa, the
battle between the *endosyms* and the Martins escalates.

Are *endosyms* real? Would you like to meet the author? Read a preview
of the next book in the series? Join in the Endosym Blog?

Visit www.endosym.com